W9-ASY-032

Date: 3/12/20

LP FIC STEVENS
Stevens, Taylor,
Liars' legacy

LIARS' LEGACY

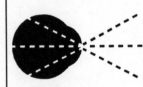

LIARS' LEGACY

TAYLOR STEVENS

THORNDIKE PRESS
A part of Gale, a Cengage Company

LIBRARY OF CONGRESS CIP DATA ON FILE.
CATALOGUING IN PUBLICATION FOR THIS BOOK
IS AVAILABLE FROM THE LIBRARY OF CONGRESS

ISBN-13: 978-1-4328-7310-3 (hardcover alk. paper)

Published in 2020 by arrangement with Kensington Books, an imprint of Kensington Publishing Corp.

Printed in Mexico
Print Number: 01   Print Year: 2020

To Kae and Kim,
who showed me what real
sibling rivalry looks like.

CHAPTER 1

DFW International Airport
Dallas–Fort Worth, Texas, USA

Holden

If one measured killers by appearance, she wasn't much of a threat, the young woman with her back to the pillar near the boarding line, short black hair, pale and petite, head bobbing slightly to some inaudible beat while thumbs, polished blacker than her hair, tapped a phone screen with game-playing rhythm.

But if one measured killers by appearance, he'd already be dead.

He didn't know her, knew only what she was.

Knew she wasn't alone, and that she'd come for him.

Another time, a different objective, he'd have laughed at the irony.

Of all the contracts and all the death, of

all he'd lived and survived, *this* — the first time the job meant more than work, the first time he had an emotional stake in the outcome — *this* was when they came for him.

Any move he made to defend his life carried an equivalent risk of alerting those he hunted to his presence, and *that* he couldn't afford.

The interference felt like raw personal theft.

One whiff of what he'd caught here and it wouldn't matter who the woman and her team had come to kill.

His targets would bolt. They'd vanish.

By the time he tracked them down again, he'd be too late.

Kill or be killed at thirty thousand feet and his hands were tied.

He leaned back, tipped the fedora low, stole another glance at the pillar.

He didn't know the woman but knew she'd die before he did.

She tucked a strand of hair behind her ear, an unconscious gesture that told him she could feel herself being watched. She had good instincts.

His gaze moved on across the boarding area, taking in body language and facial expressions from beneath the brim, just as it had in the hours leading up to departure, and as it had when she'd first strolled in, head high, cold and aloof, wheeling a thousand-dollar luggage set that pegged her somewhere between stripper and rich kid.

He wouldn't have given her much thought if she hadn't positioned herself for an uncomfortable wait with an unobstructed view and, in so doing, piqued well-honed assassin sense. So he'd observed, watching without really watching, searching for the unknown and unknowable, until betrayal had surfaced in a single wayward glance.

The object of her attention was a Caucasian male, ten, fifteen years her senior, in scuffed shoes and worn suit, dragging a beaten pilot bag toward the boarding line, but recognition and acknowledgment had flowed in that butterfly blink, followed by the furtive evasion of an actor who'd realized a heartbeat too late that she'd mistakenly looked at the camera.

She hadn't come up from her phone in the forty minutes since.

Not so much as a pause when his own target had boarded with first class, and not a hint when her partner in the well-worn suit had stood to brush off crumbs and throw away an empty sandwich wrapper. Nothing, until he himself had leaned forward to reach for a water bottle and her thumbs had stalled and shoulders tensed.

He *had* been willing to give her the benefit of the doubt.

He'd seen no reason to risk his own objective or add a fresh bull's-eye to his back if, by extreme coincidence, she'd come in pursuit of someone else.

But with that final tell he'd known, and knowledge forced him to act.

He wasn't an easy man to find, yet here she was.

Who'd sent her and why controlled his response.

He uncapped the bottle and took a long swig.

Death was never *just* death.

Eliminate a team of contract killers mid-flight, disembark before they were discovered, and that'd be the end of this; take out a government task force, and each fresh body would give rise to ten more fighting in their place.

Infinite possibilities converged into a pinprick overlap that held only one possibility: an identity used one too many times.

A compromised passport had led her to him.

He rolled the half-empty bottle between his palms.

Timing, location, and circumstance rolled into a Venn diagram inside his head.

She'd come on behalf of the United States government.

She'd come because the Broker, the man who'd played king against king and bartered souls for national secrets, who'd negotiated hits between buyers and assassins, and who'd forced order onto lawless chaos was dead. Dead without a protégé, dead without a plan for succession, dead to a sudden void in which the highly skilled killers he controlled were now unchained, free to pursue private agendas and vendettas.

The powers that be would never afford that risk.

The Broker was dead, now the ecosystem had to die with him.

This, then, was assassin's suttee — a modern take on that old Hindu tradition in which living wives threw themselves onto their husbands' funeral pyre — more specifically, the part in which unwilling wives were forcefully thrown into those flames by others. This hit squad had come to do the throwing.

Holden tucked the bottle back into the bag and took another look.

Where there were two, there would be others. Only a fool would send a pair to hunt him, and she hadn't come at the behest of fools.

Speakers overhead announced another boarding class.

The departure area emptied in the direction of the gate.

He shoved thick-rimmed glasses onto his face, stood, and wound between seats, moving with the herd.

The woman at the pillar shoved the phone into her pocket, reached for her roll-along, and fell in not far behind, lips twitching with the ventriloquist movement of throat whispers into an unseen mic. His left eye watched it happen courtesy of the pinhead camera in his hatband, watched it in the lens of those thick-rimmed glasses the way drivers watched cars in the rearview.

The line congested. He slowed. She moved in closer.

Proximity added ten well-concealed years to her face and changed the shape beneath her cropped jacket enough to confirm that, had she been a normal traveler, she'd have set off enough alarms going through security to lock down the airport.

He stepped out of line, checking pockets, scanning the floor.

By assassin standards he might as well have tipped his hat and nodded hello.

Passengers jostled him.

Legs and luggage moved forward.

He found the boarding pass that had never been missing, tucked it into his passport, and followed her down the Jetway and into the belly of the plane.

Flight attendants split the passenger feed between two aisles.

He ignored them, followed where his killer led, studying seated passengers without studying, watching those at his back as well as those ahead, searching for another glimpse of recognition or subconscious betrayal, and got nothing.

She stopped, hefted her carry-on into the overhead.

If she'd looked at him, he'd have smiled.

Instead, she squirreled in for the window, and he continued on, matching seats to faces, noting positions and patterns, ruling out young children, discounting large family groups, analyzing the old with a critical eye, and mistrusting the flight crew.

Kill or be killed at thirty thousand feet; three hundred potential threats.

A father paused to lift a kid-size suitcase into stowage.

The line stopped, and in that beat, fate looked Holden square in the face.

He'd have missed it if he'd blinked or

turned, the pupil-expanding, heart-pounding, unguarded shock that registered on the face in the aisle seat ahead.

The guy was Asian, late twenties, with straight black hair, thick black glasses, wearing a plain collared, button-up shirt, and damn near invisible in the stereotyped cliché, caught by surprise in the beat between stowing a bag at his feet and rising for the entertainment system, and coming eye to eye with the one person whose eyes should have been avoided.

He recovered fast, but Holden knew, and knowing was enough.

They were good, this team of assassin hunters.

They'd boarded the airplane armed.

He'd come empty-handed.

They had him outnumbered no idea how many to one, and if their kill skills came anywhere close to their ability to hide and blend, then he was vulnerable here, in what would soon be a dark, pressurized aluminum tube hurtling through the sky at five hundred miles an hour.

CHAPTER 2

Flughafen Frankfurt am Main
Frankfurt Airport, Germany

Kara

She shoved shoulder first between a wide man and a slower-moving elderly couple and swerved around a lanky teenager, fighting against foot traffic, pushing to keep pace with a target that slipped farther and farther away.

An errant suitcase drifted into her path, shifting the obstacle course.

She ducked, sidestepped, nearly stepped on a kid, and knocked into the plywood construction barrier that walled off half the corridor.

Heads turned and murmurs rose in her wake. She was aware of that somewhere on the edge of focus, knew she was moving too aggressively and drawing unwanted attention, but it didn't really matter anymore.

15

The target had most certainly made her, had probably made the whole team.

These weren't the evasive movements of a man dodging suppositions and shadows because he *suspected* being followed. He was bolting.

She had to close the gap, *had* to get close enough to tag him.

Twenty feet ahead a cluster of women in burkas moved to the right.

The jostling crowd parted long enough for her to see him slip behind them.

A suitcase wheeled into her knees.

She glanced down to avoid tripping and in that second lost sight of him.

She elbowed forward, pushing against slower walkers, eyes fixed where she'd last seen him. She projected his path, searched heads and shoulders, clothing, shoes.

Her lips mouthed, *Come on, come on, come on.*

Nothing. And more nothing.

She wove toward a seating area, boosted herself up onto an armrest, and scanned the crowd. To the mic at her collar she said, "I've lost visual."

She had watched it happen and had no idea what she'd seen.

Nick's voice answered. "Talk to me, Angel," he said. "Give me something."

16

Desk jockeys across the ocean chased camera feeds, hunting facial recognition and body measurements, trying to grab hold of a target who'd become his own rabbit in his own magician's vanishing hat.

Kara dropped back to the floor, glanced at the ceiling.

Bodies and suitcases, sounds and color continued on in a blur of motion.

She turned a slow circle, measuring distance, and continued in the direction he'd gone. They'd already lost him. She knew it in her gut, knew it from the way the anxiety racing through her system outshouted the adrenaline.

He'd slipped away like a raft pulled by a riptide out into the ocean.

Her feet kept moving, eyes scanning, but her thoughts had already rushed headlong into the mental underbrush, a fierce little four-legged creature chasing scent along a labyrinth of thorny tunnels, searching for an answer as to how this had happened in an international airport with cameras every few meters and a crackerjack team working the feeds.

Angel's familiar voice said, "Target at gate twenty-four."

Kara's brain froze, and her steps hitched mid-stride.

She said, "No, that's too far, too fast. It's not him."

Angel spoke over her, irritation bleeding between syllables in an unarticulated reminder that opinions — Kara's *specifically* — were unwelcome and unwanted. "Target confirmed at gate twenty-four," she said.

Kara stopped moving.

Words muddled in her head.

She could only process so much so fast, and she struggled, searching for sentences that would make Angel listen. This new data was wrong.

Frustration welled on top of frustration.

Hers was a world of facts, of cause and effect, of stray threads that tied together in ways most didn't see. She said what she thought and meant what she said, and that earned her no favors, especially not with people like Angel, who mistook hyper-focus on accuracy and pointing out logic errors as a personal affront, as if the job had anything to do with her at all. Mission objective should matter most, ability, not personality, and priorities, not politics, but that's never the way things worked.

She wasn't good with people.

She should keep quiet, let Nick handle coms.

But she was on the ground. She'd been

18

closest. She had a physical sense of time multiplied by distance, and every part of her rebelled against losing target because Angel, for whatever reasons, insisted on sending limited manpower in the wrong direction. Kara was right and knew she was right.

She said, "Gate twenty-four means he covered two hundred yards in ten seconds. Whatever you're seeing at that gate is not our guy."

Nick said, "Where is he, Angel?"

Kara heard frustration and, behind his frustration, doubt.

Nick would question headquarters before he questioned her.

She appreciated that about him.

He didn't care that she was missing the "be nice," "find a friendly way to say things indirectly" chip most women seemed to be gifted at birth.

He respected her and trusted her implicitly, which was why he'd insisted on bringing her onto his team in place of others better suited for boots-on-the-ground hunt and chase and why she'd agreed to do it.

Angel said, "Hold."

Nick said, "We're losing the window."

No, they'd already lost the window.

Airports were great for taking targets

unaware if the targets weren't smart enough to see you coming, but were damn shitty places for quick, quiet elimination of those who did. There were too many witnesses. Too many cameras documenting what needed to remain unseen.

If they couldn't get him clean in the international zone, they'd have to nab him on the other side, and getting to him clean in here meant getting up close, and that wasn't gonna happen now.

They'd have been better off if they'd arranged to have German intelligence on-site, already briefed and ready to assist before the flight landed. Even if they had missed him on deplaning, they'd have been able to grab him at any of the exit-slash-choke points, but he wasn't *that* kind of target, and this wasn't that kind of assignment. Heck, they were on the outer end of normal even for a black op.

They'd known *what* their target was but not *who* he was.

They'd had his flight number, moderate confidence he'd be in first or business class, and that was all. No name, no nationality, no description or history or prior connections. Not even age or gender. Only a critical window of opportunity and the urgency of a national security threat if he boarded without them.

They'd had a couple hours to make the flight.

Headquarters had snagged Nick a seat in first.

They'd put her and Juan on opposite ends of business, which had gotten them both relatively close on deplaning. Aaron had taken the rear in coach on the chance they were wrong on target's position within the aircraft. The cost of last-minute tickets alone must have been more than all of them made in a month combined, but the intel had been solid. Target had been seated two rows behind Nick.

Headquarters had confirmed that detail while they were over the Atlantic and that had been their first look at what they hunted. The rest of what little they had on him had been waiting when the wheels touched down.

Seat number had gotten the war room a corresponding passport.

Passport had gotten a name, age, and face.

Other than that, they were running blind.

Nick had been first off the plane, and he'd gotten ahead of target.

Kara had been first to tail him.

If she couldn't get close enough, she'd hand him over to Juan, who waited on the other side of transfers, and if Juan couldn't get him there, he'd hand him off to Nick at the connecting departure gate. They'd left Aaron behind in the arrival terminal to account for the possibility of target looping back, and that had left a hole at passport control, which was where target would head if, instead of continuing to the connecting flight to Berlin, he turned Frankfurt into the final destination.

The war room, watching and analyzing airport-security feeds in real time, was supposed to provide that cover, but they'd done a shit job so far.

Transfers was a choke point.

Boarding the connection was a choke point.

Deplaning in Berlin was a choke point.

Target knew they were looking for him, and there was no more chance he'd head to any of those choke points than that he was at gate twenty-four right now.

Passport control was the weak spot.

In a perfect world, digital alerts would start pinging as soon as he handed over his documents, but someone able to disappear the way he had wouldn't rely on a single passport. The information they had on him was now effectively worthless.

He'd already become someone else.

Kara diverted, following the pictograph signage that would take her through immigration.

Nick said, "Angel, confirm status on gate twenty-four."

Angel said, "Confirm. Target seated in waiting area."

Kara's insides protested.

The confirmation made absolutely no sense. Angel saw what they couldn't, and yet insisted on sending them where target couldn't possibly be.

Nick, as if reading her mind, said, "What's the recognition match?"

Angel said, "No match available."

This airport was too big, had too many exits to run an effective picket, and now Nick was headed in the opposite direction of where they needed him.

Angel was wrong, and because she was wrong, they'd lose target.

Kara clamped her mouth shut and focused on the crowd. Arguing it out with Nick over open coms would raise an apocalyptic shit storm. This was his call to make.

He was good with people, he understood when facts mattered less than appearance, and he knew they had nothing to gain and everything to lose by ignoring Angel. She listened to him, respected him — well-deserved respect — Kara didn't begrudge that, though she did begrudge the way a guy would be lauded for saying the exact same things in the exact same ways that earned her a reputation for being rough around the edges and a poor team player.

Nick said, "Kilo, redirect to immigration. Juliet, take my gate."

Kara was a step ahead of him, already in line, searching for anything familiar, watching bodies and faces in the ebb and flow while stamps thudded into passports and the crowd moved steadily forward.

Juan confirmed approach to connecting departure gate, the flight their target should have been on, the flight *they* should have been on.

Kara reached the immigration desk.

The official glanced at her, then the photo page.

She'd put on a few pounds since the photo was taken, but she was still brown hair, hazel eyes, wide cheekbones, and skin just dark enough that strangers usually assumed Mexican or Puerto Rican ancestry, and she never bothered to clarify, because those assumptions required less effort than explaining blood quantum.

The official stamped her passport and handed it back.

She continued into the luggage hall, where waiting passengers milled around dozens of carousels, and she meandered between them, knowing she wouldn't find what she was looking for, searching for the sake of being thorough, and moved on toward customs. She had nothing to declare.

They'd traveled light, but even hauling the one backpack while in pursuit would have made her too obvious, too visible, so she'd left her stuff with Aaron in the arrival terminal. Not that hunting without it ended up mattering in the long run.

In her ear, Nick confirmed his arrival at gate twenty-four.

Ice in his voice said no sign of target.

Silence followed. Angel returned with an update that sent him rushing the crowded corridors ten gates back the way he'd just come, and a minute later she corrected with another change of course that wasted their most critical minutes.

Nick, normally calm, unflappable, said, "Whatever the hell is going on in there, get it fixed, and get it fixed now."

Angel bit back, and the two of them argued in clipped code-speak.

The tension created anxiety, made Kara want to pull the earpiece out.

Angel wasn't Nick's boss, though she

often spoke to him as if she was.

Liv Wilson was her real name, and Liv was a politics-playing, ass-kissing ladder climber who'd say one thing to your face and something else entirely in committee meetings, which left work-oriented, non-game-playing people like Kara confused and wary and often looking a little bit crazy. Liv was every girl in high school who'd maintained social status by tormenting the awkward misfit who'd just wanted to be left alone, and she was every adult woman who saw competence in other women as a threat to her own position and who'd sabotage in a hundred petty ways, even if that damaged the team itself.

Kara despised her, but personal feelings had nothing to do with work.

Liv ran headquarters support and had the war room at her disposal — the engineers and analysts, the specialists tied directly into foreign and domestic intelligence and law-enforcement databases — she had front-door access to aggregated consumer data and financial institutions and a worldwide network of Internet-connected cameras and devices, and for anything not willingly shared, her team had backdoor channels to take what they wanted. Liv had the ability to tap information most people didn't know existed, and they needed her fully vested in the operation, not sabotaging from the back end.

In Kara's ear, Nick said, "Give me eyes on the connection."

Angel said, "Boarding in fifteen. No sign of target."

Kara exited customs without luggage, without even a purse.

Officials, curious, pulled her aside.

She answered their questions with the truth, said she'd rushed ahead of her travel partner to meet a friend and that her stuff was still coming. They nodded her on in a way that would never happen when entering the United States.

Germany was so much more relaxed in that way.

She passed through automatic glass doors for the outside, where fall air already had a winter bite, and she scanned the sidewalk in both directions.

The decision to exit had been a roll of the dice.

Target could have routed for the skyline and hopped terminals, headed for rail transit, or chosen to sit out the hours in a lounge or restaurant, waiting for the storm to pass, but if he was planning to leave and hadn't already, he'd have to come this way, and it'd be easier to spot him coming through the doors than milling among the crowds inside. Mind searching, she glanced toward the taxi stand. There, her focus snagged like a hangnail on a shag carpet, ripping her out of one hunt and yanking her back for a stomach-churning double take at the woman at the head of the line.

Her hair was black instead of blond.

She wore tight jeans instead of slacks, had on a cropped designer jacket better suited for someone ten years younger, and dragged expensive luggage to round out the look, but there was no mistaking who she was. Of the many possibilities Kara had accounted for on this op, running into Emilia Flynn wasn't one.

Confusion collided with wariness and a hint of protective jealousy.

She had met Emilia twice, both times in a professional capacity, knew her better by reputation than in person, but Emilia wasn't a person one forgot, unless, of course, that's what Emilia wanted. At headquarters she was all long legs and sly nods. Gazes shifted when she walked into a room, and starstruck stutters started up in her wake.

She was beautiful, graceful, likable. Everything Kara wasn't.

Rumor had it Emilia and Nick had been a

thing for a while, which wouldn't have been the least bit surprising. Nick had a lot of women gunning for him.

He was charming. Good looking. Had a bad boy edge about him.

Women were stupid.

Kara had no issue with Emilia personally, not any more than she had with people in general. Emilia wasn't a fake-laugh, patronizing backstabber, and she wasn't cruel, just self-centered and indifferent, which was par for the course since Kara registered so low on most people's attention meter they often forgot they'd met her, but she did have a big issue spotting Emilia right here, right now.

Emilia, like Nick, led a tactical team.

She'd been working for headquarters longer than Nick had.

But where Nick's team was mostly renditions, Emilia was strictly wet work — liquidating terroristic individuals, the ones who posed too great a threat to national security and were too dangerous to risk putting into the hands of traditional law enforcement — liquidation operations like the one Kara was on now.

Emilia reached for the taxi door.

She stepped a foot off the curb, and in the beat before her body slid into the car, her head ticked up and she looked right at Kara.

It seemed, for a second, that their eyes had met, but no.

Emilia had stared right through her.

And then the door shut and the taxi pulled away from the curb, and Kara stood frozen, caught between two worlds, half of her chasing their target, the other half running the odds of two special units crossing paths in the same time-space junction.

She dug through her pockets, retrieved a pack of cigarettes, and lit one.

She hated the smoke and hated the smell, but she needed the cover.

In her head she saw Emilia again, Emilia in that final glance, wearing a look of terror and death. *That* was an Emilia she'd never seen before.

Nick's voice in her ear jolted her back.

Kara scanned the length of the terminal, hunting for any sign of target and searching for the other members of Emilia's team.

Travelers passed by. Cars and buses came and went.

Her skin prickled with the sensation of being watched, and she strolled to the end of the sidewalk and back again, glancing at her phone like an impatient traveler who'd been left waiting, searching for the source of the disquiet.

She found nothing and dug for another cigarette.

Nick said, "How's the weather?"

Kara tapped ash into a receptacle. "Gray. Bleak."

Juan reported in. The departure gate for the Berlin flight had closed.

There'd been no sign of target.

It'd now been forty-five minutes since they'd lost him.

They'd need to adapt and do it quickly.

She'd have said as much if it'd just been Nick on coms.

She stubbed out the cigarette and glanced back toward the taxi stand, toward the glimpse of Emilia she'd caught, and tried to make sense out of what made no sense.

Juan exited the terminal.

Aaron followed fifteen minutes later with his gear and hers.

Nick was the last to make it out.

They were tired, all of them, tired from jet lag and the transatlantic flight, tired from the adrenaline dump that followed the fruitless chase, tired from disappointment and failure. Nick nodded toward a hotel in the near distance.

Kara raised an eyebrow.

"We're rebooked on an afternoon flight," he said. "Was the best we could get. Headquarters is pulling resources. Angel thinks we've got a lead on where our guy will show up next, and we'll try to get ahead of him." Nick heaved a strap over his shoulder. "In the meantime we clean up and get some shut-eye."

The hotel was a few minutes on foot from the terminal.

Nick headed for the nearest crosswalk. The rest of the team followed him, and Kara followed them, distracted, detached, oblivious to her surroundings, oblivious to anything but the images playing out inside her head.

Somewhere on the dim, foggy periphery, they reached the lobby.

She was aware, vaguely, that Nick checked them in.

Knew it for certain when he stuck a room key in her hand.

Nick paused, took a good look at her face, pointed a finger at Juan and then at her, as if tethering the two of them. "Don't let kiddo here get lost," he said.

Kara's cheeks flushed.

Nick was only half joking.

Her thoughts bolted back into the mental underbrush like terriers after a rat, and this time they caught something.

The guys had come for a shower and sleep.

All she wanted was the Internet connection.

Chapter 3

Kara

She sat cross-legged on the bed closest to the window, laptop in front of her, earbuds in her ears. Music drowned out the world, which in this case meant Juan toweling off wet hair and puttering from bedroom to bathroom and back again. She'd offered him first go at the shower, figuring that would get him out of her way faster.

Not that he was in her *way*, per se. Just that the room — a clean, efficient standard chain affair of bathroom, two beds, and a strip of window ledge that doubled as a desk — had a knee-knockingly small amount of floor area. She felt every nudge, every footstep, and the movement pulled her out of focus, made it harder to grip concepts she could feel and understand on a meta-level and turn them into something articulable.

Juan leaned in behind the computer and waved.

She glanced up.

He gestured toward the window.

She motioned him on ahead.

They'd been working together long enough now that he recognized the signs, knew she'd already started down the rabbit hole and might not surface for hours.

She didn't need the light, but he never just assumed.

She liked that about him, the politeness. It mattered a whole heck of a lot on days they were cooped up and stir-crazy, and just generally made having another person up in her space far less stressful than it could have been, which was helpful considering this was the way the rooming always went when Angel put them two-in-one the way she had here.

Kara and Nick in separate rooms at Nick's request because the two of them bunking together inflamed old rumors that refused to die. And Kara and Juan together at Kara's request because even after eight months of living, working, and breathing as a team, Aaron Jefferson Lewis just couldn't get with the idea that she was Nick's number two due to her particular skill set and not some kind of favoritism.

She didn't hold that ignorance against him.

Anyone who spent more than five minutes with them knew they were close.

She loved Nick — if *love* was the right word — as much as Nick loved her, and because of that, assumptions they were sleeping together were easy to come by.

They weren't and never had and probably never would.

Not that the chemistry wasn't there, and not that they hadn't discussed it more than once, just that neither of them wanted to risk destroying the friendship if the relationship soured. So he mostly kept his relationships out of sight, and she mostly kept hers off his radar, and that kept everything else on the table, including respect.

Aaron would figure it out eventually.

He was a smart kid. Quick. Funny. A marine sniper who'd more than earned his place. If shit ever met fan, she'd put her life in his hands without a second thought, but he was also young and cocky, in the same way a lot of guys were before life-altering mistakes handed humility a two-by-four and an invitation to knock them on their asses. Until then she preferred downtime that wasn't filled with petty sniping and passive-aggressive humor.

Juan Marino was none of that.

At forty, he was older than Nick, calmer than Aaron, and had seen enough death to live by the rule that no amount of life energy was worth wasting on drama. He wasn't a friend, exactly — mostly because she wasn't the type that people wanted to have as a friend — but he rolled with her quirks and gave her space to do her thing, and she was happy to let him do his.

Juan shut the blinds, and the room went dark.

He scooted past her bed and toppled onto his own.

They were rebooked on the four-thirty to Berlin.

Accounting for check-in and security, they had about three hours before they needed to bug out. He'd use the time to sleep. Ideally, she would, too, but with the speed her mind was running, any attempt in that regard would be an exercise in frustration. She'd missed something in that terminal.

It had been fog of war, heat of the moment.

She needed to go back and see.

She cranked up the music, set the secure line, and patched in.

She didn't have the bandwidth to pull all the data that'd be waiting now, but ten minutes of footage from the three cameras she'd noted right after target had vanished should get her what she wanted. She located target's primary file.

Front matter that had been empty now had a high-res scan of his passport.

The photo stopped her before she even got started.

She zoomed in until his face filled the screen.

There was enough familiarity to say that possibly, maybe, this was the face she'd seen in those airport corridors, but not enough that she'd have argued it with any certainty. She clicked through to the file itself.

The war room had added information while her team was over the ocean, including a short, lightly redacted summary of the SIGINT and HUMINT that had pointed headquarters to him, all of it Russian sourced.

That was a potential problem.

Moscow was notorious for pushing disinformation in ways that made it difficult to differentiate truth from fiction, but right here and now that issue was above her pay grade. These details pointed to a planned political assassination, and they came with a high analytic confidence rating, which was as good as it got.

No details on where or when or who.

She scanned down the war room's query timeline.

They were gunning for leads on target through informant networks.

They'd run his gait through Next Generation Identification and pushed his passport photo and multiple variants of the passport name and birth date through aggregated social media and commercial data, financial and credit histories, and law-enforcement databases, but so far the guy was as much of a vanishing act in real life as he'd been at the airport. That just didn't seem right. Even the best of the best of the killers on the Broker list had some kind of footprint.

She clicked through for the airport security feeds, which, helpfully, had already been labeled according to a corresponding site map.

Images filled her screen in a sort of spliced quick time.

One world faded and another filled its space, and she settled into a rhythm, clicking, scanning, enhancing until her target came into view.

He was impossible to miss.

He glowed on-screen. Well, not a glow, exactly.

The hat he wore was reflectable- or

infrared-equipped — possibly both or something else altogether — and light that had been invisible on the ground was a blinding patch of white on screen.

It was a curious choice, the hat.

The only practical reason to wear something like that was to prevent facial recognition from picking up his nodal points, but that made no sense in this environment. The same tech that kept his face out of the data systems created an obvious digital beacon that screamed, "Look at me," to anyone watching the monitors.

A person with the ability to slip between shadows the way he did should have been more concerned with avoiding attention than drawing a line straight to him.

Target moved off-screen.

She jotted a note, marked the time stamp, continued to the second feed, and accelerated the frame rate until the lighted hat came into view. She was there, too, in that sequence, not nearly as blunderous as she remembered but just as slow.

She tracked target digitally in ways she couldn't from the ground, and then, one step to the next, he vanished, just as he had in real life.

The speed of it left her breathless and searching for words.

She rewound, halved the frame rate, and watched it again.

Shifting crowds hid him from the camera in that critical beat.

She switched to the third feed.

The angle put him as a dot in the background.

He knew what he was doing. He'd made the switch where he'd cover the least amount of screen real estate. She touched the image, circling the group of burka-clad women, and physically traced the path he'd take.

This time she caught the action.

She cut the speed by yet half again and, finger on the screen, tracked each painstakingly slow sliver, waited for him to shift, and hit PAUSE.

What she couldn't see — hadn't seen — from the ground was the ebb of foot traffic, the way it had stalled, and how close two European men had followed behind the women. Like a magician performing an in-your-face, blink-and-you'll-miss-it sleight of hand, target had slipped shoulder first between those two groups and, in one continuous movement, had swiped off the hat, rolled out of his jacket, and turned on his heels.

Just like that, the two-man group had

become three.

He'd walked right past her.

She hadn't seen him, because she'd been looking somewhere else. The desk jockeys at headquarters hadn't seen him, because they'd been looking for something else.

Angel and her crew weren't easy to fool, but that hadn't mattered here.

He had known he was being watched and had set them up.

He hadn't worn that hat to hide from facial recognition, he'd worn it for misdirection, to focus their attention where he wanted it. The light had been a beacon — the mind just couldn't help itself — and they'd have searched for that first when he vanished. They would have realized the mistake almost immediately and adjusted for it, but by then they'd have had nothing else to reference what they were looking for.

He wasn't in the same clothes.

He was carrying a bag he hadn't been carrying before.

And he was no longer a male traveling alone.

She rewound and watched the vanishing act again.

The birth date on his passport put him at twenty-six.

The file put him somewhere between

twenty-four and twenty-eight.

But this high-level tradecraft shit made him look like he'd just walked out of the late eighties, the time before portable technology had become such a critical part of daily life that even the world's most wanted cycled through burners or put phones in other people's names rather than do without.

Nobody did without anymore, except this guy.

One active device to act as a digital signature was all they'd have needed for today to have had a different ending. He was an analog agent working in a digital world, the embodiment of the ghost stories old-timers liked to tell.

You kids these days have no idea how good you've got it.

Advanced technology, digital tracking.

In my day . . .

She'd give just about anything to see one of those old geezers handle what her team had experienced this morning.

She went back to the first feed, forwarded past the vanishing act, and caught target on the rebound. His pants hadn't changed. His shoes hadn't changed.

They hadn't needed to.

The human tendency was to watch at eye

level, heads, hands, and torsos, especially in a crowd. No one followed feet in a crowd — it took too much time and was too obvious — and that's what allowed his quick-change trick to work.

She pulled more feeds and tracked him from camera to camera, following him through the airport, until frustration hit concern and kept on rising from there.

Target had shadowed her.

He'd stood five passengers behind her in the line through passport control.

He'd followed her out of the terminal and watched her as she'd lingered.

He'd caught her interest in Emilia.

And he'd waited until the guys had joined her.

He'd known exactly how many were on the team and who they were.

Nick, Juan, Aaron, they weren't strangers to this game — they each had a heightened sense of situational awareness that she would never have — and target had walked right past them. They'd seen him and looked right through him.

But the sequence that set her heart racing wasn't at the airport.

The last image she had of him was the back of his jacket within a crowd on the crosswalk as he trailed their group to the hotel.

CHAPTER 4

Kara

Her fingers hurried over keyboard and trackpad, searching the war room's databases, hoping headquarters had already tied into the hotel's security system, while the specter of unmitigated disaster burned its way from her gut into her throat.

She found the lobby cameras, located Nick's arrival, enhanced the sequence to focus in on the reception desk, and started from there.

With every forward frame, clarity formed and trepidation grew.

Target had waited just off the lobby until they'd gone for the elevators, and then worked the desk clerks. He had their room numbers, might even have their passport information. This was insanity.

The war room had access to these feeds in real time, and there'd been no alert, and not a goddamn thing in the dossier to account for the fact that target *was in their hotel.* He knew why they wanted him.

The next logical step was a preemptive strike.

Nick needed to know — needed to know now — needed to see it for himself, and it'd take longer for her to get the equipment to his room, resecure credentials, and start over than to get him here.

She searched for the feeds by floor and found their hallway.

Empty.

That didn't mean clear.

She leaned over, picked up the room phone, and dialed.

Nick answered with a voice somewhere between dead asleep and panicked alert.

She said, "Sorry to wake you. There's something you need to see. Urgent."

He said, "Give me two minutes —"

She stopped him. "Nick. He's here. In the hotel. He followed us out of the terminal."

Silence followed.

She said, "The hallway looks clear, but I don't know. Be careful."

She dropped the phone into the cradle and returned to the screen.

She needed to get ahead of this.

Target had been conscious of the cameras from the beginning, which made it hard to get a lock on him, but between the various angles she could build a composite of his face, and there were segments that included his gait.

She pushed what she had into the system.

The algorithms churned.

Facial recognition spit back fifty partial matches, not one of which pinged the passport photo. She scrolled through the hits, looking for anything that fit the profile, saved the array, and closed it out. She didn't have time or bandwidth to pore through the results for clues and missing pieces, so she clipped images from the camera feeds, attached them for high priority, and sent a requisition to headquarters.

The war room had the manpower and computing power, this was their job, and if they'd done it properly in the first place, she wouldn't be left doing their work.

That was the frustration and irony of where she was this very moment.

She was an analyst, not a field operative. Her skills were a better fit for a war room than a hotel room, but here she was, and that was Nick's doing.

He was the one who'd talked her into the career fork from naval intelligence specialist to special unit analyst, and if not for him, she'd probably be back to working out of a windowless room in Norfolk, assembling confidence judgments into briefs that more often than not found their way into the circular file than onto a desk.

He had called her up, said he was in town for the night, had invited her out and buttered her up with a few beers and greasy food, and had then dropped the mother of all requests on her.

He was putting together a team, he'd said, and wanted her on it.

She'd laughed.

She could handle a rifle as well as the next guy, was actually a better marksman than most — growing up poor and hunting to supplement the dinner table did that for a person — but she'd be an awful field operative.

"You're serious," she said.

"As I live and breathe."

She swigged from the longneck. "Even if I wanted to say yes, my next reenlistment doesn't come up for another year and a half." She clinked the bottom of her bottle against the side of his. "Kind of out of luck there, buddy, but let me know if you're still hiring in eighteen months."

He took a swig of his own. "It'd be a deployment change," he said. "Same NOS on paper but with a rate bump, which is long overdue, if you ask me." He patted his chest, as if indicating a pocket inside his jacket. "Orders from higher up, a little document shuffling, and done."

She scrutinized him over the bottle.

Nick wasn't, had never been navy. He was a jarhead, Force Recon.

They'd met on the *USS Boxer* when she was in the middle of her first tour. He'd been charming as all get-out and kind in a way most people weren't, and she'd gone out of her way to avoid him because, in her experience, accepting kindness from a popular kid now meant paying with hell and humiliation later.

Turned out he was a nerd in a jock's body.

And the body was more of a recent development.

His high school stories weren't as traumatic as hers, but they'd been enough to connect over and a friendship had been built and they'd stayed in touch.

She was in for twenty, gunning for retirement. He'd done eight and decommissioned for the private sector and then contract work.

This team he was talking about wasn't within any of the military branches, and yet if he was to be believed — and she had no reason to doubt him — she'd be working for him while still on Uncle Sam's payroll.

She said, "What kind of team, exactly?"

He hemmed and hedged.

She was smart enough to convert the inference to statement of fact.

Any job that didn't exist while keeping her on the navy payroll meant a whole lot of risk, and if anything did go wrong, there'd be denial and disownment, and she'd be kissing away a retirement that was close enough she could almost taste it.

She drew another long drag and swallowed.

"I could do the job, might even be decent at it," she said, "but that'd be testament to sheer force of will and my delightful nature. I'm an analyst, Nick. I'm not built for fieldwork, and you know it."

"I need an analyst," he said.

She snorted. "I know how this shit works. Whatever you've gotten yourself into comes with a voyeur's wet dream of twenty-four-seven crackerjack support."

"Whatever I've gotten myself into," he said, "will at times put me — us — into situations that make accessing that support difficult, if not impossible. I need your brain, Kara. I don't want you as a field operative. I want you as an analyst — your eyes and ears, on the ground, right there in the moment — because when shit gets real, we're going to be on our own, running blind, and there isn't anyone else I trust to get me where I need to go the way I trust you. You've already got the clearance. You have a proven record. I can get the transfer green-lit and fast-tracked. Please."

"Still a hard sell, Nick."

"Double hazard pay, five million in life insurance, which you can line up to take care of your sisters if that's what you're worried about, and guaranteed retirement."

"That's not how things work."

"Okay, everything minus the guarantee."

She sighed.

"You're dying where you are," he said. "Your skills are wasted. You're doing time, counting the days to freedom."

"What's my commitment?"

"Give me six months. If you don't like it, then quit and pick your duty."

"Nick, you can't make promises like that."

"I absolutely can."

"See," she said, "now you're starting to scare me."

"Good," he said. "That means you're curious."

"It means you're a motherlovin' conniving asshole is what it is."

Four weeks later she was on a flight to

Langley, and two months of field training after that, she was headed to Rome. Two months bled into three, then six, then a year.

The work left her ambivalent.

She hadn't been naive when Nick had asked her to sign on.

She'd known what she'd be part of, but she wasn't like him or Emilia.

They had no moral issue with the killing. To them, this was war, and they were soldiers following orders, but it wasn't really the same. This was a murderous bent masked by terms like *patriotism* and *national security.* She didn't deny that they were patriotic, she just didn't buy they were doing it only for country.

They enjoyed the thrill of the hunt.

She didn't.

And the civic side of her had a hard time wrapping her head around extrajudicial killings, especially when those killed were US citizens.

She'd brought that up with Nick after her first six months ended.

He'd said, "It's not like we're targeting innocent people."

She had issues with that, too.

"Who gets to decide what innocent is?" she said. "I mean, what does *innocent* even mean? Because you can't tell me the people we go after don't say the same thing about the people they go after. That's like saying if a murderer murders only other murderers that negates murder."

He thought for a bit. "I'm okay with that."

"Then that makes innocence a variable that changes by day or dictum."

"Don't do the philosophical thing on me," he said. "I'm not that fucking smart."

"You're a fucking liar is what you are."

He clinked his glass against hers.

She stayed with the job for him, to watch his back, and did the job because it was her job, but any thrill she found was as a puzzle solver discovering connections other people missed and running her pack ahead of the prey. That was what she was good at, was *supposed* to be good at anyway. This target called it all into question.

She rechecked the hallway cameras.

Nick's door opened. He stepped out and into center screen.

No movement elsewhere.

She stretched a foot from her bed to Juan's and nudged him.

He opened an eye.

"Nick's on his way," she said. "Get the door."

"What time is it?"

"Move-your-ass time."

Juan groaned himself up.

The room echoed with the rap of knuckles on wood.

Juan slid his feet to the floor. Two steps took him to the door.

He said, "That you, Mary?"

Nick's voice said, "Just the sheep."

Juan turned the tumbler, held the door open long enough for Nick to wedge his way inside. Juan returned to his bed, and Nick rounded over to hers. He sat.

He said, "Show me what you've got."

She scooted over to make room, started with the vanishing point, and traced target's trajectory with her finger. "Watch him," she said.

Nick leaned in closer.

"Show me again," he said.

She stopped, rewound, replayed. They went at it like that, round after round after round, and finally he said, "Have you seen something like that before?"

"Never exactly like that."

"Similar?"

"It's like Cold War tradecraft mixed with stage magic."

He said, "You don't pull off a stunt like that without a lot of practice."

"Nope. But this isn't what I called you for."

"There's more?"

She shut down half the tabs and started over with the others, tracing time stamps for Nick the way she'd done on her own. She showed him how their target had followed her into passport control and out of the terminal, and how he had loitered within throwing distance of the crew as they gathered, and the way he'd trailed them to the hotel, and then she played the footage from the lobby cameras that had made her reach for the phone.

Nick sucked in air. "He still in the building?"

"Hard to tell. He hasn't left the way he came, but last time stamp I've got on him is from over an hour ago, and the cameras aren't mapped, so I haven't been able to locate all the exits yet."

"What's the war room got on it?"

She dragged her gaze from the screen to his face and let silence do the talking.

"Goddammit," he said.

He swung his feet to the floor. "See if you can get a trace on him, figure out if he's still in the building and, if not, what exit he took and when."

She said, "Nick."

He said, "Yeah, I know. Just do what you can."

"Nick."

He stopped. "Look, due diligence, okay? If you can't ping him within the next few minutes, package it. This is their fuckup. They need to fix it."

She clicked over to the array of camera feeds.

If target was still in the hotel, then they had a very narrow window of opportunity to find him, and she didn't have the speed, access, or manpower to make meaningful use of that time. But by the time she got it to the war room, he might already be gone.

Nick headed toward the door, stopped, and said, "Hey."

She glanced up.

"You did good work," he said. "Make sure your name's attached."

Her fingers paused. Few people realized how hard it was to be recognized for the work she did. Where the best of them wouldn't try to steal credit, Nick went out of his way to ensure bias didn't mistakenly misappropriate to him what belonged to her. That he was still conscious of it while running under pressure made her love him that much more, but Liv Wilson would be among the first to get anything she sent, and there was always a chance someone higher up the food chain would see it, and to anyone who truly looked — or cared — the details highlighted war-room incompetence, or worse.

Both made Liv look bad, and Liv already despised her.

The team didn't need that kind of poison.

She said, "Maybe not this time."

Nick understood. He might not agree, but he understood.

He circled a finger and to Juan said, "Get your gear. Let's go."

CHAPTER 5

Jack

The aisle stretched into forever, row after row of heads and seatbacks beneath recessed lights, passenger after passenger boarded and seated but no sign at all of *the* passenger. She should have been here first. That was the plan. But three minutes to scheduled departure and she was God only knew where, while he was stuck in this metal tube, with no way to make contact and no line of sight.

He shoved earbuds into his ears and cranked up the volume.

A cabin attendant moved down the aisle, shutting luggage compartments.

Inside his head, information blocks shifted and reordered.

She was in the airport, or at least she *had* been when his flight out of Dallas had deplaned, watching for him and watching for those who watched him and watching

59

for those who watched for whoever else might be watching for him. He'd detoured for the flight board and then for coffee, giving her time, and she'd leapfrogged to where he had a line of sight, communicated what she'd observed, and slipped away.

She'd had one job, just one simple job.

All she'd needed to do after was lay low and board this flight.

That she was missing now said either she'd been grabbed or this was her deliberately taunting him. The first worried him a whole lot less than the second.

God help any team that tried to grab her.

God help him if they hadn't.

She was the most capable person he knew, at the top of the game when the game was in play — so long as the game was in play — but lulls and in-between silences led to situations like this, and she'd had five hours.

He glanced at the time.

Two minutes past scheduled departure and the doors were still open.

Flight attendants at the front turned plastic smiles toward the Jet bridge.

A young couple boarded, and after them a woman, followed by an older gentleman, and then *she* materialized in boyfriend jeans and jacket, wearing sunglasses atop short-cropped hair and looking nothing like the middle-aged matron who'd been waiting for his Dallas flight, and he knew just what she'd done.

Her lanky body entered the space between the first-class seats.

He watched her make that long walk, as if watching a reflection in the mirror.

He knew her voice, her gait, her mannerisms, knew her many iterations and could imitate them at will. He was taller by two inches, and her features were softer by millimeters, but they were closer to true doppelgängers than fraternal twins had any right to be, similarities and nodal points so evenly matched that, with a few subtle tweaks, even facial recognition often pegged them for the same person.

She caught his eye and winked, teasing and testing his temperament.

He stared through her as though he hadn't seen it happen.

The captain's voice came over the intercom.

Flight attendants moved through the cabin in preparation for departure.

She reached his row, glanced at the empty space beside him, and swung into the open seat across the aisle. Neither spot was hers — not on the pass she'd boarded with anyway — but they'd paid for enough

61

tickets under enough identities to guarantee proximity without drawing the attention of database hunters who might be looking for exactly this kind of connection. That was the difference between buying tickets and using them, and the benefit of flying where carriers didn't overbook to the same degree as in the United States. Any name would do for a reservation if you were willing to burn the cash and there weren't thirty people on standby waiting for the first open seat.

Jack removed the earbuds.

She shoved her bag down by her feet and said, "Hey."

Hey, as if she was right on time, playing this according to plan.

Hey, as if she hadn't sought out a tight connecting flight, become part of the group rushing to make the next leg, and nearly missed this one in the process.

Hey, because hers had been a tri-purposed strategy that kept her invisible to watching eyes while tormenting him to the last minute while leaving him no way to confront her about the second, because the first was in itself perfect.

He said, "You got tagged?"

She searched for the seat-belt ends. "Just lost track of time."

The lie exploded inside his head.

If she'd truly lost track of time, she'd have never admitted to it. And if there'd been a legitimate reason for the delay, it'd have cost her nothing to give it. She lied when there was no need to lie, lied *because* she knew he'd know it as a lie.

This was the game she played.

This was how she maintained control.

He leaned back, shut his eyes, and blocked her out.

Voice low, she said, "Those weren't Russians, John."

Her words were a question, not a statement, but he was in no mood to share his mental toys. He pushed the first earbud back into place.

She jabbed his arm. He refused to look.

She punched him harder, and knowing she'd keep it up even if that meant drawing attention until she sabotaged this whole thing, he turned and glared.

Her hands uttered words her mouth left silent.

What the fuck?

His said, *Agreed. They weren't Russians.*

The cabin jolted, and the plane began to move.

Her hands demanded explanation.

Training and old grudges split him down the middle.

63

Withholding what he knew could get either one of them killed, but cooperation was a two-way street that she'd just blown up.

His said, *Later.*

Tell me now.

That was the thing, though. Tell her what exactly?

They'd expected he'd be shadowed the moment he showed up on radar.

His ticket had been bought and paid for by a man they knew only over the phone. He'd claimed to speak for Dmitry Vasiliev, a person who didn't technically exist — ghost of a former KGB officer, present-day enigma, father they'd never met — and they'd have been a disgrace to the blood running through their veins if they'd accepted the invitation at face value. But that was obvious, and the obvious was easy, and easy made for carelessness and created blindness to what the obvious obfuscated.

It was never the trap you could see that snared you.

That was Clare 101.

To see the obfuscated, they'd need an unknown observer, and so Jill had flown out a day early to get that observer's vantage, and he'd been the lure, traveling on the ticket Dmitry's guy had sent, a ticket purchased in a name that, until last week, they'd believed only they and Clare had known. So it wasn't *that* he'd drawn attention that had come as a surprise, it was *whom* he'd drawn attention from, and what she really wanted to know was why the US government had sent a kill team after him.

He'd like to have had that answer for himself.

She said, "Someone went through a lot of trouble to put that team on your flight, John, but I just don't get it. Those guys were slow to adapt, got panicky over losing visual, and moved like they were wading through knee-deep mud. The woman has your level of pain-in-the-ass potential, but other than that they didn't exactly send their best, so why bother? Some sort of dry run? A setup for distraction?"

Jack weighed his response.

By any measure they should have had to work harder to shake what was, he assumed, a highly trained operative team. But that didn't mean the killers were second rate or lacked skills, it meant their own frames of reference were skewed. Compared to what Clare had thrown at them, anything else *would* be easy. That had been the whole point of their insane childhoods — day after week after month trapped inside her paranoid nightmare of psych-outs and blindsiding tests — never knowing what would come at them or when, because her whole purpose in life was to prepare them for a war she saw coming but that never arrived.

"Just their first taste of what they're chasing," he said. "Took them by surprise, is all. It's going to get harder."

Jill gave him a heavy dose of side-eye. "Why would anyone come after us in the first place if they didn't already know what they were chasing?"

He didn't have an answer for that, either.

"I marked four," she said. "How many you think we missed?"

He shrugged in noncommittal nonanswer.

There was no *we* here. He knew exactly how many operatives had followed him off that flight, and he also knew they weren't the only ones who'd come looking. There'd been another spotter in the waiting area — he'd made the guy right about the time he'd caught sight of Jill — and where there was one, there'd be others. Priorities had forced him to keep moving and trust that she'd find what needed finding and let him know the rest later.

The whole truth required quid pro quo, and she was holding out.

The aircraft started forward under its own

power, and the long taxi to the runway began. Tarmac and grassy areas and position markings filled the windows. He said, "When were you planning to tell me about the Russians?"

The corners of her lips twitched in that way they always did when she realized she'd overplayed her hand. "Not Russians," she said. "Russian. Singular."

His brain measured her assessment against a history of half-truths and lies.

"Nobody sends one-man surveillance," he said. "Not for people like us."

Her tone caught a corner and edged toward offense. She said, "Well, if he *did* have partners, they were better than anything Clare's thrown our way, because I sure as hell didn't make them."

"Clearly."

She sniffed in disdain. "A little credit, dickface. If I was gonna lie about it, I'd offer you something plausible."

Jack pinched the bridge of his nose.

That in itself was a lie, but she was right about the Russian, not that he believed her, per se, but her version confirmed what he'd seen for himself, even if he still questioned what he'd seen exactly. The spotter had been aware of him — recognized him — and hadn't tried to hide it, and he'd seemed to be aware of the kill team and seemed to be there simply to observe.

Jack said, "The guy knew I was being hunted?"

She leaned back with a wistful exhale. "Yeah. He saw it all. He was good, old school. Like Clare in the body of a sixty-something-year-old man."

Jack let the description settle.

Disguise was personal, not some generic Halloween costume that anyone could pull on and off at will. Age, body structure, physical agility created constraints, and those constraints made it a whole lot easier to pass off a woman in her late fifties as a male of similar age than to give a sixty-year-old man the swagger of a teenage gangbanger.

Jill was too smart, had too much of Clare in her, to assume what she saw was anything other than what she was meant to see, which was why she hadn't identified the spotter by age or gender and had instead identified the tradecraft.

The tradecraft was an issue.

He said, "You sure it wasn't Clare?"

"Thought crossed my mind more than once, but no, wasn't her." She leaned into the aisle. "He knew who I was, knew I'd made him, and never once tried to evade. If anything, he was amused by the whole thing, like we were both in on a private joke."

"Amused," Jack said. "By watching killers try to take out your brother."

"Ohhh, your little girl feelings are hurt."

"No, my big girl feelings are appalled."

"Oh, for fuck's sake, you were fine — you knew it, he knew it, I knew it — and now you're missing the point. Forget about the *estadounidense* for a minute and try explaining that Russian super-tradecraft spy guy, singular."

"I can't."

"Such a drama queen."

He waved her off.

"Think he was Dmitry's guy who bought the tickets?"

Her fingers punctuated *Dmitry* with air quotes, but the question still assumed there even was a Dmitry in the first place — that the KGB agent who'd donned the persona of Dmitry Vasiliev twenty-seven years ago was who'd extended the meet-and-greet invitation that had brought them here — and not someone else using his name and familial connection.

He said, "Anyone else would have tried to put a bullet in your back, the same way the Americans tried to put one in mine."

Voice singsong and teasing, she said, "Clare would beg to differ."

As if two weeks ago they hadn't both valued Clare's opinion somewhere between dementia and psychosis. But that had been before mercenaries had stormed her house and she'd been abducted, and assassins had come after the two of them, and overnight a lying, paranoid, delusional narcissist had morphed into an information repository critical to survival. Even Clare hadn't known who'd put the hit out on her. Or them.

"The past doesn't forget," she'd said. "I had a lot of time to make a lot of enemies, and there's not one among them who wouldn't kill you to get to me. The Broker, knowing who'd pay most for that information, is at the head of the line."

Clare had left them to cut off that head.

She'd promised to let them know if she made it out alive, but promises for her were as situational as her ethics. They hadn't heard from her — might never hear from her — because Clare did what Clare wanted, when she wanted, for reasons only she understood, and none of that changed the baseline. The world's underbelly now knew she had children, and knew where those children had last been seen.

The possibilities as to who might be interested in their movements were endless, reliable information on those movements was valuable, and just because someone didn't want to kill them here and now didn't mean they weren't planning to kill them later.

He didn't have the energy to articulate all that, so he said nothing.

Jill said, "Fine, I'll try one for size. We get a call from someone claiming to be Dmitry. You fly on the ticket he bought, and somehow *coincidentally* there's an *American* hit squad on that same flight. My bet is that the spotter was there to confirm the pieces were falling into place. You only need a single pair of eyes for that."

Jack rolled his eyes.

She said, "What?"

He said, "The Russian was amused, like you were both in on the same joke."

"Yeah."

"And he knew I had killers at my back."

"Yeah."

"You don't call in a hit squad for shits and giggles, and a joke is only an inside joke if everyone in on it is amused by the same thing, so either he didn't want me dead or you did. Which was it?"

The aircraft slowed and turned. She said,

"He knew the Americans were outclassed. We both did. That's what made it funny."

Jack held up a finger.

He needed her to stop talking.

In his head he saw the hit squad, saw their picket pattern in the airport like beacons inside a cubed map. It would have made better logistical and strategic sense for them to have picked up the trail in Frankfurt than to fly a four-person crew with him across the Atlantic with no ground support on the receiving end. But to get ahead of him like that, they'd have had to have had his itinerary in advance or known who they were looking for ahead of time. They hadn't.

This had been last minute.

He mentally returned to the gate area and watched the flight deplane, and he searched the waiting passengers, saw his sister among them, and the Russian, and he followed his own path into the terminal. The pieces came at him, over and over.

Kill team. Russian. Him. Jill.

Time and again he got stuck on Jill.

What was it she'd just said?

We get a call . . . There was no we.

The hit squad hadn't come after *them,* it'd come after *him.*

They'd picked him up in Dallas, followed him through Frankfurt, staked out his connecting flight to Berlin, and all the while there'd been not a whiff of surveillance on Jill, not in Frankfurt, and not in Dallas the day before, when he'd played observer on the outbound side of her flight.

But the Russian spotter had known them *both.*

If, intentionally or unintentionally, Dmitry-in-finger-quotes had pointed the Americans to him, the Americans would have also known them both. And if it hadn't been Dmitry, then Jill should have been the one with a target on her back, not him.

She was the one who'd taken contracts.

She was the one who, in defiance of everything Clare had taught them, had gone off to work for the Broker. He hadn't pinged that underworld radar, she had.

But if not for Dmitry's invitation, he'd have remained invisible.

This flight was what had drawn him out into the open, and that left Dmitry seeming not so *that* Dmitry, after all. And that took him back to the beginning and back to questions without answers.

Jill said, "So?"

He shook his head. "All I've got is mud."

It was, perhaps, the most honest thing either of them had offered since leaving Dallas.

She said, "Come on, John, stop with the bullshit. You left the terminal. You're holding out on me. Quid pro quo, brother dearest. How far did you get?"

Resentment he'd held back during the long wait for her to arrive morphed into anger over her button-pushing hypocrisy, and against his better judgment, it came rolling out his mouth. "You want to call bullshit?" he said. "I made it around the airport and back and still managed to get to my seat before you. What took you so long?"

She said, "I needed a drink."

"Oh, sure, you had *a* drink. A White Russian, singular?"

"Clever."

He raised his wrist and tapped his watch. "How many guys did you hit up? Four? Five? Or did you manage to score the harder stuff this time?"

She cocked her head, as if running numbers, let the questions go without comment, and reached for a book.

He clenched his jaw and bit back spite.

She knew better than to carry drugs when she traveled, and he'd gone behind her back to search her luggage to make sure she hadn't tried to smuggle them along anyway, but that didn't mean she'd stay clean after they arrived.

The intercom dinged, signaling cabin attendants that takeoff was imminent.

Shoulder inching into the aisle, he said, "You almost missed the flight."

The aircraft picked up speed.

He said, "Where. Were. You."

She leaned toward him, close enough that they were nearly face-to-face, patted his cheek, and said, "I'm here, John. I made the flight. Let it go."

Frustration ground to a hard stop at a sudden fork.

Her eyes were clear. There was no alcohol on her breath, or foreign smells on her skin or clothes or hair. Drink and drugs were predictable if worrying variables, but she hadn't been drinking and she wasn't high, and the absence of explanation was worse than the one he'd imagined. "What are you not telling me?" he said.

She smiled a dangerous, power-flaunting smile.

The core of him shut down.

He knew better than to trust her, knew better than to accept at face value that she wanted this trip for the same reason he did, knew that setting himself up to depend on her was the same as putting money in front of a thief and drugs in front of an addict — knew it the way he knew his lungs needed air and his stomach needed food — and had done it anyway because she'd promised this time would be different, and he'd wanted so much to believe.

But this was who she was, and all she'd ever be, a woman who treated jobs, friends, lovers like collectible trophies in a winner-takes-all game of life in which nothing could ever hurt as long as she didn't care enough for it to matter. In her reductive, zero-sum way of thinking, not losing was the same as winning, and Dmitry was a prize she'd rather watch slip away than risk letting him have.

His hands demanded what his vocal cords couldn't.

She said, "Don't pick a fight you can't win."

In a different mood she might have slugged him, and if she had, he'd have been forced to take the beating, because to retaliate was to escalate, and she was twisted enough to set the world on fire even if that meant burning in the flames.

He couldn't out-crazy her crazy. He cared too much to take that risk.

He shoved the second earbud into place, and turned the volume up, way up.

The wheels lifted off the ground.

Pressure in the cabin built alongside the

pressure in his head.

For her, this search for Dmitry might, at best, put meaning to their mother's past and make some sense of an upturned childhood.

Answers would be nothing more than potential weapons.

But for him they were atonement, a way to avoid repeating the mistakes of a past in which he'd taken time and opportunity for granted and lost the man who'd been the closest thing he'd known to a father.

He was willing to pay just about any price to get them.

And his sister, by forcing him to cede, had just forced his hand.

Chapter 6

Frankfurt (Main) Hauptbahnhof
Frankfurt, Germany

Holden

He nudged the plate toward the table's center and angled for a better view of the promenade. They were out there, three would-be killers, one browsing magazines at the newsstand across the walkway, another in the curio shop next door, the third somewhere in the direction of the long-distance tracks.

They didn't care if he saw them.

He'd tipped his hat and said hello, and they in turn had moved on to the pack predator strategy of tundra wolves nipping at the edges to keep the herd running until exhaustion singled out weakness. They had the resources to keep him moving, sleep deprived, until he wore down and made mistakes.

Better to get this over with now.

He ordered espresso, one final round before the chase, and he retrieved a packet of SIM cards from his jacket liner. They were burner numbers, activated over time as part of the ongoing process required to stay connected in a life that called for complete disconnection. They were utterly worthless without phones, but about the only thing that'd have drawn more unwanted attention than hauling a bag of cell phones through airport security was if he'd tried a bag of cash or a bottle of water, so he'd split the difference with minis, unlocked GSM devices about the size of a pack of gum.

They were shit quality and had no Wi-Fi capability, but they were cheap, disposable, easy to hide, and right now they were all he had.

One SIM, one location, one call, that was the burn rate of attrition.

He had started with three, had burned one at the airport to give his would-be murderers a signal to follow, and had led them here.

He didn't want to kill them, not on any personal level.

He wanted to be left alone — wanted to get to Berlin — *needed* to get to Berlin before he lost the twins and the trail went cold, and dealing with this ate away time he didn't have and would cost them a whole lot more than they thought it would.

They'd have been better served waiting for another day.

He'd warned them.

He'd taken one of their team while on the flight, the one with the pilot bag.

Had waited until the meal service was done and the cabin lights went off and the woman in the seat behind him had left to use the restroom, and he'd slipped in to take her place. In a dark filled with noise-reduction headphones, face masks, and movie screens, no one had noticed — hadn't noticed him, or the gloved hand between seatbacks, or the piece of gauze as it rested against the man's skin.

A few seconds was all he'd needed.

There was no ego in sneaking in and sneaking away, but that's why he still breathed when others more skilled didn't.

In his world longevity required invisibility.

He'd been content to let carfentanil do his work.

The big-game tranquilizer was a hundred times more potent than fentanyl, which was in itself fifty times more potent than heroin. It didn't need to be injected or imbibed to work, and a dose no larger than a couple grains of salt brushed up against unprotected skin was enough to shut down the involuntary nervous system.

No violence. No sense of foul play.

Until an autopsy showed otherwise, he'd have simply gone to sleep and never woken — an easier, happier death than Holden could have expected had the roles been reversed — but the man's teammates would understand and know.

Holden's mistake was hoping they'd heed the warning.

He found the French SIM and nudged it into a waiting slot.

Every niche, no matter how small, had someone willing to supply the market.

Assassins were perhaps the smallest niche of all.

He powered up and dialed.

A gruff voice answered in Euskara-tinged French.

There weren't many people Holden would trust with his location or his life, but the wiry sixty-year-old Basque who ran Janssens Outfitting out of Brussels was among them. Holden said, "Do you still offer courier service?"

"This depends on the location and the order."

"Bonn. Germany," Holden said. "Forty-nine and fifty-two."

Silence hung over the line for a surprised beat, followed by a laugh — spontaneous laughter, which Holden read as relief — and Itzal said, "It is good to know you are alive, my friend. Much bad weather this week, so many accidents. You've heard?"

"I've heard."

"A difficult season, fewer customers, the couriers don't come to work. But give me the address. For you, I make delivery my-self."

A delivery would put the man directly in the crosshairs, and Holden couldn't in good conscience allow that. Not that Itzal couldn't hold his own — he'd been fighting one war or other since he was a young teenager among the Basque separatists — but this wasn't his war to wage.

Holden said, "I'm not well. A drop would be better."

"Then you should rest. I will come to you."

Message received, message rejected.

Itzal would do what Itzal would do.

Holden said, "Be safe like Mozart, my friend."

"There's no one safer."

Given the man's life and all he'd survived, that was probably true.

Holden ended the call.

The SIM was trash, the phone was trash.

He had fifteen minutes to make the train.

He dropped the steak knife off the table's edge, slid it up his sleeve, and when the server cleared the plate, he smiled his most charming, distracting smile.

He paid the bill, waited for a group at a nearby table to finish, and followed them toward the long-distance tracks and high-speed trains.

The assassin hunters fell in not far behind.

He could feel them at his elbows, woman at the right, short black hair now long and brown, jeans and jacket converted to slacks and a chic blouse, and the hipster to his left, flannel shirt and jeans, easy to pick out of the crowd because no self-respecting German would be caught looking like a lumberjack from early last century.

The Asian guy was ahead, by the tracks.

Voices echoed beneath the towering glass arch.

Pigeons squabbled and scattered in a rush of aerial acrobatics.

The restaurant group veered off for an exit, leaving him exposed.

He walked faster, senses heightened, adrenaline rushing up his skin.

Crowds were his protection.

Cameras were his protection.

United States operatives, guests on foreign soil working without the cooperation of their local hosts, required invisibility more than he did. They'd need to come in close, clean and quiet, with no witnesses, no collateral damage.

Human shields deprived them of opportunity.

That was why he'd gone from terminal to public transportation to Frankfurt's central station. That and he needed an alternate route to the old capital.

Holden turned down a track, boarded a train, destination Berlin, and hurried the aisle from car to car. The woman kept pace along the platform.

The Asian guy had gotten on the train ahead.

The hipster boarded behind, boxing him in the middle.

Holden's walk became a run. The cars were still near empty, not enough witnesses to prevent a bullet in his back. Distance ticked out inside his head, distance and speed and the rate at which they closed in.

A vestibule loomed ahead, the space between cars where a metal floor and an accordion of thick rubber were all that separated passengers from the tracks. He tugged a hairpiece from his sleeve, slid the door open, shut it behind him, and off to the side of its small window, he shrugged out of the jacket, flipped it inside itself, stuffed his hat down into the mix, and pulled tight.

Jacket and hat became canvas bag.

Backpack went into bag.

Short black hair became straggly blond.

Glasses went from pocket to face.

Ripped fingerless wool gloves went on both hands, and a spritz of *au de garbage* across his chest. Shoulders slumped, focus to the floor, he pulled the door open and lurched back the way he'd come, moving slowly, drunkenly, searching seats and picking up stray newspapers and magazines.

The hipster dude caught a whiff, stepped aside to let him pass.

Holden dropped steak knife into palm and, with the same feral will that had consumed his thirteen-year-old self in Calamar, sent the knife plunging, stab after stab, in a train-car version of the prison-yard rush. He gripped the hipster's arms to steady him, dropped him into the empty seat at his knees, rolled him over to drift into forever sleep, and continued on.

He took no pleasure in the kill and felt no pain.

They were a tactical team doing a job, just

as he'd done similar jobs. He'd have been content to walk away if they'd been willing to leave him alone.

A life for a life.

It didn't have to be this way.

He limped to the end of the car, hobbled down to the platform, and shuffled back to the concourse. Inside his head the clock ticked down.

Three minutes until departure to Bonn.

He still had half the tracks to cross.

The inexperienced would be tempted to hurry.

He'd been surviving longer than the hipster had been alive.

He limped steadily forward, consistent, never breaking character.

Far behind him, the woman shouted.

He reached the track, the train to Bonn, closed in on the rear car, gripped the handrail, hauled himself slowly up the stairs, and hitched down the aisle for an empty seat that put distance between his body and the window.

He could see them still, the two of them, running full out across the terminal, closing in on him in a race against time.

The car lurched.

The carriage moved, picking up speed.

He slid closer to the window and watched

the chase, human against train, and last he saw them they were halfway down the platform, trying to catch their breath.

CHAPTER 7

Hotel Mozart
Bonn, Germany

Holden

A five-minute walk from the station took him to the boutique hotel, a stately prewar house in a quiet neighborhood of similar stately homes, and he jogged its stairs for private doors that led to a reception area that might have been a parlor in more genteel times. Itzal had arrived first. Holden caught sight of him in the hall, seated on an upholstered high-backed bench, with hard cases on the floor beside each leg and, Holden knew, handguns strapped to each shin, and two more at least beneath the leather coat.

The old Basque wore time like a badge of honor. His dark eyes and weathered face tracked Holden from door to desk to check-in to stairs and Holden finally lost sight of him on the first landing. He continued up, testing carpet tread and bannister strength, and made a full run of the third-floor hallways before looping back for his own door.

The room, small, updated, modern, had a street-facing window.

He dumped his bag on the bed, rounded for the curtains, and scanned left and right. The hotel sat at the bend of a Y junction, he had only a partial view, and the seven minutes between entering hotel and entering room were an eternity in shooter years, which left him working blind.

The killers would come — might already be here — he'd guaranteed it by calling ahead from the train to confirm the reservation, adding another radar blip to the same phone and same SIM he'd used to make the booking at Frankfurt Airport.

They knew he wasn't careless.

They'd recognize the call as the lure it was.

But they had already shown him they had no choice but to pursue and so they'd come, and they'd compensate with resources he couldn't see — drones, satellite access, database connections to every repository known to man.

What they wouldn't have was on-the-ground resources.

There'd be no local police or SWAT equivalent tossing flash bangs through the windows, not unless those who ran these killers were ready to loop a diplomatic ally in on the fact they'd been running a dark op under their noses *after* the thing had gone to shit, and he didn't think they were ready to burn that bridge quite *yet*.

They'd come quietly.

He hoped they'd come quickly.

He had two hours before the next departure to Berlin. One way or the other, he was going to be on that train, preferably without his executioners in tow.

Knuckles beat a knock-pause-knock on wood.

Holden left the window, opened the door.

Itzal carried the two cases in, set them on the bed, stretched a hand in Holden's direction, and when Holden took it, the old man pulled him in tight for a hug.

Holden gripped the man's forearms, released them, and carried the cases to the window, where he could unload supplies while keeping an eye on the street.

Itzal said, "What do we face?"

Holden rummaged through the first case. "There's no *we* in this, my brother."

Itzal, soft, plainspoken, said, "To this *con-*

90

nerie, I say *non.*"

Holden withdrew a couple passports, thirty thousand in cash, and a SIG Sauer P226 semiautomatic. "All the same," he said. He retrieved two spare magazines, several boxes of ammunition. "This is my problem. My war."

"You can say with *confiance* who is on this target list?"

"No," Holden said. "No confidence at all."

"This is, yes, also my war," Itzal said. "After first priority like you are gone, they come for the second, and after the second is gone, they come for me. You die today. I die tomorrow. You live today, there are fewer killers tomorrow. It is *our* war."

Holden opened the second case, retrieved the Arctic Warfare rifle and a Bullet Blocker fleece vest. He needed to get to Berlin. He needed to be there for the rendezvous, needed to pick up whatever trail remained of the twins before it went completely cold, and pride was a waste of time. He said, "Okay."

He stood, emptied his jacket pockets, removed its liner, pulled off the hairpiece, and handed both jacket and hairpiece over. "Give me three minutes to get to the roof. Then go be me down on the restaurant patio."

91

Itzal pointed to the rifle. "I thought my help is more like so."

Holden zipped into the vest, stuffed what he couldn't carry back into the cases, and snapped the lids. "I know what I'm looking for," he said. "Putting you up top will get me killed." He dumped ammunition from a box and fed the first SIG magazine.

Itzal said, "And what is this you look for?"

Holden spoke in time to rounds clicking into place. "One male, Asian. One hundred seventy-eight centimeters. One female, Caucasian. One hundred seventy centimeters. Changing faces, changing costumes. Semiautomatic handguns. Possibly a sniper, though I haven't spotted one yet. Possible reinforcements. Intel off-site. Unlimited resources overhead. I've already taken half their team. They're angry. Now it's personal."

The corners of Itzal's lips turned up in sly understanding.

Caring was dangerous. Anger was worse. Both clouded thinking, both could get a person killed, and with half their team dead, they'd be too far in on both to go back on either. Holden counted on that. He snapped the magazine into the SIG and started loading the next. "They know I want them here," he said. "They might wait for me at the station."

Itzal slipped out of his coat and replaced it with Holden's jacket.

He said, "They know you'll return?"

"They know where I need to get."

The old man tsked. "There are other ways to travel. Only fools assume." He motioned to Holden's weaponry. "But you do not see them as fools."

"No," Holden said. "Not fools."

He dug into the jacket's liner, pulled out the mini phone he'd burned to call the hotel, and shoved the accompanying SIM back into place. The kill team had a better chance of getting to him here than they would at the station. They had to know that, but another nudge wouldn't hurt. He tossed the device toward Itzal. "That links to me," he said. "If there's anyone you hate, now would be a really good time to call."

Itzal rolled the phone over in his hand. "I keep this?"

Holden said, "Be my guest." He shoved the cases under the bed, holstered the SIG, and picked up the rifle. "Did you come by car?"

"Of course."

"How close are you?"

"Close enough."

"Close enough to run?"

93

"There will be no running."

Holden strode to the door and paused, hand on the hardware.

There were two killers headed his way, possibly more. He needed a clean here and gone, couldn't afford a protracted firefight that locked him into the neighborhood, and every minute after the first round, and every extra round beyond the first, exponentially cut the chances of extracting without complications. The odds of lining up two clean shots directly correlated to how much risk Itzal assumed.

The prospects frustrated him.

He should have ended all four killers while he was on that plane.

He left the room without a word, continued to the access door at the end of the hall, and climbed a ladder up, methodically, rhythmically, counting time in a careful balance between the need to hurry and the need to keep his heartbeat steady.

He let himself out onto asphalt tiles.

Unlike the gables that topped every other house in sight, the Mozart's rooftop was nearly flat, and unlike the window in his room, the rooftop gave him access to a 270-degree bird's-eye vantage over the Y junction.

He belly crawled toward the edge and

scanned the streets, seeking movement in windows and tiny side yards, searching between parallel-parked cars and manicured hedges. Time wore on, and with time came impatience.

Late afternoon brought a slow increase in bicycles, pedestrians, and vehicles.

He fought against himself, and he fought to clear his head.

Below, Itzal left the patio, crossed the street, and placed himself in Holden's direct line of site. He was a horrible body double. The hairpiece and jacket looked ridiculous on him, embarrassing really, but the imitation didn't need to be good, just good enough to be seen. Cigarette in one hand, miniature phone in the other, Itzal dialed.

The line answered, and the conversation grew animated and agitated, dragging on longer than Holden expected, but whoever Itzal had called and whatever was said produced a reaction that time, on its own, hadn't, and Holden, intent on protecting the old man from threat on the ground, nearly missed the threat on the rooftop at his right.

Shadow alerted him.

Instinct rolled him left.

Adrenaline slowed time to the metronome beat inside his chest.

A sound-suppressed rifle crack dissipated with the city noise.

A bullet struck where he'd been lying.

Instinct kept him rolling.

Another crack, another near miss.

The human psyche, primed for survival, urged him to evade, and the human psyche under attack screamed for retaliation. Instinct stopped him on his back. Rifle stock to shoulder, he searched for the source of fire. Experience, logic, and the four-pound fleece vest with its stitched Kevlar plates held him fast.

He had nowhere to shelter, couldn't afford to miss.

He waited, exposed, daring a bullet to find him.

A shadow and hint of out-of-place color tripped his focus to a gable peak.

The color shifted and time stretched out into a long warp between life and death, filling the space between heartbeats, and hair became forehead, and forehead became eyebrows, and Holden's finger reacted.

The rifle report thundered through the quiet.

Red mist filled the crosshairs.

He rolled back to face the street and a world on pause, suspended in the half-second uncertainty that lay between vehicle ackfire and reason to run. But someone down there had known that sound. He hunted for that anomaly.

He found it on a bicycle. The woman with the black hair was a redhead now, twenty years older, twenty pounds heavier, grocery bags in the basket, pedaling forward with the weariness of a long day on her feet. He hesitated, mistrusting judgment, unsure of recognition, unwilling to risk civilian casualties.

She continued in Itzal's direction because Itzal was along her path.

Nothing about her indicated interest in him, nothing indicated threat.

Holden followed her with the scope, waiting.

She reached into the basket.

He found black in her hand.

He controlled his breathing, controlled his heart rate, and waited longer to ensure this thing she had reached for wasn't a phone or wallet, waited, knowing that waiting too long meant Itzal would be dead, waited until her gaze rose and focused on Itzal's jacket.

Holden shifted crosshairs from head to thigh and pulled.

For the second time, the rifle crack ripped through silence.

The woman fell. Her bike clattered. Itzal hurried toward her with all the urgency of a passerby running to help, and it was help, but of a different sort.

The decision to take a nonfatal shot came from trust.

Itzal, on the ground, was in a better position to assess her true threat.

His hands worked fast. Her head dropped. He called for help, and the front staff rushed from the hotel, and in the confusion, Itzal slipped away.

Holden inched back from the edge.

Time, unspooling, made movement feel like slogging through sludge.

He found the spent shell casings, pocketed them. Crawled back to the access ladder, raced the rungs down, and hurried to the room to collect his cases.

The *Polizei* would have already been called.

He had to be gone before they arrived.

He disassembled the rifle and shoved each piece securely into foam, snapped the cases shut, grabbed the handles, left the room, and jogged down past the now-empty first-floor lobby, down to the hotel's basement, and pushed out the door into a small parking garage. If things were otherwise, he'd head for the border and spend the next week out of sight, laying low, waiting for the drama to die down, but he didn't have that luxury.

An engine revved. Tires squealed.

A black BMW 6 Series backed up and stopped in front of him.

The passenger window rolled down.

Itzal said, "There will be no running. Come."

CHAPTER 8

Savignyplatz
Berlin, Germany

Jack

He stepped from train to open-air platform, out of stale air into a drizzling damp and the must of aged stone, wet concrete, and hints of exhaust from late afternoon traffic. He pulled the old jacket tight against the chill and followed the transit crowd, moving slow, head low, shoulders stooped, right leg hitching with a slight limp he'd picked up just outside Berlin's Hauptbahnhof.

Train doors hissed and closed.

The carriage gave way to empty tracks.

A sparse crowd waited on the opposite platform.

He veered out of the pedestrian flow for an empty bench, groaned stiff joints toward the seat, and leaned forward to tie wayward laces.

Loafers, sandals, heels, and sports shoes strode past his head.

He analyzed gaits and soles and sizes, searching for the familiar and for the out of place, and he scrutinized the shape and height of bodies and clothing across the tracks, looking for signs of the same — an amateur maneuver, obvious and sloppy by old-school standards — anachronistic cloak-and-dagger theater in a world where station cameras and city cameras, facial recognition, gait recognition, and the predictive software they tied to posed a more realistic threat.

Would have, anyway, if subterfuge wasn't as much about showing a hand as hiding one, and digital surveillance didn't still have exploitable weaknesses.

As far as electronic eyes were concerned, he'd never gotten off the plane.

What concerned him in the here and now were the human eyes belonging to those who knew better, those who knew where and how to look.

His sister's words kept him tied to that past and dying art.

"Old school," was what she'd said.

Clare in the body of a sixty-something-year-old man.

He'd detoured through public spaces,

down underground walkways, up empty side streets, into covered shopping areas, and out parking garages to ensure the only way those eyes could stay on him was to follow on foot. He'd moved slowly enough, obviously enough to avoid losing the tail, attempting to force errors and flush whoever followed him so he could see for himself what he was up against and how many were out there, or convince himself he hadn't been followed at all.

Three hours of wasted time.

He was as certain of being alone as certainty would allow and doubted the certainty. Anyone capable of eluding him this far was capable of eluding still, but neither could he find what didn't exist, and therein lay the madness.

Absent proof, he found remnants of a ghost in everything.

He just wasn't sure *whose* ghost, exactly.

He stretched arthritic fingers toward his shoe and secured the laces, waited until another train rolled in, and joined the departing crowd headed toward Else-Ury-Bogen. Shielded by movement and numbers, he shed his limp and shed the hat, converted jacket to coat, swapped chipped and aged glasses for big, black, bulky frames, and exited out onto the street a good twenty years younger than he'd gone in.

And he followed the old cobblestones parallel to the tracks, scanning windows and doors, searching camera angles, feeding distance calculations and route possibilities to the multidimensional maze inside his head, a maze in which he could travel only forward, never back, and every move toward one opponent rotated layers within time and space, creating blind spots, opening weakness, and shutting off access to the others.

His primary goal was survival.

The goal of survival was to find Dmitry, the real Dmitry. And every other person within the maze was an adversary intent on thwarting that goal.

The US hit squad was close and closing in.

They'd had proxies waiting for him at the Berlin airport, local operatives assembled out of the embassy in a hurry, on the barest of need to know. He'd seen that in their hair and clothing styles, their familiarity with the airport, and in the way they wore dumb cluelessness like a group of teenagers who'd stumbled from bed to kitchen in search of coffee and found themselves in an airport, playing facial Whac-A-Mole. It hadn't been a fair match, not by any stretch, those four officers, agents — whatever they were —

with real world training, put up against a pair whose entire lives had been preparation to survive the worst of Clare's paranoid fantasies.

If he'd been a different kind of target, they'd already be dead.

But that they were there at all, *that* was a problem.

He'd expected a welcome committee of some sort.

With the way his original itinerary had been booked through to Berlin, it'd have been incompetence of the highest order for them not to have someone on the ground watching as a just in case, but this hadn't been that. These three, with their luggage, neck pillows, electronic distractions, and the basic accoutrements of a long layover, were too starched, too food and drink free, too directly focused on one specific gate — his specific gate — to have already spent hours watching a succession of flights deplane.

They'd come in a hurry. Recently. Specifically.

They were watching for *his* flight.

Which meant that at some point in the hour and a half between the departure gate closing in Frankfurt and the arrival gate opening in Berlin, someone had connected the dots linking him from one flight to the next, and for that to have happened, there'd have had to have been vast resources and top analysts working to make him dead.

He had no idea why.

And he'd had no time to pursue that tangent, because in the hierarchy of what mattered most, finding Dmitry took priority, and the Russians had been waiting, too. There'd been two of them this time, nowhere near as skilled as the solitary spotter in Frankfurt but skilled enough. They'd been aware of the American presence and aware of Jill and aware of him, and he'd seen for himself what his sister had described:

One team hunted him.

The second observed the hunt.

The whole of it had been déjà vu, which had sent blood rushing to his head and certainty careening into chaos. Time had split, dropping him into an alternate reality in which the invitation from Dmitry had never happened and these operatives weren't Americans or Russians and none of this was real — not in any true sense — because this was Clare again, Clare manipulating perception and manufacturing truth, Clare putting his mind under fire and his body in the crosshairs, Clare testing response and reaction time, just as she'd done his whole damn life, and in that alternate reality this entire thing was an elaborate show-and-tell, live-demonstration field test, to which outsiders had come to witness what he and his sister could do.

Hate and disgust and rebellion had risen from deep buried grudges.

Hate for the woman who should have been his mother, disgust at himself for being so goddamn gullible, and adamant refusal to be her unwitting puppet.

He'd stood there a second, two, maybe three, brain numb, limbs immobile, committing the unforgivable of unforgivable sins, while his heart raced and his stomach lurched and his mind spiraled in a grasp for any single point in time to which he could anchor reality. Training had smacked him upside the head, forcing him to move and blend and be, and he'd recovered from a failure that would have been fatal had he been up against more hardened opponents.

He'd retreated the way he'd come, and he'd left the terminal on an employee shuttle with a crew changing shifts, his body functioning on habit while his mind rewound and replayed every explosion, every bullet, and every conversation that filled the past two weeks, rewriting what he thought he knew into a different version of the same story, one in which Clare, the master puppeteer, pulled all the strings.

But he hadn't been able to make the performance work.

Not all the characters anyway, and so the pressure had eased and reality had shifted back to the way it had been, but the hate and disgust and rebellion had remained.

He blamed Clare.

Even if this wasn't her doing, she'd still put him here, all those years of fucking with his head, of never letting his mind shut down, of turning every location and every encounter into a potential threat to be outmaneuvered when, really, the only threat had ever come from her. This was her legacy, this life of lies, in which up was never up and down never down and every action and every word existed in two or more states at once.

Her paranoid delusions had spawned his own.

Now he saw *her* hand in everything.

That kind of mind-fuckery would be what got him killed in the end.

He shoved his hands into his pockets, pushed her as far out of his head as he could get her, and rounded toward Savignyplatz, a rectangle of prewar buildings and quaint high-end stores and restaurants that formed a town square of sorts around a small park, and he followed past awning-covered tables and waitstaff wiping off the last of the passing rain, observing the clientele, absorbing the ambience, and eavesdropping on conversations. These were his markers, the sounds, sights, and smells he'd need to replicate when the time came to vanish again. And he moved north, to Kantstrasse, the thoroughfare that divided the park where he traded euros with a street vendor for an umbrella, and followed Stilwerk, a furniture mall, around the corner.

Buildings rose beside him, five-, six-, seven-story structures standing shoulder to shoulder, outlining a city block and forming a hollow core: ground floors occupied by restaurants and mom-and-pop stores, which opened to the street, and apartments above them, which were accessed through the *Hof* — the communal center courtyard, which, in this case, had been turned into tenant parking. He knew it from satellite images that he'd measured to the meter, and knew it by scent-triggered memories he couldn't quite grasp.

The Berlin Savoy was through that courtyard, face to the parallel street.

It didn't seem possible that out of all the

hotels in Berlin, Dmitry would have chosen this one by chance. He assumed it was another nod, some secret handshake, like the way their birth names had been used for the Lufthansa tickets.

But Jack had been nine the last time they'd lived in Berlin.

The Savoy was where they'd stayed at first.

The hotel had a long history of secrets and spies, Clare had said, and she'd navigated the halls like she'd been there before, moving through staff-only spaces as if they belonged to her.

She owed someone a favor, she'd told them, and she'd left them for two days. Even then he'd known *favors* meant someone would die. Or live, depending on the circumstances and whose side she'd taken in whatever war went on inside her head.

They'd lived in the city another three months, he and his sister confined to a flat not far from here, assigned a stack of schoolwork, while Clare disappeared for weeks at a time. That apartment had been his prison until he'd mastered what Clare said should be mastered and knowledge had earned him freedom. For him, Berlin had been two weeks of running wild, and then they'd moved again. If this hotel choice was a message, he didn't have the means to decode it. For that, he'd need Clare and, well . . .

For all he knew, it was Clare who'd sent the message in the first place.

CHAPTER 9

Jack

He reached a gap between buildings, a driveway of sorts, and followed it in toward the courtyard center, cautious of windows and balconies and rooftop positions he'd have taken if it were he waiting for someone like him to arrive.

The sound of engine and tires approached from behind.

He tracked the vehicle's path, keying location, distance, speed.

A silver Mercedes passed by, and he quickened his stride.

The vehicle pulled into a reserved parking space. The driver exited for an inner entrance, and Jack followed, mental radar spinning. This was exactly the type of scenario Clare would have used to pop him in the back.

He reached the door, grabbed it before it shut, stepped inside.

The foyer became its multiple parts.

Mailboxes, garbage bin, umbrella holder, elevator, stairs.

Stairs up, stairs down.

The driver thumbed the elevator call button.

Jack headed up, climbing slowly, until the elevator arrived and the doors closed, and then he jogged back to the entry and down again.

The basement door stood unlocked and open and led to a matrix of wood-framed, chain-link storage units. To the far, far left was bicycle parking and a door to the outside, and to the immediate right a laundry room.

Twenty machines, one for each apartment above his head.

He removed the trench coat, which had started out as a bomber jacket, removed the glasses, stuffed them into the coat pocket, tied the arms into a bundle, and strode between storage units, searching the contents from between the wood slats until he found one that looked like stuff had been thrown in at random until it'd reached capacity. He dropped the bundle over the transom where it blended in with the rest, and he continued on to the bicycles, to the basement exit, which led out to a ramp and a small set of stairs, and he stuffed paper into the door's strike-plate hole to keep the automatic lock from engaging and then carried the umbrella back to the laundry room.

Overhead, the elevator dinged.

He paused, tracking footsteps across the foyer and out the front, then pressed the umbrella handle tight above a hinge and tugged the laundry room door.

Pressure became a vise that cracked plastic.

He tossed the pieces into the trash, shoved the bare aluminum tube against the hinge, and slammed the door. Tube became a shiv that, with enough quick force, would punch a hole between ribs. He hoped to never need it. At the sink he ran the water, traced wet fingers through his hair to strip out the gray, and then he headed up the stairs.

The rooftop was empty but for a small seating area, where a collection of carefully tended patio trees and plants framed otherwise weatherworn cushions.

It'd been a while, it seemed, since anyone had visited.

He peered over the wall into the courtyard proper, and into the small private gardens and patios that nudged into it, and had a clear view of adjacent rooftops and interior-facing windows, and he stood there breathing in the cold, damp air, returning to days he'd been forced to evade Clare in an environment much like this, forced to find her before her nonlethal rounds found him.

He'd been seven the first time she'd shot him.

She'd brushed aside his brokenhearted protests and poked his still welting bruise. "Of course it hurt," she'd said. "That's how you remember there are consequences to failure. If you're smart, you'll learn to avoid getting hit."

He'd gone up against her time after time, driven by the hope of hurting the thing that hurt him most. It'd taken nearly five years before he'd managed to do it, and like an animal taunted for years by those he couldn't reach, he hadn't been kind when he'd managed to break free. All he'd had to do was tag her. He'd knocked her out cold with the butt of his rifle and left her cuffed to the underside of an engine block.

She'd shown up a day later, never said a word about it, but she'd upped the stakes for the next round, proving yet again that winning was never the end and that the only way to truly win was to refuse to play.

He hadn't had that choice back then.

Her world had been all he knew and all he had, and bruising, bleeding, and breaking had been easier than facing the push-pull of love and rejection, which she'd honed into a precision weapon. To rebel had always hurt more in the end, so he'd complied.

He'd hated her and loved her — hated and loved her still.

Had wanted to destroy her and had wanted to make her proud.

This hunt for Dmitry was a different side of that multifaceted coin.

He turned and headed back to the stairs and down to ground level, and all the while Clare's voice, in his head, echoed variations of itself over the years.

You're answering the wrong question, John.

No, this isn't about tactics, it's about strategy.

He angled across the courtyard and past the Savoy's restaurant garden, guarded against the hit squad, against Dmitry and, most of all, against his own damn mother, still unconvinced this wasn't her tugging at his strings. He exited onto Fasanenstrasse, a full diagonal from where he'd gone in, and strolled the tree-lined sidewalk, past boutiques and restaurants, and pushed through gilded glass doors into a throwback world of marble floors and wood-paneled walls.

He spotted the first target at the edge of the lounge just off the lobby, six feet flat, well fed, poorly exercised, earpiece, bored, and only partially attentive, but no name badge and suit too nice for hotel security. Jack threaded past a large central floral display and pressed on toward the restaurant. He found his second target beside the elevator bank, five feet nine, not quite as well fed, better exercised, identical earpiece, similar suit, equally bored, and twice as attentive.

This guy's jacket was open, his holster partly visible.

Sloppy.

They were a different kind of crew than what had waited at the airports, had a different feel about them, and were easy to find because they'd made themselves easy to find. Not to scare him off, but as an invitation to approach.

Curious.

He made a quick pass through the restaurant and patio, returned to the cashier station, where a lean brunette in a pencil skirt flipped through a ledger. He pointed to the phone beside the register and made a go of rusty German.

"Darf ich Anruf zu die Rezeption machen?"

She smiled, polite and patiently forced, lifted the handset, punched in a quick code, and offered the handset to him. In his ear, a crisp male voice welcomed him to the Savoy with Teutonic efficiency.

Jack said, "English?"

If English wasn't an option, French surely would be. That was the beauty of Europe, where even the lowest patron-facing staff members were trilingual at least.

In his ear the accent remained, but the language changed.

Jack said, "There is a man standing near the lounge. He has a shaved head, dark blue suit, and brown shoes. Could you please tell him Mr. Lefevre and his sister are waiting on the restaurant patio? We are the couple with the red dress and light blue jacket. He may not understand in English. Try Russian if you can."

That last request was a long shot, but it let the messenger know there might be trouble communicating and gave him a chance to accommodate.

Jack tabbed his watch and started the clock.

The front-desk messenger would relay information to Lounge Guy, and Lounge Guy would relay information to Elevator Guy. They couldn't both abandon their posts, and the lobby was a critical no-miss juncture, so Elevator Guy would be the one who came creeping in.

Two minutes from front desk to patio was his bet.

He counted down a minute, turned back toward the restaurant tables, and made a slow return to the double French patio doors.

Rushed footsteps at his back announced his quarry's arrival.

Senses engaged, feeding a composite picture into his brain, and when the body was broadside, Jack dropped umbrella shiv from sleeve into hand, jabbed shiv into waist, reached right arm over torso and into holster, gripped weapon, retrieved it, pressed muzzle to gut.

One second.

The speed felt unnatural, like moving on fast-forward in a world that paused to let him by. In his head he knew the difference between a lifetime of torment under Clare's paranoid tutelage and moderate skills that had grown rusty through infrequent use, but it felt wrong all the same. Clare had taught him to hunt, to hide to kill; had desensitized him to death and pain and fear so that if, God forbid, the time came, he'd have that edge; and had then forced him to deny what he was capable of.

Training said hide first and fight last, that

the best fights were those won by never having to fight at all, and he couldn't count the times he'd taken blows from bullies and strangers, refusing to engage, because drawing attention to his skills would result in far greater pain than getting hit.

What he'd just done directly violated everything he knew.

There was a thrill in that, and danger in the thrill.

Elevator Guy stiffened.

Jack nudged him forward, out the doors, onto the patio, past a woman in a red dress and a man in a blue jacket, who were oblivious to how helpful they'd been, and to a table in the rear that backed up against the ivy trellises, where a boost would get him over the wall as the fastest means of escape.

Jack pointed to a chair.

Elevator Guy sat.

Jack took a catty-corner position, out of arm's reach, weapon in his lap and a clear view of the door and anyone who came through it. He said, "English?"

The guy shrugged.

"Français?"

Guy said, *"Un petit peu."*

Good enough.

He'd have tried Spanish next, but no way in hell was he giving up Russian. There wasn't a disguise in the world that could compensate for being able to understand what others thought you couldn't. Clare had taught him that, and just because she'd turned his life into one long psychotic break didn't make her wrong.

Jack said, "What do you want from me?"

Guy struggled with syntax and word choice but got the point across.

Dmitry was delayed in Prague. He wouldn't arrive in Berlin in time for tomorrow's breakfast. He had made new arrangements and left the details with the front desk. This man and his partner were to confirm when the information had been delivered.

Jack said, "Dmitry told you all this personally?"

Guy said, "Marinov, who works for Dmitry."

Jack's thumb caressed the weapon grip.

This was all such transparent bullshit.

Marinov or Dmitry or Clare, or whoever the hell was bankrolling this thing, knew what he was and knew suspicion, evasion, and self-preservation were part of that package. They might have hoped he'd swing by out of curiosity, just as he had, but they couldn't guarantee it and would have never believed for a minute that he'd actually give up his location by staying in a hotel someone else had booked. If he'd never shown up, there'd have been no message. The men themselves *were* the message.

Jack said, "Tell *Monsieur Marinov* I'll be there tomorrow, as arranged. Anything he has to say, he can say to my face."

Guy hesitated, as if he wasn't quite sure if he'd been dismissed.

Jack said, "Go."

The man backed halfway across the patio, and when he turned, Jack boosted himself from chair to table to wall and dropped over into the center courtyard.

He ran between cars and past the entrance he'd followed the Mercedes driver into, around the corner, down the stairs, and through the basement bicycle door. And he hurried between storage units, climbed chain link to grab his bundle back from over the transom, and raced the stairs up. He was on the rooftop by the time Lounge Guy and Elevator Guy made it to the courtyard, and he watched them search, knocking on doors and disturbing neighbors long past the point of diminishing return, and his sister's words were in his head again, what she'd said about the Russian in Frankfurt.

He knew who I was.

That solitary spotter had known them

both.

The men at the Berlin airport had also known who they searched for.

But these two had stared right through him when he'd walked in.

They didn't know him.

Inside his head the maze shifted so hard, so fast, it almost hurt.

— Dmitry was either Dmitry or not.

— The solitary spotter was connected to Dmitry or not.

— These two were something else, related but not the same.

In response to that understanding, another beacon joined the mental maze, and Jack sighed and pressed the heels of his palms against his eyes.

The enigma of Dmitry had now split into three.

The US government wanted to kill him.

His sister was sabotaging him for entertainment.

And his mother, God only knew what she was up to.

She shouldn't even be part of the equation.

To survive the hit squad, he needed her out of his head. To get answers on Dmitry, he needed Jill out of the way. Last he'd seen of *her,* she'd been dragging her suitcase up the aisle to the front of the plane, the few things he genuinely needed but couldn't carry stuffed in it. The angry half of him, the half that wanted to guarantee he got them back, had begged to GPS collar her, but she'd figure it out, and he couldn't afford the full-blown conflict that'd hit as soon as she did, so he'd watched her go.

The part of him that trusted her knew it was better that way.

The part of him that didn't trust her knew it, too.

The maze tilted, rotated. Strategy formed.

Here, in old West Berlin, he'd found the trail that would lead to Dmitry.

And here he'd start another, one that would draw the hit squad to him.

CHAPTER 10

Friedenau
Berlin, Germany

Jill

She found the door, though not without effort. The streets were all so much the same, four-story apartment next to four-story apartment, balconies and windows and more balconies and windows, similar colors and shapes, and tiny tidy landscaped spaces, corner stores, neighborhood pocket parks, sidewalk cafés, and tree after tree, with leaves that had turned color weeks ago and were now mostly fallen.

The butcher shop jogged her memory.

The awning was gone and the colors had changed, but the rest was familiar enough in the cold, wet drizzle that she found her way.

She recognized the door soon as she saw it — door and postage-stamp garden, which wasn't so much a garden as a few flowerpots and a trimmed-up hedge — and the ornamental gate that set the entry off from the sidewalk.

The only thing that had changed was the graffiti.

Even nice neighborhoods like this couldn't escape the graffiti.

Or the dog shit.

That, too, was a thing with Berlin, the dog shit on sidewalks.

She loved this city. Had loved it then and loved it now, place of outcasts and misfits, where no one belonged and everyone did, where anarchists and old Nazis, hipsters and club kids, street artists, actors, slackers, and thieves should all be at war but weren't, because the city never let you forget what happened when intolerance set in.

The wall was right there, and Stasi headquarters, in the starkest reminders.

Of all the cities they'd traveled, this was the only one that had drawn her back, but never this neighborhood.

She made another pass, searching for signs the place was no longer Clare's. Best as she could tell, nobody was there *right now.*

That was good enough.

Patience had never been her thing.

She pushed through the ornamental gate,

moved the largest flowerpot, and traced a finger in the grooves between the garden stones. The dirt was compact, a lot of rain, a lot of heat and cold and passing seasons since anyone had last messed with it.

Fingers were all she had to do the work.

She'd left the suitcase in a storage locker at the Berlin Hauptbahnhof — regrettable but unavoidable. Luggage was difficult to disguise and impossible to hide, and last thing she needed was to draw attention to this door.

She'd go back for it if she had to.

But if all went the way she hoped, then even what Jack had given to her for safe-keeping would become redundant, because this was Berlin, and Berlin had *stuff* most cities they'd lived in didn't. Well, *had* in the past tense.

Seventeen years was a long, long time, even for someone like Clare.

The groove in the dirt got deeper.

The center stone loosened. With a bit of prying, she got it free.

Beneath the stone was the silicone sleeve; and inside the sleeve, the key.

Jill slipped the metal into the dead bolt.

The lock turned, and the lever gave way.

She opened the door a crack, did a quick check, caught a whiff of stale, dusty air, and knew even before she saw that this was exactly what she wanted.

She shut herself inside the dark, flipped the light, and got nothing.

Her hand fumbled while groping for glow sticks, which should have been left hanging from a hook on the wall. She found one. Grabbed it. Cracked it.

The space lit up in ambient green.

She opened the nearest cupboard in search of bulbs, pulled out a four-pack, screwed one into the naked socket, and tried again. With light came the memories, and a wave of nostalgia as confusing as it was annoying. The room was exactly as her nine-year-old self remembered, albeit half the size, about as big as the cheapest cabin on a cruise ship's lower level, and laid out near the same, with a bunk along the left wall — the type found in tight sleeping quarters, upper level folded up, bottom doubling as a storage locker — and on the right closets and a self-contained bathroom, in which toilet, sink, and shower all occupied the same tiny molded-plastic cubicle.

Clare had quite a few of these across Europe and the Americas, not so much safe houses as safe places. She also had drops in every city they'd lived in and in quite a few they'd only passed through, but those were just boxes or lockers with money, ID, maybe a weapon if it was small enough to fit. The hideaways contained enough to lay low for a few weeks, longer if a situation was dire enough to put up with the conditions that long, as well as everything needed to completely reinvent and vanish.

Each had a carefully crafted story to go with it, and well-paid caretakers who kept watchful eyes on the lights and the owner's keys, and who knew how to get a message through if the unexpected happened.

Jill checked the bathroom, confirmed it still had running water, left the glow stick in the sink, and dragged a hand over the bottom bunk to examine the dust trail.

It hadn't been that long since someone had been here — a few years, if that, definitely not seventeen — Clare, most likely, since Jack tended to avoid available resources for the same reason he avoided anything that kept him tethered to Clare.

Jill didn't have that problem.

She'd made visits to several drops over the years, mostly because pilfering the cash out of them and arguing with Clare after the fact was easier than asking for money up front. Not that Clare ever said no — Clare fucking owed her and knew it, and guilt was useful in that way — but the ordeal of getting to yes meant paying Clare a visit, and it would take a whole lot more than Clare was willing to offer to make *that* worth it.

Jill lifted the plywood that held the bottom mattress and latched it in place.

Beneath was the lid to a metal storage locker, secured with a five-digit combination lock — nothing that couldn't be snipped with bolt cutters or cracked with a little bit of patience — just a basic deterrent against curiosity should someone manage to accidentally stumble in.

Jill pressed the tumblers and rolled the numbers.

The lock was sticky, but it opened.

She raised the lid and secured it to the plywood.

Soft emergency lighting lit up the interior. That was new.

The rest was a time capsule of life on the run.

On the right, watertight, fireproof cases that held passports, driver's licenses, birth certificates, all the paperwork necessary to backstop them, and a shitload of cash in multiple currencies. The rest were firearm and munition cases, sorted by purpose and stopping power, because Clare was, if nothing else, a hypocrite.

She'd started her kids with pellet-gun target practice when they were four, gotten them friendly with knives, fuck all lethal with a crossbow, decent with a compound bow, and to where they could play convincingly with any number of martial arts weapons, but she had never allowed them to keep or carry their own.

Her goal was knowledge and skill, not dependency.

In her view, they'd never be able to predict when or where an attack would come, and they traveled too much, crossed too many borders, and carried so little that they could never know what they'd have on them when *it* struck.

She wanted them smart, capable of thinking on their feet, able to anticipate and avoid confrontation in the first place, but for all that talk, Clare wasn't big on following her own advice and always had reasons for playing by different rules.

She couldn't safely transport weapons and ammunition across the globe, so she stockpiled and stashed them instead. They were her tools, she'd said, and she couldn't afford to have to hunt them down through old contacts when she needed them in a hurry.

At the time, it'd been just one more

convenient lie in an ever-changing story.

Nuance had been wasted on the young.

Jill understood it now.

The same reasoning that had driven Clare to bury her tools propelled Jill to raid this hideaway now. She reached for the fireproof cases, pulled them free, unlocked them, rifled through documents and identification, and retrieved the passports.

Like the dust that had been disturbed in the not-so-distant past, some of the photos and expiration dates pointed to Clare having returned within the past several years.

Jill pocketed two of Clare's older passports.

The resemblance between mother and daughter, which was unmistakable enough to have drawn out killers from Clare's past, made swapping ID a given.

She thumbed through the cash, about two hundred thousand dollars split between euros, Swiss francs, and US currency.

She took about half the dollars and most of the euros.

She would have emptied the bank if that wouldn't have required notifying both brother and mother that the stash had been compromised. It was a safeguard meant to ensure the others didn't get screwed over by expecting to rely on matériel that no longer existed. No way in hell was she giving brother dearest that kind of heads-up on her movements. Same went for Clare. But fail to follow through and Clare would make it a priority to change the locks and codes on every hideaway from here to Timbuktu.

She couldn't take it all, but half was fair game.

By taking no more than half she could leave Jack out of the notification scheme and put off letting Clare know until after this whole thing was finished.

Jill slipped a thousand euros into one of the extra envelopes made available for the purpose and slid the envelope beneath the boarded-up door that separated this room from the house itself.

That was the arrangement.

The money let those on the other side know that whoever had entered belonged there. Without it, they'd alert Clare, and Clare would assume the hideaway had been burned, and it'd be a fantastic way to fuck with her if it wouldn't also mean losing access to all of Clare's hideaways and drops forever, and even *she* wasn't "don't give a shit" crazy enough to pick that kind of fight.

Jill moved to the closet and pulled the doors open.

She'd left the airport buxom and blond.

She was back to being a brown-haired tomboy now.

She'd traveled light, as they always had, planning to pick up what she needed as she went, but the American killers and Russian game players had run out the clock faster than expected, so she'd come for weapons, cash, and ID, but mostly she'd come for Clare's costuming.

Appearance was a better weapon than any bullet or blade. That's what Clare had taught, and it's what had made her dangerous, even to her children.

She could be anyone, anything.

Sometimes it was hard to tell where the real Clare began or ended.

Sometimes it was hard to tell if even Clare knew.

"All self-betrayal comes from mannerism, habit, appearance, or speech," she'd say. "Of those, appearance is easiest to control, and only an idiot would let that be what gave them up."

There wasn't much from the past worth claiming.

This, though, was hard to let go.

Jill liked the high, the power it gave to slip between persona and personality and play with perception, but there was a particular thrill in moving through enemy territory while in disguise that made everyday interaction feel like cosplay.

She lived for this shit.

Only in life-or-death stakes did she truly feel alive, and that it might be feasible to escape Clare's shadow, and that there could possibly be such a thing as free will.

No weak-ass chemical alternative could ever come close, which made a joke out of Jack's accusations in Frankfurt.

She'd have thought he'd have figured that out by now.

She'd been late for the flight, true. And, sure, she knew where his assumptions would travel, and hadn't gone out of her way to dispel them, because it'd been amusing to watch him squirm. But that had all been a bonus, not the goal.

While he'd been off gathering intel on the Americans, which he wasn't willing to share, she'd set out in search of the old-school spy guy. It'd taken her forty-eight minutes, but she'd found him, travel documents in one hand and phone to his ear, people watching over the rim of his glasses like a man absentmindedly staring at nothing in the middle of a call. His beard was gone. His jacket was a different color. He had more hair.

Unlike the Americans, he'd had nobody in his ear.

She had been certain by the end that he was really alone and relying entirely on tradecraft, and had become convinced that he was indeed male. His age had been impossible to pin down, but she'd gotten close enough to hear him speak, which had confirmed he was Russian.

She'd stuck with him until he'd boarded a flight for Vienna.

More challenging had been getting the flight manifest.

That list of names had almost caused her to miss her own boarding, but she had it with her. Subtract the women, and subtract those so clearly foreign or unique that no self-respecting spy would dare travel on them, and she had twenty-eight ways to go hunting in Moscow. Nine, if only the Slavic ones mattered.

She'd have given the information to Jack if he hadn't been such an asshole.

No. That wasn't true.

He had his secrets, she had hers.

She took two wigs off the shelf, one as replacement for what she'd left in the suitcase at the station, the second for variety. And she perused the hangers, pulled out pieces that she recognized and others that were new, and held them close, sniffing the age and dust. The smell would be a problem if getting in close for a surprise strike became a thing. She'd have to deal with that in its own time.

She opened drawers, sorted through random accessories and added a few select pieces to the growing pile, and then turned to the bags and suitcases. There were two wheeled carry-ons where there should have been three, a guitar case with a guitar shell inside, and an accordion case with the false accordion missing. They'd never had the real things while growing up.

Clare was a classically trained violist.

They knew that because she'd told them, and believed it because Raymond Chance had confirmed it, and they trusted that his stories were real, but Clare couldn't be bothered to find out if her kids had an interest in music, and in all those years they'd never once heard her play. Instruments were impractical and learning required practice, and practice made noise, and unless they were looking at a harmonica or something of equal size, they weren't about to carry a thing from city to city as she dragged them across the planet. But if one needed to move an arsenal from one place to the next, particularly if one was a young teen, hopping on a bike and wheeling across town with a guitar case on one's back was an inconspicuous way to do it.

Jill pulled a battered duffel bag off the top shelf and dragged it toward the guns and ammunition. Where she was going, a guitar case would just get in the way.

She opened the firearms cases, studied their contents, reached for the Blaser Long Range Tactical, and paused. It was a German sniper rifle used by armed forces, counterterrorist operations, and law enforcement across Europe and Asia.

It belonged to Clare.

Taking money and clothes and ID was one thing.

Removing firearms was another.

You didn't touch Clare's guns except in an emergency.

And this wasn't an emergency. Not justifiably. Not yet.

But if she didn't take the weapons, there'd damn sure be an emergency, and the only way she wouldn't get them back in place before Clare realized they were missing was if there *was* an emergency. Even Clare couldn't argue with that logic.

Jack would argue. That's why Jack didn't need to know.

She took two pieces.

The Blaser for precision work.

A Glock 23 for close range.

More would only slow her down.

That was the thing about firearms in movies and news stories that had always baffled her, the way a trunkful of guns was supposed to show a well-armed team, and how nutjobs hauled around suitcases filled with them. Twenty firearms were nothing but twenty clubs if you didn't have the ammunition to use them.

Ammunition was heavy.

Guns were heavy *and* bulky.

She'd take two good working pieces and as much ammunition as she could carry over a dozen different weapons any day. She pulled out a box of bullets and eight spare magazines, set them on the floor, and sat beside them.

Rendezvous was set for nine in the morning, and Jack planned to walk right into a potential trap without any defense. He made her crazy at times, crazy enough to want to choke him out, crazy enough to want to hurt him — fuck, she'd hurt him now if she had half a chance — but hell if she was going to stand by while someone tried to kill him.

She might be an asshole, but she was his asshole.

She picked up the first magazine and started loading.

He wanted her as an observer? Fine, these were her terms.

If this were any other scenario, she'd trust he knew what he was doing. She'd argue with him just to be an irritating dick, but she'd still trust him.

But this wasn't like other times.

For the first time since they were kids he truly wanted and needed something for his own reasons, reasons beyond survival or a need to win, almost as if down in his murky center, where the deep, dark thoughts were buried, a lying voice kept telling him that tracking down the past could change what had happened. He wanted it so badly, he was blind to the way it was changing him, making him dumber.

The Russians, the Americans, they were peripheral problems.

Jack losing his grip on reality was the real nightmare.

CHAPTER 11

Alexanderplatz
Mitte, Berlin, Germany

Kara

The room faded into a dark, cool, quiet background, and the information on the screen became everything. The little ratter tugged her along, leading her down into the underbrush trails, while the rest of her sat cross-legged on the bed in front of the laptop.

Another hotel, another round of hurry up and wait.

The guys were out, all three of them, securing equipment headquarters had shipped in. Not that they all *needed* to be out. But this time the war room had booked them four to a single room, beds arranged along the walls almost hostel-like, and clearing the guys out had been Nick's way of giving her space to work.

She had a few hours, maybe, before they returned.

She was racing the clock.

They were all racing the clock.

The war room had located target and lost him again.

Angel had called, confirming he was en route to Berlin — no small consolation considering Nick, Juan, and Aaron had wasted an hour hunting for him in the hotel — and headquarters had drawn on the Berlin station to mobilize a surveillance unit to the terminal. They'd managed to get an officer on board before the passengers deplaned, but hadn't been able to confirm target arrival.

So either the war room was wrong about target boarding that flight or the Berlin operatives had missed him. She was willing to let time bear that one out.

Her questions went a different direction.

She returned to the Frankfurt Airport footage, all the way back to when she'd first realized they were dealing with something different, and searched the cameras at gate twenty-four for whatever had made Angel so certain, she'd wantonly wasted their time and squandered their resources.

She found the answer in a bright patch of white.

Her fingers froze.

Thoughts scattered, and anger rose.

There, in the boarding area, exactly where Angel had directed Nick, was a passenger wearing a hat identical to the one target had worn right before he'd vanished. Nick wouldn't have seen the light in person, just as she hadn't seen it on the concourse. But Angel, watching through the screen, most certainly had.

Kara could see how, in the fog of war, two individuals with identical markings could appear the same on-screen and how, without an accurate sense of on-the-ground distance, it would have been easy to get confused. That the war room had stumbled wasn't worth the anger, but that they'd gotten back into the race without ever allowing the team on the ground to account for the mistake most certainly was.

Their target had had an accomplice.

That factored into everything.

A person, even the wrong person, didn't simply get up from their seat, walk into the restroom, and vanish, and Nick had been right *there.*

He'd needed to know about it while it was happening.

Instead the war room had let him walk away.

If she hadn't taken to analyzing footage, they still wouldn't know target had followed them to their hotel, and now there was this.

These were failures so egregious, they felt deliberate.

Kara tapped the trackpad and watched the hat in half time. The accomplice waited until Nick had gone, then entered the men's toilet and never emerged.

She ran the segment through gait analysis, got nothing, so searched the manual way, tracking every single body that had exited that door within a thirty-minute time frame — forty-two men in all — and then she traced every single one, jotting notes and time stamps, locations and interactions, until each had left the airport or boarded a new flight. The work was tedious and consuming and failed to point fingers.

But four of the men had boarded flights to Berlin, so camera feeds for those departures came next, and on the third, recognition hammered through her chest, and for the second time in as many hours, she sat back and stared.

This was the flight headquarters had flagged.

While she and her team had been preoccupied, hunting for target in their hotel, he'd walked back to the terminal, through security, and boarded that flight.

The realization felt personal, in the way feeling stupid always felt personal, but also intriguing. The accomplice had indirectly led her to where the war room had already gone, but the desk jockeys would have followed a different path to get there.

She went back to the file notes, looking for it, found the connection in a gait match that linked target on the concourse, before he'd disappeared, to an unknown individual at the Berlin flight departure gate. The hit had come after the plane was already in the air, which was why they'd called up the Berlin station.

She'd have done the same if the decision had been hers.

But that's all they'd had, just that flash of a match and no identity to go with it. The war room had scraped photos, birth dates, places of birth — addresses when available — off each travel document linked to that Berlin manifest and had dumped them into a mix-and-match search through national and international driver's licenses, identity cards, mug shots, social media profiles, cellular records, insurance providers, Internet providers, utility companies, hotel chains, credit card companies, marketing aggregators, and law-enforcement databases. Hits had come back in the thousands. Those required human interaction. The desk jockeys would have to follow each lead, even the most absurd, in a laborious process of elimination. They'd find him, eventually.

Nobody was truly invisible.

People who did disappear didn't get there through lack of data but rather because of low prioritization, and the resources required to find the connections.

The data itself was always there.

Commercial surveillance through banking, telecommunications, and travel alone was such an integrated part of life that, but for the most disenfranchised, it couldn't be avoided. Staying off radar wasn't something a person did for six months out of the year. It was a fully committed disconnected lifestyle, in which a single sloppy move last month was all it took for the truly persistent to find you today.

The average person couldn't do it.

The average *professional* couldn't do it.

This guy might be good, but no one anywhere was *that* good. Friends, family, habits, patterns, he had them, and the war room would find them. What jumped at her now wasn't what the queries were pulling, but what was missing.

Nowhere in any of this did anything point

145

to the accomplice.

And also, nowhere was there an obvious link to Emilia Flynn.

Kara clicked over from cameras to the internal data system.

She stopped.

There was a fine line between watching out for her team and the accusations of misuse of authority that could arise because of it. But combine a query on Emilia with the Emilia-and-Nick rumors, add in the Kara-and-Nick rumors, and doing this would mean handing Liv Wilson a knife and asking her to stab her whole team in the back with it. She'd have to stick to looking in places she'd already been.

She went back to the cameras instead, found Emilia at the taxi stand, and worked a reverse search through the feeds, tracing a backward journey through the airport, right into the Jetway of their own flight out of Dallas.

She should have been surprised. Wasn't. She searched for context.

Emilia had deplaned late, had seemed oblivious to their target's existence, and whatever had put that look of death on her had happened before arrival, because the distress was already obvious from her first step into the terminal.

Kara shifted to stretch, looked up into Nick's face, and yelped.

She hadn't heard or seen him come in.

Had no idea how long he'd been watching her.

He raised his eyebrows and gave her *that* look, the one offering pity while also laughing at the way she lost sense of time or place.

Aaron and Juan trooped in, carrying a plastic locker.

She pulled the buds out of her ears.

Nick nudged the bed with his knee, said, "You get something?"

She glanced toward the door.

The pieces she'd found made lies out of what the war room had given them, but she didn't have enough yet to know what truth might look like, and these weren't things she could discuss in front of the others.

Nick motioned her up and out.

Kara shut the laptop and carried it toward the door. Behind her, Aaron made a kissy noise, just loud enough that she wasn't sure she'd heard right.

But Nick had heard it, too. He stopped short, doubled back and, voice low, almost a whisper, said, "Do that again, you'll be using those lips for teeth."

Kara, one foot over the threshold, froze.

Juan, arm buried elbow deep in the locker,

stopped moving.

Nick didn't anger easily, and a quiet Nick was a terrifying Nick.

Aaron put both hands up, defensive, apologetic.

Nick turned without a word, and Kara followed him down the hallway, toward the stairwell, conflicted, concerned. Belittling behavior like Aaron's was everywhere. She'd had a lifetime to grow inured to it. More here wouldn't make much difference to her, but a rift between Nick and his men certainly would, and to a kid like Aaron, what had just happened wasn't a superior quashing insubordination and disrespect so much as white knighting. That would make things worse.

Nick reached the stairwell. He said, "What's the damage?"

It took a second to switch from no good options to no good way to put this.

Her mouth opened. Words were slow in coming.

She said, "Did you know Emilia was in Frankfurt this morning?"

Nick's head tipped right. "Emilia Flynn, Emilia?" he said.

"Yeah. On our flight out of Dallas."

"Emilia Flynn?"

"Yes, Nick. *That* Emilia. *On* our *flight.*"

148

If they were different people, Emilia might make for a touchy conversation, but things weren't like that between them.

He said, "And you know she was on our flight because . . . ?"

"Because I saw her outside the terminal — stared right at her while she was getting into a taxi — and because she was in footage with deplaning passengers."

"Emilia alone or Emilia plus team?"

"She got into the taxi alone, but Daniel Cho and Peyton What's-his-name were on the flight. There might be someone else. Did you know?"

"No."

Kara said, "Clues to why she was there?"

"I assume she had a target of her own."

"On the *same* flight?"

Nick let out a loud frustrated exhale.

He knew exactly where she was going with this.

Frankfurt as major gateway into Europe was a logical transit hub, but two sandboxed liquidation teams in such close proximity created a high risk of right-hand, left-hand confusion. If Emilia and crew had been in pursuit of a target that *wasn't* on that flight, headquarters would have never booked them on it. But Emilia *had* been there, which meant there'd been a second target on board, or it meant more than one tactical team pursuing the same target.

Both scenarios created a shit storm of potential problems.

He said, "You didn't want me out here to ask about Emilia."

"I did," Kara said. "But there's more."

She sat on the floor, opened the laptop.

She didn't like making statements without a clear set of facts to back her up, and right now she was about to point fingers in the war room's direction while doing just that. "You need to see this to understand," she said.

Nick slid down the wall and sat beside her.

She said, "You remember the feeds earlier today, when target did that disappearing act?" She tabbed the window, zoomed in to enhance the hat.

She outlined its shape and highlighted the panel seams.

"That's him on the concourse," she said. "Now follow this. Angel sent you to gate twenty-four, and I couldn't figure that out. Too much distance in too little time, but she was convinced, confirmed it twice."

Kara flipped the feeds and enhanced the frame.

"Gate twenty-four," she said. "Same attention-grabbing hat."

Nick leaned in toward the screen. A low growl rose from his throat.

Earnestness seeped into her voice. "He has an accomplice, Nick, someone just as skilled as he is, and while we were busy hunting for him in our hotel, they *both* boarded that flight for Berlin."

He inched his shoulder away from hers and looked her in the face.

She said, "It gets even better."

She opened a new window and set both feeds running simultaneously. "The accomplice heads for gate twenty-four and sits there until — watch the time sequencing — about a minute before our target vanishes, then the accomplice flips on the light. The coordination is so on cue, it's impossible for it to be coincidental. I keep asking myself how they did it. How do you get that level of precision without communication? And that's not even the point. The point was misdirection, right? Misdirection for the *cameras,* Nick. To do this, they knew they were under . . . they were under, were under sur-surveillance *before* we left Dallas. This isn't some, some, something you plan and coordinate from twenty-eight thousand feet. And that's not even, not even, that's . . . Look, that's only half, be-because the real point . . ."

She stopped. There were too many threads.

She could see them as a matrix in her head, understood the way they intersected, but her words were choking from the same damn speech disfluencies that always rose when she got animated or agitated, the ones that had made it nigh impossible to communicate complex concepts for the first half of her life and left silence as her safest option, which had only reinforced the accepted belief that the poorest kid in a poor rural school really was a fucking moron. Panic screeched inside her head, wings beating in a wild attempt to escape pain and shame and humiliation.

Nick waited, patient, nonjudgmental, understanding.

He said, "Hey. It's okay. This is me you're talking to, right?"

She took a long, deep breath to calm the mental chaos, forced herself to think through to the end, and came back with what she'd been aiming to communicate from the beginning. "The misdirection wasn't for us on the ground," she said. "Angel caught that eventually, but right there in that realization, she had to have also realized that for misdirection to work, there needed to be a second person. You see it. I see it. She had to have seen it. She knew before we did, but *never told us.*" Kara waited and then continued. "If we'd known, Nick, if we'd known from the beginning that there were two of them, if we'd known what we were looking for, we'd have been able to get ahead of them."

Nick didn't engage the accusation. He said, "All right, so our new baseline is target plus accomplice. What do you have on accomplice?"

"As far as I can tell — and this is just preliminary — accomplice wasn't on our Dallas flight. I've followed the time stamps forward from Dallas–Frankfurt and backward from Frankfurt–Berlin, and the only trace I have is at a restaurant about fifteen minutes before accomplice heads to gate twenty-four. With enough time and energy, we might be able to get a hit on when and from where. But in an airport this crowded, with thousands of people arriving in any given hour, multiplied by an unknown number of identity changes, multiplied again by the way these guys are able to manipulate perception and toy with the cameras, I don't have the resources to do it."

"Send it all to headquarters."

"They might already have it and have

chosen not to share."

"That's their prerogative," he said. "Send it anyway. They'll know we know."

Nick started up off the floor.

Kara said, "There's something you need to consider."

He let himself back down.

She relaxed her fingers and rested them against the keyboard. She said, "When we got called up, all we had on target was a flight number, which came in last minute and left us rushing to make that departure. Then we got a seat number, which gave us passport data and, from there, name, photo, whatever. And what that means is, we knew target's seat number before we knew who was in the seat. You follow?"

"Not yet, but I'm sure I will. Keep going."

"We start out looking for just one guy, who turns into two. Headquarters knows but doesn't tell us. Emilia's team happens to be on our flight, which headquarters also knows and also fails to mention, and all this raises questions about what else they know and aren't telling. Protocol is protocol, and reasons are reasons. I'm sure it's all legit, but we got lucky in Frankfurt, Nick. We were sitting in a trap, and he left us there. We might not be as fortunate next time."

Nick's expression clouded. He said, "What are you really getting at?"

"I can't do my job unless I'm given all the data," she said. "Maybe, you know, maybe there are things you're aware of that you can't mention, and if that's the case, I respect it, but I really need to know if there's something going on with this op that's above my paygrade."

He sat silent for a beat and said, "Everything I know, you know. It's always been that way, Kara, and always will."

She accepted his words at face value. If he, the one person she truly trusted, was lying, there was no point to anything else. "Okay," she said.

He said, "I agree, there's a whole lot here that doesn't add up. But just because it doesn't fit the official narrative doesn't mean the alternative you're hinting at is accurate. This thing with Emilia doesn't have to be one or the other. It could be something else entirely. And Angel might have held back on letting us know about an accomplice because she wanted more answers herself first."

Kara shifted and eyeballed him.

She said, "Really, Nick? That's what you're going with?"

"Look, I'm just saying there are always

alternative explanations — you know that better than anyone — so let me ask around, put out some feelers, see what comes back before you go all baby bulldog on it, okay?"

The *baby bulldog* forced a hint of a smile.

It was a shortcut back to the first time Nick had jumped on her for latching onto an issue and refusing to drop it. He'd been angry and she'd hated that, but she had been right and had refused to concede.

He'd turned away from her, face red and fists clenched. "You get your teeth into something and you just can't stop until you shake the thing to fucking death," he'd said. "How about you learn some fucking tact."

Tact would never be her strong suit.

He knew it, she knew it, and this was his way of reminding her that there were ways to get questions like these answered, but they'd be better off if she wasn't the one asking about them. "You do what you do," he said. "Dig where you dig, and find what you find. That's what you're good at. But for now everything this side of the conversation stays between you and me. Clear?"

CHAPTER 12

Friedenau
Berlin, Germany

Jill

Awareness kicked in with the soft bell of an alarm, telling her the time to move had come. She dropped a foot to the floor and groaned upright. Her eyes burned. She had cotton for brains. Four hours was just enough to make her regret doing the responsible thing and wish she'd forgone sleep altogether.

She stretched chin toward toes and arms over her head.

Blood flowed where it mattered.

She dressed in the dark, finding her way into a black bodysuit that, with the right layers, could pass for real clothes when daylight came.

She had a few pieces to work with tonight.

She'd get the rest of what she needed

along the way, because the only way to avoid the mark of being an outsider was to buy local, and besides, most of Clare's stuff was old. She slid another envelope with another thousand euros beneath the boarded-up door, bookending her stay for those on the other side, then strapped on her bag of borrowed treasures, and stepped out into the deep, dark cold. Six kilometers stood between her and the rendezvous point, a two-hour walk if she didn't hurry. She locked the front and reburied the key and followed shadows along mostly empty streets and piss-fragrant underground walkways.

The need for sleep faded.

Anticipation took its place.

The early morning dark, when the strait-laced and normies slept, and the freaks and artists and addicts roamed, and the raves and parties were just getting started, these were the hours in which she truly came alive. Berghain was where she would have been, high on music and ecstasy, if this purer rush hadn't come to fill that restless space.

The club was inside a former power plant in the middle of an industrial old East Berlin estate. People traveled the world in order to try to get in. Rich people, cool people, famous people, beautiful people, turned away by tatted and pierced doormen who could smell fake and taste fear. She'd never been denied.

Berlin, Berghain, these were places she belonged, but she belonged to the thrill of a life-or-death hunt more, and so she strode on to meet it.

An hour and fifty brought her to the edge of Savignyplatz. In theory, the place was a good place for the suspicious to meet. It was easy to find, had plenty of foot traffic, and offered multiple access points. But this time of year, with leaves mostly fallen, a tightly defined space surrounded by multi-story buildings was a literal canyon gorge. Any kid who'd watched any old Western knew what that led to, and her idiot savant brother planned to set up camp down there anyway.

The part of her that loved him hoped for the small but existing chance that this whole thing with Dmitry was true, that the *real* Dmitry was alive and had been searching for his children and genuinely wanted to get to know them.

The rest of her preferred just about any other possibility.

It was easy for Jack, the Golden Son, to want this.

It was easier for her to not.

She reached the northwest corner.

Hook pick and torsion wrench let her inside the building, and she took the stairs up until she reached the ladder, and followed the rungs through an access hatch to a rooftop bathed in a half-moon glow that came and went with the clouds.

She shoved a shim between hatch and rim to ensure egress stayed open, unloaded equipment within the shelter of the rooftop wall, used a drain gap as the opening through which she minimized her heat signature to nearly nothing, and worked a slow, tight grid up the face of each park-fronting building.

If there were others, they'd come ahead of the rendezvous, just as she had.

If there were others, they'd be searching, just as she was.

She couldn't know when, couldn't know where.

Focus pulled her into a Zen trance state: she and the rifle, she and the scope, probing rooftops and windows and doorways and shadows, just as she had in the past, hunting for threat, hunting to win. A matte Mylar blanket kept her warm.

She maxed out the drain-gap range, crawled to the next, and started again.

When she reached the end, she'd start over.

This would be her routine until the sun rose.

Movement on a fourth-story balcony caught her eye.

She broke from the pattern, searching for what training and natural sight had alerted her to. Curtains and shutters blocked normal sight.

Glass, if no one was touching it, did well enough at blocking heat.

The thermal scope let her peek between the overlap.

She found the heat signature on the floor, in a narrow gap between balcony doors, and with that find, euphoria rushed in. What she saw here was too elongated for a dog or cat, looked as close to a prone sniper as she'd probably ever get, but she had no way to know if the body was Russian or American or civilian or something else.

She could put a bullet through that window.

Taking the shot was easy.

The aftermath was what had the potential to hurt.

She'd need to get closer.

She searched the streets and trees for signs of a trap, the way she would have had this been Clare's doing, then dosed a few syringes for a range of bodyweights, and tossed them into a purse, together with standard kill-kit fare. She stuffed padding up her bra, pulled a blond wig over the black cap that hid her hair, tugged on a tunic blouse with enough color and frills to belie the truth of the black skin suit underneath, and pulled on a jacket, like a normal person would in these temperatures.

She headed back down the ladder.

Jack would try to stop her if he were there.

He'd say what she was about to do was going to draw unnecessary attention and put her at unnecessary risk, and he'd offer her a half dozen brilliant but time-consuming and patience-zapping nonconfrontational options to solve what she'd just as soon fix with a few broken bones.

For him, fighting was always a last resort.

She found it a particularly useful tool as a first. Especially when the violence was dirty and unexpected. Doubly so when it came from a woman who looked the way she did — no — *because* it came from a woman who looked the way she looked.

Her targets were nearly always men.

This lifestyle seemed to draw the worst of them.

And the one thing that she'd yet to prove

wrong was the inverse relation between a man's respect for women in general and how hard he'd be to send to his knees.

Whatever faulty wiring induced a guy to tell a woman with twice his education and four times his brains that she'd get further in life if she was a little friendlier and smiled more, *and* to think he was doing her a favor, was the same faulty wiring that made a guy feel entitled to a woman's time and attention and grow abusive when she didn't give it, and the same faulty wiring that prompted a guy to laugh at the little lady when she told him to back off and then to tell her he liked 'em fired up and she should give it her best shot when she threatened to break his nose.

Same candy, different flavors.

Anyone who handicapped a person on account of double X chromosomes was also one to miss the signs that double X was about to knock them on their ass. "Hit hard, hit once," that was her motto.

Those kinds of guys never saw it coming, and her world was full of them.

She slipped out the back and into the dark, stride changing, gait loosening, shape-shifting, and stepped out into the open like a party girl finding her way home after a few drinks too many, and made her way to the entryway that would lead to her quarry. She dropped a set of keys, struggled to pick them up, and fumbled them toward the keyhole. Her fingers, sheltered by a drunken body hunched for concentration, picked another lock. She made her way up with the same uncoordinated steps and reached the apartment and pounded on the door, calling out in French, "Goddammit, Anton. I came all the way from Paris to see you, and you're going to tell me you're not here?"

They couldn't shoot her.

Not through the door, not after all the noise, and not with the neighbors, who would have taken note. Easiest way for them to resolve this would be to open up and let her in.

She counted down those seconds in her head, digging through the purse, swearing and complaining about losing her door key, punch knife between her fingers as a just in case, and then she pounded harder, making a drunk-ass ruckus.

Voices came through from the other side, one near, one far.

Russian, spoken clearly enough to grasp snippets.

". . . Some drunk bitch . . ."

". . . Make the noise stop . . ."

The door opened.

164

Head low, eyes focused on legs, she placed a playful, drunken hand on the guy's chest and, before he had a chance to speak, pushed past him into the apartment. She tossed her jacket on the couch as if she belonged there, and kept right on going for the kitchen, talking the whole way, as if the man who'd opened the door was her friend or lover or roommate, as if the second guy didn't exist, babbling nonsense about the night in a psychological maneuver so brazen, it bought her a few confused seconds and let her cross the room and round the corner for the kitchen.

She opened a cupboard and slammed it shut in an ostensible drunken search for a water glass. The man who let her in trailed behind her. She met him with a breadboard to the face and followed him to the floor with a needle to his arm. She depressed the plunger, rammed her shoulder into the wall, faked a cry for help, and was up and moving toward the second guy before he reached her.

He rounded into the kitchen.

She swung that board with every pound of force she could muster.

She clipped him beneath the jaw.

His head whiplashed back, and he went down, crumpling like a test-drive dummy in a high-speed head-on collision. She stomped his balls and got no response, pulled hand-gun from thigh holster beneath her tunic blouse and paused, waiting, listening.

The radiator rattled.

A siren in the distance wailed.

She stepped aside, pieing the corner into the living room and then into the hall, quick checked the bedrooms, and ascertained that the place was empty. If this were one of Clare's setups, there'd be a body or two rap-pelling in through the balcony doors right about now, maybe another through the kitchen window, and after she took them out, she'd still have to fight her way down the stairwell to get free.

But this wasn't Clare.

She shoved the handgun back into place.

The absence of more made it hard not to feel cheated and sad, and for a brief mo-ment she actually missed Clare and wanted to punch herself in the face.

She tugged industrial zip ties from a pocket and dragged the second guy deeper into the kitchen. She'd clipped him hard. He wouldn't need anything else. She se-cured his hands to the radiator, grabbed his partner's shoulders and pulled him in close, pushed the two of them together so they were nice and snug and nearly mouth to mouth, and secured the second set of hands. She checked pockets and shoes, looking for electronic devices and identification, and used the punch knife to slice shirts and pants to check for tattoos or distinguishing markings, and for all that trouble, the only thing she got was the apartment key.

It should have concerned her, not knowing whom they worked for, but the absence of information didn't change the situation.

These guys were Russian. Either they worked for Dmitry or they didn't, and that's exactly where they'd been with this yesterday morning.

The keys, though, those were interesting.

Keys were things people carried when they owned or rented or borrowed things, and usually not when the thing was stolen or taken by force.

These guys hadn't broken in. That added a whole new layer of context to this invitation from so-called Dmitry.

What it meant, though, was still a question.

CHAPTER 13

Savignyplatz
Berlin, Germany

Jill

Service staff and delivery vehicles marked the start of a new daily grind, and soon after came the lightening sky. Light gave color and depth to the hustle below, the workday pedestrian trickle thickened into a rush of morning commute, and from her rooftop vantage she searched slow-moving figures and fast-moving strides for her brother, for Dmitry, and for the source of unease, which had grown stronger with each passing hour.

She'd left the apartment as she'd found it — rifle, ammunition, and equipment exactly where they'd been placed — and returned to where her hunt had begun.

Morning had broken without any sign of the Americans.

No Russian presence, either, other than

168

those she'd decommissioned. But there *was* something out there, something more, something she hadn't located.

She sensed it the way wild things smelled threat on the wind.

Jack came into view across the plaza, hands stuffed into pockets, shoes shuffling along the cobblestones, slouched and sloppy in grays and browns, everything about him well worn and local, as if he'd walked into someone's house and chosen clothes straight out of their wardrobe and dresser drawers.

For all she knew, that's exactly what he'd done.

But now he was here, saying hello, letting her know he was around, and giving her a chance to communicate anything she might need him to know. That was how they operated, always had, traveling dark, carrying no electronics — not even burners, because anything capable of sending a signal was trackable if *they* knew where to look, and in Clare's paranoid world, *they* always knew where to look — leapfrogging and leap-of-faithing, trusting that the other would do what needed doing. In the best of times they'd handed off the same position as if they were a single person.

They'd had some fun, the two of them.

The memories hurt and they made her smile.

She hated her brother and loved him and couldn't escape him.

He crossed the plaza and rounded the corner that led off toward the station.

She rescanned windows and doorways, rooftops and rail lines, tracking commuters and service staff, trying to locate the source of unease.

Minutes ticked on. Her insides itched.

Jack reentered the plaza from the opposite side, different clothes, different shoes, different demeanor, and he crossed to the corner café, ordered coffee, and chose an outside table, newspaper in hand. He sat fully exposed with his back to the sun, offering a clean shot to about half the buildings on the square, his way of telling her that, all evidence to the contrary, he didn't perceive a terminal threat.

Time to rendezvous counted down in her head.

She studied faces and clothing and shoes and gait.

Her skin tingled in subconscious recognition, and it took a beat for logic to process what instinct had homed in on.

The subject was male, late forties to early fifties, balding, five feet six if he stretched,

170

and carrying forty pounds of genuine paunch around the middle. He wore a midrange suit and low-end dress shoes and carried a satchel like any other cubicle slave heading to the station for the weekday commute, but he didn't fit.

He was similar, but not the same.

He read as a well-fed bureaucrat shielded by two degrees of deniability.

The only way to avoid the tells of being an outsider was to buy local, and he didn't belong, even by Berlin standards.

He made a direct line for Jack's table.

Jack stood, shook hands.

The bureaucrat sat.

Jill loathed his face, not for lack of aesthetics but because he wasn't Dmitry — at least not Dmitry in the photos she'd seen — and he wasn't the spotter in Frankfurt, and he wasn't one of the two who'd been waiting for their flight in Berlin, and they hadn't crossed the ocean and dodged assassins to meet with this joke of a man.

She scanned the periphery, scanned him over.

She found no nervous tics, no subconscious gestures to send adrenaline dripping or betray this rendezvous as more than a conversation, but without a doubt, he was a new variable, and new was a problem. She

171

still didn't know what Jack had learned about the kill team in Frankfurt, didn't trust he'd give her a full accounting of this, either, and she didn't have enough of an angle to play bad lipreading to figure out for herself what went on below. Away from the action was not where she wanted to be.

She inched back from the edge, paused, and debated.

Jack would be vulnerable until she got out of the building, but he'd stated his opinion by putting himself out in the open, and she'd already taken out the immediate threat. Well, except for the sense of more, which still itched her insides, but hours of searching hadn't given her its source and overactive instinct was as much an explanation as anything.

If she hurried, she could get to ground in sixty seconds.

She could take a handgun, come back for the rest later.

Jack stopped her, Jack running his fingers through his hair, absentmindedly scratching the back of his neck, asking her to join him at the table, and just like that, he'd taken what had been her idea and made it his.

She swore under her breath, packed up the rifle, stashed her kit behind an electrical box, where it'd be days, or forever, before someone noticed it, and she jogged down to street level empty-handed, all big blue eyes and big blond hair, extra padding still up in her bra, looking a whole lot more like Barbie than Beatrix Kiddo.

She rounded into the open at an angle that kept her out of Jack's line of sight and put her dead-on for collision with the guy across from him, and she strode forward, eyes locked, fists clenched, coming in hard and fast like a brawler looking for a fight.

The man caught sight of her, tensed, as if he couldn't decide whether to bolt or stay, and that told her more than any interrogation would have.

Told her brother she'd arrived, too.

Jack's right hand dropped off his lap. Fingers dangling toward the ground, he signed to her the way she'd signed to him in the airport, spelling out *Belmopan,* taking her back to a time and place where unified silence had netted information.

He pointed to the chair at his right.

She slapped his shoulder, slid around him, said, "Sorry I'm late."

The newcomer stood and stretched a hand in her direction.

"Luka Marinov," he said. "I've come on behalf of your father."

He had the easy fluency of Moscow buried

under decades of London and was about ten years and two countries removed from the voice on the phone that'd arranged to get them to Berlin.

She gripped his hand in a power grab.

He wasn't Dmitry, wasn't the solitary spotter, wasn't either of the superspy wannabes at the Berlin airport, most definitely wasn't the voice that had started this all, and wasn't connected to any of them, because the one thing they all had in common was that they knew exactly what they were looking for.

This guy hadn't recognized her from Eve.

She let go, sat, crossed her arms.

Marinov cleared his throat. "As I was telling your brother," he said, "you came to meet your father, and clearly, I'm not your father, and for that I apologize." He chuckled, more fake than nervous. "It's not a good look, is it? A last-minute change like this? I assure you it's not what your father had in mind, either."

She stayed silent, expressionless, but it grated on her, the way he kept repeating *your father,* as if the matter had already been settled. Belaboring was what Clare would call it, a clumsy, transparent attempt to bully a baseline understanding.

That wasn't a good look.

174

Marinov said, "He was forced to detour to Prague for a work emergency. We tried to reach you, but our previous communication channel was already disconnected. This" — he finger-drew a circle around the table — "the sudden notice, and the suspicion it would cast over his motives, was what he most wanted to avoid. The Savoy was the only remaining option, but it seems the message was . . ." He paused. "Not well received?"

Jill studied him, unblinking, neutral.

Not a good look had shifted from trying to force a baseline understanding into attempting to preempt objections, or as Clare would put it, showing a person the horseshit up front so they stopped looking for a bull. But the bit about the message did explain Jack's request for silence. He didn't want the guy across the table to know she didn't know whatever she didn't know.

This whole who's-your-daddy adventure had shunted hard off the rails.

Marinov reached into the satchel, retrieved several pages, nudged them across the table in Jack's direction, and rested his hand atop them to keep the breeze from carrying them away. "I sent these express to the Savoy, expecting you'd already have them before this morning," he said. "Your father still

175

very much wants to meet, but it will be a week, possibly longer, before he can leave Prague. He asked me to arrange for travel and a hotel, hoping you'd understand this was a situation over which he had no control."

Jill tugged the pages from beneath his hand and glanced at them.

The hotel was Kings Court Prague, prepaid for a week as of tomorrow.

The tickets were Eurail Passes, which would allow them to plan their own routes.

She handed both to Jack who, still looking at Marinov, said, "I'd prefer to skip dealing with the messengers and speak with Dmitry directly."

Marinov said, "That's perfectly understandable and I'll be sure to tell him. His English isn't very good, though, so it's possible he thinks he'll make a better impression by first communicating face-to-face. That said" — Marinov dragged a cell phone from the satchel — "as a way to avoid repeating today, he did want you to have this. Maybe it'll give him a chance to — as you said — skip the messengers. My number is in there. If you run into trouble, have questions, need anything, feel free to give a call. The lock-key code is your birth date."

He slid the phone in Jack's direction, just

as he'd done with the papers — not toward the middle of the table, where they both would have access to it — directly to Jack, as if this was Jack's decision to make.

Jill eyed the device with the hunger of permanent second place, and all those years under Clare's hand — of Jack, the favored child, getting what little approval Clare dished out — left her wishing Dmitry had never found them and that they'd never come to Europe, because if he *was* real, this right here showed where the story went, and she hated him for it already. She said, "We were curious enough about Dmitry to make one trip. You're insane if you expect us to follow you down this rabbit hole."

Marinov smiled slyly. "Do you speak for yourself or for your brother?"

The provocation was a gut-punch trigger that sent anger to her fingertips and made her want to hop the table, straddle his fat lap, and strangle him blind.

Jack rested a hand on her knee before she could act.

He said, "The phone doesn't substitute for a time, date, and place."

Marinov raised a finger, as if chiding himself for a memory lapse, dug for another sheet, slid it in the same direction, and said, "Do you have a preference?"

177

A gust of wind lifted the page slightly.

Jack shifted the phone to weight it down, dropped his finger onto a nine-in-the-morning time slot three days out, and said, "That one."

Marinov hesitated, as if this felt too abrupt to be the end, as if he expected more, an explanation perhaps, or to have to cajole or convince, and then, realizing that's all there was or all there'd be, said, "I'll pass along the message." He waited again, understood he'd effectively been dismissed, wished them good day, and left.

They sat in silence long after he'd gone.

Jill, first to speak, said, "Do you trust him?"

Jack snorted.

There was relief in that, at least.

He flipped through the rail tickets and the hotel reservation.

Part statement, part sigh, he said, "Prague," and she knew then that he'd already made up his mind, and that nothing she did or said would dissuade him, and that he planned to go through with this with or without her.

She said, "If you make this trip after being fed that line of bullshit, whoever is behind this will know you're all in. You'll just be trading one set of strings for another."

He offered her the pages.

She waved them aside.

She'd seen the rendezvous time, place, and date. The rest was superfluous. She said, "Prague, John? Come on, seriously? They had us here in Berlin right *now*. They've got no guarantee we won't vanish. That they'd abandon a sure thing for the risk of trying to lure us out of Germany is all the proof you need."

Jack said, "Maybe."

She glared. Now he was just being obstinate. The Czech Republic, with its long ties to Moscow, played host to a larger Russian diplomatic mission than any other country in Central Europe, most of it in the capital. Prague was a hotbed of spies and covert operations and about the closest thing they could get to a lion's den in the West. Whatever they found there wasn't going to be Dmitry.

Jack reached for the phone, a sealed model that didn't allow for battery removal. He said, "It's the only way to find out if he's alive or even real."

His thumb caressed the power switch.

She fought the urge to snatch the thing out of his hands.

He pulled a paper clip from his pocket, sprung the SIM free, and held the card between finger and thumb, as if pondering its possibilities.

"You've been here before," she said. "You know exactly how this game is played, and yet you're letting them rope you in anyway."

"I refuse to spend the rest of my life repeating Clare's mistakes," he said. "I can't have this hanging over my head like some zombie issue that refuses to die, the way it refused to die for her."

Jill leaned up on the table and into his line of sight.

He didn't respond, so she reached for the SIM to take it.

He snatched his hand away, and focusing on the phone, the papers, he said, "You visited the safe house."

She didn't really want to have *that* conversation, but now wasn't the time to evade or lie. She said, "Yes."

"How much was left?"

"Pretty much everything."

"How much did you take?"

"Half the cash. Some costuming. A few weapons."

He said, "I could use some of the cash."

She waited.

"Maybe a quarter of what you've got."

180

"Fine," she said. "I'll trade you cash for that SIM."

He held up the card, angled it against the sun. "Can't afford that," he said. "Too much risk of you losing or misplacing it."

The words were so much like Clare's, always assuming the worst, and with so little respect for what she was capable of.

"I'm not going to lose or misplace it," she said.

"Can't afford to have you use it against me, either."

She bit her tongue, drew blood, forced her hands to relax. "The fuck makes you think I'm going to use it against you?"

He raised an eyebrow.

She sighed. "Look, I wasn't deliberately late for that flight, okay?"

"Then where were you?"

She didn't want to have *this* conversation, either, but she was all in now. "On the other side of the terminal," she said, "trying to see if I could find any more of our Russian friends, and just like I told you on the plane, I fucking lost track of time."

"And?"

"Only one Russian, John, same as I said before."

He eyed her with the suspicion of someone for whom disbelief was a baseline response,

181

but she'd told the truth, if not the whole truth.

She said, "Don't make me fight you for it."

And that was the thing.

She could take the SIM if she wanted. He knew it, she knew it. She'd never be able to compete with him brain to brain or make Clare love her the way Clare loved him, but she didn't need to when she could take him down in two quick seconds. That'd always been the reason for training hard, fighting harder, and getting beat by bigger assholes. But using force here guaranteed he'd vanish to seek Dmitry on his own, and letting him walk into the jaws of death alone meant that good-bye now possibly meant good-bye for forever, and she wasn't ready for that.

He said, "Look, you want the card, you can have it. But I need a promise from you — not manipulation — a one-hundred-percent, honest-to-God real promise."

The irony almost made her laugh.

"Coming from the guy who claims I've never kept a promise in my life."

"Do you want it or not?"

"Fine," she said. "What's the promise?"

"That you stop sabotaging me."

"I'm not sabotaging you."

"That's not the answer I'm looking for."

She held up her pinkie.

He hooked his with hers, then dropped the SIM on the table and nudged it in her direction. She picked it up before he'd have a chance to change his mind, pulled a small square pill case from her pocket, and dropped the SIM in together with the others.

He said, "No matter what happens with Dmitry, there's still the kill team, and that's not going to stop until we put an end to it."

"How close are they?"

"Close."

"Bonus for Prague," she said. "Might buy us some breathing room."

"Or an opportunity."

"You see an intersection between the two."

"If you're willing to provide cover at the rendezvous and let me take point with a body double, then yeah."

The suggestion made her bristle.

A plan like that would put him down on the ground again, same as it had here, and if Dmitry was real and this thing in Prague turned out to be legit, it meant he'd be meeting their father first, alone, without her, and that raised the same damn issue that had pushed her back from the rooftop edge to join this conversation and made her want the SIM. But if one of them had to be down

183

in the gorge, she'd rather it be her covering Jack than the other way around.

"I don't like it," she said. "But I can work with it."

His finger traced the edge of the coffee cup.

He said, "Have you heard from Clare?"

This was the second time since Frankfurt that he'd asked about Clare, and it wasn't like Clare hadn't been worming around in her head, too.

Clare was a problem.

Jack had always been the favorite — was still the favorite — and being the favorite meant it'd taken him longer to rebel, and meant Clare had fought harder against letting him go. Nonviolent resistance had been his way of breaking free. She'd watched him take a knife to the gut, a bat to his knees, a bullet to a thankfully Kevlar-protected chest, and so much else in his absolute refusal to let Clare bait him into engagement. Not that Clare had deliberately done those things herself. Jack had refused to play war with the combatants she'd sent, and the damage had been done before Clare could call them off. But at least she *had* called them off. If he thought this was Clare now and it wasn't, nonviolent resistance would truly get him killed dead.

She said, "You can't have it both ways, you know that."

His finger continued tracing circles.

"I'm serious," she said. "This might be the only time you ever get serious out of me, John, so don't screw it up. Look at me."

He stared her dead on in mocking over-attentiveness.

She said, "If you think there's a chance this is Clare, then we stop right here, right now. Because if you go forward harboring the slightest doubt in that pigheaded skull of yours, you're going to get us *both* killed."

His head tipped left and right, like he was half agreeing with her and half agreeing with whatever weird debate went on in his brain, which meant he wasn't agreeing with anything.

She slapped him. "I will knock the shit out of you if that's what it takes."

He snatched her wrist. Gripped it hard. Glared.

She said, "That's a little better."

He let go and shoved her arm aside.

"I'll put a line out tonight," he said. "I'll see if I can find her."

CHAPTER 14

Holden

Four dining-room chairs pushed edge to edge created a platform that kept him off the floor and allowed him to angle off the kitchen window in a way that kept most of his heat profile shielded behind the wall. Fifteen hours he'd been on this improvised bench, waiting for this, brother and sister together for the first time since leaving Dallas, out in the open, easy marks for a long shot.

He had a clear view of the plaza, target in the crosshairs, and he breathed a slow in and out, finger resting beside the trigger guard, the whole of him suspended in the space that hung between kill and no kill.

They were brazen, foolish, two high-value assets with a high price on their heads, sitting exposed like this. No matter how skilled they were, they weren't invincible and the sister hadn't found every threat last night.

She hadn't found him.

He'd been watching when she'd entered the plaza; watching when she'd reemerged blond and drunk hours later; watching when the brother arrived; and was now watching the rendezvous he'd spent so much energy to reach.

Itzal had driven him to Dortmund.

Deutsche Bahn had gotten him the rest of the way.

He'd made it to Savignyplatz by after-dinner dark.

There, he had scouted apartment entrances, searching for full mail slots, which pointed to occupants being away, and had found a unit with an advantageous view, let himself in, and spent the intermittent stillness hashing and rehashing a confluence that grew bigger by the day.

There were five, maybe six players in motion now.

— The twins tracking their father.

— The Russians tracking the twins.

— The Americans tracking the twins.

— Himself tracking the twins.

— The Americans who *had* been tracking him.

Clare, the mother, was still a question mark.

He hadn't seen signs of her, but that

didn't mean she wasn't around.

And now, down at the table, the wrong man had shown up at the right time and right place. Not Dmitry. Not the father. Something else.

The man offered the brother documents.

Body language spoke of irritation, agitation, and a contest of will.

Holden reached for a spotting scope, secured the adapter, snapped a phone into the holder, and captured a photo array — not of the same quality he'd have gotten with a telescopic lens but good enough to get a record of the man's face.

A breeze lifted the pages and showed him Eurail Passes, a hotel, a city.

Whatever came next involved travel, and travel created a new set of issues.

The man followed the documents with a phone, and then the conversation, barely ten minutes old, showed signs of ending. Holden packed up his gear, hands moving quickly, methodically, while his focus stayed on that café.

He'd been willing to lose the siblings in Frankfurt, because he'd already had the rendezvous details, but if he lost them now, this would be the end.

The twins would never check into that hotel.

Odds of randomly finding either of them in a city of one and a quarter million people weren't odds he wanted to gamble on. Anyone else, it'd be different.

Life and the simple acts required to sustain it inevitably left a footprint.

Connections tethered humanity to routine.

The most cautious varied where they slept, avoided establishing daily patterns, left no digital trail, to make it difficult for someone like him to get ahead of them, but there were still groceries to buy, bills to pay, birthdays and anniversaries to celebrate, meetings to attend. With enough time and patience, he always found a lead.

But these two had no home, no family, no friends, no employer, and they had a lifetime of turning invisibility into an art form, and a kill team at their backs.

Once they were on the move again, they'd untether completely.

He'd have about fifteen seconds from the time they stood to the time they vanished, and he'd need ten to get out the door and another forty to get to the ground floor. He scooped the few items he still had out into his bag, grabbed the straps, shoved the chairs away from the window, and headed for the door.

There was no time to put things the way he'd found them, and it didn't matter anyway. He hadn't stolen anything. Hadn't killed anyone.

Other than a few misplaced items, he'd never been here.

He raced the steps down to ground level and caught sight of the table through the glass. The man stood, hesitated, then turned and walked off.

There'd been no handshakes, no formal good-byes.

The siblings stayed seated, watched him leave.

Tree trunks and bushes partially blocked the view.

Holden stepped outside, and strolled the sidewalk while the twins argued.

To any passing observer it was just a casual conversation, but the two weeks he'd spent tracking them, learning them, told him what it was.

The sister pushed back, left the table.

Dilemma chewed through him.

He needed to follow, and could follow only one.

Logic pushed one way. Desire, the other.

The brother was predictable — not in the strategic sense. His ability to think in multiple directions made him unpredictably dangerous. But he was predictable in his reliability, which would make him easier to shadow.

The sister was a few sane days shy of crazy.

He had no good options for sticking with her for the long haul.

Holden tracked her parallel from across the plaza because he wanted to.

Want.

Want was a dangerous, dangerous word.

He knew better than to give in to it and did anyway.

He glanced back at the table.

The brother was gone.

One second to the next, just like that, decision settled.

Holden followed the cobblestones to where he had a view of both exits to the building she'd entered. His luggage was an issue. He'd condensed the items from Itzal's cases into a single bag, but even one bag, no matter how bland, would stand out over time and make him visible, in the same way patterned shoes and bright clothing made a person visible. He couldn't afford to be seen with the weapons, couldn't afford to leave them.

Down the street the basement door opened.

The sister trotted up the stairs, clothes a

different color, body a different shape.

He gave her time, space, and started up after her.

She looked so much like her mother.

There were buyers who'd want the children for no other reason than revenge.

Clare — Catherine — Catalina — Karen . . .

One didn't easily escape a legacy like that.

"They'll find you," he'd told them. "You'll end up running hard. You could use an ally, a friend."

He wanted them alive, wanted *her* alive.

And want was a dangerous, dangerous thing.

CHAPTER 15

Alexanderplatz
Mitte, Berlin, Germany

Kara

She thumped the return key in frustration, hard enough that the laptop jumped. Nick stopped pacing. Aaron stopped bouncing the stress ball. Juan opened his eyes.

She hadn't been going for attention but had it now regardless.

She waved them off and went back to trying to ignore them.

They were too many bodies in too tight a space, an entire kill team sequestered and on edge, waiting for go, while the sense of impotence mounted.

Every repetitive motion, even those she couldn't directly see, was a gust of wind over a sand mandala, turning what should have been straightforward if tedious work into a struggle to keep big-picture focus.

She was tired, desperately needed sleep.

Obsession wouldn't let her mind shut down.

As of last night target was in Berlin.

The war room had picked him up outside the central station and then lost him again. There'd been no sign of him this morning, but he was still here, of that she was certain. SIGINT and HUMINT both pointed to an early meeting with a Russian handler, and this guy hadn't gone through all the effort of misdirecting attention just so he could up and leave before he got what he came for.

The intelligence channels had all gone quiet.

They had the time but not location.

The war room was hunting, and her team was on standby, and where the others had taken to pacing and sleeping, she had gone digging and had found an anomaly in the Berlin flight manifest.

She wasn't an expert on predictive modeling.

Didn't know what the standard deviation for no-shows looked like on this particular route at this time of year, at this time of day, but an Internet search gave her rough averages, and by appearances, that flight out of Frankfurt had taken off with an inordinately high number of empty paid-for seats.

Eyes closed, Vivaldi rolling through her brain, Kara willed herself through to the other side, trying to understand from target's perspective why buying out a third of the flight would have been worth the trouble.

The expenditure would have run into the high four figures.

The time investment, too, would have been considerable.

Most of the bookings had been for individuals or couples rather than large traveling groups, and keeping that many names, birth dates, phone numbers, e-mail addresses, and passport details realistic and pointing to unique IP addresses required incredible attention to detail. For all of that, he gained . . . ?

— Multiple tickets, multiple names.

— A whole heck of a lot of obfuscation.

The possibilities forked, and she followed the tangents.

Headquarters had scraped the manifest, pushed the data through software analysis, turned up thousands of hits. They'd followed each one in a time-consuming process of elimination, but every name on that list, whether on the flight or not, had led to a legitimate person with a fully backstopped,

195

ordinary, boring life.

— Borrowed identities.

Target could have moved through security with travel documents and identification for a different flight and used a borrowed identity to board this one.

Gate agents rarely confirmed identification as part of a domestic boarding process, but on the chance they did, a quality fake would be enough. The photo wouldn't even need to match, because nobody ever looked closely, and if the war room ever did manage to link a name to his body, all they'd find at the end of the rainbow was a random stranger with no idea how he'd been pulled into this game of intrigue.

— Wasted resources.

— Wasted attention.

Liv Wilson and team had spent the past twenty-four hours immersed in a game of which one of these is not like the others. If Kara's hypothesis held, the war room still wouldn't have found him, because, in a repeat of the same damn strategy that had led to chasing a hat in Frankfurt, they weren't looking for the real *him.*

Kara rested her fingers on the keyboard and let the adrenaline pass.

The dutiful part of her wanted to alert the war room to the anomaly.

The rest of her knew she'd be wasting her time.

She returned instead to the camera feeds in the Berlin airport.

She'd been through the deplaning footage once already, a quick pass to confirm with her own eyes what others had already reported.

But target *had* boarded that flight.

He wasn't a ghost, and he didn't have superpowers.

He was just as human as she was.

If he'd walked on that plane, he'd most certainly walked off. They were all just looking in the wrong place or for the wrong thing.

Illusion and misdirection were his comfort zones.

That's where she'd find him.

She located footage for the secured areas and started where the war room had long ago stopped. This was stale data. Locating him in the past wouldn't lead to him in the present, but for her, it didn't have to.

Tracking him to current location was the war room's job.

What she wanted was to understand.

She searched among the baggage handlers and fuel suppliers and food-service personnel, running feed after feed, laboriously enhancing images and pushing stills through recognition software.

The system finally spit out a partial match.

Its face belonged to one of the ground crew.

He worked the job as if he'd been doing it for years, but she knew him by the way he slipped away. The entirety of start to finish filled her with awe and concern.

To make this happen, he had to have known airlines and routes and have had the uniform in advance, and he had to have made the switch while their operative was on the aircraft, all of which meant he'd already anticipated and prepared against someone waiting to snag him in Berlin before her team had even known they'd be tracking him out of Dallas.

With that level of foresight, they could be chasing him indefinitely.

— No.

— Illusion *and* misdirection.

Everything they'd seen thus far was what he'd wanted them to see, which meant even in this, he expected to be seen, which meant he was directing their attention away from something else.

— The accomplice.

Nobody watching the flight had been looking for a second person, because she hadn't discovered the second until after the flight had landed.

The accomplice, too, *had* been there.

Kara went back to the Frankfurt boarding footage and watched the passengers, ignoring faces, focusing on attributes, and notating key characteristics, and she returned to the Berlin arrival to study the process in reverse. Over and over she watched and replayed, and each time the woman with lush blond hair drew her attention. She was young, stylish, haughty in a way that reminded her of the girls at school who'd thought they were better than everyone else and deserved special treatment because their parents had money. The worst had also been beautiful.

That's what this blonde was, and she had no match on the outbound side.

Kara moved the footage back thirty seconds, lifted a still out of the frame, enhanced the image, and ran it through the databases. Just as had happened with the guy in the ground-crew uniform, facial recognition came back with a partial match on target's passport photo, and what should have been the lucky break that confirmed they were hunting a male and female team instead led to the impossible.

She'd already found target below the

aircraft in a ground-crew uniform.

The same person couldn't be in two places at the same time.

Frustration squeezed her from the inside.

Facial recognition software wasn't infallible.

There were always false positives and false negatives, and this hit was a low enough match that the war room, having not seen what she'd just seen, would have likely discarded it. But it wasn't a fluke, wasn't a mistake.

And yet two partial matches for the same person so close together?

The only way that made sense was if they were dealing with two people who understood the way the algorithms worked well enough to pass themselves off as the same person — unlikely — or they were two people with nearly identical facial features.

She sat motionless, staring through the image, thoughts racing from possibility to possibility. Target had used quick change in Frankfurt — basic disguise, no masks, no prosthetics, just a well-planned series of clothing swaps performed with incredible timing — and, by appearance, the accomplice entering and exiting the restroom had done the same. But basic disguise had limits.

Passing a woman off as a man was straightforward enough.

Going male to female was a whole different level of difficult.

For this kind of nodal match, they were looking at identical twins. But target was male, and what she had here on-screen was either the best goddamn drag she'd ever seen or this was an honest-to-God woman.

— Target was female.

— Or, best guess, this was a brother-sister team.

She needed space from it, time and space to let the subconscious percolate on what else between the layers she might be missing. She set aside one analysis track in favor of another and returned to the departure out of Dallas.

She sorted through the angles for a view that would allow her to convince the waiting area to give up its secrets, and when she found it, she grabbed her notepad, and flipped to a clean page. She diagrammed the waiting area, marking out each key figure, like in a football play schematic, tracking physical movement and eye movement, until she had a map that told a story she only half understood.

She'd found target, but no sign of accomplice.

She'd also found Emilia Flynn, Daniel Cho, Peyton What's-his-name, and Bill Wright, a full four-person crew, and seeing them there, observing them from a distance, answered the question of why Emilia had been in Frankfurt.

— One flight.

— Two liquidation teams.

— Two targets.

That would have been really helpful to know *before* they'd boarded.

The men and women they sought to liquidate were assassins for hire, top-tier names on the Broker list, the ones smart enough, invisible enough, dangerous enough to become national security threats if the right money came along. Odds that two of them coincidentally happened to be on the same flight were about the same as getting struck by lightning while getting bitten by a rabid shark in the middle of the desert.

Their target was on his way to a rendez-vous in Berlin.

A second assassin along for the ride meant that somewhere out there, a third party had a vested interest in seeing he never made that meeting. A second assassin also meant a killer would be robbed of payment if Nick's crew hit target first, which made Nick & Co. the competition, which meant that unless Emilia was successful, there'd be an assassin gunning for *them,* and from the look on Emilia's face, as of Frankfurt, that killer was most definitely alive and roaming free.

Kara narrowed person-of-interest possibilities down to three, closed out the Dallas feeds, and switched back to the Frankfurt arrival. This time, she stuck with a single camera and watched the entire flight deplane.

She found target, and found Daniel, Peyton, and Emilia, and found the three persons of interest, but still no accomplice.

More curiously, there was also no Bill Wright.

She let the footage roll long past the deplaning.

Motion out on the tarmac, beyond the window, caught her attention.

She switched feeds for a better angle.

A stretcher wheeled a body from aircraft to ambulance. New data layered over old, and Kara understood, and she felt so very, very small.

What had seemed like war-room incompetence had been distraction in the juggle between crises. Emilia's target had struck preemptively on the flight.

She'd lost a man before the wheels had

ever touched down.

Hers would have been a very different hunt through the airport, and all of this while Nick's team had been tracking their man through the concourse.

Kara's throat tightened, and emotion built like water welling in a blowhole.

She hadn't known Bill personally, but she'd known of him, and known he was good people. She was overtired, needed sleep, was useless on this now.

She nudged the mouse to close down the camera feeds.

A flash of color at the edge of the frame gave her pause, and she stopped, pointer hovering over box, mind processing, trying to grasp what she'd just seen.

She pushed the time stamps backward and rewatched at the edge of the lounge.

The accomplice was there, acting as lookout.

She hadn't been on that Dallas flight, because she was already in the terminal, waiting for the flight to arrive. This explained how events in Frankfurt had spun so quickly out of control, and explained target's foresight and preparation.

This was a team that expected to be trailed.

By whom, she didn't know — Emilia's assassin, the Russians, both, something else altogether — but these two had come prepared for high-level evasion, and her own team had stepped right into the middle of that.

Were still in the middle of whatever *it* was.

That raised the exponential risk of getting caught in existing cross fire.

The weight of the implication must have shown on her face, because Nick crossed her field of vision and nudged the bed. She pulled earbuds out.

He said, "What'd you find?"

She scooted over, made room for him.

Aaron stopped bouncing the ball.

Juan rolled over and opened one eye.

Ringing interrupted before she had a chance to get to show and tell.

Attention riveted in Nick's direction, the entire room reverent and focused.

The conversation was one sided.

They waited.

Nick said, "Understood," and ended the call.

"Pack up," he said. "Rendezvous has moved to Prague."

CHAPTER 16

Eglise Ambérieu-en-Bugey
Ambérieu-en-Bugey, France

Holden

The church filled one side of the small plaza, two vaulted stories of quarried limestone blocks and lead-paned windows that led off the main street in a solid wall. Narrow homes and old stone buildings edged the rest — solid doors, wooden shutters, sun-bleached plaster — in neat, crisp lines, hemming in a few trees, tidily parked cars, and the cobblestone center. Clean. Calm. Quiet.

The only thing that moved was water spurting from the center fountain.

Not the kind of place a person could sit for a while and go unnoticed.

Stores, cafés, banks, all the busy places he'd have utilized to blend into the background, were a few blocks over.

It would have been easier to kill her here than it was to surveil her.

Ironic, considering she wasn't an easy person to kill.

Also ironic, considering this was the first time killing *wasn't* the objective.

The bell tower, twenty, thirty feet above the church peak, with a clean line of sight on the *mairie* — the town hall — was where he would have gone if it had been. What he'd needed was a fast, clean exit. The belfry couldn't give him that, and the plaza was too exposed, too naked to hang around in an attempt to observe both sides of the *mairie,* which was how he'd gotten to where he was now, holed up in a place of worship, staring out a window and watching the entrance like a trusting dog convinced its person would walk back through that door any second.

She might. She might not.

She'd been in there two hours, at least he believed she was still in there.

Two hours for God only knew what.

The destination *had* been Prague.

This wasn't Prague.

This was everything opposite Prague. Opposite direction, opposite feel, and if he'd read the signals right — and he was pretty damn sure he had — opposite the plans she'd made with her brother.

Whatever she was doing here, she was doing behind her brother's back.

As if there weren't already enough warning signs.

He had followed her on foot out of Savignyplatz, a six-kilometer trek across town, through high-traffic areas and appearance changes, into a residential area, where she'd disappeared through a nondescript door and reemerged a half hour later as a woman twice her age, drab and unnoticeable, but for a carry-on suitcase, and had followed her out of Berlin by train in a jagged route that detoured through Frankfurt and Paris. He'd been able to stay with her because he *was* her, another iteration of her, ghost and chameleon, familiar with the ways in which a person stood and walked and gestured identified them as much as any individual piece of clothing did. But mostly he'd been able to stay with her because her disguise was flawed.

The carry-on was her weakness and his touchstone.

No matter how she disguised the thing or where she left it, she always circled back to claim it, and what should have been a prop, a transition piece, or a distraction to facilitate shedding one persona for another had become a homing beacon instead.

From her very first abandon-and-return, he'd understood.

She'd perceived enough of a tangible, credible threat at that outdoor table in Berlin to assemble an arsenal. She was traveling armed and traveling heavy.

But whatever she'd prepared to fight wasn't in this French village. He knew *that* because she'd left the suitcase behind, tucked out of sight in the station's tiny ticket-master office, a courtesy she shouldn't have been granted but had been because few were capable of telling her no.

If patterns prevailed, she'd return to collect it.

That was the only logical thing he had to hold on to in this illogical venture, and the only thing stronger than the nagging possibility she'd brought him to this location to lose him. Well, not *just* to lose him.

There were a hundred faster, easier ways to get rid of him if ditching him was what she wanted, and none of them involved a daylong detour into the foothills southeast of Geneva.

No, this village, this town hall, was too specific. She'd come here looking for someone or something. But letting him believe he had the drop on her the whole long way, setting him up in an impossible surveillance position, and leaving him waiting and watching at the front while she slipped out the back and caught the last train out for the night, knowing he'd be stranded in a town with limited transportation options, *that* was exactly the kind of thing she'd do for personal entertainment.

The longer she strung him along the more hilarious she'd find the payoff.

She was twisted like that.

Unpredictable, raw, electric, alive.

It made her a new kind of danger and a different kind of challenge, which was why he was still standing here, watching that damn door, ignoring the Klaxon sounding through his head. That, and he wanted to know what in this small town possibly mattered enough for her to risk betraying her brother's trust when trust was what they needed most to keep each other alive.

He stole another glance at the time.

The persistent nagging grew stronger.

This whole thing would have been so much easier if he could just talk with her, but that was out of the question and also nonnegotiable. He'd observed enough targets through the crosshairs to know that even she, manipulative, emotional chameleon that she was, wasn't a good enough actress to prevent subconscious body language from telegraphing the presence of an armed companion.

For him to be of any value, she couldn't know.

That had been fine enough in concept when he'd first set out in Houston.

In practicality, he felt like a voyeuristic creep.

That surprised him — a lifetime spent peering into people's lives, and *now* he was uncomfortable? But he should have seen it coming. Nobody, guilty or innocent, took kindly to learning they'd been spied upon, and hunting someone he cared about to protect her when she didn't believe she needed protecting was a far cry from picking pockets, as he'd done as a kid on the streets from Calamar to Cartagena, or running skip traces for pocket money after a promise made to the father he'd never met resulted in a new life in the United States, or tracking down those outside as he followed that trailhead into the world's underbelly to where he observed the most intimate moments through the crosshairs.

The last thing he wanted was for her to feel repulsed by him.

That's what this would earn him if she knew.

So, no. And also, no.

Murmurs and footsteps reverberated in the solemn acoustics. Parishioners came and went, lighting candles, counting rosary beads, whispering prayers.

It'd been two hours and forty minutes now.

The *mairie* would close soon.

The next train departed shortly after that.

Even if she walked out now — assuming she hadn't already slipped out the back — he no longer had enough time to find out what she'd been after.

He'd reached the self-imposed cutoff.

He would return to the station and look for her suitcase.

Either it'd be there or it wouldn't, and then he'd know.

Reluctance held him at the window, refused to let him go.

To leave now was to acknowledge the possibility she'd absconded.

Every minute he delayed was a minute he didn't have to face that truth.

The pragmatic part of him grew angry at the self-delusion. He gripped the bag and stepped away from the window, but the glass door opened, and *she* was there, head down, stride long, moving fast across the plaza with the focus of someone who had no time to waste. Nothing in her presence, her posture, said she was aware of his.

But nothing about her could ever be taken at face value.

He turned for the rear, for the small door behind the offices, which would let him out to a side street. His hurry was a different kind of hurry. He knew where she was headed, knew she wouldn't leave town without that suitcase, but once she had it, there was no telling what she'd do next.

CHAPTER 17

Hotel Galileo
Prague, Czech Republic

Kara

She stepped off the elevator and strolled toward the lobby, conscious of her posture, of every step, trying not to overcompensate, like someone trying to pretend they weren't pretending to look relaxed and normal. This was just her, on the way out to grab a bite to eat, exactly like she'd told Juan as she'd walked out the door.

Food and coffee, that's all she needed to think about.

Coffee, food, coffee, food, around the corner, then past the front desk.

Lying was never meant to be part of the job.

Nor was keeping Nick in the dark, but traitorous as it felt, she saw no way around it. Her priority was watching her back and watching Nick's, and two assassins on the same flight out of Dallas wasn't a co-incidence.

The war room had missed it — which she highly doubted — or intelligence was deliberately being withheld, and the reason didn't really matter if the end result was the same. Her team was being primed for failure, maybe worse. The only way to protect them and protect herself was to know what they were up against.

She'd seen an Internet café a couple blocks down on their way to the hotel. That usually meant international calls, as well, and that was where she headed.

One number, ten minutes, that's all she needed.

She pushed out the hotel doors into a biting wind, turned her coat collar up, dug her chin down into the warmth of body heat, and followed the cobblestones.

She'd left her department-issued phone behind, out in the open, on the bed, beside the laptop, where, if it came to it, no one could deny seeing it, and she hoped like hell she'd never need the alibi. Not that she was doing anything illegal, but the way she was going about it could be spun as such, and she'd rather not lose years of her life to the brig at the hands of someone like Liv, who'd gladly frame carrying either of those devices on this jaunt as an attempt at unauthorized disclosure of classified information.

Familiar outdoor signage welcomed her, and she stepped off the street into a cozy room with a bakery and coffee bar at the back, computer-laden tables at the windows, and a menu on the wall that priced out phone and Internet services.

A few words, a handful of koruny got her a phone line.

Four in the afternoon in Prague meant ten in the morning on the East Coast.

To do this meant pretty much now or never.

She dialed from memory.

She didn't have friends, tried hard not to make enemies, and filled the in-between by collecting and nurturing favors like her career depended on them, because it pretty much did. Twenty-nine-year-old Bartholomew Baker, whose drunken, beer-bottle-brave mouth may or may not have gotten him a hair's breadth from losing his clearance, position, and career, was one of those who owed her.

Bart worked at headquarters, a separate department, one in which Liv Wilson's tentacles had far less suction.

He answered with a gruff hello.

216

Kara said, "I'm calling in my favor."

No pleasantries, no introduction, no need to make her life more difficult. He knew who she was, and he'd give her what she wanted, not just because she was the one asking, but because she was letting him off easy.

She said, "I need you to run a flight manifest against the Broker list for me."

A pause hung in the air. Typing clicked across the line. He said, "Something happened with your clearance?"

"No."

The typing stopped. The phone shifted from one ear to the next. His voice lowered, turned cautious. He said, "Then why are you coming to me for this?"

"Because I need it done."

Silence followed. She could hear the mental gears grinding and didn't fault him for that. There'd be less room for confusion and suspicion if she'd asked for something that'd get him fired or jailed.

He said, "You're burning your chit to have me access something you can just get yourself?"

"Yes."

"Why?"

"Because none of your business."

"Look," he said. "I'll get you what you

217

want, but at least let me know what it is I'm not seeing here, so I can keep my own ass covered."

"There's nothing to cover. I just don't want my name on the requisition."

"Yeah, well, I don't think one favor's gonna solve *that* problem."

The attempt at humor fell flat.

She said, "You're burning my daylight."

"Whatever you say, boss lady. How soon do you need it?"

"How soon can you run it?"

"Now if you want."

She gave him the Dallas–Fort Worth flight information.

A minute passed. Bart said, "Manifest against the Broker list gives me one match. Christopher Holden. You know the name?"

Kara's thoughts slowed to a crawl. That wasn't right.

She said, "Only one match?"

"Just the one."

"Where's he rank?"

"Third, but the first two are placeholders — no aliases, nothing but kills and skills. Need me to dig around and see if we've got any other links?"

"Nah," she said.

The higher up the list, the greater the threat and more urgent the liquidation priority, but you couldn't liquidate what you couldn't find, and there were killers up and down that list who'd been smart enough to stay anonymous, even to the Broker. Placeholders meant the war room knew they existed, but hadn't identified them yet. They weren't her problem.

Jacques Lefevre was her problem.

And now, apparently, so was Christopher Holden.

Bart let out a low whistle. "This mother's a piece of work."

Kara wanted details, didn't have time for a verbal lesson, and would need to see them with her own eyes anyway. "Send me the Broker's original op file," she said, "and everything we've got on him."

"Same e-mail?"

She didn't care if the war room knew she was looking, she just didn't want them to know *right now,* and her official work account was the only way to protect herself against a clearance violation. She said, "Yeah, but rename before you send, something generic, and then I need to know where Jacques Lefevre ranks on the Broker list."

A beat of silence followed and lengthened. Bart said, "The name shows up on the flight manifest but not on the list. Maybe he's one of the placeholders."

No, that wasn't right, either.

The war room had known what this guy was even before they'd known who he was, and the whole reason headquarters had mobilized Nick's team as fast as they had was *that* he was on the Broker list. Now that they'd locked in on him, the name he'd flown under, even if it was an alias, should still point back to the list.

She said, "I've got a second manifest for you to run."

Bart grunted. "This favor's turning into multiple favors."

"And you're turning into a whiny baby, so I'd say that makes us even."

"I'm just saying."

"So am I."

He grunted again. She gave him the information for the Frankfurt to Berlin flight and waited, focus jumping from street to silence and back again.

He said, "I'm not pulling up any matches."

"Not a single one?"

"I didn't stutter."

"One more," she said, "and then I'm done."

"So you say."

"Go back to the Dallas–Frankfurt manifest. Run every name on it against the war room's op files, including personnel."

"Oh, now we get to the part where I need to cover my ass."

"Just run the fucking manifest, Bart."

Bart typed and clicked. He said, "You know, if you weren't such a ballbuster, you wouldn't have to work so hard to get people to do things for you."

"I'll come see you for congeniality lessons when this is over."

He said, "Flight out of Dallas to war-room op files and personnel files gets me your original Christopher Holden guy."

"That's it?"

"You slay me with the questions. There's also Emilia Flynn, your buddies Nick Carson, Juan Marino, and . . . Oh, this is cute. Looks like a whole party of your kind was on that flight."

"How many?"

"Eight, including you."

That accounted for Nick's and Emilia's teams and ruled out anyone else working for headquarters who might have tagged along, but it still got her only a single liquidation target, and the wrong one at that. She said, "Send me the op files on the placeholders and the next eight names down the list."

Bart paused. The silence thickened, and

she could hear the hesitancy.

She said, "I'm searching for a needle in a haystack right now, so unless there's been an adjustment to my clearance that I don't know about, there's no reason why there'd be any heat on this. Man up and send me the damn data already."

"And then we're settled?"

"Then we're settled."

"Need about ten minutes to pull it together," he said.

She hung up without a good-bye, squared her bill at the coffee bar, purchased a couple pastries and caffeine to go, and made her way back to the hotel, Styrofoam in hand, focus on the pavement, thoughts bolting like a herd of spooked horses in a multidirectional gallop.

She was familiar with need to know, and accepted her place in that hierarchy.

That her team's target wasn't on the liquidation list for the reasons headquarters claimed didn't matter. Why he'd made the list didn't change the objective or her obligation to shut up, follow orders, and do the job, but it mattered a whole heck of a lot in terms of being successful at her job.

Who the target was, what he was, determined how they pursued him and how they took him down. The information headquarters withheld could make the difference between putting him in their crosshairs or winding up in his — and that was just one target — it didn't even factor for a second assassin competing with them for the kill.

Christopher Holden was a whole other issue.

Top of the list meant he was highly dangerous and a high liquidation priority.

Probably why they'd sent Emilia after him.

She wouldn't begrudge that truth, Emilia *was* good.

But unless she'd already managed to put him down — and the look on her face outside the Frankfurt terminal was anything but assuring — Christopher Holden was an assassin with a liquidation team at his back, competing for a kill on their target, who may or may not be aware of the assassin tailing him. Meanwhile, headquarters had failed to notify the two teams of the others' objectives or presence and had put them all on a collision course, with a hundred ways to die.

Beautiful.

Her thoughts turned in that direction, spinning off threads that left her so preoccupied, she didn't register the real-world patterns until they were nearly close enough to touch. The color jolted her first.

Three times now she'd seen that same red

and black coat.

She'd seen it across the street when she left the hotel.

She'd seen it pass the window when she was in the Internet café.

And here she caught it in her peripheral vision while checking for cars before crossing. She resisted the natural urge to look again and pushed on with the same distracted stride, fighting hard to keep realization from seeping into her posture.

She was vulnerable — unarmed, isolated from her team, didn't even have a phone on her — and was being watched, shadowed by an enemy who knew what she was here to do. She'd have felt fear — probably *should* have felt fear — but analysis wouldn't let her.

He could have killed them in Frankfurt.

He could kill her now.

But if he was half as good as she knew he was, she never would have become aware of his presence unless he wanted her to know he was there. Hell, if she'd been more aware of what went on outside her head, she'd have registered him the first time, and he'd have moved on.

But she hadn't, and so he'd come incrementally closer.

What was he gonna do next? Walk up and

shake her hand?

She reached the hotel doors, caught a glimpse of him in the glass.

He was close enough to touch.

Close enough that she could have accomplished what she'd failed to get close enough to do in Frankfurt, but of all the scenarios she'd thought of before leaving the hotel, bringing a weapon because the target she'd spent days trying to locate would instead locate her wasn't one of them.

She kept her gaze low to avoid accidental eye contact, pushed into the lobby, strode for the elevators, and lingered there.

He never followed.

To the best of her knowledge, he never set foot inside.

She returned to the room and found it dark and quiet, as she'd left it.

Juan, splayed out on the nearest bed, watched television with the volume too low to hear. She handed him a coffee and pastry.

"Anything new?" she said.

He shook his head and raised the cup in a salute of thanks.

She slid back onto her bed and woke the laptop.

The enormity of what had just happened settled like a cold, wet quilt.

She blanked at the screen, fingers moving

slowly of their own accord.

Thirty minutes ago she would have been antsy, waiting for news so they could be on their way again. Now all she wanted was for minutes to multiply.

She didn't have enough of them.

Nick needed to know about target having been outside their hotel.

The longer she waited to tell him, the more questions there'd be over why she hadn't said something sooner. But to tell him now would require time. And telling him now would result in resources and attention turning to something that mattered less than the overall objective. Target was their objective.

He'd come and gone.

To find him, she needed to get ahead of him.

She needed to track him before the clues died.

The computer booted.

E-mail from Bart waited for her.

Her thoughts scattered, and pressure built.

There was too much too fast.

She ignored the e-mail and followed a hierarchy of links to the hotel cameras and any Internet-connected cameras nearby, and she searched the street outside the hotel, searched for visual proof that she wasn't imagining this, that she wasn't crazy.

For thirty minutes she hunted, and she finally found him at that damn Internet café, and she traced him from there to the nearest streetcar, and from streetcar toward the old city and into Náměstí Republiky — Republic Square — and caught a glimpse of him crossing the wide-open center space and turning down a side street, like a burglar casing a joint, and lost him within Hotel Kings Court.

Try as she might, she failed to pick up the trail.

The urgency of informing Nick faded.

Even if she'd gone to him immediately, they'd have already been too late.

She summarized the find, collected time stamps and screen grabs, packaged the material, and sent it to headquarters. She copied Nick, was tempted to copy Steven Hayes, Liv's supervisor, because the logical thing to do when one didn't trust that material was being put in the right hands was to put it in someone else's, but logic didn't work in a bureaucracy. Logic wasn't prudent. Emotions, personalities, politics, hierarchy, they all got in the way of logic, and of the objective, and made the world a messy place.

She hit SEND, and the mental chaos eased up.

She could let target go for now and return to what had sent her out the door in the first place. She opened Bart's e-mail and clicked through to the data dump. Both files were there, as requested. The first contained the Broker's raw data, the second everything the war room had reconciled against it, and that's what she wanted first:

Holden, Christopher – Alias
Name: Unknown
Age: 36, est
Nationality: Venezuelan, presumed

Headquarters placed him as working for the Broker for at least six years. She scanned a list of weapons, skills, and potential sightings, kept going along a blood trail of confirmed kills, suspected kills, kidnappings, and assisted assignments.

Some of the names she recognized, most she didn't.

The most recent activity had been two weeks ago outside Austin, Texas — abduction, not a kill — contract origination out of Russia, target Karen McFadden.

She grabbed her notebook, flipped to a fresh page.

There was something familiar about the name, something she couldn't place.

She added it to the diagram of unknowns.

Headquarters had no decrypted match for the buyer's code name.

But Russia . . .

Russia by itself meant nothing.

Like China, like the United States, Russia was a global player meddling anywhere it could to advance its interests, but timing and current circumstances . . .

She returned to the material.

The Broker's data put Christopher Holden's last known location as Houston.

That was a trail she could follow without hiding behind a proxy, but the information was stale, which made it low priority.

The war room had connected him to four confirmed aliases.

She had to assume there were more.

The file contained twelve photos: one from the Broker's file, in which his face was distance-blurry and concealed by cap and glasses, four lifted from the alias-identification documents, and a series that would have come from Emilia prior to boarding out of Dallas. He had dark hair, a strong jaw, was easy on the eyes in a masculine Enrique Iglesias sort of way.

A knock on the door jerked her out of the hunt.

Juan dragged himself off the bed to answer and returned with Nick and Aaron. The look on Nick's face said there was news.

She said, "Rendezvous confirmed?"

"Nine tomorrow," Nick said. "Republic Square, near Old Town. We bug out in an hour for recon."

Kara's body froze, and her thoughts raced from video feed to video feed, recalibrating everything she'd seen — target's lack of fear, the way he treated as a game the threat they posed to his life — and where those feeds had led.

She said, "No. It's a trap."

The room went pin-drop silent.

The gears in her head locked up.

She should have waited. Should have kept her mouth shut.

She glanced at Nick. "Have you checked your e-mail?"

"I've been on the phone."

All three of them stared at her, waiting.

Nick said, "On a confidence scale of one to ten."

"Nine."

"We move out in an hour. You don't have time to tell it twice. Go."

Her mouth opened. No words came out.

She struggled to break the interconnected puzzle into separate pieces that would be easy for logic to follow, that wouldn't create accusations and set off a time bomb of cascading repercussions. She started at the end.

"He followed us here," she said. "Like he did in Frankfurt."

The room erupted in an echo of "What? When? You didn't tell us. Why?"

She dug fingers into the bedspread to keep them still, focused on the foot of the bed to avoid eye contact. "Went out for coffee about an hour ago," she said. "Spotted someone I thought was him on my way back, wasn't sure, had to confirm, and by the time I found him in the feeds, he was already gone."

Juan said, "So he's running recon for a hit."

Kara said, "If he wanted to hit us, he would have already done it."

Aaron said, "Riiight. Cuz assassin dude totes just wants to be friends."

The sarcasm shorted her train of thought.

A joke, maybe, but a joke he'd never have thrown at Nick or Juan if they'd offered the same assessment under similar circumstances, and that made it not a joke; made her the joke. For a brief second her cheeks burned and her skin flushed with the shame of old humiliation. She was that kid again, mom in prison, dad unable to cope, sneaking out with the .22 before school to hunt rabbits and squirrels to provide a semblance of dinner for her sisters, showing up in clothes too big and shoes too small and sometimes mucky, because she didn't always have time to wash off before the bus arrived. The kid tormented by teachers and bullied by classmates, and written off as stupid by everyone who should have cared because she was poor and dirty and afraid to speak. But at least they'd had the balls to come right out with it.

She'd known where she stood with them.

This thing Aaron did, that so many men did, passing off belittlement as humor, slithering down an escape-hatch variant of *learn to lighten up* if called out, spinning their own bias as her personal failing, that was just chickenshit cowardice.

She said, "Walk us through your thought process, Aaron. Explain how you got to that conclusion. Help me see what I'm missing."

He smirked, almost winked. "It's not that important."

"It was important enough to interrupt. Clearly, we need to hear this."

Aaron glanced at Nick and then Juan.

Said, "You know, with the thing about how you didn't think our guy was running recon."

Kara waited.

Aaron placed hands behind his back and stood military at ease.

"Doesn't matter," he said.

She said, "Well, when you do have something that matters, let us know."

That was as close to subtlety as she was capable of getting and probably should have earned her a goddamn medal. She turned to Nick, said, "We're dealing with a guy who knows what we are, knows why we're here, who is capable of getting close enough to strike first, and hasn't. Once is a coincidence. Twice is a pattern. He utilizes misdirection as a weapon. Everything we've seen, we've seen because that's what he wanted. Think of it as elaborate, high-end stage magic — sleight-of-hand, disappearing acts — every step thought through in advance, focusing your attention where he wants it so the illusion seems real. He wanted us to know he was with us in Frankfurt, and he wants us to know how to find him here in Prague."

Juan said, "Why? He's a dead man walking, so if he's as good as all that, why stick around? Why not just take off and be done with us?"

She said, "Why does anyone refuse to walk away from something they know might kill them?"

"Because he's an overconfident prick."

"No, forget about him for a minute," she said. "What about you? You know this job might kill you, so why are you here?"

Juan hesitated.

Nick said, "Something matters to him more than the immediate risk."

"Right," Kara said. "So, Frankfurt was him assessing that risk, and we gave him a baseline gauge of our threat level. Then he got in close, showed us what he could do. We didn't take the warning, and that told him we're predictable, dependable."

The room went quiet.

"I tracked him through camera feeds from here to Republic Square," she said. "So the real question is why a guy who uses misdirection as a weapon went out of his way to ensure we know where to find him for a rendezvous that matters more to him than the risk we pose."

Juan said, "He wants us there?"

"Yes. He wants us there. But that's just problem one." She took a long, deep breath. "Problem two is that our guy wasn't the only assassin on that Dallas flight."

234

For the second time, the room erupted in a chorus of questions, and she fought to find the line between giving them the information critical to the moment and accidentally pointing fingers of betrayal at headquarters.

Anything to do with Emilia's team was a no-go.

So was anything to do with their target having an accomplice.

And especially anything to do with the war room having withheld information. Nick knew about all three, he'd pick up the inference. From the stricken look on his face, he'd already recognized where this was going.

She said, "Best as I can tell from the information currently available, we've got one target heading into the rendezvous at Republic Square and a second right behind him, hired to make sure it doesn't happen."

Juan said, "Hold up a minute. You're saying we've got someone out there competing with us for the kill?"

"By appearances, yes, and that takes us back to the question of why our target would have gone out of his way to ensure we know where to find him, and that answers Aaron's original point. Just because he left us alive doesn't mean he intends to *keep* us alive. Either he knows there's a threat bigger than us gunning for him, or he expects some kind of foul play from the people he's meeting tomorrow, maybe both. Regardless, we're firepower and distraction. He's setting us up to do his work for him."

With that she stopped. There was nothing more to say.

Nick stayed silent.

The room stayed silent.

The silence grew until it took on a life of its own.

Aaron was the first to speak. He said, "Republic Square, that's a busy, kind of high-end shopping part of town, isn't it? If anything goes down that requires more than a round or two, we're going to blow our cover. I mean, there's really not much worse we could do to announce to the Czechs that we're here, right? So does keeping this operation dark rank higher or lower than taking out target?"

The question sucked what little oxygen was left out of the room and proved Aaron was capable of thinking strategically when he wanted to, which made Kara detest him a little less, but his question wasn't really *the* question.

He knew, they all knew, that if the op went sideways, they were on their own.

This was the tact in him finally surfacing, asking if they'd just been deliberately fucked over. She answered yes the only way she knew how.

"Target takes priority," she said.

Nick said, "You sent all this in?"

She glanced at her wrist. "About an hour ago."

He said, "We recon. We set up for the hit. I'll take this to command for clarification, but unless something changes, we're still go."

CHAPTER 18

Hradčany
Prague, Czech Republic

Holden

The bar was small and narrow, a recently updated affair in a centuries-old building, the type of place that catered to neighborhood regulars by the generation, which guaranteed his face stood out the moment he stepped in, but the bar was the fastest way behind the walls. He paused at the threshold in a beat of acknowledgment for the sideways glances, a beat that placed every barstool and beer mug in snapshot threat assessment.

Three men at the counter, focus on the television at the far end.

Young couple preoccupied at a tiny table against the right wall.

Early evening. Sparse crowd.

That would change as the night wore on.

238

The bartender was a woman in her late fifties, with arms men half her age would envy. She glanced his way, sized him up the way he sized up the room, and he continued in her direction, navigating the tight walkway between bar top and tables. He asked for *svařák* — mulled wine, popular in the colder Czech months — headed out back to a small patio, where remnants of warmer times were still evident on the trellis, pulled a chair free at one of the tables not yet put up, tucked his chin into the scarf, and wrapped his hands around the mug for warmth.

Late, late fall in Prague was a shitty time to be outdoors.

A light turned on in an upper-floor bathroom window across the courtyard.

That he was out here freezing, trying to catch a glimpse of her through the back side of a youth hostel, instead of across the street, watching its entrance, was case in point for why Prague had filled Cold War legends with intrigue and spies.

Forget geography and centuries of political alliances.

The lure was in the architecture, tight streets flush up against the buildings, solid walls, solid doors, limited ground-floor windows, block after block of man-made canyons, which left pedestrians exposed to the elements and to watchful eyes, and made it difficult to hide while out on the streets but easy to disappear once off them. The real living went on in the open spaces behind the walls, which was why a cold backyard patio was as close as he could get to her right now.

He sipped the *svařák* and watched the light.

Another half hour and he'd head back around the block, walk in through the front, and inquire about a room of his own, though there was a chance, as with everything she did, that the hostel was a ruse — that the light he watched wasn't even hers — and that she'd slipped away while his back was turned.

Part of him would be relieved to discover that she had.

Trying to keep up with her was exhausting.

He tracked people to kill them and did what was necessary to stay invisible to those who wanted to kill him, but thirty-six hours of hopping trains and crossing borders, of sleeping in short bursts and second-guessing and triple-questioning every damn move, while tailing someone whose entire life had been a lesson in strategic evasion, had turned grueling patience, lateral thinking, and meticulous attention to detail into mental mush. He was ready to be done.

The upper-floor window dimmed with shadow.

He recognized its shape and averted his gaze, as if somehow *that* lessened the creep factor or made any difference at all if she knew he was watching.

Motion just beyond the patio light pulled him back to ground, footsteps he'd have heard sooner, movement he'd have caught faster if he'd been focused on the job itself rather than the person. His senses dropped into the space between life and death.

Sound slivered and light fractured.

His hand moved from table to jacket, reaching for the firepower that would put an end to threat before it began.

A male voice off the side of the patio said, "I'm unarmed, Chris."

Strategic thinking somersaulted head over heels.

The voice's body stepped into the light, all five feet, ten inches, in nineties denim and a warm winter coat, hands up, palms open, fingers waving hello.

Holden exhaled, part guffaw, part exasperation.

He was half tempted to pull the trigger

anyway. "Jesus, man," he said.

Jack moved in closer, cheeks too large and cheekbones too wide, nose and jaw too low, eyes too puffy, and — unless the light was playing tricks — skin tone a full four shades darker. That last feature, Holden knew, was specifically for facial recognition software.

Algorithms and deep learning systems were only as strong as the data sets used to train them, and facial recognition, like so much of technology, was plagued by bias and inherently prone to err with darker skin. He'd made use of the same technique for the same reasons, though this was the first he'd seen it used by someone else.

Jack clamped a brotherly hand on Holden's shoulder and slipped behind him for the opposite seat. "Miserable night to be out alone," he said. "Figured you could use the company."

Holden watched him settle, waited until reciprocal silence bordered on rudeness and, stretching one word out into two long syllables, said, "Bullshit."

Jack laughed, and with the laugh, the facade cracked and familiarity seeped through. Brother and sister. Same damn twisted sense of humor.

Jack nodded toward the *svařák*.

"That stuff any good?"

"It's warm."

"*Coffee* is warm. *Tea* is warm."

"Yeah, well, this is warm in all the right places."

Jack tipped the chair back until its front legs came off the ground, and he studied the sky. "My sister does have that effect on people," he said. "Stick around her long enough and even heroin will seem like a reasonable way to cope."

There was humor in the sibling jab and camaraderie in its delivery, and it felt as if they were old friends with years of common history, instead of recent enemies who'd been bent on killing each other and almost had.

But this wasn't a friendly visit, no matter how friendly it might be.

That wasn't how things worked in this world.

Jack, still staring at the sky, said, "Picked you up coming off the plane in Frankfurt. In case you were wondering."

Holden raised the mug in salute. "Question did cross my mind." He nudged it toward the hostel. "Your sister know I'm here?"

"Not that she's mentioned, but then, she makes a habit of not mentioning things to me, so who knows?" Jack dropped the chair forward. "Wasn't just you I picked up coming off that plane, though," he said. "Those playmates of yours made me worry when you didn't show up in Berlin."

"I was there."

Jack motioned to the hostel's upper-floor window and then toward Holden, as if drawing a link between one city and the next. "Obviously, right?"

Memory made a fast rewind to Savigny-platz, shifting context to what Holden should have realized then. *Obviously,* while he'd been busy tracking one half of the brother-sister team across town, the other half had been tracking him. Not the whole way, just enough to ascertain he was capable of keeping up, because knowing where to find one made it easy to find the other.

Simple. Elegant. Dangerous.

Jack had planned this conversation before any of them had left Berlin.

Holden rewrapped his fingers around the mug.

Heat seeped into his skin, and silence seeped into the discussion.

Jack said, "So how'd things go with your Frankfurt fan club?"

"I'm here and they're not, *obviously.*"

Jack tipped a finger forward, as if to say, "Touché."

"Dead or shook?" he said.

"Dead."

Jack leaned the chair back again. "There'll be others," he said. "They'll just keep right on coming and coming and coming."

Holden took a long sip.

The warmth reached his belly, almost reached his head.

He placed the mug on the table, stretched his legs, said, "It's cold, John, and I'm tired, and charming as I may be, I know you didn't come crawling out of the shadows for a round of small talk. What are you doing here? What do you want?"

Jack relaxed, the whole of him, as if the upper layers of a multi-layered disguise had dissolved and all that remained were base-line latex features. He dropped the chair legs. "Rendezvous is tomorrow at oh-nine-hundred." He cut his eyes toward the hostel. "Using her to lead you to it won't give you enough time to scout, won't give you much of a chance to sleep, either, and you're gonna need both, so I'm here saving you the time."

Holden's eyes narrowed in barefaced suspicion.

No way in hell had a guy fighting a four-dimensional war inside his head broken a perfectly good charade to offer intel as some altruistic gesture.

"Why?" he said.

Jack laced his fingers atop the table, waited a beat, said, "Because at some point tomorrow, after nine, several armed men will come careening through that square. They're going to grab me, haul me off, and when that happens, my sister is going to lose her goddamn mind. I need you to be there to keep her safe, mostly from herself."

Holden's mouth opened and shut.

In his head tomorrow's rendezvous played out as a mirror of what he'd seen in Berlin: sister as sniper on a rooftop, brother as bait on the ground, and between them a vast no-man's-land filled with lies and manipulation.

Danger crackled up his spine.

This right here was Jill detouring into France behind her brother's back. This was that multiplied by a thousand life-or-death twists, because it made him an explicit accomplice in their private sibling war.

He said, "You're asking a goddamn awful lot."

"Yes," Jack said. "I am."

Holden said, "Let's make sure I've got this straight. You're about to let yourself be grabbed, and your sister — the one *responsible for protecting you and keeping you safe*

— has no idea?"

"Correct."

Holden snorted. "Hell no, and no thank you."

Jack sat silent, expression fixed, undeterred.

Holden said, "You've got government-sanctioned killers coming after you on one side. There are underground assassins hunting for you on the other. This thing with the Russians is still anybody's guess, and your response is to stab your *one* ally in the back? That, my friend, is betrayal or insanity, maybe both."

"I know what it looks like," Jack said. "But that's not what it *is.*"

"It doesn't matter what it *is,* John. She's going to think it's *real,* and putting her in that position is top-level sadist shit, and I want no part of it."

Jack leaned forward. "I love my sister, okay? But sometimes love means doing the hard things, and this is one of those things."

"No, I don't think so," Holden said. He nudged the mug aside and matched Jack's posture. "I could've been killed between Frankfurt and Berlin. Your sister could have lost me a hundred times between Berlin and Prague. I can still refuse to be your tool, and nobody with any sense of probability, especially not you, rolls the dice expecting the stars to align before the numbers stop tumbling."

"All true," Jack said. "And if any of those variables hadn't fallen into place, I'd be faced with a much harder choice than asking you to look after her."

The implication settled.

Holden stared at Jack hard, sat back, crossed his arms.

If anyone could compete with these two for most screwed-up childhood, it was him — the kid who'd watched his mother die and been torn from her arms, the kid who'd been delivered as a trophy to the man who'd ordered her dead, and who'd subsisted on scraps and garbage and the kindness of strangers until he'd grown strong enough to escape to the streets, and who'd been running from emotional attachment ever since — yet somehow they made him look like the well-adjusted adult. Hell, they made their crazy-ass mother look reasonable, and that was *after* she'd ambushed his team and killed half his men.

"I've seen a lot of messed-up shit in my life," he said. "But this? This is something special."

Silence returned.

Jack said, "I can't fight a three-front war,

Chris. Whatever kill list you're on, I'm on it, too." He jabbed a thumb in the direction of the hostel. "Not her — they don't even know she exists — me, the guy who had nothing to do with the Broker, the idiot going broke trying to make a living in this stupid gig economy because I refused to utilize the only skill set I have. If I preempt this shit and kill them first, ten more will take their place. This will never end, and I'll become my mother, jumping at shadows for the rest of my life. Meanwhile, the thing with Dmitry has splintered into two directions, both of which lead to who knows where or what, I've got no idea how much of any of this is my mother fucking with my head, and my sister, bless her tar-black soul, is actively sabotaging my every move."

Jack placed palms on the table and in a slow, measured cadence said, "I can shortcut through it all, but that means letting the Russians have me for a while, and if I do that and she goes off script — something she's well known for — the whole thing blows up. For me to be able to walk out alive, I need her safe, out of their reach, and on the outside." Jack took a breath and stopped, explanation unfinished, ending abrupt.

Holden pulled a toothpick from the packet

in his pocket, shoved it between his teeth, waited for the missing pieces and, when they didn't come, said, "I'm not your windup toy, John."

Jack said, "I never —"

Holden held up a finger and stopped him.

"Maybe all those cloistered years fighting with just your mom and sister left you oblivious to how many others out here know this game and play it well." He leaned forward. "All this blah-blah-blah asking for help and trying to persuade, it's all just window dressing and performance art, John, so I can feel like a willing participant and maybe overlook the fact that you already factored in our friendship and my affinity for your sister as a given days ago. And you know what? I'm not even mad. Playing chess with people is what you do. It's who you are. Kudos and much respect. But what I hate — *hate* — is that you've dragged me into your bullshit family feud."

Holden paused for effect. "I want to say yes . . . you already know it. I don't want to see your sister messed up more than she already is. But I do this, and we get a future of escalating hurt and retaliation, the both of you trying to use me as a pawn to strike against the other. I might as well rip the Band-Aid off and walk away now, because no amount of friendship is worth that kind of drama."

"It won't be like that," Jack said.

"No? What's her reaction when she finds out I was in on your plan?"

"*If* she finds out."

"Now you're just insulting me."

"Okay, fine. She'll probably try to kill you."

"And supposing I survive that?"

"She'll try to use and manipulate you to get back at me."

"Yeah." Holden's jaw ground down, turning wood into splinters. "You drive a really hard bargain, buddy. You should probably try sales."

Jack held motionless for a second or two, lips pressed together in a not-quite-there grin, as if he was plotting the safest way through a verbal minefield. "For what it's worth," he said, "I don't feel like I've got a whole lot of choice here, either. I promise you, if I had any other way, I'd take it."

This time authentic desperation backed the words, a resolve Holden had seen in cornered animals and in men who went charging to their deaths because forward provided the only hope of escape. He said, "If I do this, I need your word that you never pull this shit on me again."

Jack breathed out long and slow relief.

"You have my word," he said.

"Even if your sister refuses to play by the same rules."

"That will be between you and her."

Holden spit out what was left of the toothpick, retrieved another, and pointed it in Jack's direction. "I want everything," he said. "Every detail of what you know and what you've set in motion for tomorrow. Leave out anything — *anything* — and your sister sabotaging you will be the least of your worries."

CHAPTER 19

Náměstí Republiky
Prague, Czech Republic

Holden

Nearly four hours he'd been on this rooftop slope, eighty feet up in temperatures that hovered near freezing, tucked in behind brick and trying to keep the wind gusts from sucking the warmth right out of him, waiting for a hint of morning and then for sunrise and then for the clock to roll around. Jill, nearly invisible beneath a black Mylar blanket, was fifty meters west atop a different building, one he'd need a running start and reasonable leap to reach. It was as close as he could get to her without giving up the ability to assess the action with his own eyes while also staying out of sight.

Another few minutes and chaos would descend on Republic Square, though it wasn't so much a square as a zag of pedestrian streets that connected Prague's grand concert hall and the Palladium shopping mall and boutiques and hotels in art nouveau buildings through a wide, empty cobblestone wedge, a center with nothing but streetcar tracks and escalators descending deep into the metro underground. On its corner, in the armpit of the zag, stood Hotel Kings Court and its awning-covered restaurant patio. Holden checked the time, swept the scope.

The cobblestone center was clear, and pedestrians were few.

There was plenty of empty space for a vehicle to maneuver.

Made sense why the Russians had booked the twins here.

If one *had* to use a hotel to facilitate an abduction in Prague, Kings Court on a cold weekday morning was about as good as it got. Assuming, of course, it made no difference if the abductee's head got blown off.

For that, the hotel was bullshit — an open patio surrounded by four-, five-, six-story buildings, every one of them with a clean line of sight on location — no one with any kind of strategical sense would put a wanted, high-value asset in that position, not even if they didn't know there were killers waiting for a chance at a headshot.

Holden shifted the scope to the five-story directly across center from the patio.

His finger twitched against the trigger guard. For the umpteenth time, the map in his head played through the series of shots he wanted to take but couldn't.

Fourth-story window.

Trigger pull.

Shift right, one floor down.

Pull.

Shift down, ground floor across the tracks.

They were there, the American killers, barely meters from where Jack had predicted they'd be. He'd diagrammed the square while back at the bar, mouth motoring as he scrawled on a napkin, marking positions, describing access points and exit strategies, and factoring cardinal coordinates against the sun's trajectory for shadow length and glare.

He'd jabbed a finger on the left edge of the improvised map. "Americans," he'd said. "Here, here, here. They're the ones coming for the kill, so they'll be the ones my sister is focused on." And he'd followed out at an angle and pointed. "Russians. They may or may not know about the Americans. May or may not know about you. But they wouldn't have gone to all the effort to get us out of Berlin if they thought this thing was going to go down easy. They'll have someone there to protect their investment, and this would be the best defensive position."

He shifted the napkin, tapped left and then right. "My sister. With her, there's no guarantee, but these two layups are my best guess."

He pointed to the Kings Court patio. "That's me." He nudged the hand-drawn map across the table. "I mean, it's not anything you wouldn't have seen for yourself if you'd had time to recon."

Holden snatched the napkin, muttered, "Smart-ass."

Jack responded with another almost smile.

"I'll have a body double with me," he said.

Holden's gaze paused in its arc toward the napkin, came back up. He raised his eyebrows in question.

Jack said, "I show up alone, they'll just drag the whole thing out. My sister never shows up at all, and they'll push things off for another day."

"Yeah, but fixing that by bringing in a civilian?"

Jack sighed. Stood. "Trust me," he said. "I hate it more than you do."

"Your sister knows?"

Jack nodded, made his way back around

the table and, like a man headed to his own funeral, slipped off into the night the same way he'd come.

But at least *he* had known what he was getting himself into.

Holden studied windows and doors, finger itching to preempt the threat laid out on that napkin. Just a half inch was all it wanted, a few pounds of pressure to turn gray matter to red mist. A delivery van entered the opposite end of the empty square, and stopped near the streetcar platform a hundred meters down.

Holden quick checked Jill's position.

She was still under Mylar, but he caught a glimpse of muzzle.

The vehicle idled.

Driver stayed seated.

The itch transferred to Holden's brain, wheedling and begging to put a bullet through the windshield, arguing that the van hadn't been accounted for on Jack's map, as if the map were some sort of step-by-step game plan instead of a concoction of reconnaissance and guesswork inked out onto a piece of trash.

In the near distance, church bells rang the nine o'clock hour.

Holden breathed a slow in and out and descended into the zone where the cold dissipated and the wind went silent, and his heartbeat swallowed him, steady and rhythmic, counting down to where all that mattered was the micrometer air buffer between metal and skin. Timing was everything.

Make a hit too soon and chaos would break loose before the plan got under way.

Wait a beat too long and the plan maker would be dead.

"They'll find you," he'd told them. "You'll end up running hard."

He'd been wrong about the running.

Not wrong about the finding, maybe not so wrong about the dying.

Jack stepped out of the restaurant, onto the patio.

The blonde at his side stole breath from Holden's lungs.

Her name was Anna, that much he knew. She was a drummer in an alternative band and, with the makeup and costuming, was closer to any living, breathing copy of Jill he'd have thought possible.

A man seated at a table on the patio stood, shook both of their hands.

Down by the streetcar platform, the van moved forward.

Light in the fourth-story window across the cobblestone wedge shifted.

Holden's index finger curled inward.

On the periphery of awareness, he heard the tires squeal.

The rifle stock recoiled into his shoulder.

Light in the fourth-story window changed color, and the world went silent, as if time had paused to catch its breath.

Pigeons scattered.

Pedestrians entering the escalators continued down.

And then came the chaos, van plowing toward the restaurant patio; armed men rushing the table, dropping hoods over heads, dragging off bodies; and a staccato of rapid fire, glass shattering, and metal zinging against metal.

He'd known the grab would happen, but it shocked the senses all the same.

Patrons screamed and pedestrians dashed for cover. The square center erupted in a chorus of battlefield crossfire, and Jill was up, running, following the van from the rooftop edge, firing, drawing attention.

Across the cobblestones, a shadow in body armor tracked a rifle in her direction.

Holden took aim. The shadow fell before he fired.

He had no time to see who'd made the hit, had no time for more.

He slung the rifle over his shoulder, cinched it tight, was up and moving, head down, skirting cover to cover until he crested the roof peak and picked up speed, chasing after Jill, who seemed to care not at all that she drew fire from two directions now.

The van careened around the corner.

She changed course.

Holden stopped short, cut left to outflank her, reached the rooftop edge, leapt.

She changed trajectory again.

He cornered in the opposite direction, chasing tiles foot to foot, collided into her, and took her down in a rolling heap.

She hooked around him, arms and legs tangling fast.

He'd been here before, not here in Prague, but here fist to fist in a fight for life. He knew what she was capable of, how quickly she could gain the upper hand, and what would happen if she did. He couldn't take that risk.

She broke free, rose up, recognized him, and in recognition hesitated.

He swung the rifle stock, caught her fast upside the head.

She went down hard.

He stood over her, lungs aching, heart pounding, fully alive and intoxicated by the fear of having accomplished the most stupidly anti-self-preserving thing he'd ever done.

This, perhaps, was what it meant to fall in love.

On the cobblestones below, the van was gone.

Pedestrians had fled.

The firefight continued in sporadic bursts, Americans and Russians fighting each other in another man's battle, as Jack had planned.

In the distance sirens wailed.

Holden knelt, got an arm beneath Jill, lifted her over his shoulder and, laden by deadweight, moved cautiously for the nearest ladder. She'd wake eventually, and when she did, she'd break his fucking heart.

CHAPTER 20

Náměstí Republiky
Prague, Czech Republic

Kara

One second to the next, a blink, a heartbeat, and the morning had gone from mission accomplished to complete and utter shit. From her perch at the square's highest point, camouflaged in drab gray-green and sheltered beneath stone wings, she'd watched, trepidation turning to horror as each new second took bad to massacre.

She'd wanted a scoped rifle instead of a spotting scope.

Had requested a position that gave her a shot at target instead of a distant eye on him, but Nick had wanted her where she'd have a bird's-eye view of the entire arena, had wanted her where she could watch and analyze, and hell if that wasn't exactly what he'd gotten.

She had watched commuters, oblivious in the daily routine, exit the underground and hurry on for the sidewalks, and had watched pigeons flock and settle, and she'd called in each movement.

Banter had run thick with gallows humor.

She'd especially watched the delivery van, blatantly out of place and the first obvious sign there was more to this morning than met the eye. And she'd watched target step out onto the patio, accomplice beside him, blond hair straying from beneath a hat and most definitely a woman. It'd been vindication seeing the two of them there like that, knowing she'd been right, that they were hunting a pair: male and female, brother and sister.

Target and accomplice had continued toward a man who sat at a table alone, and she'd watched that, too, holding her breath, willing them just another few feet forward.

They'd been that close.

But the delivery van had started forward, picking up speed in a straight line for the patio, shutting the window of opportunity at fifty miles an hour.

Aaron hadn't yet had the angle for a clean kill.

Juan had confirmed he had target.

Nick gave him the go.

The crack of a high-powered rifle had shattered the early workday morning, but it hadn't been Juan's rifle. Or Aaron's. Or Nick's.

One second to the next, just like that, everything had gone to shit.

Her focus had darted from rooftop to rooftop to window to balcony, heart pounding, adrenaline coursing, searching for what she'd missed, for what they'd all missed in the long hours leading up to the rendezvous.

A blink, a heartbeat, and bad had turned to massacre.

The van reached the patio.

Masked men leapt out, grabbed target and accomplice, pulled both in.

The rapid staccato of an automatic weapon replied.

People scattered. Glass shattered.

In her earpiece, chaos followed.

Nick and Aaron spoke over each other.

Another barrage of firepower followed and her brain pulled in each new piece of information, processing the details like an algebraic equation, canceling out on one side to cancel on the other.

She found a muzzle peering between curtains behind a flower box.

She called out coordinates.

A rifle report answered in place of words.

Shadow distracted her.

Movement below a rooftop ridge caught her eye.

Her brain circled for x. In her ear Nick grunted, and with that grunt, her stomach clenched and the whole of her screamed in protest.

Across the square a shadow moved within a window.

Another report rang out.

The van peeled away.

A barrage of bullets rained down on it, first toward the tires, then the driver's door, then the windshield, round after round ricocheting off.

She tracked the weapon fire.

Nick said, "Kilo, take coms."

Pain and struggle filled his voice. He'd been hit, was hurt bad.

Her throat closed, and she fought to breathe.

Nick had wanted her where she'd have a bird's-eye view and she'd watched it all, impotent, powerless, disbelieving. She was useless here, she had to move.

She crawled away from the ledge and angled for the hatch.

He said, "Don't you fucking dare."

He couldn't see her. Hadn't heard her. He just knew her that goddamn well.

She continued the backward crawl.

He said, "Get me eyes *now.*"

His words were raspy, like he was repositioning himself and fighting for air.

She hated him, hated his stupid stubborn loyalty, and crawled back for the ledge, because that was what he wanted.

Tires squealed. The van turned a hard corner.

Target was gone.

The man on the patio lay dead beside the table, blood from a head wound pooling between chairs. The square went silent.

Beginning to end, it'd been forty-five seconds, sixty at most.

She called for status.

Nick was silent. Juan silent.

Aaron answered. Of course it'd be Aaron who fucking answered.

All that mattered now was getting what was left of her team out and to safety, but her brain wouldn't let go of the movement she'd seen.

She knew who'd taken that shot at Nick.

If she had a rifle of her own, she'd zero in on that window and put a bullet through it, and then another and another, bleeding her soul dry through gunpowder with the same gripping urgency she'd felt on so many wee-hour mornings when going home empty handed wasn't an option.

No matter what else, that shooter would die.

She ran the scope toward the far end of the square.

Monotone, emotionless, she called in the coordinates.

Aaron said, "I don't have a clean line of sight."

She said, "Take the shot."

His rifle answered.

She scooted back from the ledge, said, "Clear out. I'll meet you for extraction."

He said, "Where are you going?"

"You know where I'm going."

"That's against orders."

She knew it. Nick knew it. They all knew before going into a job.

Injury, capture, death, if the team couldn't get to you without compromising the objective, you were on your own. Headquarters might send in a local cleanup crew after the fact. If you were lucky, they'd get to what was left of you before the enemy did.

Every extra second she spent in this square was compromising the objective, but fuck if she was leaving Nick behind if there was a chance he was still alive.

She said, "If I'm not there in an hour, break for the border without me."

Aaron said, "You —"

She unplugged, cut him off mid-syllable, scrambled for the access hatch, dropped down into the stairwell, and flung herself over the handrail. She dropped half a floor at a time in a race to ground level, burst out onto a side street, paused long enough to get a look at the obvious, and bolted between cars for the square's narrowest point.

Detouring around the kill zone would eat away minutes.

The fastest way to him was through.

She charted a trajectory broken by the tram stop and an advertising board, put her head down, ran. Bullets hit the cobblestones, ricocheted, sent projectiles flying.

She ducked and scurried.

A mosquito whine passed inches from her ear.

Her feet kept moving.

Her heart hurt, her lungs burned. She skidded into the doorway that led to Nick's position, barreled through, slammed it shut, and started up, listening for him, listening for life, but heard only her boots pounding, echoing thud against thud in an empty stairwell. She tumbled onto the third-floor landing and found him leaned against a doorframe two rooms off from where he would have been.

His vest was soaked. His hands were red. His eyes open.

She checked the hall.

All but two doors were closed. Offices.

Anyone already at work likely hiding beneath desks.

She knelt beside him, afraid to touch him, as if wishes and wanting could keep him alive and reaching for him might be the curse that expelled his final breath.

But he was already gone.

She slid beside him, pulled his shoulders into her lap.

Guilt and self-loathing chased each other around her head, taking her back to the night before, to the warning she'd given him about a trap, to his decision that regardless, the operation was go. Protest had gurgled up her throat then, nausea mixed with desperation compelling her to argue, to convince him he *had* to convince headquarters to look at the bigger picture and postpone the hit, but she'd clenched her jaw to keep the words from forming. She couldn't press him in front of the team and had known it'd do no good to argue with him in private, either.

If Nick had a fault, it was loyalty, so she had consigned herself to confronting whatever fate had to offer, and hadn't spoken.

Hadn't spoken, hadn't spoken, hadn't spoken.

She rocked forward and back, forward and back.

Didn't matter if he would have listened or not. She hadn't tried.

A part of her split and calved, ice shelf shearing off into the sea.

On the barren cliff behind, there were no tears, only cold.

She smoothed his hair, closed his eyes, wiped the blood off his face, pulled herself free, and lowered his head to the floor.

She checked his ears, his neck, his chest.

The earpiece was missing, as was the receiver unit, and it took a few minutes to find them, and a few minutes more to find his weapon and kit. He'd stashed it all and dragged his body as far away as he could before he'd gone under, his final moments spent trying to protect his team from whoever came looking for ways to trace them.

He'd been a foot soldier in a machine that didn't deserve him.

She picked up the rifle, shouldered his gear.

Her feet moved her toward the window with a will of their own.

She zeroed in on the last coordinates she'd given Aaron.

He hadn't had a clean line of sight, hadn't confirmed the kill.

Patience rewarded her with movement.

Shadows danced, her brain reacted, and her finger kissed the trigger. Thunder rolled out from beneath her cheek. Red spattered against the curtain.

Another report rang out, and self-defense kicked in.

She retreated behind the wall, shoved the rifle into its custom-built case, strapped it to her back, stepped over Nick on her way into the hall, and started down the way she'd come. There'd be a time for grief, a lifetime for self-recrimination, but no matter how much blame she laid at her own feet, she wasn't so gluttonous for punishment that she forgot where true responsibility belonged.

— Information withheld.

— Missing pieces.

Nick was just as dead as if headquarters had planned this.

With each step, anger and rage and hate grew stronger. She no longer cared about the objective. She wished Jacques Lefevre and Christopher Holden, or whoever the hell they were, long and happy lives. At least someone would escape this tragedy.

She'd find a way to do right by Nick,

would be patient and smart and would ensure nothing led back to her, because the only way to avenge him in death was to honor him with her best-lived life. She paused on the ground floor.

Sirens reached the square. Shouting followed.

Law enforcement fanned out.

Juan was one building over, four flights up. There was nothing she could do for him. She gripped the straps at her shoulders. Leaving the rifle behind would make it a whole lot easier to slip away, but this was all she had of Nick.

She wasn't letting go.

CHAPTER 21

Prague 9, near Kolbenova Metro Station
Prague, Czech Republic

Jack

The world was dark, and time uncertain, same as they'd been since the pillowcase went over his head. He sat motionless in that uncertain dark, chin to chest, wrists shackled to armrests and ankles to chair legs, listening to acoustic patterns that spoke of empty walls and empty floors with just enough furniture that the three men who guarded him weren't playing musical chairs for a place to sit. He was in a ground-floor room in an empty office or industrial building somewhere near Prague.

They hadn't driven fast enough or long enough to get farther than that.

And the air was too sterile, absent the cooking grease, body oil, and cleaning chemicals that lingered in curtains and

273

furniture, for it to be a home or hotel, and too still and quiet to be an embassy or other building under diplomatic cover, and it had none of the baseline stench of body fluids and fear that would have pointed to a black site. Whatever *here* was, it was temporary, outside the apparatus purview, and away from spying eyes. Just he and the men who'd grabbed him, waiting in silence.

No television, or radio, nothing but an occasional whisper.

They'd hit him hard, these men.

They'd shoved him to the floor of the van, and tossed Anna in through the back, and her high-pitched terror had bounced within the enclosed space as they careened across cobblestones, and bullets ricocheted off the panels.

He'd tried to crawl toward her, to comfort her.

Their boots had responded with vicious kicks.

He'd seen them, their hands and feet. He'd seen through sound and movement, just as he did now, and he'd tracked them like Doppler tracking a storm. His senses, running on overdrive and fueled with post-Clare trauma, had driven him to his knees in a retaliatory strike he hadn't planned.

He'd punched his elbow back into the

nearest face.

Had felt the crunch, and smelled the blood.

The van lurched, knocking him off balance, and a sap struck his ribs, landing blow after pummeling blow.

He swiveled, hooked a leg over a shoulder, locked thighs around a ropy neck.

The van peeled around a corner.

He took the neck with him into the side panel.

More bullets hit. Anna's screams drowned out everything else.

They beat him until he let go, and then they grabbed her by the hair and stuffed a rag in her mouth. He inched in her direction, and they boot stomped him every time. The van braked to a hard stop soon after, and they hauled him away, and her muffled screams went silent.

He never did have a chance to talk to her or apologize or explain.

He wasn't sure what they'd done with her — assumed she was in a room similar to this — knew she was hurt and scared, and for that, the fault was all his.

He'd counted on professionals, not goddamn sadists.

That miscalculation raised the possibility of others and dredged the murky subconscious depths, churning up self-loathing and fear. He'd factored for exponential possibilities, but he could never know what he didn't know. There'd always been a chance that the Russians, with their enormous network of spies, were three steps ahead of him. There was *still* the chance these weren't Russians at all.

That final thought pushed self-loathing into anger.

He shoved Clare out of his head, same as he'd been shoving her for the past ten years, and his focus homed in on the patter of soles against tile, and tracked footsteps from the wall at his left across the floor.

Minutia in movement betrayed breathing behind his back.

In his mind's eye he saw the man whose neck he'd locked onto, face not far from his, staring at his head.

Seconds dragged on like minutes.

A metal tip pressed through the pillowcase, against his throat, and a ragged voice whispered, "When is end, you pay. Urvan does not forget."

Jack pressed against the knife, fast enough, deep enough for the point to draw blood. The blade jerked away.

Urvan hissed, *"Psikh yebanutyi."*

There were a handful of ways to interpret that.

Psycho motherfucker was what the guy had meant.

Mocking laughter followed.

Urvan returned to where he'd started, and silence settled, and pain at Jack's throat joined pain in his head and the burn of stiffening muscles and a thirst that had started with the fight and had only grown more intense since, comforting discomfort in the way so much of the hell from his childhood was comforting, because pain was familiar and he understood what was familiar and he'd been here before — a dozen times in a dozen places — inter-rogated, sleep deprived, beaten, starved, until reality turned inside out and his own mind betrayed him.

He'd been thirteen the first time, snatched off the streets of Bucaramanga by two men on a motorbike, and thrown into the back of a truck before he'd had a chance to react. Faces hidden by bandanna masks, camou-flage and boots, AKs pointed at his head had all kept him on his stomach against the rusted floorboards.

The kidnappers had stashed him in an old storage tank, where day and night had blended together and solitude had been broken by cruelty. They had said they'd release him only if ransom was paid, had threatened to cut off toes and fingers, and had demanded information he couldn't give. He'd relived and replayed that first half hour over and over, all the things he could have done, should have done, instead of panicking and losing track of place and time the way he had.

He hadn't known if it was real or another of Clare's tests.

He had been forced to conquer fear in that damp, dank dark, and he'd drawn upon his training, searching for ways to turn their habits and patterns to his advantage.

But he hadn't escaped, not that first time.

Clare had come for him in the dead of night.

She'd shoved a knife in one hand, a garrote in the other, and crept him past the sleeping sentries, gotten him home, fed him, debriefed him, and then vanished for a week. The only thing he had to point to her involvement was that she hadn't summarily executed the men who'd guarded him, but Clare's immediate choices didn't always make immediate sense. "You still have a lot to learn," was all she'd said about it. "There'll come a time when I won't be able to protect you."

He had sworn he'd never give her another chance, and never had.

He'd talked, lied, wrangled, tricked, traded, cut, dug, broken and, as a last resort, fought his own way to freedom every damn time, and he'd have done it again here, too, if he didn't already know they'd set him free of their own accord.

Voices from within the building brought him back to the present.

At his back clothing rustled and chairs scraped tile.

The door opened, stayed opened several long seconds, and shut.

Three, possibly four people had entered.

Conversation followed, too low to hear but with none of the braggadocio or fist-bumping camaraderie that would come with a change of guard or a simple message delivery. Rank had arrived with an entourage.

This was whom his captors had been waiting on.

Bodies drew near.

Hands pulled the pillowcase off his head, and ten thousand lumens hit his face.

Eyes smarting, tears forming, he winced against the light.

A shadow dulled the brightness and morphed into the backlit outline of a man in a suit. The man tugged his pant legs and squatted to eye level and studied Jack's face for a few long, silent seconds, then shifted to examine the neck wound and followed the trail of blood.

In accented English, he said, "You are shot?"

The question arrived more as surprise than concern, but that it had been asked at all was a message of its own. Jack tipped his head in the knife-wielder's direction.

"Urvan stabbed me," he said. The words scratched out like cotton dragged through brush.

The man motioned to the right.

Someone Jack couldn't see put a bottle to his lips.

Water sloshed into his face, painted a patina over the desert in his mouth, and dribbled down his chin. Whoever held the bottle stepped aside.

Jack said, "My sister. Where is she?"

The man in the suit leaned in closer and looked at the neck wound again.

"She is near," he said.

The reply was as much a nonanswer as the inquiry had been a non-question.

The suit tipped his chin toward someone off to the side.

The light cut off.

Jack's eyes adjusted.

He faced a windowless wall, and the odd shadows on it spoke of table lamps on the floor and folding chairs and emptiness.

The man in the suit stood, flicked a finger toward the opposite wall.

Footsteps shuffled, the room emptied, and the door shut.

The man motioned to the restraints and then the chair.

"Is not meant to be like this," he said. "Even so, we meet at last."

The words implied *Dmitry* where Dmitry didn't fit — where he didn't *want* Dmitry to fit — and Jack scrutinized the face, searching for clarity.

The man said, "You are not recognizing me?"

Jack said, "I don't know."

In all twenty-six of his years, he'd only ever seen two photos of the man he assumed was his father, both of which had been taken before he was born, and neither of which had come from Clare. They'd arrived as bona fides together with the tickets to Berlin, sent by the voice who'd claimed to speak for Dmitry.

This man was anywhere between late fifties and late sixties, six feet, give or take, with a head of thick brown hair, a solid build, and the clear skin of a man who went heavy on clean eating and light on booze relative to a hard-drinking culture, but any resemblance he had to those photos was far off and faint, muddied by time and questionable provenance.

Jack didn't believe this was Dmitry.

He also didn't *want* to believe this was Dmitry.

And, like a therapist struggling to diagnose his own delusion, he was forced to give credence to a possibility he'd have otherwise rejected.

The suit pulled a key from his pocket and dangled it off a finger.

He said, "You like the chair?"

"I love the chair," Jack said. "I also love redundant questions."

The suit chuffed. He said, "If I unlock, we sit, we talk, have food, some drink, and you sleep in nice bed tonight. Or you fight, run, and men outside door put you back in chair, maybe use knife more on neck."

Jack forced a patient smile. "If we were interested in fighting or running, we wouldn't have let you pick us up in the first place."

"Let?"

"Allow."

"I know the meaning."

Jack's shoulders drooped, and he sighed loud and long, as if these were just so many wasted words. He said, "We traveled to Europe to meet Dmitry. You used that to bring us here, to this." He tugged the shackles for emphasis. "There's nothing you could possibly want from us badly enough to go through the effort you've gone through if you actually thought we were dumb enough to believe we'd find Dmitry waiting for us in Prague. That's why you sent those Spetsnaz rejects to collect us, instead of showing up yourself. And we knew you'd pull some stupid stunt like this and came to Prague anyway, which means there's also something we want from you. So why would we run or fight if we don't yet have what we came to get?"

The suit stayed silent for a bit, as if weighing each word, and then he leaned in to unlock a single wrist and stepped out of reach.

Jack shook his hand free and rubbed itching skin hard against his thigh.

The man tossed him the key.

Jack snatched metal from the air, put his arm back into the position in which it'd been shackled, opened his fist, and there, with the key nestled neatly in the center of his palm, he winked. All those years of hell, the broken bones, stitches, concussions, welts, bruises, and scars, they'd never been about bullets and blood. They'd been about *this*.

Legerdemain.

Mental prestidigitation.

That's what Clare had always been after.

The rest had been to support the illusion, the way a gun supported the badge.

Anyone could be taught to vanish or fight or plan an ambush.

Anyone could point and shoot, and most anyone could even be good at it.

Hell, if there was one thing Clare refused to let him forget, it was that there wasn't a single skill he had that someone else couldn't do better, and the only thing that would give him an edge was being able to think ahead of the enemy. "True skill lies in convincing your opponent that he believes what you want him to believe," she'd said. "And that he believes it of his own free will."

Jack left the key resting in his palm.

He dragged his gaze from his free hand to the shackled one.

The man in the suit followed along.

Jack tugged the shackled wrist for emphasis, and those imprisoned fingers scratched that imprisoned thumb, each movement obvious, deliberate, theatrical, tearing through a layer of latex. He couldn't begin to guess at how many hours he and Jill had entertained themselves during Clare's long absences by playing Harry Houdini vs. David Blaine, locking each other up in increasingly impossible configurations and finding more devious ways to cheat. What his captors had done by securing him to the chair was a small step above the dumb-assery they'd have committed by securing his hands behind his back. For this, he didn't even need a key.

But performance made a point while concealing a point.

That was legerdemain.

Jack leaned forward and drew the formerly hidden sliver of molded plastic from his thumb into his mouth, and with his teeth, he released the cuff that restrained the left hand, unlocked both ankles with ambidextrous flair, and tossed both keys back the direction the first had come.

The man in the suit caught them, examined them, pocketed them.

He heaved off the wall, motioned toward the door, as if inviting a guest to go on ahead, and said, "Come. We talk."

Jack swiveled in the chair.

He said, "I want to see my sister first."

The suit took a step forward. "Soon. Come."

Jack stayed seated. He knew what he knew. He didn't know what the suit man knew.

Didn't know if, in spite of his best efforts to keep his sister out of this, they'd gotten to her anyway, didn't know if they'd yet figured out that Anna was but a well-paid look-alike, but performance required he push. Because, if it *had* been Jill who'd been gag-stuffed and dragged out of that van, he'd have killed to get to her — and she was trained for this and could take care of herself. A traumatized and terrified near stranger in her place didn't change his response, only the reason.

He was the one who'd put Anna here.

A different burden, but a burden all the same.

They'd use Jill against him if they had her.

They'd do the same with Anna if at any point they believed his concern for her was more than a ploy to convince them she was his sister.

That was the risk of playing liar's bluff.

Jack said, "I'm being polite, but it's not really a request."

The man said, "First we eat. Then we talk. Then we see."

Jack leaned forward, picked one of the

freed cuffs up off the floor, and played the metal between thumb and finger, as if debating its suitability as a weapon. "I *will* see her," he said. "And if you've hurt her, I'll know, and I'll spend whatever's left of my life hunting you down in payback."

The man's lips turned up ever so slightly, but amusement never reached his eyes. He said, "There is, as you say, no hurting."

Jack exposed his neck, pointed to the knife wound.

"Is that what you're telling her about me?"

"No. This is unintended. Unfortunate."

"It felt pretty damn intentional when it happened."

A flash of angry irritation broke through the facade and faded half as fast, the tell of a man unused to being threatened or challenged, a man for whom stating a thing once was effort enough and being forced to repeat it would send the oxygen waster to the morgue. He said, "I give my word, personal guarantee, she is not harmed."

Jack let the cuff drop and slowly stood.

There were compromises to be had.

For now.

CHAPTER 22

Jack

The room opened to a narrow hall that dead-ended left and forced foot traffic right. Jack followed the man in the suit, squeezing between sentries stationed at the door, and the suit man's bodyguard entourage in turn followed him.

They were a different type, these bodyguards, different from the gumshoes who'd staked out positions at the Savoy in Berlin, different again from the psychos who'd run the snatch-and-grab in Republic Square. They were the type who missed nothing while ignoring everything, slow to engage, because they'd earned their composure, the type Clare would have sent if control truly mattered.

The hall led to an overlarge opening lit by shoddily hung fluorescent tubes, a hub of sorts, with no clear exit, no windows, no obvious doors, but from which several halls branched off. The man took a hard left into the nearest hall, which widened out into several steps that led down to a cavernous room supported by concrete pillars. What might have been a warehouse receiving area in a former life was bare and empty except for the ridiculous juxtaposition of a living room set up in the nearest corner — sofas and tables and wall art against an industrial landscape — as if someone had walked into a furniture showroom, drawn a square around an ensemble, and had the whole thing moved exactly as is, right down to the rugs, vases, and lamps.

The obvious difference was the bottle of Beluga Noble at the table's center, and the *zakuski* spread and, less obvious, the diplomatic pouch on the sofa seat, like an ugly stain on the soft blue palette. The man in the suit motioned for Jack to take the oversize chair, as if this was a friendly social event and there weren't bodyguards posted on the steps, blocking the only way out. "Please," he said. "Please, sit."

Jack eyed the plates filled with drinking food and then the bottle.

Whatever this man wasn't, he *was* Russian, and Russian drinking culture was consistent and homogenous, and in Russian drinking culture, vodka wasn't something drunk alone or as an everyday thing, like wine with meals. Vodka needed an occasion, even if an occasion required creative invention. The bottle was never left unfinished, and he was parched and thirsty, his stomach empty, and there wasn't another soul or sound in this whole damn building. It was a lot of vodka.

"Sit," the man said again.

Jack did as he was told.

The suit took a seat within reach of the black-blotch pouch.

He picked up the bottle, poured vodka into two small tumblers, handed one to Jack, lifted his glass, and said, *"Za vstrechu."*

To our meeting.

Vodka required an occasion, and meeting was just the first of them.

Jack mimicked the raised glass.

"*Za* something, something," he said.

The suit exhaled loud and obvious and tipped the liquor down his throat. He followed the vodka with a pickled green tomato.

Jack eyed the tumbler.

Drinking culture said nothing else happened until everyone at the table had emptied their glass, but that was Russian culture, and he wasn't Russian.

The man said, "Drink."

Jack said, "I'd rather not."

"Drink, or you insult me. You do not wish to insult me."

Jack tossed back the vodka.

The liquor went down nice and smooth, counterfeit water to desperate thirst in a way that left him dangerously wanting more.

The man in the suit nudged a plate of piroshki forward. "Eat," he said.

Jack picked up a pastry, shoved it in his mouth, and took a second for good measure, bolting meaty-greasy goodness down faster than he should have in an effort to get ahead of the alcohol.

The suit poured another round. He raised his glass. *"Budem zdorovy,"* he said — another toast, another occasion for vodka.

He swallowed the liquor and thumped the glass down hard.

Jack raised his own in kind and then returned the tumbler to the table, vodka untouched. He said, "Perhaps some water?"

The man barked out a laugh. "Water is for women. Drink."

Jack pushed the liquor toward the table's center.

One shot and he was already feeling the warmth enough to want to call shenanigans on *water is for women* and introduce the guy to his real sister.

Jill was capable of a lot of things. Copious drinking was way up that list. She'd put this guy under the table. But she wasn't here, and he couldn't call her, and for him, there'd be no winning, definitely not while dehydrated on an empty stomach.

He picked up a cucumber, stuffed it in his mouth, raised the glass in mock toast, and said, "There's vodka thirst, and there's water thirst. I've got both kinds."

The man in the suit leaned in. "You offend me with refusal."

Anyone who'd spent time drinking with Russians knew the difference between cultural insistence and true offense, but an American kid whose entire experience with Russia was limited Hollywoodized tropes wouldn't.

Jack had backed himself into a corner on that one.

He tossed back the alcohol and helped himself to pickled herring.

Bottle touched glass in yet another pour.

The man in the suit said, "Now you make toast."

Jack tipped the glass forward. He said, "Cheers."

The man growled. "This is not *toast*. For *what* we do drink?"

Jack waited until silence begged for interruption. "Truth," he said. "We drink to truth."

The man in the suit nodded appreciatively. "Yes, this is reason to drink."

Jack brought the alcohol to his lips and paused.

He said, "Answer me a question."

"Drink."

"One question first."

The boss man emptied his glass, followed alcohol with a pickle, exhaled, and said, "What is question?"

Jack returned the untouched liquor to the table. "Why?" he said.

The suit man laughed. "Why is very *big* question. Make smaller."

"There's a man," Jack said, "a Russian man. He has a woman, an American woman. She gets pregnant but leaves the country before the baby is born. The man doesn't know where to find her. Time passes. The man learns the woman birthed twins, a boy and a girl. He searches for them, but they are gone. Years later he gets news. His grown children have been located. He asks them to visit. They make the trip at his invitation, but when they arrive, they discover another person has taken his place. Why?"

The man in the suit pushed a plate in

Jack's direction, and when Jack didn't respond, took a canapé for himself, ate it slowly, wiped his fingers on a napkin, and said, "This is the story, you think?"

Tone earnest and honest, Jack said, "I don't *think*. I know. The part where the story gets hazy is at what point you got involved."

"Is good question. Is all good question." The man nodded toward the untouched vodka. "Drink."

Jack answered with silence.

"Okay," the man said. "American boy wants to talk American way."

Jack raised the glass in salute. "A toast to business."

The man said, "What are you called in America? Your name."

The question had no right answer, so Jack gave him the truth insofar as any name was truth, and offered what the man most likely already knew.

"John," he said. "Jonathan. Smith."

"Smith. Is nice, simple name, yes?"

"Bland. Boring."

"Easy to be invisible. Is good name." The boss man reached for the pouch, opened it, retrieved a packet, and tossed it across the table. He snapped for the bodyguard's attention, and motioned to Jack. *"Prinesi vody,"* he said.

294

Jack ignored the summons for water, as if the thing he wanted most in the moment had no meaning at all. He picked up the packet, slipped a finger through the seal, and pulled out a stack of documents about thirty pages thick.

They were photocopies, all of them, more than half of which related to Clare: photographs in which he wouldn't have recognized her if she hadn't been pointed out, and segments of classified material that had been lifted out of both US and Soviet files, and a history that documented a hole-filled variant of the stories she'd told throughout their childhood. And there were copies of his and Jill's true birth certificates, and a trail of documented sightings, and crossed-out dead ends littered with handwritten margin notes, which ended abruptly at the Savoy in Berlin when he and Jill were nine, and picked up again with a single entry in Houston two weeks back.

What was left constituted a separate dossier that ran nearly as long as Clare's, a convoluted web of legends and lies surrounding a man who, given the contents, could only have been the Broker, a man whose history had intertwined with Clare's starting years before he and Jill were born and had remained intertwined until a series of macabre photos that, if genuine, pointed to the night Clare had left them.

Noticeably absent was any detail on Clare's current status or location, and in that absence he found answers he hadn't deliberately come here to find.

Clare hadn't died that night.

She'd made it out. She was alive.

Jack flipped back to the beginning, searching for and confirming what his subconscious had grabbed on the first pass.

He hadn't been handed intelligence documents.

If that was the case, Clare's file alone would be six inches thick on the light side. This hand-notated, curated collection had been extracted and distilled from multiple sources slowly over time, and that said nearly as much about the person who'd put it together as it did about the subjects within.

This wasn't Clare's handiwork, and wasn't the product of a bureaucratic intelligence-gathering machine in some basement-level government office. What he held here was the persistent decade-spanning quest of someone who cared about what had happened to Clare and her children and who had a personal reason to find them.

These were Dmitry's files.

Everything, except the final page.

Jack tugged that piece of paper free, laid it flat, and studied a photo that had no earthly business being in this packet — an image so far removed from reality that if he didn't know better, he'd assume it had been sitting in the photocopy tray when these copies were made and had been gathered up by mistake.

It had no label and no explanation, but he knew the face.

Everyone knew the face.

Clean. Wholesome. American.

US senator Alex Ford Kenyon.

The man was an outspoken, polarizing firebrand, a pro-Russian populist heading into a huge political win in an election that half the country believed was already hacked by the Russians, and *this* was his assassination order.

Jack tapped the pages to align them and flipped to the beginning again, because any kind of movement was better than sitting in dumb silence while the man in the suit scrutinized him. He would have asked why — why now, why this target, why him as the assassin — but his brain, on fire, drew all his body's wattage and left his mouth with nothing to operate it. The questions were pointless, anyway, because he'd already been given the answers.

These pages collectively, in totality, were a map, a chronology that walked down a chain of decision-making logic the same way comic book panels walked readers through a story, all of it leading to that final, incongruent photograph. Except this story didn't start at the beginning — it started at the end, started with the Broker's death — and this story had never been about him or his sister, not at first, not even now.

This was about chaos.

The maze inside his head snapped and reformed.

Clare vanished from it completely.

The tightness constricting his chest, the sense of entrapment and double-blind doubt that had made it hard to think dissipated, and for the first time since he'd stepped off that flight in Frankfurt, he understood that whatever mistakes he made going forward, were his mistakes to own completely.

Clare had had nothing to do with this.

He'd been set free.

The man in the suit said, "Your mother was intelligent woman."

"Is," Jack said. "She *is* an intelligent woman."

And that was part of what kept him

298

tongue tied.

The story in these pages, Clare had seen it all years ago.

She had known fate would snag him and had tried to warn him.

Not the micro-level stuff that related to this particular target in this particular scenario. Even if she'd had *that* kind of foresight, she wouldn't have cared.

Clare didn't give a shit about politics or politicians.

To her, they were glorified bureaucrats, interchangeable, replaceable self-serving pawns in love with the idea of importance, for whom she held varying degrees of contempt and animosity, and not without good reason.

Her own government had turned its back on her, had labeled her a traitor and an enemy of the state, so she'd become one, hiring out to anyone if the money was right, but she was a patriot all the same. She was loyal not to any flag or nation-state, but to the ideals her country was founded on and that she'd sworn to uphold.

She'd have put a bullet in any assassin foolish enough to take this job.

He could hear her in his head even now, the paranoid rants he'd tried so hard to tune out, the desperation that bled into her insistence that he listen and learn, as if what he believed or didn't had any bearing on reality.

But it made sense now, all of it.

She'd known this day would come, and needed him to understand. "Democracy isn't perfect," she'd say, "but it's better than the alternative. Freedom of speech, freedom of the press, due process, a government of the people by the people, everything that makes us strong makes us weak, and the Russians are experts at exploiting that weakness."

"Masters of the long game" was what she'd called them.

They were fully vested in American politics, but not the way most people thought. They didn't care which party won or lost or who lived in the White House.

They didn't have a "side."

Their goal was to erode trust in elected officials, to erode trust in democracy itself, their target was the American voter, and their wet dream an ungovernable America, because what better way to convince less powerful nations that democracy was dangerous than to point to its beacon as it tore itself apart from within?

Political warfare.

The Russian intelligence apparatus had

been at it for years.

"Active measures" was what she called it, a term that combined the ideology with the methods — propaganda, disinformation, deception, assassinations, counterfeit documents, political front organizations, nonprofit research. Anything and everything that targeted the human condition was fair game.

"Vietnam," she'd said. "The protests you see in old news footage don't do justice to the anger and unrest on the ground at the time. The energy was raw and electric, *felt* organic . . . hundreds of thousands of people fighting for a cause. The Soviets were pouring millions into activist and political organizations to keep the antiwar movement going, but who would want to believe that? It's psychological suicide to admit this thing you were willing to die for wasn't actually *yours*. That's what makes the Russians so successful, so dangerous. They're experts at finding divisive issues and feeding and fueling fear and anger until they take hold, and once they have taken hold, a person would sooner attack someone trying to save them than admit that their beliefs weren't their own."

Legerdemain.

According to Clare, Russian psyops were

responsible for all the biggest conspiracy theories running amok in antigovernment communities. Fluoride in the water as a plot to control the population? Russian psyops. Moon landings as a hoax? Also the Russians. "Don't even get me started on AIDS as a CIA-manufactured virus," she'd said. "For that one, they forged documents, turned that paper trail loose in academia and political circles, and let democracy give it wings."

He'd listened, but he hadn't really *listened*.

Clare had so many paranoid fantasies of her own that it'd been hard to know where hers ended and others began, but that was the thing he understood now and hadn't then. Clare might be paranoid, but she wasn't delusional.

The Cold War had ended, but the world hadn't changed.

Russia's end goal was still the same. Everywhere you looked, active measures were on display: fear stoked into outrage, ideological differences reinforced until they turned violent, the worst of human nature fed and nurtured until some no longer saw their opponents as human at all.

And now they wanted him to kill their biggest proponent.

This wasn't an assassination. This was the

start of a second Civil War.

Brilliant, really. Or at least it had been until the Broker had pissed Clare off, and she'd gone rogue and killed him, and the world's underbelly had lost its shock collar, and governments, panicked at the idea of assassins running amok, sent out their own hit squads in preemptive strikes, and now every killer for hire with the skills and smarts to carry out this kind of job had a target on their back.

He bet these genius masterminds hadn't seen *that* coming.

Not that the Kremlin lacked for killers, per se.

Journalists and dissidents and people who knew things suffered such a high rate of clumsiness that their deaths barely blipped the news anymore.

But European borders were small and porous.

Getting into the United States meant crossing an ocean or a whole heck of a lot of land, and acquiring legal transportation and accommodation and vanishing within a surveillance state on high alert were whole other issues. Whoever they'd lined up was either dead or suddenly unable to get within a hundred miles of a US border.

Dmitry, intentionally or not, had handed

them the perfect Moscow-connected, familial replacement. But that's where Jack's understanding stopped and where the data didn't fit. He slid the senator's face toward the man in the suit.

The bodyguard approached, a liter of bottled water in one hand, drinking glass in the other, interrupting where interruption was least appreciated.

Jack skipped the glass, cracked the seal, and drank straight from the plastic, downing gulp after gulp in an attempt to drown the desert, and set the half-empty bottle on the table. "I'm useless to you on this," he said.

The man shrugged. "Maybe yes. Maybe no."

"To pull this off, you need someone who can slip undetected through the American landscape, and I've already got one of their kill teams chasing me. In my position I'd be better off using this information as a bargaining chip."

The man in the suit harrumphed and leaned forward. "We talk like Americans, okay? Business. No more pretend."

"All right," Jack said. "No more pretend."

"The woman with you, she is not sister, Jillian."

"Correct," Jack said. "And you are not Dmitry."

"This also is true."

Jack placed his finger in the center of Senator Kenyon's forehead. "You want an assassination," he said. "I want Dmitry."

The man nodded toward the vodka. "Drink."

Jack dumped the liquor into his mouth. Swallowed, ate, rolled the glass between his palms, and held on to it to prevent another refill.

The man said, "There is work, and when work is done, you have Dmitry."

"But, as I said, I'm useless to you on this."

"Is only part true," the man said. "There is work, and is other work. We speak with Jillian also."

Those words, so casually spoken, implied that all the effort he'd gone through to keep Jill away had been wasted, but inferring that her compliance was a done deal was where the suit man went wrong. "You don't have her," Jack said.

The man made a mewling sound, as if to say, "Who knows?"

No, they didn't have her, but they *would* speak with her.

In his head, he could see it, the table in Berlin, the way the emissary had pushed the phone toward him — specifically toward him — and the way his sister's body had tensed. He'd needed her to have it for reasons of his own, but it'd been the emissary who'd manipulated her into wanting it.

The maze snapped again, ordered and reordered, and the kill team that had followed him out of Dallas blinked to the far edge. He knew now exactly how they'd found him, and why it'd been him, not Jill, that they'd pursued.

To the suit, he said, "My sister won't be easy to convince."

"We have you," the man said. "This is enough."

Chapter 23

Hradčany
Prague, Czech Republic

Jill

She came to slowly, falling in and out of consciousness, with each rise a little more cognizant, a little more confused. She knew the room, its texture and smells and size, knew the single bed, the small table that doubled as a desk, and the hardback wooden chair. Knowing amplified the anxiety. All of this was wrong.

She'd left this room. She shouldn't be here.

And she drifted down again, grasping for a sense of time within space.

Somewhere in the fog, a voice said, "How's your head?"

She knew that voice, warm and cozy. She liked that voice.

But that, too, was wrong, and her thoughts

startled, scattering with the beat of a thousand wings. She struggled to see, to think.

A shadow filled the blur, the outline of a face.

The voice said, "Here, drink this. It'll help you feel better."

Warm, sweet liquid touched her lips.

A hand slipped behind her neck to support her head, and she drank, and with each swallow, awareness built and memories returned — Jack down in the square, the van, the gunfire, the blur of madness and motion — and everything she knew was wrong collided in panic, and she lunged to swing off the bed.

Liquid splashed down her chin.

Her torso caught, and she heaved, struggling to move, until understanding dawned and the desperate need to find her brother morphed into rage. Her hands and feet — her fucking chest and thighs — were all strapped to a fucking bed.

The voice with the face came in closer.

She hated that voice and that lying, lying rat-bastard face, with its assurances and promises that no matter how big the contracts got, he had no interest in the money, and all that talk about wanting to be friends and keeping them alive.

She should have killed him when she had

the chance.

He put his hands up, placating, soothing, like he was caught somewhere between trying to shush a baby and being terrified it'd breathe fire and burn him alive. "John's okay," he said. "He's okay. You're okay. You're not hurt. Everything's good."

Memory shoved her back on that rooftop, and she was there again, legs scrambling, adrenaline coursing, anger rising, the whole of her racing toward that van, and then a tackle out of the blur and she was rolling, fighting, and a rifle stock swung toward her face, and the world went black.

That had been nine in the morning.

Ambient light in the room said this was late afternoon.

The dry mouth, the discombobulation said she was coming to after sedation.

Inside her head a megaton bomb rained fire down into a debris field of revenge, but she needed out of these restraints, and so her body lay passive, and her brows furrowed in innocent confusion.

Befuddled, perplexed, she said, "I don't understand."

No, that was wrong. The tone was too gentle.

Gentle was unbelievable.

She added an edge. "What are you doing

here, Chris? I mean, not just *here*" — she raised her wrists as far as the binding would allow and tugged for emphasis — "but here in Prague, and what have you done to my fucking brother?"

"That wasn't me," he said. "Had absolutely nothing to do with me."

The words made no sense.

And then they made too much sense.

Her brother, her own goddamn, son-of-a-shit-face, quisling-ass brother had cut her out and let her drown. She should have seen it, him being so goddamn nice last night, pulling out a deck of cards like when they were kids, trying to pretend that they even knew how to just be siblings, and that Clare, for everything else she'd taught them, hadn't failed to teach them how to be a family. He had known what was coming — no, had *planned* what was coming — and had roped in an accomplice to handle the dirty work, and that bullshit hurt worse than if he'd just been his usual asshole self.

Holden pulled the chair out from the tiny side table, spun the seat away from the bed, straddled it, draped his forearms across the high back, and studied her.

She couldn't stomach looking at him.

She turned to the window, said, "Where is he?"

"Wherever it is he wanted to be, I'd guess."

"You guess?"

"I'm not working with him, Julia. Not siding with him against you, either."

She glanced at him, went back to staring at the window, and summoned enough water for a few tears to leak visibly down her face.

He said, "Not that it likely matters from your perspective, but I hate doing this just as much as you hate it being done."

"You're not the one duct-taped and zip-tied to a bed."

"That was for my protection," he said. "I like being alive."

The subtle admission within admission almost made her smile, reminded her of why she liked him — God — no — stupid, stupid, what the stupid — *had* — reminded her why she *had* liked him enough not to kill him when killing him was all that mattered.

What a fucking mistake that'd been.

She summoned another round of leaky eye faucet.

He said, "Couldn't afford to have you swinging at me as soon as you opened your eyes. I'm cutting you free. Just need you to hear me out first."

311

She refused to give him the satisfaction of a reaction, *any* reaction.

He reached round to the back of his waistband, pulled out a SIG, set it on the desk. "Show of good faith," he said. "That'll be there waiting when you're loose."

She had nothing to lose by calling his bluff. "Show me," she said.

He picked up the weapon, released the magazine, turned it round-count forward for inspection. Eased back the slide, showed her the chambered round, let the slide go, snapped the magazine back into place, and set the SIG back on the desk. She watched his hands, big hands, capable hands in strong, smooth, fluid movement, and caught herself.

No, that was *not* where her head needed to be.

He said, "I told you in Houston you were going to need an ally, told you I wanted to be your friend. That's what I'm doing here. I tagged along as an extra set of eyes and an extra rifle in case shit went sideways. Figured if you got lucky, if everything turned out on the level, I'd say hello, say good-bye, and bow out unless invited to stay. But the venue changed and you two split up, and the only way to find the next rendezvous was by following one of you to it."

She cast him a side-eye glare.

"I'm already on your shit list," he said. "Thought I should put it all out there in one go. Yes, I followed you into France. No, I didn't mention your little detour to your brother. He spotted me in Frankfurt, confirmed me again in Savignyplatz, knew I was following you, and used that to find me once you got to Prague."

"Let me guess," she said. "He told you what was going to happen. Said he *had* to do it alone because he couldn't trust me, and you went right along with it, because what kind of a dick would you be if you didn't show up?"

Holden sighed.

She coughed out a mirthless laugh. "Dangle a princess, threaten some dragons, and the big dumb knight goes charging in. Goddamn story of my life. My mother, brother, now you . . . everyone making decisions on my behalf, choosing what they think is best for me like they're God's gift to an incapable half-wit."

Holden looked at her funny.

She could read the hurt right off him.

He said, "You think I didn't see your brother's bullshit and call him on it?" The tone in his voice edged up. "We could have gone in circles, playing *I know you know* all

313

night. I didn't do this for you or for him. I did it for me."

His word choice threw her, forced a pause. She said, "I never took you for a sadist."

"And I never took you for an idiot."

She kicked the bed and thrashed, left, right, left, attention-drawing racket that forced the legs up off the floor and scooted the frame out of place.

He watched impassively, as if she'd finally given him what he expected and now he waited for her to tire herself out. She didn't care. He'd said his piece, he'd made his promise. Either his word was good or his word was trash. It made no difference, because the two things she could count on were that big boy here wouldn't kill her, and that he couldn't keep her tied up forever.

Holden pulled a knife off his belt and waited.

She slowed and stopped, out of breath, out of strength.

God, she hated the way sedation messed with energy like that.

He said, "You finished?"

She glared.

He unfolded the blade, knelt by her right foot, slipped the tip between zip tie and tape and cut the zip tie free. Tension released.

With just the tape, she had stretch and room to move. That was a start.

He said, "I've watched you work, Julia, and I spent days pent up with Robert, forced to listen to him pine for you. I know you far better than one stranger has a right to know another." He stepped around to the other side of the bed. "There are a handful of people in this world capable of understanding what we've lived and how we think, even fewer who'd accept that truth exactly as it is. That matters for something."

He cut through the zip tie on her right foot and, as with the first, left the tape in place. "I hated your brother's plan," he said. "Hated it on principle, hated the unfairness to you. But mostly, I hated it because any hope of friendship is impossible so long as I'm considered a tool and a weapon in your sibling war."

He sliced through the tape that bound her thighs and chest.

"I didn't care that he tried to play me, I cared that he tried to play me against *you*. What I wanted was his word. I wanted off his board for good."

He reached for her left hand, cut the zip tie, moved back around to her right, and did the same there. "I upheld my end of the deal," he said. "So now, here we are."

She rolled her eyes and met his gaze.

He snapped the knife closed.

He'd cut the zip ties, but she was still taped to the bed.

"A quarter-inch strip," he said. He motioned from hand to foot with the knife. "Leave the rest of you like that and cut your left hand mostly free. A quarter-inch strip will buy me all the time I need to clear the room before you get loose. Gun's on the other side of the bed. By the time you reach it and aim for the door, I'll be gone. So the question I'm asking myself is, Do I act the fool and stick around, hoping you want a friend as much as I do, or do I walk now and spend the rest of my life thinking back on this moment, wondering what might have been if I'd remained?"

She shut her eyes to block him out.

This vulnerable honesty thing he did made it really damn hard to stay angry.

Not that she didn't know how to handle an occasional bout of sincerity. Just that with anyone else, she'd have used it to crawl inside their head, and here it crawled inside hers, forcing her to acknowledge the anguish that made her want to lash out, reminding her that what burned on the inside was Jack's doing, and projecting his betrayal onto someone else only made her the bigger asshole.

Holden re-straddled the chair.

She cursed him inside her head.

She didn't know what she wanted, but she did know she didn't want him to leave, and that was twice the mindfuck because Jack knew it, too, would have counted on it, which meant more was coming and Jack was *still* making decisions on her behalf and the only way to free herself from him was to choose a path she didn't want.

She clenched her jaw shut and, muted, screamed.

She said, "I hate him, Chris. Sometimes I truly, truly hate him."

"I don't blame you," he said. "But where does that leave me?"

She didn't know the answer to that. Honestly, she didn't.

"I don't want to kill you," she said.

He said, "That's hardly reassuring."

"I do still want to hurt you."

He pondered for a beat. "Fair enough, I suppose."

He stepped around the bed for her left hand, unfolded the blade and, for the first time, cut through tape. She waited, watching, rage and frustration, exhaustion and emotional overload colliding into a need for control, watching until the blade cut clean through, and she lunged to snatch the knife.

He was faster than expected, but he flinched, nicked her wrist, and for a fraction of a second, his expression hovered between horror and panic.

That alone was worth shedding blood for.

She laughed, she couldn't help it.

And with the laughter, rage and tension eased.

Holden stared at her, mouth agape.

That only made her laugh harder, silent, body-racking manic laughter that sent relief flooding her system and real tears streaming down her face.

He said, "You're an asshole."

Her one free hand wiped her face. "Yeah," she said. "I am."

He placed the knife tip against her left foot.

"Stop moving," he said.

She stilled to let him do his thing, and once she was fully loose, seriousness descended as quickly as the laughter had. She scooted into a seated position, tore the tape mittens off her fingers, and rubbed her wrists and ankles.

"Do this to me again," she said, "I'll slit your throat."

She wasn't kidding, and he knew she wasn't.

He nodded, and silence and emptiness followed, as if reaching this truce was as far as either of them had thought out. There was no "What next?" No purpose.

At least she sure as hell didn't have one.

Holden offered her a bottle of water, said, "You hungry?"

She said, "I'm not going to do it."

He said, "Do what?"

"Tell me I'm wrong," she said. "God, please tell me I'm wrong. But I'm not. I know I'm not. My brother did not go to all this trouble to push you and me together and get himself abducted just so he could walk off alone into the sunset. No. Today was the beginning." She swung her legs off the bed. "He told you more than you've told me." She searched the floor, looking for footwear. "There's more coming, and whatever he has planned, I'm not doing it."

Holden pointed toward the opposite wall, where her boots were lined up neatly, toe to baseboards, beside his gear. She stood, wobbled the couple steps it took to reach them. She struggled to get a foot inserted, gave up, and sat on the floor.

He said, "I don't know what John has planned, but I think he thinks you do.

Something about how having you on the outside was the only way he'd get back out alive. Said the reason he couldn't tell you ahead of time was that you'd sabotage the whole thing to keep him from going."

"Well, I guess now he gets to learn how right he was."

"You're serious?"

She loosened the laces. "One hundred percent."

Holden slid down the wall and sat beside her. "I don't know what it's like to grow up with a sibling," he said. "Closest I got is the guy who's been my best friend since we were fourteen, but he's my brother, you know? In the truest sense he's my brother, just like John is your brother, and it wouldn't matter if he sold me down the river for thirty-three pieces. I'd still rather die than leave him in the hands of people who'd grabbed him. The rest, we sort out after."

She shoved foot into boot. "John will be fine. He can take care of himself."

"So can Baxter, but that doesn't give me a reason to abandon him."

She tightened the laces.

"If John wanted my help, he should've included me in."

Holden shifted to put space between them

and looked at her hard. "Is it me you're lying to, or is this just something you do to yourself?"

She grabbed the second boot, shoved it on.

He said, "You *know* you do shit behind his back to sabotage him, and yet somehow you can't see that maybe because of the constant war, he felt he had no choice?"

She tied off the laces. "He had a choice."

"So did you when you went to France."

"Totally different."

"How different?"

"Doesn't matter." She stopped. Looked at him. "Listen," she said. "I know you're just trying to help, and I get how, from your perspective, this makes no sense. But there's history here — a lot of fucking history — if you'd lived it, you'd understand, and I assure you, John understands."

"Make it make sense, then. Make me understand."

She sighed. Debated. Some things just weren't worth the effort.

"It's just words," she said. "It's not the same."

"Try me."

She answered out of spite more than anything. "Clare pitched us against each other constantly," she said. "She played favorites. Didn't matter if I outshot, out-fought, outperformed my brother. He was brilliant, and I was the fuckup. I guess a person can only handle so much of that before they buy into the belief, and he bought into it hard enough to carry it into adulthood. He makes decisions on my behalf that aren't his to make, believes he has that right, because he thinks he knows what's better for me than I do. We've drawn blood over it. He's well aware of where the line is and what happens if he crosses it."

She wrapped her arm around her knees. "I've made a lot of shit choices in my life, Chris, but every single one has been deliberate, and I've always been aware of the consequences. John, on the other hand, is so used to being Mr. Good Guy that he's blind to his own blind spots. We should have bailed in Berlin the moment that fucktard offered new tickets, but John, he's like this abandoned street urchin who just heard a rumor about parents searching for him. He wants this thing with Dmitry more than he's ever wanted anything, wants it so badly that he's lying to himself about what he sees. He would have gone with or without me, so I came to make sure he had someone watching his back. He thanked me by pulling this shit, so yeah, I'm done."

Holden took a long time to answer.

"I get why you're angry," he said. "I do. I just can't wrap my head around hating him so much, you'd rather let him die than suck it up and deal with it later."

"I don't hate him," she said. "I mean, yes, I do. Especially right now. But it's not him I hate. It's . . . it's everything else. I don't *want* him dead."

"Want, indifference, it's all the same thing, really."

"No, *want* would be me actively seeking to make him dead. *Indifference* is me refusing to let him drag me into more of the same old shit."

"So there's no changing your mind?"

"No."

"All right," Holden said. "I tried." He heaved up off the floor, reached for his bag, pitched the strap over his shoulder, and moved for the door.

She studied him, confused. "You're going somewhere?"

"Like I told you, I tagged along as an extra set of eyes and extra rifle in case shit went sideways, and we've gone straight past sideways into upside down. If your brother can't count on you, then someone's gotta save his ass, and I guess that someone's me."

She said, "Wait. Hang on."

Holden paused, hand on the door hard-ware.

She pulled in detail, reading him the way she'd read people her whole damn life, and inside her chest the first anxiety flutter rose. He wasn't bluffing, and this wasn't a power play or negotiation. It simply was. And when he left, he'd be gone.

She wasn't ready for that, not like this, not with everything on his terms right after she'd spilled her guts. She said, "You don't have to save him right this second."

Holden smiled wryly, as if he knew exactly how this worked and was amused enough that under other circumstances, he might have humored her.

He depressed the handle.

The anxiety fluttered harder.

There was *always* room for negotiation if the motivation was right. The one thing she had that he wanted was information. She patted the floor and, offering the secret that would cost least to give up, said, "I'll explain France."

He released his thumb. He didn't sit.

She said, "How much do you know about Dmitry?"

"Only that supposedly, he's your father."

"But *who* he is or was?"

"No."

"Nobody does. Clare's version of events — believe it at your own risk — was she was deep-cover CIA in Moscow, running a guy who was KGB and actually running her. They had a real-life thing for each other, which is how she got pregnant. Yada yada yada, skip a lot of drama, she ends up cut off from her people, Dmitry gets her out of Moscow, tells her he'll follow, and asks her to wait for him. She never hears from him again. Clare being Clare, she tries to contact him, which is when she discovers Dmitry — KGB or otherwise — never existed. She has no idea whose body she was having a thing with. She's tried to get that answered a few times but always ended up almost dead for it. Lots of years pass, more yada yada, and then two weeks ago the hit goes out on her, you enter the picture, and out of nowhere this so-called Dmitry turns up with tickets to Berlin. We have no idea if he's our DNA donor, only that he says he is."

She paused. Holden nodded, as if to say, "Go on."

"Clare was seven months pregnant when she vanished. I suppose if the same thing happened today, she'd risk an unassisted birth, but back then her version of off-grid was a seventy-year-old midwife in a small

325

French town, and that meant birth records, which meant birth certificates, and the names on those birth certificates — our actual true given names — have never been used for anything, ever. Hell, John and I had never even heard our own fucking names until Clare handed us those documents as a 'Happy sweet sixteen, you should probably know about this.' For the longest time we thought it was just another made-up identity, but the punch line, the reason I went to France, was that whoever bought our tickets used our birth names."

"So, Dmitry has your birth certificates?"

"Well, someone in Moscow does, or this is Clare fucking with us again. Even in the digital age, there's no single French repository for birth information. To get those certificates, someone had to know what name Clare was using, the day we were born, and the town itself. There are only three people on this planet who have that information, and it didn't come from me or John. Even if, for the sake of argument, someone had the time, resources, and motivation to track those details down, he'd have still had to show up in person to get the actual certificates. So I went to the *mairie* to see if there were margin notes — stuff that's recorded but doesn't show up anywhere else — maybe something about Clare or her babies or a father, and if there was nothing, I wanted to see that nothing for myself."

"I assume you found the nothing."

"Far as I know, yeah. The records clerks have both been working there for over fifteen years, so at this point all I know is that if this wasn't Clare's doing, whoever tracked that information down did it over fifteen years ago."

"That's a long time to wait to use it."

"Right?"

"You told John?"

"No."

"But if you had found something?"

She shrugged. "I don't know. It's complicated."

"Your brother wants this more than anything in the world, but the closer he gets to finding answers, the less you care if something goes wrong? It's not *that* complicated."

She said, "If this friendship thing is going to work, you're going to have to learn to lie more. The honesty stuff freaks me out."

Holden snorted and smiled. "You should think about that."

He stretched a hand toward her. She reached up. His fingers swallowed hers, and he pulled her off the floor, and she stood, her hand in his, caught off guard and off balance. Her cheeks flushed. She tugged away.

She said, "You're really going to go after him?"

"Yes."

"Ah, fuck it," she said. "Why exactly does John think I know his plan?"

"He said once you settled down enough to get over wanting to kill me, and once you'd had a good meal and got beyond wanting to kill him, that'd probably be about the same time they realized the woman with him wasn't you. He said they'd be eager to talk with you, and you'd know how to make that happen."

Her mouth opened. Shut. She knocked the back of her head hard into the wall and then did it again, and again, until the aftermath of sedation mixed with the pain of skull against stone and the throbbing muted the need to hurt something.

She saw the pieces now, Jack's strategy.

The brilliance of it made her want to smother him.

She kicked her head back again, harder. Holden moved to stop her. She held up a hand to warn him off. "You were in Berlin," she said. "You saw what the guy gave us."

His eyes narrowed in accusation.

"Are you stupid?" she said. "No, I'm not carrying the phone." She reached beneath her waistband, fiddled with her pants, pulled out a SIM case, and held it palm forward. "He made me think it was my idea."

Holden plucked the case from her hand. Examined it.

"John wants you to call them?"

"Yeah."

"I've got a spare burner you can have, but you load this up and it won't matter what steps your brother took to keep you on the outside. They're going to beeline right for you."

She cocked her head puppy dog–style and gave his bicep a pitying, patronizing squeeze. "That's so cute," she said. "You actually believed John wanted you at Republic Square to save me from myself?" She let the inference dangle like baitfish above a shark tank, then leaned in and whispered, "No, you see, John, in his 'control other people for the best' wisdom, foresaw that the Russians wanted me and him both, which meant they have plans for us both, and the only way to keep me on the outside *and* utilize that plan was if I made contact from the outside. So he made sure I had the means to do that."

She snatched the SIM case back. "He also knew that if I *did* call, they'd try to grab me the way they'd grabbed him, and that it'd take more than just one of me to keep me out of their hands."

She paused for emphasis. "What he *really* pulled you in for, big guy, was *that* two-man job."

CHAPTER 24

Jack

He sat on the floor in the near dark, table lamp at his side, door at his back, attuned to movement and conversation in the hall, while his fingers traced up the plastic base to the bulb, to the metal guard that had, until a few hours ago, secured the shade, and back down again, biding time.

He'd been promised freedom.

The suit man's bodyguards had brought him here instead, marching him through the same windowless walls and windowless hub to the same tiled, windowless room with the same single exit locked from the outside.

Not that he'd confirmed the door was locked.

Some things could be safely assumed.

The room had a bed now, a shoddy

331

bargain-basement contraption topped with a foam mattress, which might, with luck, hold up a few nights before pancaking. Rough, overbleached sheets and a thin blanket had been dumped at its foot, and on the floor near the wall sat a liter of water and a Styrofoam takeaway box, which he assumed held something edible.

The bodyguards had had him strip, and they had examined his fingers and toes, and then taken his watch, wallet, and belt — shoes, too, though they'd eventually given shoes and clothes back — and had left him then, unsecured, alone, and had turned control of the building over to the crew who'd abducted him.

Two of them were in the hall outside.

They were on the floor now, the thug with the knife seated beside the door, the other somewhere along the opposite wall. They had been standing when they started, and they'd been generous with gossip at the beginning, too, speaking with the seditious freedom of men who had no expectation of being recorded or observed or understood.

They'd mocked him for the easy target he made, growing creative in the ways they could torment him, and griping about the limitations placed on them by their boss. And they'd moved on to verbally undressing Anna, crude and graphic in their descriptions of what they'd do to her if they could just convince Vadik to swap positions for a few hours.

The conversation had thinned and would stop completely as late night descended and the body's need for sleep took over. He waited for that, killing time inside a mental maze that had twice shifted and shrunk in the past five hours.

He knew Dmitry was alive.

Knew Dmitry was aware of present circumstances, if not the particulars, knew that no matter how high Dmitry had climbed within the bureaucratic apparatus, this thing had come from higher still, and knew this abduction hadn't been Dmitry's doing.

Clare inside his head, Clare, who'd taught him to do better than believe, saturated that knowledge with doubt.

They give you just enough truth for wishful thinking to take over.

They give you the idea of hope because hope creates fear of losing what you imagine you have, and that keeps you pliable.

He knew the training, knew the warnings, but this wasn't the time.

He needed to believe.

Silence behind the door deepened.

It'd been an hour since the last spoken word.

He stood, took a deep breath, and pounded both fists hard against the door.

The hits reverberated through the room, shocking the quiet, and drove both men in the hall, swearing, to their feet. A fist punched the door back.

The same voice that held the knife threatened to bash his skull in.

Jack said, "I need the toilet."

Both men laughed.

The man with the knife said, "Shit your bed."

Jack waited for silence to settle, waited until the men had settled, and he pounded again, harder. The men swore at him, at each other.

One of them kicked the door.

He waited again and pounded again, mimicking with his fists the mental torture of dripping water and random squeaks, interruptive noises spaced just far enough apart that a tired brain begging to relax got just that close, only to be jarred and startled — *pound* wait *pound* wait *pound* — until the voice with the knife ordered the other to unlock the door and debate ensued and angry frustration won out over reason.

Keys jostled. The doorknob rattled.

The world slowed, and time fell between its cracks.

Jack reached for the lamp.

The door opened. Light spread through the widening gap and shifted, replaced by shadow. Jack drove the lamp upward, metal shade support as a spear tip, up beneath the chin of an angry oncoming face and through soft flesh.

He threw his full weight upward behind that thrust, tore knife from hand, stabbed into neck, and yanked down through the carotid triangle, severing muscle, windpipe.

He let the body drop, stepped into the hallway, into a rising PYa Grach.

Instinct took over, hands blocking wrist, slamming handgun into doorframe, shoving blade into throat to guarantee silence.

The sentry fought for control of the semiautomatic and clawed at Jack's face, fingers fighting to reach his eyes.

Blade sliced wrist tendons.

Firearm clattered to the floor.

Jack dropped the knife, gripped head, rotated hard, fast, and took the neck with him. The man's legs went out. The body fell.

Jack stood over the lifeless form, sucking air, catching his breath.

Two dead. No gunshots.

Fifteen seconds, which had felt like fifteen minutes.

You need to know your opponent to outthink him.

Understand your enemy and you'll know his plans before he does.

If these were the suit man's bodyguards, he would have needed a different strategy, would have had a much harder fight.

But they weren't. That was their first, second, third mistake.

He reached for the knife, sliced a strip off the sentry's shirt, used the cloth to wipe blood spatter off his own face, his arms, cleaned the blade, and picked up the semi-automatic. Russian military sidearm. Standard issue.

He pulled the slide, checked the chamber.

Released the magazine, checked ammunition.

Eighteen 7N21 armor-piercing rounds, like they expected some kind of rescue attempt by Kevlar-wearing ninjas. He snapped the magazine back into place, checked both men for keys, money, identification, turned up a pack of cigarettes, a couple hundred euros, enough koruny for a decent meal, and two security badges with names that bore no relation to the names they'd called each other. He left the cigarettes and took the rest, nudged both weapons out of sight, and headed for the hub.

He didn't know how many men were in the building or where they were, had no way to confirm the absence of cameras in the halls and hub, and wasn't sure how far sound from pounding on the door had traveled.

Didn't care.

He'd felt drafts while being marched one place to the next.

In a building like this, that meant doors or windows.

And he also knew Anna was close and only a single sentry guarded her. *Vadik,* they'd called him — the familiar form of Vadim — similar to the way Jimmy was a diminutive of James used by family, friends, and peers, or as deliberate condescension to put a lesser in his place.

In this case maybe a bit of both.

They considered him a stick-up-the-butt rule follower.

He could work with that.

He reached the end of the hall and followed a hint of cigarette smoke into a perpendicular entryway. A man in his early twenties, in civilian dress, stood military at ease three meters down. Jack strode toward him, purposeful, direct.

The sentry's hand moved toward his side-arm.

Jack said, *"Zdraviya zhelayu."*

A militarized greeting, uncommon, out of place.

The sentry's hand hesitated, rose an inch, as if he wasn't sure whether to salute or draw, and that bought another meter.

The sentry's posture shifted.

Jack gripped handgun, gripped the knife, rushed the remaining distance, got muzzle to temple and knife to shooting hand before the guy's finger slipped past trigger guard. "Your friends are dead," he whispered. "Don't join them."

The sentry understood the intent, if not the words.

He stopped fighting.

Jack backed the blade up off his fingers.

The sentry released his grip.

Jack knocked the weapon to the floor, kicked it beyond reach, gripped the sentry's arm, spun him hard, shoved him into the door, and with the muzzle to the back of the man's head, said, "Unlock it."

The man did as instructed.

Jack snatched the keys, grabbed the sentry's collar, and used him as a human shield as he went through the door. He cleared the space, shoved the man into the far corner, and quietly shut them in.

The room was much like the one he'd been in, repartitioned office space, if he had to guess, and he found Anna on a bed much like his, with her right ankle cuffed to a chain and the chain cuffed to the frame.

She had startled awake when the door opened and let out a muffled scream, and she stared now, mouth slack, body immobile, as if not quite sure this was real.

Jack scanned the length of her.

Her eyes were red, puffy from crying, and her hair was a matted disaster, but her clothes were intact, and if she'd been hit or hurt, the cuts and bruises didn't show. He kept the muzzle trained on the corner, flipped through the keys, found what he needed, and released her ankle.

Anna slipped off the bed and stood.

He nudged her behind him, nodded the sentry over to where she'd been, cuffed his foot as Anna's had been cuffed, pulled her in tight, and backed toward the door.

He twisted the handle slowly, opened a crack, peered out into an empty hall, pulled Anna after him, relocked the door, put a finger to his lips, and led her back the way he'd come, pausing every few feet in search of airflow.

He felt the first draft at the edge of the

hub, knelt, sniffed, followed toward the source, and a few feet farther found the outline of a door.

Palm to the wall, he pushed.

The segment gave way, opening a crack in an inward swing.

He nudged Anna to the side. "Wait here."

Her eyes widened. She held on to his arm, and shook her head.

She didn't want to be left behind or risk getting grabbed again.

"One minute," he said. "Maybe less."

Definitely less.

He was as vested in keeping her free as she was in getting free — different motive, sure, but just as much at stake — but had no time to persuade fear with logic.

He gripped her wrist, removed her hand.

This close to the outside, he no longer cared about noise or weapon reports.

This was full commitment right into the fatal tunnel, and the only thing that mattered was speed. He pushed through, weapon relaxed, low ready.

Information, details filled his head in rapid sequence.

Drab reception room. Small windows. Double front door.

Armed guard at the desk. Twenty feet.

Armed guard at the door. Twenty-five feet.

He fired toward the desk. Double tap to the chest. The guy went down, out of sight. Jack shifted left. Target at the door, reaching.

Jack pulled the trigger. Hit center chest.

The guy struggled to stay standing.

A shaking hand brought the muzzle upward.

Jack fired again.

The guard stumbled backward into the glass, slid to the floor.

Jack strode forward, pulled the trigger, single tap to the head.

He shifted right, weapon high ready, toward the security desk, and he sidestepped for a view behind the counter. The guard was on the floor, bleeding, gasping, struggling up, reaching for the underside of the desk, for what Jack assumed was an alarm.

Trigger pull.

Silence.

Jack patted down the body, searching pockets, neck, hands.

He snatched security badge and wallet, left the service weapon.

He would have rummaged through drawers and the computer system but didn't have the time, so retraced his steps back to the wall that shielded Anna.

From this side, the hub entrance had a handle.

He pulled the door a few inches, cleared the breach, and pushed through. The hub was empty, and the hall, except for Anna.

He grabbed her hand, tugged her into the reception room.

The door closed behind her.

She followed a few feet in and stopped, legs immobile, focus riveted on the body propped up against the window. Jack left her for the love seat on the opposite wall, shoved furniture across the floor, and blocked the hub entrance. The piece wasn't bulky enough to stop someone from getting through, but it would keep them from sneaking in the way he just had. He returned to the front door, dragged the guard from the glass to behind the desk, and, there, where Anna couldn't see, searched the body the way he had with the first.

He took cash from the wallet, took the security badge, and scurried out.

Anna stayed where she'd stopped, jaw slack, arms at her sides.

The only part of her that moved was her eyes, and they tracked him relentlessly.

He reached for her hand, tugged gently, tugged harder until she took a step, and then pulled her along, out the front, into a small courtyard with limited parking, blocked off from whatever lay beyond the high surrounding wall by a metal gate. Cold, deep night air tinged with hints of diesel fumes indicated a nearby road.

He spun back for a glimpse of the building, old and factory-like, a single-story structure that looked like it had been gutted by fire and was under renovation. The updates included modernization, not least of which was the security pad to access the front door. Not a secure facility, a temporarily abandoned one.

He crossed the courtyard with Anna in tow, found the access pad for the gate, and tapped one of the four badges against it. Gears whirred, mechanics groaned, and metal pulled sideways. Jack slipped through the widening gap, and Anna followed onto the shouldered edge of a dark and quiet two-lane road that ran between mom-and-pop businesses and houses and industrial buildings similar to this. The area was more open, less tightly packed than the city proper, but urban all the same.

He paused, trying to get compass bearings.

Anna pointed right. "That way," she said.

He followed her finger to near-distance signage, which he couldn't quite make out, but he understood. They were past midnight, when the last of the restaurants and cafés shut down, but bars sometimes stayed open until the early morning hours.

"Go," he said, and she walked, and he followed.

He knew even before they reached the place that it still hummed.

If he could guarantee Anna would find her way to safety alone, he'd leave her there, but abandoning her, only to find her grabbed again, wasn't worth the risk. He said, "Do you have a friend with a car? Someone you can call to come get you, to help you?"

"Help only me?" she said.

"Only you."

"I can call. Ask. What happens next, I don't know."

"Try," he said.

She moved toward the door.

He pointed to her hair. "You have to fix that first."

She ran her fingers through the tangled strands, smoothing, if not straightening them, turned for the door and, realizing he wasn't coming, stopped.

"It's better if I wait outside," he said.

Less attention, fewer people to get a good look at his face — and with the condition she was in, they *would* look — and fewer chances of being picked up on CCTV.

He said, "I'm not leaving. I'm right here."

She studied him for a long second. Unspoken accusations and unasked questions filled the silence, and she sighed and opened the door. Music, noise, and light spilled out onto the sidewalk, and she stepped out of sight.

A minute or two dragged into five.

Five minutes dragged into ten.

He leaned against the wall, gaze toward the pavement, fighting against impatience and the unknown, and was debating the need to follow her in when the door opened and Anna stepped out, alone. He couldn't tell if she'd succeeded or not.

She joined him against the wall.

"Maybe twenty minutes," she said. "My friend will come."

"This is someone you trust? With your life?"

Her expression, incredulous, said there was no possible way someone willing to come help her in the dead of night could screw up her life any more than he already had.

He said, "This wasn't meant to happen. I'm sorry."

She sniffed, effectively calling him a liar.

She said, "I thought first, maybe this was big mistake, or maybe something with mafia or drugs that goes bad. But I see how you move. You kill like execution, and a man who moves like this, who kills like this, who asks stranger to be girlfriend for a day, maybe this man does not *intend,* but he knows this is all possibility."

She was right, of course, and nicer, kinder than he deserved.

He'd known they'd be grabbed. Just hadn't expected the rough treatment.

Denying it would only make him a bigger dick.

He said, "Is there anywhere you can go? To leave Prague for a month?"

She studied the pavement, took a moment to answer and, voice soft, said, "There is going, and there is paying for the going."

It'd have been easy to interpret her statement the way his sister would have intended it, as a passive-aggressive, guilt-inducing shakedown that said no matter how well he'd paid her to accompany him to that meeting, it didn't come close to touching the damage he'd done, and that he owed her. But this wasn't that. Even if she had a place she could go, even if she worked her own hours and didn't have to worry about losing a job, there were still costs associated with keeping a roof over her head and perhaps homing a pet. Even the semi-transient couldn't uproot as easily as he could.

He said, "You're not safe here."

"One month is enough?"

He nodded. "Should be enough."

Her face filled with doubt. He couldn't explain how he knew, or why, and it'd be ludicrous after all this to ask her to trust him, so he said nothing.

Headlamps rounded the distant curve, lighting what had otherwise been a traffic-free stretch of road. Anna leaned forward for a better view, a position that drew attention and ensured anyone who knew her or was looking for her would recognize her without help. He put a hand on her arm and held her back.

She jerked loose and glared.

He said, "It's only been fifteen minutes."

The vehicle slowed, approaching too directly to be random.

They were targets against a wall, waiting for a firing squad.

Jack reached for the small of his back. Gripped the handgun.

Anna said, "That is him, my friend."

Jack said, "Just wait. Give it time."

An old beige Opel hatchback ran its tires

up onto the sidewalk and stopped a meter away. Anna moved to take a step forward. Jack, gripping her arm, held her in place. The passenger window rolled down.

Anna tugged and, forcefully this time, said, "It is my friend."

Jack walked with her, put himself between her and the passenger door, leaned down, scanned the interior, confirmed the backseat was empty, and loosened his grip. "Don't go home," he said. "You know Petřín?"

She answered with a confused shrug.

Of course she knew. Everyone knew.

Petřín was a hill near the center of Prague, a popular recreational area for the locals and a destination for tourists, who sought out its Eiffel-like lookout tower for the views. "Go there," he said. "Go to the statue of Mácha. Search in the trees behind it. You'll find a brown paint mark. Upturn the largest stone near that tree. There's money. It will get you what you need for clothes and shoes and personal items. It'll get you a ticket out of town." He pulled the stolen euros and koruny from his pocket, shoved it in her hand. "So you don't run out of petrol along the way."

She took the money, squeezed his biceps, leaned in, and kissed him on the cheek. She said, "Maybe this bad thing is intended, or maybe you know is only a possibility, but you care enough to come get me and make me free. So. Thank you."

He opened the door for her. Nudged her inside. Closed it behind her.

"Go to Petřín," he said. "Leave Prague."

The window rolled up, the tires pulled off the curb, and the Opel hung a U-turn. He watched the taillights until they faded, stashed the pistol behind his back, and weight dropped off his shoulders, lifted off his chest.

He'd warned her, and provided the money she'd need to run. He'd done what he could, but more than that, she'd forgiven him and absolved him.

The absolution mattered.

He shoved hands into pockets and began a long, slow stroll back the way he'd come. The gate was closed when he reached it. The security badge opened it for a second time, and the badge got him past the glass and into the drab reception room.

He detoured for the security desk, rifled through drawers that offered paper and pens and standard office fare, and studied the monitors. The feeds came from cameras that pointed outward, presumably to protect the building from vandals and thieves and record the comings and goings at the front.

There'd be footage of him somewhere, of him and Anna strolling out and, an hour or so later, of his solo return. His face would be grainy because of the dark, and difficult to enhance because keeping his head down was second nature, and if the footage existed, someone somewhere would try to make use of it, and he wished them luck with that.

He left the security badges on the desk.

The love seat was exactly where he'd shoved it, to the inch.

He pushed it back across the room, righted it into place.

And he returned to the hub and headed for his bed, conscious of the way silence and solitude amplified each step. Other than Vadik, whom he'd left shackled in Anna's place, he was alone in this building. He wiped down the PYa Grach, and returned it to the hand of the sentry to whom it belonged. He did the same with the knife and grabbed the shoulders of the body lying across the threshold, lamp metal still protruding from beneath the chin, dragged it into the hall, and propped it up. And he returned to the room, to his bed, slipped off his shoes, lay back, hands behind his head, and closed his eyes.

They'd promised him freedom and

brought him here instead.

They hadn't let him see Anna.

He didn't respond well to force or threats — he'd said so plainly — but those most used to giving orders were often deafest to warnings.

Some people needed shouting.

"Sleep," the man in the suit had said. "We talk in the morning."

Indeed they would.

Chapter 25

Wien Hauptbahnhof
Vienna, Austria

Kara

She wove past sleek signage and modern departure boards, head down, fists clenched, into the main concourse, where translucent panels and recessed lights played contrast against the folded lines and open spaces of the tracks. Vienna station was an architectural playground, but all she saw was shoes and floor.

She needed to get in, get to a phone, get out.

That was the mantra cycling through her brain.

This call was an obligation, a duty that now fell on her.

Failing to follow through would invite questions and suspicions and make her a scapegoat for the fiasco in Prague.

Making the call portended the same out-come.

Vienna had never been part of the plan.

She'd made a judgment call and taken what was left of her team off-line. She'd expected to have to fight Aaron and his bickering the whole way, but he'd followed her lead without protest. He'd been docile enough, really, that under other circum-stances she'd have fast-tracked his way to a psych appointment.

Struggling to hold her own shit together, as she was, she didn't have the bandwidth for his mental health, too, so the ride out of Prague had been five hours of silence: silent pain, silent questions, silently buying tickets and finding tracks and seats and, upon ar-riving, silently finding a place to sit tight. She'd gotten him settled in the food court, and waited until he'd begun to pick at his meal before telling him she was going for answers. He'd put a hand on her arm and stopped her.

He'd pushed a plate in her direction. Voice breaking, he'd said, "You need to eat. You need to take care of yourself, too."

The concern — from him, of all people — had threatened to rupture the membrane that contained the flood. She'd squeezed his hand and hurried away before what was left of her spilled all over the floor, which was how she'd gotten to where she was now, striding beneath skylights under a dark sky, call card in hand, fighting back tears on her way to the public phones. Their own equipment was in a Prague luggage locker, left behind for the same reason she'd gone to ground, and the same reason she already had tickets in hand for the next train to Bratislava. She didn't know what the hell had gone down in Republic Square, but she damn sure knew headquarters had withheld information and that withholding it had gotten half her team killed. She wasn't willing to bet against a cleanup crew coming for the two that got away.

She'd chosen Wien for its flexibility.

This new central station had turned Vienna into a major artery on the European rail lines, which meant quick access to trains in any cardinal direction, and the station wasn't far from both international airport and highway, and Austria itself was small, which meant nearby land borders, all of which mattered if she was forced to run.

But first, she had to make this call.

She reached the phone bank, chose the handset with the best view of the concourse and, using the number Nick had given her for emergencies, bypassed Liv Wilson for

Steven Hayes, the man at the apex of whatever headquarters was.

She'd met him just once at a briefing, a handshake the extent of their interaction. He was smart, short, balding, and buzzed with the low hum of a burned-out fluorescent bulb, which she'd chalked up to a decade of substituting neurotropics and edible caffeine for sleep. Calling him directly was a breach of protocol that would get someone far more important shitcanned, but she was beyond caring.

She was loyal to Nick, loyal to family and to country, and she'd saluted enough men and women undeserving of the uniform to mistake loyalty for obedience.

Hayes answered with a clipped hello.

She said, "Novak calling on behalf of Carson."

"Novak," he said.

The repeat wasn't a statement, wasn't a question, and wasn't a greeting.

It was information for someone else's benefit, and in her mind's eye, she saw him snapping for attention, circling fingers, summoning the desk jockeys to get a real-time trace. He said, "Are you secure?"

"Not the line," she said.

"Go ahead," he said.

She checked her surroundings, scanned

the concourse.

"Carson and Marino, KIA. I'll have IRR and analysis within twenty-four hours. I'm resigning position and requesting a return to station."

Hayes said, "We're still working on building the complete timeline. I'd like to bring you in, have you fill in the gaps on what we're missing. Let's discuss exit options in person after you're finished."

Kara parsed his words, struggling to read implied meaning between lines she'd never been good at seeing in the first place.

There was threat, and maybe warning.

She hadn't been naive enough to assume this would be easy.

People like her didn't just walk away, and any possibility she had of a smooth transition had died with Nick. Without Hayes's blessing, best case might find her facing a dishonorable discharge, and worst case, she'd be dead within the month. The only protection she had was what she knew, and she wasn't ready to give that up just yet.

"Unable to exfil at this time, sir," she said. "It'll all be in the report."

The clock in her head said a minute since the line had connected.

Nearest embassy was seventeen minutes door-to-door. Thirteen if operatives were on standby and traffic and traffic lights were inconsequential. Zero if the war room had pinged her departure out of Prague and already had a team on-site.

In her head she counted down.

Hayes said, "Give me a second."

The need to hurry intensified, amplifying the mental chatter inside her head, making it hard to focus. In her ear, the ambient noise changed, as if Hayes had stepped somewhere quiet and shut the door behind him.

The sense of privacy brought a change in tone.

His language slipped from formal to casual, and exhaustion bled through, and that was all an illusion, because the call was recorded anyway.

"I'm sorry to hear about Carson," he said. "It's never easy losing a partner, but when you're tight like the two of you were, the gut punch wrecks you to the core."

She struggled for a response, knew one was required.

Logic protested, questioning why the grieving party owed anything.

She stayed silent.

Hayes said, "I've been reading your op reports and requisitions. You've got a good head for abstract connections and a keen eye for detail. It's fair to want out, but target is still at large and remains high priority, and we can't afford to lose you until the team closes out. I want you to take lead."

Kara fought for words, fought to breathe.

She didn't want this, wasn't cut out for fieldwork.

She was an analyst, not an operative and not a leader.

Her thoughts scattered. She struggled to bring them back to the concourse.

No sign of field officers yet.

Didn't mean they weren't coming. Just meant they hadn't already been on-site. Her mind bolted again, jumping over probabilities, racing through possibilities.

She was screwed no matter what she did.

She said, "You may feel differently after you receive the report."

He said, "You can speak frankly."

Five minutes. She could do this in five minutes.

This was suicide. Or this was rescue.

At least she'd know one way or the other.

She said, "I'm an analyst, sir. I can only do my job if I'm given all available data, and with all due respect, to ask me to continue against an advanced, persistent threat without allowing me all-source access is asking me to continue the losses. I'll pull that pin and fall on that grenade, sir, if that's what you're looking for, but I'd still be more effective with access to all the data."

Hayes stayed silent for a few seconds, and she struggled to gauge what the silence meant but was too far in now to change course, so she, too, kept quiet.

When he spoke, his words were perfunctory. "You already have full, unlimited access to everything that's relevant," he said.

Not so much a lie as an equivocation.

Relevant was interpretive.

Relevant was a man in a suit protecting his own interests, or sandboxing operations to prevent one blowing back on another, or holding on to classified intelligence above her clearance level, but reasons that might matter stateside, or might matter to long-term survival, didn't matter right here and now.

Headquarters had failed her. The war room had failed her.

If she couldn't have access to information from *all* available data sources, she would fail and her team would die. She said, "Identity and objective are always relevant, sir. Our man is not on *the* list, and we weren't informed that another who is on it would be there. If we'd had accurate intelligence, Carson and Marino would still be alive."

Hayes's tone caught an edge. "That's quite an accusation," he said.

"Not an accusation, sir. You're asking me to lead an operation under the same parameters that killed half my team. It does no favors for either of us if I pretend otherwise. Like I said, you want me to pull the pin and throw myself on that grenade, I'll do it, but if you want my team to close out, then I need to know who we're chasing and everything you know about him, relevant or not, classified or not."

Hayes waited a beat.

"This is an unsecured line," he said.

"Understood," she said.

He wasn't stating the obvious or reminding her of what he thought she'd forgotten. He was telling her this conversation had already breached protocol and that he was about to charge right through that breach in a good-faith gesture. He said, "First, you understand why we're working from the top of that list?"

"Yes," she said.

Well, she *had* understood until she'd discovered their target wasn't on it.

She added, "I no longer understand how this op is connected."

"Everything as briefed," Hayes said. "But a new actor."

Her gaze dropped to her feet. Inside her head, the pieces snapped.

She'd been aware that the Broker's death had come as some form of coup within that underbelly world, and that the aftermath had been a bloodbath in which the assassins themselves had shortened the list considerably by killing each other. Same briefing, new actor meant the details that had launched the op were the same, but the original assassin was either dead or had gone to ground.

Jacques Lefevre, the man they hunted now, was the replacement.

That put sense to why headquarters had known his seat number before they'd known his name, but a whole lot else still needed answers.

She said, "Who is he?"

Hayes said, "We don't know."

She didn't believe for a minute that headquarters was working entirely dark. "There's always something," she said.

He said, "You've heard of Karen McFadden?"

She forced the neurons to connect, drew up the memories.

The name had shown up in Christopher

Holden's files as last known target.

"I've heard the name," she said. "I don't know who or what it is."

"McFadden was deep cover in a clandestine op out of Moscow at the tail end of the Cold War," Hayes said. "Officially, she was rolled up by the KGB. Unofficially, file's still open. Her handler was a double, triple who-really-knows, and you've already heard of him. We're working from his list. Intel we're pulling says she's the one who unplugged him. For as long as there've been rumors about McFadden, there've also been rumors she had a child. The chatter we're picking up points in that direction. You can infer the rest and deduce the urgency."

She could, yes.

She'd seen a strong operative skill set and a man capable of slipping back into the United States unnoticed, which made him a true threat if a political assassination was in play. But this little slice of history didn't explain why him, why now.

And it didn't explain target's accomplice-slash-sibling.

Or how Christopher Holden factored in.

Or why target seemed ambivalent to their presence.

And for all that mess, the assassination theory seemed a little too tidy and complete, but she had limited time and Hayes had limited patience, and what worried her most was getting lured into assassin-on-assassin cross fire, the way her team had been lured to Republic Square in Prague. Or, worse, having her team played against Emilia Flynn. She needed the lines clearly delineated or needed more access.

She said as much to Hayes.

Hayes said, "All four Tea Team, KIA."

The words stole thought from her head and breath from her lungs, and she was, for a few seconds, speechless. New meaning layered over old, and thinking of Emilia now led to thinking of Nick, and that he'd died without knowing and *that* he was dead, and the world closed in on her again.

She forced agreement up her throat and out her lips.

"I need equipment," she said. "And I'm going to need the rest of my team."

The departure to Bratislava was coming up fast. She needed to get to Aaron, needed to get him on that train. She dropped handset into cradle.

She would, without a doubt, find her target.

What she did when she found him was yet to be determined.

CHAPTER 26

Toledo Executive Airport
South of Toledo, Ohio, USA

Jack

He stepped from airstairs to tarmac, fuel fumes and winter cold kissing his lungs, the whine of the Gulfstream engines fading as he followed the cabin crew's finger-pointing instruction toward the center of a squat, metal-topped structure, where administration offices and government offices combined under a single roof into a terminal of sorts.

Not that he needed directions to find it.

The building was the only one in sight, the only *thing* in sight, really.

This airport, with a runway just long enough to handle private jets and prop planes, was but a blip on the map. There were railway tracks in the near distance, and a freeway not too far off, and not much else for miles around.

He'd flown Prague to Toledo on Moscow's dime.

Toledo was his choice, as was the detour through Nassau that allowed him to preclear US airspace in the Bahamas.

The Russians had set the time frame, handled logistics.

He was traveling on their papers — a French passport with a backstopped legend that would have made Clare weep in envy — genuine documents for a genuine individual with impeccable references but, more importantly, a travel history limited to the European continent.

A visit to any of the Five Eyes countries would have ruled him out. Australia, Canada, New Zealand, United Kingdom, United States, they all shared signals intelligence and biometric data.

Several Pacific nations posed a similar risk for different reasons.

Every year the world's borders grew less porous. Every year it got harder to slip between the cracks. But the world hadn't yet united in a single biometric database, and so Jack's face and Jack's voice had been the first of this traveler's records siphoned into US biometric repositories. He'd set the baseline. A new hairline, prosthetic facial adjustments, the man's own fingerprints covering his, and a set of balls forged in the pits of hell had been enough to get him a few cursory questions, a quick declaration, and the thump in his passport that sent him on.

This stop now was just a pass-through formality.

He rolled the small carry-on into the terminal, toiletries and clothing he hadn't asked for but that the Russians had insisted he take because empty-handed globe-trotting drew attention. He checked his watch and set a five-hour countdown.

That was about how long he figured, give or take, before the Russians who'd been so eager to make friends, provide flawless credentials, and shell out heavy cash to get him into the country, started leaking those same details through the same communications channels they'd used to leak his travel itinerary out of Dallas and put the kill team on his trail.

Life, it seemed, was destined to run on constant replay.

It hadn't been Clare's doing, but it was still another damn test.

The Russians had already known what Jill was capable of from her work for the Broker but they'd had no reference point for him.

By their reasoning, if he wasn't skilled enough to outsmart a kill team following him into Europe, he wasn't smart enough to play decoy for her within the United States.

That's what he'd been from the moment he checked in solo on that Dallas flight, a political assassin leaked to Washington by supposed Kremlin defectors, an offering borne out of a temporary ideological alliance for the sake of greater global good. And while the US government pursued him, Jill, always the deadlier one, would continue on undetected.

She'd make a kill of her own, and the world would recoil.

The media machine, in a race to be first to report, would rush unverified details into the tinderbox, and the troll farms would feed the partisan frenzy, and the country would devour itself from the inside. Such was the treachery of spies.

Jack exited the building.

A black Yukon waited at the curb, placard with his name on it in the window, a Russian-arranged private car to get him to Detroit, where he'd catch a Russian-booked commercial flight to DC and check into a Russian-booked hotel.

As if he'd be fool enough to put his life in

their hands.

As if they were fool enough to believe that he would.

Mental games upon mental games, so easy to get lost among them.

The driver was African American, male, late fifties, shaved head, barrel chest, starched shirt, sharp tie, and shoes mirrored to a high-polish shine. Not the look or feel of an undercover Russian operative, but assumptions were what got a person killed.

He opened the rear door, stashed Jack's suitcase in the trunk, slid in behind the wheel, and lifted a large manila envelope off the passenger seat. "Delivered by courier about ten minutes ago," he said. He handed it back.

The envelope was blank.

No name, no address, not that there'd ever be a question as to who'd sent it.

The Yukon pulled away from the curb.

Jack opened the seal, pulled the pages out far enough to leaf through them, and nudged them back. He glanced at the rearview for a glimpse of the driver, who appeared about as interested in him as a contractor would be in watching paint dry. Jack plied a French accent to match the name and passport. He said, "You have done this *chauffeur* for much time?"

The driver's focus stayed on the road.

" 'Bout six years now."

"Is good work?"

"Pays the bills. Helps put my sons through college."

"Toledo College?"

The driver looked up briefly. Spontaneous parental pride oozed from every part of him in a way even Clare, the mynah bird of human emotions, couldn't mimic.

"Stanford," he said. "Cornell."

Jack said, "The father is very proud, yes?"

"Proud as hell. Boys worked hard. Earned it."

The guy was authentic.

That didn't rule him out as an operative, but most of the cards stacked the other way. Odds of a Russian cleanup crew coming in from behind weren't zero, but United States intelligence building a trail forward from here was likelier. Jack didn't trust either, but any warning realistic enough to be taken seriously carried an equal risk of causing erratic behavior, which would draw enough attention to become a self-fulfilling prophecy. It was a shit position to be in, made worse because those who pursued him likely knew and would use the weakness against him.

Jack said, "This small airport, you do

much work here?"

The driver said, "Mostly Toledo Express. Sometimes Detroit."

Jack nudged the envelope into the driver's field of vision. "And this courier for documents, this is regular thing?"

The driver dipped the blinker, changed lanes. "See 'em a couple times a month, though I can't say I've ever had a plain envelope handed through a window like that."

"But is the same company to bring this, yes?"

The driver checked the mirror, met Jack's gaze.

He was slow to answer. "Just an old, beat-down guy in an old gray Buick," he said. "Asked if I was waiting on you, said he'd been paid to courier a package, handed me that, and said to give it when you got in."

Jack held eye contact, said nothing.

These questions weren't for him — he already knew the answers.

He let time do the explaining, and said, "I am sorry, my friend. We must change destination to Cleveland."

The driver's fingers tapped along the steering wheel.

He checked the mirrors, and adjusted the temperature. They were the motions of a man who, realizing he was heading into uncharted territory, was buying time.

This was good.

The driver said, "Cleveland is an extra hour in the opposite direction. I'll need to call in to dispatch, make sure the vehicle has that kind of availability."

Jack dug into his jacket, pulled out a grand in crisp, clean Benjamins, and slid the Russian pocket money between bucket seats. He said, "We can perhaps skip formalities to make for the easier trip?"

The driver glanced at the bills.

Debate marched across his face.

This was also good.

Jack offered another couple thousand and then reassurance that the destination wasn't the issue. "Cleveland is not so far," he said. "But a difficult passenger with many demands makes a good reason to take the rest of the day from work, yes?"

The driver sighed, took the cash.

Jack tugged a single page a few inches out of the envelope and, as if reading off an address, said, "Downtown. West Tenth Street. Aloft Hotel. You know it?"

The driver reached for the GPS. "Shouldn't be too hard."

The Yukon neared Interstate 280. The driver took them south. They rode in silence, incremental miles putting distance between Moscow's plan and Jack's own, and he emptied the envelope and perused months of detailed surveillance — times, dates, and locations meticulously tracking the senator's movements, a record of cell phones and vehicle plates, home and office addresses, the wife's routine and kids' after-school schedule, and a hefty dose of kompromat on the staff members — all of it information someone preparing for a hit would find helpful in getting up close in a hurry and getting away faster still.

No question as to where it'd come from, only why.

He was the decoy, tasked with a kill the Russians didn't expect him to make on a mission they didn't expect him to survive.

Not that they'd exactly put it that way.

The suit and his bodyguards had returned in the morning, as promised.

He'd been on the bed, staring at the ceiling, watching them in his mind's eye, as they made their way through the front and into the hub and down the hall, passing one body after the next. They'd entered his room, weapons drawn.

He'd said, "Have a seat. Let's talk."

It'd been a very different conversation from the one they'd planned.

The suit had asked him about Anna, and he'd told the truth, said he didn't like people suffering unnecessarily and he didn't trust them not to hurt her. And he'd asked again to meet Dmitry, which the suit had refused outright.

No surprise.

Dmitry was the control mechanism, the one piece of leverage they held, a threat that didn't need to be spoken to be understood. *Maybe don't go getting your father killed before you even have a chance to meet the man.*

What the suit *had* offered was a hero's welcome from Mother Russia when this was over. Citizenship. A house and stipend. A country in which Jack would have safe haven, an obvious need because, clearly, the Americans no longer wanted him as one of their own, and what kind of country was the USA anyway if the government sanctioned extrajudicial killing of its own citizens?

As if the same thing and worse didn't happen in Russia.

But that was different.

Of course it was different. Russia wasn't a democracy. Russia didn't hold itself out as a beacon of morality to the rest of the world, active measures and all that.

Their offer was only partially true.

They never expected to have to fill their end of the bargain.

For him, the only way out was to die or to fake his own death, and faking death meant the rest of his life on the run. Easy enough in principle. He had no roots, no home, no family and, child of the world that he was, he was capable of adapting anywhere. But that left him with a mother he couldn't trust, a sister who hated him, killers at his back, and a half-cocked, fucked-up plan that would make him persona non grata in every connected country he tried to enter.

That was Clare's legacy, not his.

He had been running his whole damn life and was over it.

He wanted to go where he wanted, when he wanted, for reasons he wanted, not because his mother or father or sister or the goddamn Kremlin had made their own set of plans. If he hadn't been willing to be Clare's puppet, he damn sure wasn't about to start performing for someone else, and so he'd agreed to the job for the same reason he'd returned after setting Anna free.

It was the fastest way to get what he wanted.

Or the dumbest way to die.

He shoved the papers back, folded the

envelope, and stuffed it inside his jacket.

Intelligence, like a parachute, was only as good as the hands that had packed it, and this was more of a tangled death trap than the means to a safe landing.

Didn't mean he couldn't repurpose it, though.

He leaned back, shut his eyes, and puzzled through the mental maze in a search for Jill and couldn't find her. Instead of the positional awareness that connected him to her when their fates intertwined, he had the guilty memory of her loping across the plaza with that damn SIM in her pocket, and the fatalistic acceptance that the laugh-filled hour they'd spent playing cards in her room in Prague might be the last of their shared bond.

He'd taken from her what he had no right to take.

One day, maybe, he'd earn her forgiveness.

One day, maybe, everything with her wouldn't have to be so damn hard.

He pushed her away, sunk deeper into the seat, and let his mind drift through the two hours that separated the runway from the mirrored multistory hotel in downtown Cleveland. He lost another forty minutes at Walmart in between, time that was expensive and hard to spend, but a single detour that netted burner phones, tools, and change-making supplies had no substitute.

The driver left him at the hotel curb.

He waited, suitcase by his side and newly acquired goods in hand, for the Yukon to swing out of sight and then turned for the hotel's front doors.

He had two hours to lose everything that connected him to Russia and to lose himself. For that, he didn't need a room, per se.

He needed a focal point those hunting him could focus in on, and a hotel worked as well as anything else. This hotel or another, it didn't matter. This had just been the first one to come to mind. The check-in process ate another ten minutes.

In the room he emptied the suitcase out onto the bed, grabbed toilet paper, toiletries, and hotel towels from the bathroom, courtesy of the Russians, who didn't yet know they'd be paying for them, and divided the pile between three shopping bags.

He added those items to the supplies he'd purchased, stuffed it all into a larger duffel bag, and walked out into a late afternoon chill with everything but the travel documents and the empty suitcase.

Not the wisest course of action.

He was bleeding time faster than money, but to leave anything in the room was to throw it away, and he couldn't bring himself to do that, not even now.

He had Clare to thank for that, too, he supposed, a lifetime of uprooting and abandoning most of what he owned, and starting over somewhere new, again, and again, and again.

"Belongings are chains," Clare would say. "They mark you as a stranger, slow you down when you carry them, make it hard to move."

But they were kids, and like other kids, they hated not having.

Worse was having to give up what little they did have, and so in compromise, each departure came with the promise of something new on arrival, always temporary, always to be left behind when the time came again, and the time *always* came again.

In the days and hours counting down, Clare would ferry them into slums, orphanages, prisons that housed young children with their mothers and would have them hand off what they treasured to those who had even less.

He had grown up detached to things but respectful of their value and could count on one hand the items he'd owned that hadn't lived a second life with someone who needed them more. That was the one thing Clare had taught him that had been worth keeping, perhaps the only thing he'd deliberately adopted for himself.

A few-minute walk took him to the Westgate Transit Center, and a bus took him toward his destination. At the halfway point, he stepped off in a detour for a nearby homeless shelter, and he walked the streets, searching for signs of those who preferred to live rough, handing off the grocery bags to those he met, shedding, adapting along the way, swapping the clothes and shoes he wore for what he'd purchased, and swapping again, all the while putting anything of value into the hands of those who could use it most.

He was cautious of cameras and social interactions, passing in one door and out another, cutting through backyards and down side streets, as he made his way to Edgewater Park, and by the time he arrived, he had nothing but cash and the few purchased items he still needed.

The park itself was 150 acres of fishing pier and public beach, picnic areas and walking trails, stretched out along the shores of Lake Erie. Not a big early-winter destination, but home to one of Clare's drops, and that was why he'd chosen Toledo as an entry point, and why he'd made the run to Cleveland itself.

He'd prefer to avoid raiding her cupboards.

Anything that came from her was another string he'd have to cut, but he needed a clean identity, didn't have time to build one of his own, and no matter how many of his own deliberate decisions had brought him here, this mess was still on her. If ever there was a scenario for which a drop was buried, he was in it.

And that was the thing about this one, it was *literally* buried.

To find it, he'd have to dig.

A lot of work for a small box.

But of all the resources she'd hidden in the United States, this was the closest he could get on the axis of *least likely to have been raided by Jill* and *near a municipal airport he could afford to burn.*

He strode along the bike path in its direction, hands stuffed in pockets, chin tucked into a scarf to ward against the biting wind blowing in off the lake, searching for the statue that would guide his way.

Clare had a thing for statues.

"They're usually cared for," she'd said.

Trees died. Creeks rose. Buildings got

renovated. Businesses closed.

But statues were meant to last generations, and even in cases of war or uprising or shifting politics, where the statue itself might be removed, the pedestal or evidence of its existence still remained.

Clare was a lot of things, but she wasn't stupid.

Proving her point was Richard Wagner, all thirty feet of him, standing where he'd stood for over a hundred years in spite of recent calls for his removal.

Jack reached the base, counted off the paces.

In the cold ground beneath bare deciduous branches, he found the box he'd come for, and in it ten thousand dollars cash and a full set of ID.

Passport, driver's license — now expired — library card, and Social Security card, but every piece tied to a single identity: Clare.

That's all there was.

He removed the contents, dumped the box into his backpack.

Refilled the hole, folded the camping shovel, and put that away, too.

He'd notify Clare that the stash had been cleared out, though at this point he wasn't sure why he should bother. He'd put out lines, trying to make contact.

He'd heard nothing back.

She had her reasons, always had her reasons.

A betting man could make good money on long odds that even if she hadn't been responsible for Dmitry's invitation or involved in the Russians' scheming, she was aware of it. He wouldn't want to be the man in the suit right now.

What he did want to be, though . . .

He'd had one opportunity to grab a clean identity, and all it had netted him was Clare and Clare and more Clare. He didn't have time to make a run on another stash.

He flipped through the ID pieces again, pondering the options.

Swapping genders was a pain in the ass that required a lot more work for him than it ever did for Jill, but he'd done it often enough that he could convincingly become her. And Jill looked so much like a younger Clare that if not for the way photos aged, it'd be easy to mistake them for each other in pictures.

He tapped the plastic against his fingers.

Pondered some more.

A woman inevitably drew less suspicion than a man.

And a woman had more costuming options — massive sunglasses, stylish hats, the ability to wear dresses or pants, not to mention the oversize purses, which were so ubiquitous they were near invisible, making it possible to haul all kinds of shit as an inconspicuous matter of course in a way a man never could. The more he thought about it, the more he liked the idea, and the more he laughed.

For years he'd done everything possible to get Clare out of his head.

Now he'd willingly become her.

CHAPTER 27

Aloft Hotel, Cleveland
Ohio, USA

Kara

She lost herself in the water's flow, head drooping, eyes closed, palms braced against the shower tiles while wet heat pounded down her neck and back, easing the ache at center chest that made it hard to breathe. Steam filled the bathroom.

Solitude brought relief, release.

The water took what it wanted, washing pieces of her down the drain.

She was stopped, again, for however long this new pause lasted, mobilized in haste out of Bratislava to Cleveland, where target had been reliably identified. She'd known even before boarding that he'd have already vanished before their wheels lifted off, and now she waited for the reinforcements promised by headquarters, she in this room,

Aaron next door, both of them two floors up from where target had spent all of eight minutes before walking out again.

— Jacques Lefevre.

— Jack, as he'd come to reside in her head.

Chasing him was like chasing summer fireflies as a kid, running barefoot through the backyard, following blips of focus-grabbing light that changed direction in no predictable pattern, showing up again but never quite where you'd been looking.

The unpredictability that had captured her attention as a child captivated her now — blips of focus-grabbing light — a series of actions that didn't fit the official narrative. She explained the inconsistencies to Nick in her head the way she'd have explained them to him in person.

This guy, this assassin, he comes into town on clean papers.

Never would have known he was here if not for the chatter.

He has a connecting flight in Detroit that will take him to DC.

But instead of catching the flight, he changes destination, divests himself of everything he brought, including the papers, and then disappears.

Why?

She wasn't an investigator.

Interacting with and questioning witnesses wasn't her thing, the war room sent others for that. But she had access to the raw data in real time now.

They'd tracked down the Gulfstream flight crew while she was in the air.

They'd found the driver who'd delivered target to this hotel.

They'd spoken to desk staff and cleaning staff and followed a physical trail out of downtown toward Edgewater, and then, in a routine with which she'd grown well acquainted, target had disappeared.

Like a firefly.

War-room analysis said he'd gotten wind of his cover being blown, that his actions in Prague spoke to inflexibility and aversion to plan deviation, and that he'd still be on his way to DC. They were working to pinpoint whom he'd been sent to kill and, as a precaution, had put out a general alert to the Secret Service and the Capitol Police. Alerting all of Congress was nonviable. The news would inevitably leak, and a media frenzy would follow, and the resulting panic would complicate their job and make it easier for the assassin to carry out his objective.

Analysis of competing hypotheses said the flight to DC had been misdirection, that heavy security at the capitol made DC a less than ideal location, and that because round-the-clock protection was provided only to congressional leadership, non-leadership senators and representatives were softer targets, especially vulnerable while away from the capitol and in their home states. He could have gone anywhere.

She couldn't fault either analysis.

But something more, something abstract wasn't showing up in available data. At its most basic, it was what she'd told Nick before they'd left to recon Republic Square. Target had gone to great lengths to reach that rendezvous, but he didn't trust whomever he'd gone to see. Didn't trust them in Prague and didn't trust them now.

— Didn't trust *who*, exactly?

— Didn't trust them, *why?*

— Because, logically, his employers would want him to succeed.

These actions created inconsistency. What didn't add up in the present somehow tied to the inconsistencies in Republic Square *and* to the shooting in Prague that had taken place the following day.

She'd gotten wind of *that* while she was in Slovakia, holed up in a ski resort, scouring raw data, trying to force logic over senselessness. It'd come in as an unrelated alert, and it'd added another layer of context.

The timing had been too close, the details too similar to Republic Square, to have been coincidental, and so she'd swapped one search for another and found Charles Square, a park that formed the center of a large downtown rectangle not far from Old Town, and she'd found police-scanner transcripts and camera feeds.

The two dead in that shooting were Russian.

They'd been long-distance kills, sniper kills.

And if she'd had any doubt that two shootings in two squares over two days in Prague involving Russians might be coincidence, a glimpse of a blonde — the accomplice, the sister — in the corner of a two-second frame had obliterated doubt and everything else she thought she knew about the day Nick died.

She'd sat there, frozen, staring.

And when she could move again, she enhanced the footage and replayed it, and her own words to Nick came back home.

Everything we've seen, we've seen because that's what he wanted.

First time she'd seen the blonde had been in footage at the Berlin airport.

It'd been *that* footage that had connected

accomplice to target.

Second time she'd seen the blonde had been at Hotel Kings Court.

It was vindication, then, proving she'd been right about the accomplice.

But the same vindication that fed her ego blinded her to what should have been glaringly obvious. The master of disguise had chosen no disguise at all for that distinguishing head of hair.

We've seen because that's what he wanted.

The woman thrown into the van at Hotel Kings Court hadn't been the sister.

The blonde was the misdirection.

— An illusion set up all the way back before Berlin.

But if the blonde was the misdirection, what was she not meant to notice?

— No, not her. The illusion wasn't just for her.

She could see it in her head then, target and body double, misdirection for whoever had grabbed him. The sister had still been running loose. She would have been vindictive, would have wanted her brother back, and it explained how the drama would have carried over into the next day.

— Except the blonde was the one in that two-second frame.

— They'd been long-distance kills, sniper kills.

— The sister hadn't been the one to make them.

— So if not the sister, then who?

For the second time, her words to Nick came home.

Our guy wasn't the only assassin on that Dallas flight.

It made no sense, but the evidence was there, staring her in the face. Christopher Holden, the assassin whose last confirmed target was Karen McFadden, had aligned himself with McFadden's children.

They were dealing with a trifecta.

Not one assassin, three — three who wanted something badly enough to lure her team into that rendezvous — three who trusted the Russians so little, they had expected betrayal and had set up a long-game misdirection to avoid it and then had killed two in retaliation — three who were likely now in the United States, or would be soon, to carry out an assassination, and meanwhile the SIGINT and HUMINT pointing headquarters to target continued to be Russian sourced. . . .

She shut the computer down.

Disconnected. Disengaged. Quit.

Nick's death still sat on her chest like a

hundred-pound weight, and these convolutions were more complex than she had the emotional and mental capacity to process. But that was then.

If she'd been on speaking terms with Hayes or headquarters, if she'd been willing to offer the thoughts inside her head, she'd have said that while Jack very well might have returned to the United States as an assassin, nothing he did was ever straightforward or simple. He was lining up to play them all against each other.

Just like Prague.

She stretched her neck and stretched her arms, adjusted the temperature hotter, and let her mind free-fall, becoming him, trying to see want and fear through his eyes.

Ringing from the room, incessant, persistent, refused to give her that space.

She shut off the shower, pulled a towel off the rack, buried her face in it, and wiped water from her eyes.

The ringing stopped.

She toweled off her hair, slowly, in no hurry.

The war room knew where she was.

For something urgent, they'd call back.

The ringing started up again.

She wrapped the towel around her hair, stepped from steam to the shock of cold, carried the phone back into the bathroom, sat on the toilet lid and, with a puddle pooling around her feet, answered there.

She'd expected Liv Wilson or one of Liv's deputies.

Instead she got Steven Hayes.

He said, "We have a match on target in Dallas, Texas."

The news seeped into her brain, filling the cracks between what she already understood. She hadn't seen the footage, wouldn't conclude prematurely — target may have finally made a mistake and unwittingly pinged their radar, as statistically it was inevitable that he'd eventually slip — but she'd seen enough of this now to know that if it wasn't accidental, and with him it was really damn hard to know what was an accident, then they were meant to see this.

She said, "Where and when?"

"Greyhound. Bus departed for Houston ten minutes ago."

Just like a firefly.

She did the math in her head. Dallas to Houston by bus . . . Depending on stops and average speed, they were looking at roughly four or five hours, give or take.

Hayes said, "We've got a plane on its way to Burke Lakefront. Should be landing within the hour. Equipment and new team members all on board. Briefing material will be to you shortly. Be on the tarmac to meet it."

She ran those numbers, too.

Adding an hour for the plane to arrive and time for departure, Cleveland to Houston was also four or five hours, give or take. Factor in travel within Houston and they'd still be behind him, too slow, too late, chasing blips of light.

There was also the issue of Christopher Holden and the blonde.

They hadn't been spotted since Prague, but that didn't mean they'd vanished. If her theory about the three of them working together held up, then they, too, were headed for the United States, and Jack showing up in Texas pointed to the southern border as their entry point, and what they had on their hands here was a tri-assassin rendezvous, and she was headed straight for that mix.

She said, "This will lead us into another trap."

"We have a terrorist on American soil, preparing to assassinate one of our political leaders," Hayes said. "We don't have the luxury of waiting for ideal circumstances."

The answer made her bristle, not its bite or the condescension that treated her concern as cowardliness, but that, terrorist or not, assassination plot or not, the same foreign operation that had already taken her best friend and half her team *had* moved to US soil, and there were now jurisdictional issues at play and the potential complication of interagency collision or an accidental bullet in her back from local law enforcement responding to the scene of a perceived crime.

None of that seemed to matter.

She chose her words with as much caution as someone used to speaking her mind could summon. "Is the operation still dark?" she said. "Because extrajudicial killing of a US citizen in a high-density urban area carries high risk of civilian injury and heightened exposure to scrutiny."

Hayes said, "We have no record of target as a US citizen."

Kara's breath caught at the flagrant denial.

Data analysis and fact-checking kicked in.

She opened her mouth and shut it again.

This wasn't about facts. Hayes already had the facts.

This was one of those between-the-lines things that people not like her easily grasped, and in catching that, everything she knew, everything she'd experienced, everything she'd learned from Frankfurt to

Vienna flooded her head, reconfiguring and reshaping memory. She understood now, in this instant, the indisputable fact that Hayes, in asking her to fill Nick's shoes, hadn't overlooked the ways not being good with people made her a poor choice for team lead. He'd taken advantage of it.

Her head pounded.

She fought to prevent awareness from seeping into her voice and continued on as if he'd never spoken. "What about jurisdiction?" she said.

"We've got a twenty-four-hour lock. After that, it'll be touch and go."

"Understood," she said, and he ended the call, and she threw the phone hard onto the bed. So much brainpower, so much ability to work with data, and yet only now she *finally* fucking understood.

Nick had wanted her on his team specifically because she was an analyst.

As far as the rest of headquarters was concerned, that made her redundant.

And Aaron, he was new, just a kid, so no great loss to them there.

They'd both just become the sacrificial offering to flush a target.

They were reverse bait playing bait for the trap.

And they were there to take the fall if the

rails collapsed.

She stared at the phone as if it was toxic, trying to find a way through.

She didn't know where the new guys fit into this, didn't care. Far as she was concerned, they were on their way to facilitate the plan that would get her killed. But Aaron, she cared about Aaron. He had every right to know what was about to go down, and telling him would be treason.

CHAPTER 28

Rio Grande Valley, East of Matamoros
Tamaulipas, Mexico

Jill

She crept toward the riverbank, careful to avoid disturbing the marsh grass and desert foliage that grew lush off the rich water supply, and stopped just short of the edge. Behind her, to the left, Holden squatted low, and beside him, José Luis guarded the open-deck kayak he'd carried on foot from where they'd left the truck.

They were about fifteen miles inland from the ocean.

Desert to the south.

Irrigated farmland to the north.

The outskirts of Matamoros, city of half a million, a few miles to the west.

Here the land was quiet and parched and sunbaked, even in winter, even at the banks of the Rio Grande, where the river, nearing

the end of its eighteen-hundred-mile journey to the ocean, meandered in long, lan-
guid curves. The slow-moving water separated border from border.

At this spot it was maybe thirty feet from
bank to bank.

Not much to cross, and yet it was everything.

Four days she'd been on the move, dodging Russians who wanted to control her,
avoiding Americans who wanted to kill her,
hopscotching across Europe, out of Spain,
into the Dominican Republic, and then to
Mexico, traveling dark, until she and Holden
had reached Matamoros, and she'd lost a
day trying to find José Luis.

She'd been forced to use a phone to track
him down.

She was dirty. Tired. Hungry.

Still had no idea what had happened to
her brother, and everything she needed and
wanted was on the other side of a river that
the full might and weight of the United
States worked to prevent people from crossing.

She needed over it tonight.

Not tomorrow, not the day after.

Tonight.

And the problem with urgency, as she
knew well from pain and personal experi-

ence, was it upped the chance of getting caught.

Insects crawled up her legs and biting gnats swarmed her head.

She powered on the drone.

Fingers working the remote control, she sent the little beast with its little burden high up over the water, where it would be hard to see and harder to hear. Twenty-five minutes flying time start to finish was all she'd get.

The sun, low in the sky, would give her less.

Dusk, that perfect mix of low light, which caused detail to blur, and ambient light, which kept night vision from being of much use, was her opportunity window.

She angled the drone, searching the road for border patrol.

Ground sensors worried her less, they were easier to avoid.

The camera picked up a small dirt plume a half mile or so west.

She figured five minutes, give or take, before the border patrol vehicle turned and headed back. Another minute or two before it reached this spot.

She motioned José Luis forward.

The boy picked up the kayak with gangly arms and hauled it toward the water, brushing off Holden's offer to help, insisting again that no one touched the boat but him.

A dead-serious sixteen-year-old warding off a grown man twice his size and with the skills to break him in half made it hard to keep a straight face.

She wouldn't laugh.

The kid had been her gatekeeper since she'd caught his thirteen-year-old hands in her twenty-three-year-old pocket, trying to relieve her of her decoy wallet.

He'd tried to fight her, and she'd knocked him out, then bought him a meal, and after he'd eaten enough to kill a horse, she had insisted he take her to meet his parents, which had turned out to be parent, singular. He'd been the oldest of five living out of a roughshod two-room home that more resembled a shack than a house. She'd left a month's worth of grocery money with his mother, conversing in Spanish, which she'd once spoken more fluently than English, and then hired the kid on as her eyes and ears.

It'd been nearly a year since she'd last seen him, a lifetime for a teenage hustler. She hadn't known if he'd still be around, or alive. He'd rolled up to his mother's place at noon, six inches taller than she remembered, pants too short, shoes too small, wary of Holden like a jealous lover facing competition, and she hadn't known whether to hug him or feed him and had ended up doing both.

Her route would be the same with or without him, but tracking him down had saved her the extra time she'd have needed to go it alone, and had avoided the risk of bringing on someone new.

He settled the kayak broadside against the bank and held it steady against the current. She watched the camera, seconds ticking down inside her head.

Holden boarded.

She tossed him her rucksack and two push poles, handed the remote off to José Luis, clipped a carabiner onto a custom ring at the kayak's tail, double-checked that the line was secure, clipped the line to José Luis's belt, and monkey crawled onto the craft.

Push poles to muddy bottom, she and Holden guided the kayak across, working in tandem, moving three times faster than when she made the crossing alone.

A couple minutes, maybe less, that's all it took.

Behind them, José Luis, eyes in the sky, watched the road.

They reached the northern bank.

José Luis chirped, alerting them to border

patrol approach.

Jill slid from kayak to United States soil, held the craft in place while Holden tossed their belongings off and scurried for land, and she secured the poles to it and let the boat go. The kayak drifted off, nearly the same color as the water, difficult to see in the lowering dusk, and she and Holden lay flat in the foliage, hidden by grasses, silent, killing time in the wait for the all clear.

An engine approached. Wheels against dirt and gravel rolled slowly past.

Another couple minutes ticked by.

José Luis chirped again.

She stood and led Holden on, through the foliage and onto the road, as if she belonged — which she did — and across to a fallow field, and from there to a footpath. Behind her, somewhere in the dark, José Luis brought the drone back to its starting place and hauled the kayak out of the water, and he'd soon be strapping the watercraft into the back of his thirty-year-old F-150 and returning to his mother's cinder-block house on the outskirts of town. And in the coming weeks, construction on the last room would be finished, and the exterior would be plastered and painted, and a new pump on the well would go in, and he'd have made his mother proud. This was why it didn't matter if another year passed before she saw him again, or if she never saw him again.

The kayak would be waiting, as would the drone.

She led Holden a quarter mile northwest, to a well-lit, low-slung farmhouse surrounded by irrigated land. Three well-fed dogs came to greet her, circling, tails wagging, checking out Holden's legs and shoes, and when the butt sniffing had gone on long enough, she continued around to the back, where a forty-foot fifth wheel was parked on a concrete pad, up against a recently stained deck.

Beside the deck stood a small carport, a five-year-old Fiesta beneath.

She strolled past the car and up to the deck, ran her fingers beneath the handrail, found the key hooked in place — signal that no one had come asking questions — and she unlocked the trailer door, flipped on a light, swept a hand forward in welcome and, speaking the first words in hours, said, "Home, sweet home."

Holden stepped inside.

She followed him in.

Temperatures in the valley rarely dropped below fifty, even in the heart of winter, and the trailer, having been closed up for the past several months, had a sunbaked, stale-air, mold-tinged taste to it. She powered up the air conditioner.

"Give it a few minutes," she said. "It'll clear out pretty fast."

She reached into a cabinet and pulled out a clean towel, offered it to him. "A little musty," she said. "Humidity is hard to fight down here."

Holden took the towel, and his gaze tracked along the interior.

If thought bubbles could appear above a person's head, his would have read, *Cozy, clean, all the necessities of home, but not a home.*

Humans were pack rats by nature.

Small, tight spaces were difficult to keep tidy.

The lack of life detritus was a giveaway.

She pointed him toward the bathroom. "Shower's in there, if you don't mind cold water. I'll get the heater pilot light lit soon as I've said hi to the parents and let them know it's me."

He looked at her funny, but *parents* wasn't something she wanted to explain.

Clare had her stashes, Holden had safe houses — surely, he did — Jack had safety valves she couldn't even pretend to guess at, and she had Paul and Janet Moore, parents without living children, grand-parents with two grown grandbabies now out of state, fifth- and sixth-generation Texans, who years ago had found their home in a sudden no-man's-land when one of the first border fences, a tall, slatted metal monstrosity, cut a swath through their property.

They weren't naive enough to think of her as the daughter they'd lost, and she wasn't innocent enough to view them as the parents she never had, but they were retirees on a fixed income, and she had more than enough money to share, and she needed a legitimate reason to hang out on this side of the fence when she needed access to the river, and they were content to let her come and go as she pleased.

The situation worked out well for everyone for as long as it did.

She knocked on the back door, waited for an answer and, when none was forthcoming, checked the garage. The truck was gone, they were out.

She continued around to the front porch, turned the door knocker up, and returned to the trailer or, more specifically, to the Fiesta under the carport and its key beneath the passenger seat. She tried the ignition, got nothing, and so lugged the battery charger and extension cord out from trailer storage, hooked that up, and returned inside to now-conditioned air and a chance to catch her breath and finally stop moving.

Holden was out of the shower when she walked in. Hair wet, towel low around his waist, chiseled abs still damp as he dug through his bag on the dining table.

She paused at the threshold, glanced at him, sighed on the inside, and turned away.

He said, "Got the tank heater going. Water's not hot yet, but not cold, either."

She pulled a drawer open, grabbed a clean T-shirt and sweats.

"Thanks," she said.

He said, "Your parents okay?"

She kept her back to him. "They're out. I'll check in on them in the morning. Battery on the Fiesta was dead. I've got it charging."

He said, "The car yours?"

She glanced over her shoulder. He'd added a shirt, was still wearing the towel, and damn if she didn't still want to rip it off with her teeth.

"Define *yours,*" she said. "I have free use of it."

He nodded appreciatively. "I like it," he said. "Mostly farmland, not a lot of eyes, United States soil but south of the fence.

There's an unmanned pass-through, right? Motorized gates, keypads, secret codes, so citizens who live this side can get into town?"

"Nearest gate's right down the road that-away," she said.

"You have the code?"

"Of course."

"And that's linked to Homeland Security records for . . . ?"

She returned to digging through the drawer. "A girl's gotta have some secrets," she said. "I'm sure you've got your own backdoor route."

"Canada sometimes. Usually through the islands into South Florida."

"You have a boat?"

"Same way you have a car."

"Cars."

"Well, just one boat."

She turned. The towel had been replaced with track pants.

She moved next to him and hip bumped him away from the table. "Need to get something out of storage," she said.

He dragged his bag to the floor and stepped aside.

She lifted the dinette bench. Boxes of unused equipment waited below, phones and laptops mostly, most of them of dubious provenance, bought cheap for quick cash, and accumulated over time.

Holden let out a low whistle. "What's on the other side?"

She tipped her chin in its direction, inviting him to look.

He raised the bench to a small armory.

She pulled an iPad mini from inventory, closed the bench, and sat on it.

Priorities were priorities, and one final obligation stood between her and washing off the road stench and crawling into bed.

She unboxed the device.

Holden watched her.

She motioned to the weapons. "Take a few pieces, if it'll help you sleep better." She wasn't being facetious or patronizing.

Utilizing air travel had meant leaving all the firepower behind in Madrid.

Holden had made a few calls, had told her he would put the weapons in the hands of someone he trusted, had given her a number and a name, and had promised they'd be waiting whenever she was ready to collect them, which would be sooner than later, because she still needed to get them back to Berlin before Clare discovered them missing.

This was her returning the favor.

Holden picked up the Desert Eagle,

turned it over, glanced at her, and she nodded. He added a couple magazines, a box of ammunition, and lowered the bench.

She tuned him out.

Four days of traveling dark meant four days of not knowing if brother dearest had attempted contact. If Jack was alive and if he was free — as Holden believed he would be — then there would be a message for her out there somewhere. To check just this once, and to respond once, a VPN and TOR browser on a clean device over a borrowed satellite connection was enough to avoid worrying about drawing the cavalry to her door.

Holden encroached on her peripheral space.

He said, "May I?"

She scooted over to make room and continued with the setup, loaded the browser, and began the search, hunting through gig-economy Web sites and message boards — Fiverr, TaskRabbit, Craigslist — searching for Dallas–Fort Worth postings when possible, because that was the last place stateside she and Jack had seen each other face-to-face, and that was how these things worked.

She found him in a miscellaneous Craigslist post.

Seeing his words, knowing without a doubt he was alive brought just enough relief to piss her off and make her angry again.

She said, "John wants to rendezvous in San Antonio day after tomorrow, and his grand strategy is playing bait and catch with the bad guys."

Holden squinted at the screen, as if trying to make sense of tea leaves.

She shifted the device so he had a better view of what she'd read.

Looking for someone with an archeological background or who specializes in South American history to check out an artifact my grandfather brought back from Bolivia when he was a kid. Photo is for attention. Will send pictures of the actual artifact once we have a chance to discuss. Willing to compensate for time and travel (if necessary). Need this done within the next three days. Best time to call is evenings, after 7:00.

Holden whispered each word out loud. In his distraction the accent broke through, the one from the life before, which normally stayed buried beneath the American years, the one she'd first heard when he'd taunted her from the upper floor on the day she'd gone after him to kill him.

He leaned sideways and looked at her, bewildered.

"This, you've got to explain," he said.

His tone held admiration and respect.

Both flooded her senses with warning and the urgent need to fight or flee.

She focused on the screen, rested her fingers on the table, trying to reconcile the conflict between mind and body that made it difficult to stay as they were, with skin nearly touching skin. Twenty-six years of Clare's tutelage and its aftermath had taught her how to hide, how to kill, and how to keep anguish at bay.

She knew hate and knew hunger.

Knew rejection and how to suffocate pain.

What she didn't know was what it meant to be accepted as enough, and Holden's words, the way he spoke, and the way he looked at her triggered every need to fend off threat, because this *shouldn't be.*

He shifted to give her space. "Archeology?" he said.

Instinct took over, the cunning that let her give others what they needed to see and hear. A slow smile lifted her expression, and with the eagerness of a kid asked to explain an art project after the first day of school, she said, "It's one of several words that let us search without getting a ton of false hits."

She scrolled for the attached photo, a watermarked image of Japanese macaques in a hot spring. "To anyone else, this is just random stock photography," she said, "but it references an inside joke from when we were kids that only I would know. It's a secret handshake. Between that and the words, there's no doubt it's him. As for the timing, he posted the message yesterday. *Three days* is self-explanatory. *Travel, if necessary,* means he isn't certain where we actually are. Basically, he's hoping we see this and that we can make it there in time. The artifact stuff, that's all throwaway language, but Bolivia is a reference to when we were fourteen and Clare threw us into a live-fire ambush, using a mercenary team for the first time.

"I mean, we'd worked under live fire before, and we'd been ambushed before, but never both by strangers at the same time. We were in this small town north of La Paz. Clare had gone off to do whatever Clare did, and we thought we were settled in for a typical wait. We had supplies and money, but not much in the way of weapons. That was the thing about her. She trained us incessantly in how to use them, but she never actually let us carry, so when the ambush hit, we were completely outgunned. We'd been trained hard enough at that point that we got out of the house fairly easily. We carried bags, tool bags . . . God, I can't believe I'm telling you all this. It's embarrassing."

"No," he said. "It's fascinating. Please don't stop."

She sighed. "Okay. So, tool bags were the essentials. We could live for weeks, months with everything in them. We made it out with those and not a lot else and headed farther up the highlands. But these guys, they were hard core, and we were tired of being fucked with. John didn't want to spend the next few weeks on the rough if this was just more of Clare's bullshit. The way he saw it, these guys knew we were kids, and they were fighting for money, so the easiest way to end it was to figure out their lead and snatch him — torture him if we had to — to find out who'd hired him. John figured if it was Clare they were working for, we could kick the guy in the nuts and send him on his way, and if it was someone else, we'd cut off his nuts and save them for Clare."

"That's it?"

"Yeah, that was it."

"No, what happened?"

"Oh. Well, we set a trap, used me as bait — I was always the bait — and worked our way up the food chain. Once we had one of them, we had access to their coms and we used that to lure in their commander. Once we had him, we rigged a pulley system and roped him upside down off a tree. Jack lit a fire beneath him and just kept adding sticks. Didn't take long before the guy offered up the number Clare used to communicate with him and gave us the city she'd hired him out of. It took a bit of sleuthing on our part to hunt her down, but the story ended with us waiting for her in her hotel room and me putting a gun to her head."

Holden stared.

"Yeah, fucked up, I know. For what it's worth, the gun wasn't loaded. I did shoot her later, but that's another story. Anyway, Bolivia is John's strategy." She tapped the contact information link. "The phone number has a San Antonio area code. Hundred bucks says it rings to a real location and gives us our rendezvous point."

Holden said, "And we meet at seven in the evening."

"Yep. Easy peasy. I'll call the number tomorrow. See where it leads."

She closed the browser, as if that was all,

413

but it wasn't all.

The post was missing context for who they'd be baiting or, more specifically, what the endgame might be. Jack wasn't the type to inadvertently leave out that kind of detail, which meant he was handling it, and as much as she trusted the strategist in him the way she always had, she also didn't. Not just because he had gone rogue in Prague and cut her out and was now forcing her to fly blind, but because Bolivia was a one-off scenario. It'd worked because they were fourteen, and because they were up against mercenaries, not patriots defending their homeland, and because no matter how lucky they might have been that Clare hadn't accidentally gotten them dead, they'd always been able to count on knowing that in her own messed-up way, she was trying to keep them alive. This was different.

She'd warned him that trying to play it both ways was going to get them killed. This would be so much easier without Clare as an unknown.

Holden said, "Whatever it is you're not saying, it's only fair I know."

He was right, but that was more than she had energy to deal with, so she gave him the half-truth. "I've posted a few of these for Clare," she said. "I'm sure John has done the same. There's been no response. Part of me is certain that once we get to the end of this, there'll be no Dmitry, just her and another lecture on everything I did wrong, and John will get the credit for the successes, and whether we win or lose, I lose and he wins. Again."

Holden nudged his shoulder into hers.

She looked over at him.

"You were dealt a shitty hand," he said. "For your sake, I'm sorry. But selfishly, what you lived through made you who you are, and I happen to like who you are. I mean, I hate that you had to go through it, but there's this version of you on the other side . . ."

She put a finger to his lips and shushed him.

She knew where this was headed, and it set off all the same fire alarms as before. She wasn't ready to go there now or maybe ever. She said, "What were you up to at fourteen? Pickpocketing tourists in Bogotá?"

He chuckled. "*That* story needs more time than we've got tonight."

"Oh, you're gonna make me fight you for it?"

He slid off the bench. "You'd need a tree

branch, pulley system, and a fire. Nothing less."

She scooted out behind him, pulled a clean towel from the cupboard, waited till his back was turned, and mock lunged in his direction.

His reflexes were faster than she remembered.

He caught her wrist, spun her round, and locked an arm around her neck.

Instinct overrode playfulness.

She flipped him hard onto his back.

He took her down with him.

The whole trailer shook, and the floor groaned.

She froze, tight up against his side, half on top of him, half on the floor.

In stillness there was his breathing and hers, his heartbeat and hers, and the terrifying sense of losing control. She let go and pulled herself up, grabbed the towel and clean clothes, and strode for the bathroom.

He called after her.

She stopped. Didn't turn.

He said, "Are you planning to play fair when we meet your brother?"

The question, out of the blue, threw her.

She could lie, but they both knew she wasn't yet ready to forgive.

She'd gone along with Jack's plan in

Prague and called the Russians because Jiminy Cricket here wouldn't stop reminding her that her brother hadn't acted in a vacuum and that, as much as she hated what he'd done and what he'd continue to do, she didn't want him dead. But what Jack had asked of her wasn't just a phone call. The Russians wanted an assassination, and until she knew Jack was clear, that meant following through, which meant going to the trouble and expense of sneaking back into the United States so she could put a bullet between the eyes of the goddamn Speaker of the House, all to support whatever he'd gotten himself into behind her back.

So much depended on if his explanation matched this bullshit.

"I don't know," she said, and she started forward again, frustrated, irritated at Holden, at her brother, at the world.

Holden said, "Hey."

She stopped again. This time she turned.

He was still on the floor, on his back, where he'd fallen.

"What?" she said.

He propped up on an elbow, glanced at the fifth-wheel overhang, said, "There's only one bed up there." He nodded toward the sofa in the slide out. "If you've got extra sheets . . . ?"

She debated. Long and hard, she debated.

"Bed up there is big enough for two," she said, "but keep to your side. Much as I want to shoot you, I don't want to do it in my sleep."

CHAPTER 29

San Antonio Museum of Art
San Antonio, Texas, USA

Holden

She turned the Fiesta off the street into a half-empty lot across from the museum, pulled into the nearest parking spot, and shut off the engine, then flashed a teasing smile, leaned over the center console, put her head in his lap, reached between his legs, and stuffed the keys up under the seat, somewhere in the cushion. She took her sweet time about it, too, as if she didn't know what she was doing and as if trying to get a reaction wasn't her idea of entertainment.

She was bad in that way, relentless, and he loved that about her, just hated that it came as part of another rotation through a revolving personality door.

That had started yesterday morning.

The farther they'd gotten from the border, the worse the cycling had become.

She'd been real, honest, and genuinely human one moment, shut off, brusque, and sullen the next, and twenty miles later out had come the flirtatious coquette.

Confusing as hell, but what he minded more was the way she'd also become evasive, doling out information as control and reward, twisting truth to where it became difficult to tell where the lie began, making it hard to figure out what exactly was going on inside that head of hers and even harder to trust her.

He'd known she'd eventually slip into that mode.

Just hadn't expected it this soon.

She disentangled from his lap, offered a mischievous smile, grabbed a purse off the backseat, and stepped out of the car.

He followed her lead.

She looked nice — stunning, really — dark brown hair, mid-thigh, figure-hugging dress with over-the-knee boots that she'd picked up during the same shopping spree that had put him in a button-down shirt, jeans, and dress shoes.

He'd cleaned up okay.

Not as nicely as she had, but more eyes on her meant fewer on him, and under the circumstances, he preferred it that way.

She linked her arm in his and led him toward the museum.

They were a good thirty-minute walk from where they needed to be in the city center. With her in heels, that might be a generous estimate. She hadn't explained why she'd brought him here instead, and he hadn't asked, because he had no tolerance for the head games, and every request he made gave her another opportunity to withhold information and lie.

He reached the museum door, held it open. She squeezed his bicep, headed past him for the admission desk, and paid the entry for two.

It was five in the afternoon now.

Museum doors stayed open till nine.

Rendezvous was at seven, at a restaurant in the heart of downtown, not far from the Alamo, right smack in the heart of the city's tourist mecca. He knew that much because two hours out of Brownsville, she'd pulled off the road and called the number on the Craigslist post and, after she'd hung up, said, "River Walk. You ever been there?"

He'd seen pictures.

As far as he'd been concerned, that was as close as he needed to get — to the River Walk or the Alamo or anywhere else that at-

421

tracted slow-moving, selfie-snapping hordes by the thousands. If the point of a place was in the experience, he'd had enough of that to satisfy two lifetimes. He'd suspected it'd be much the same for Jack, which had raised questions about why he'd choose the most tourist-infested part of town over a quiet resort or a nature trail or, heck, even a museum.

Jill, tracing her finger in a daisy-chain loop along the edge of the steering wheel, had answered the unasked. "He knows that if we meet in private, I'd greet him with a punch in the face and possibly break his arm. He figures the more public the place, the better chance he has of me behaving. Having you there is a backup, because he thinks me causing a scene in front of you would embarrass me enough not to do it."

Holden ignored what was written between those lines.

He said, "Is he right?"

Her finger continued tracing. "I'd much rather meet him alone than with you there, so yeah, probably."

Holden took her hand, held her fingers, waiting for her to look at him, and when her gaze tracked over to his, said, "Listen, if you need to fight him to make it better, by all means get it out of your system. But

422

that's going to create exposure that puts us all at risk — me included — and I don't want to be there when it happens."

"I'll behave in public," she said.

"I have your word?"

She had given him that, but hadn't given him the name of the rendezvous location until they'd settled in at the rental secured off Airbnb, a one-bed, one-bath rural cabin on the north edge of town that didn't require ID verification and had keyless check-in. She'd tossed the restaurant name out in passing, as if she'd already mentioned it hours ago, as if he'd automatically know what she was talking about.

Which he had, but that had been beside the point.

He'd stood, picked up his jacket.

She said, "Where are you going?"

"Need to see the river," he said. "Map the area."

She cocked her head and studied him. "John's not going to sell us out."

He strapped on the Desert Eagle. "It's not him I worry about."

"We weren't tracked here, either."

He leaned down and kissed her forehead. "You, my dear, might be fully comfortable walking into unfamiliar territory and improvising your way out, but I like to know where the exits are."

She stretched out on the bed like a long cat exposing its belly, daring a hand to touch it, and said, "Are you coming back? Or do I have to come find you?"

"Would you?" he said.

She offered a sly smile. "I think so."

That was probably the last bit of truth he'd gotten out of her.

She led him now in a slow stroll through the museum, down hallways and past exhibits, then out the back and along a walkway toward the river.

He understood then.

The museum provided free parking, a place to stash the car. The river taxi that passed by once an hour provided a way into town that bypassed the traffic and the camera grid. A simple plan. Easy. Convenient. It'd have been simpler and easier and more convenient if she hadn't tried to turn it into a power play.

The flat-bottomed boat took them south along landscaped hike trails and bike trails, past overlooks and beneath pedestrian bridges, then through floodgates into the downtown loop, where the roar of music rose and crowds thickened and colorful seasonal lights draped bridges and filled the branches of hundred-year-old cypress trees, and let them out a stone's throw from their destination.

The boarding zone and the bridge became bottlenecks.

Bodies clustered, hemming him in.

His insides tensed, the whole of him uneasy in the thick, where the human press made it possible for an unknown assailant to get in tight for an up-close kill.

She glanced back, grabbed his hand, threaded her fingers between his, and pulled him along, navigating the throng like a shark through territorial waters. She'd flipped again, offering a warm, playful version of herself, not so much real as needing him to believe it was real, and she led him off the walking path onto a sectioned-off patio, where, putting on airs for the young twentysomething at the hostess station, she plied a drawl so thick he'd only ever heard similar in movies and on ranches and in sororities.

"We're here to meet someone?" she said. "Bolivia, I think?"

They were early, even with the stroll through the museum, the wait for the taxi, the slow ride into town, and fighting to move through the Friday evening throng. But the hostess smiled, as if she knew exactly what Jill intended, and handed them off to a server, who led them away from the low, rumbling roar to a quiet interior, where the decor and dishes were high end, and the tables spaced widely enough to allow room to breathe.

Tension eased. Holden's hands relaxed.

He followed around a wall to the far back corner, where a Hispanic brunette in a maxi dress sat alone, looking over a menu, nails impeccable, makeup flawless, and Holden recognized the face, because its twin currently led him by the hand.

In the shock of the unexpected, a laugh escaped.

Jack glanced up, smiled, and stood, every movement perfect.

He leaned out to hug his sister, and surprisingly, Jill let him.

And he offered a feminine hand in Holden's direction.

Holden shook, and only then did the facade break.

Eyes that had been smiling hardened. Delicate grip turned firm. "Thank you," Jack said. "I appreciate you coming." The sincerity beneath the words was a gut punch that spoke of a man who'd truly believed he'd lost his sister and who credited Holden for bringing her to him.

Holden clasped left hand over right. Lips tight, he nodded.

Nothing needed to be said.

It was what it was, and that was enough.

Jack let go and sat.

Jill leaned over him and, in a low growl, said, "Apologize."

The server, catching the mood, said she'd be right back.

Jack flipped tresses over his shoulder.

"I'll apologize properly when I can," he said. "Words will have to do for now." He paused for emphasis. "I'm sorry. I hope one day you'll let me explain, and maybe one day after that, forgive me."

The anger went out of her like air in a deflating balloon.

She sat, and Holden followed, and he made a finger circle in Jack's direction and said, "What's with the . . . ?"

Jack went back to studying the menu. "Drag makes the best disguises." And after a disbelieving beat, "My choices were either do this using Clare's ID or ride the hobo rails. I've gone soft for pillows, so Clare it was."

Jill said, "Which stash did you raid?"

"Cleveland."

"Clear it all out?"

"Every bit of it."

"Clare knows?"

"I'll tell her after, assuming we live."

"Still no word from her?"

"No. But this isn't her doing."

Jill looked askance at him, as if she wanted to believe but couldn't, and that brought a pause to the rapid-fire volley, which would've felt like the lead-up to a fight if Holden hadn't seen it before and known it as a high-speed debriefing.

He shifted, got comfortable, kept quiet.

If the past was any indication, these two were just getting started.

Jack said, "I'm not saying she doesn't know. She very well might be hanging around, watching the whole thing unfold. Hell, for all I know, she's got a line tapped right into it, but one hundred percent, no doubt, she's not the one driving it."

The server returned, interrupting the conversation before it had a chance to get going again. Jack handed his menu to her and, without the slightest bit of apology, placed an order for the table. He waited until she'd gone, said, "We don't have a lot of time, and there's a lot to cover." Then, turning to Jill and picking up where he'd left off, said, "Dmitry, the DNA donor, exists. He was the source of our tickets and the original invitation. I don't know who he is and don't know where he is. But he *is* alive, and he's not our enemy."

Jill said, "Proof."

"A collection of documents that go back fifteen, twenty years — birth certificates, handwritten notes, times, dates, sightings — curated with the meticulous detail of someone who had a personal interest in finding us."

Jill said, "Source."

"Emotional blackmail handed to me by the guys who sideswiped him."

She said, "Source."

"Kremlin. Maybe GRU. Can't confirm."

She said, "Motive."

"Active measures."

She sighed. Sat back, slouched, and crossed her arms.

Jack said, "And I'm near certain the solitary spotter in Frankfurt was Dmitry."

Jill's eyebrows lifted in question.

He said, "Once all the other pieces connect, I can't see it any other way. Clare might have dropped off radar within the US intelligence community, but Moscow hasn't forgotten. In their eyes she extends to her kids. So going back to the beginning, right? Dmitry's high enough up the food chain that he can afford the risk of ignoring policy in regards to her as long as no one takes an interest in what he's done, so he sends us an invite. We say yes. But then, oops, the

429

Broker gets dead.

"That throws Moscow into turmoil.

"They've had a long-game strategy in play and an assassination about to go down, but every intelligence agency is now out for blood, and their go is now no-go. They're looking for a way to salvage it. Enter Clare's kids, whom they know how to find — thank you, Dmitry — and whom they feel they have dibs on because of Clare's past. Not only are these kids American, but they've also been trained by one of the best, and Moscow knows this — thank you, renegade sister working favors for the Broker.

"The invitation has been sent. The kids are *already* on their way to meet a father they've never met. So, whoever's managing the now no-go operation inserts into Dmitry's business. Dmitry's not untouchable. He doesn't have the power to complain, not if he doesn't want to get dead, too, so the scenario shifts. The guy who metaphorically stood in the midst of a battle and raised a white flag to force a cease-fire so the kids he's been looking for since birth didn't die before he had a chance to meet them, has the whole thing yanked out of his hands by overlords who've gotten other ideas. What's someone in a position like that do?"

"I don't know about him," Jill said, "but I

430

know Clare would have counted on us being smart enough to figure out what was happening and probably would have found a way to follow close, ready to interfere if things got out of hand."

"Ergo, Dmitry in Frankfurt," he said. "But then the Americans showed up, and that complicated things beyond his ability to meddle. I can't prove it, but I think the Russians waiting at the Berlin airport were his guys, too. That's as far as he gets."

"What about Clare?"

"She's got more vested in finding Dmitry than we ever did. If I had to put money on it, I'd say she's in Moscow, and the reason we haven't heard from her is that, well, she's in Moscow."

The siblings glanced at each other. A pall fell over the table, and in that break of silence, the server arrived with drinks and appetizers, and Jill's assessment of Jack filled Holden's head.

John wants this thing with Dmitry more than he's ever wanted anything.

He understood now why Jack had gone to the effort of bringing them all together face-to-face. Dmitry, the question the twins had set out to Europe to answer, had become Dmitry the sword hanging over their heads.

Holden said, "Who's your target, John?"

"Senator Kenyon, but it doesn't really matter. Moscow sacrificed me as a decoy within hours of touching down. Who they really want dead is" — he looked at Jill — "who exactly?"

"Speaker of the House."

Jack let out a low whistle. He glanced at his nails. "Gonna be a whole something else trying to pull that off. It's almost like Moscow had some backward idea about which one of us was made for the harder stuff."

She kicked him under the table but grinned as she did it.

Holden studied brother, then sister and pondered the dilemma.

Assassination wouldn't weigh heavy on the conscience — certainly not on his or Jill's — and whatever it weighed on Jack's wouldn't be enough to offset the risk to someone he cared about. But they were also smart enough to understand that in doing this, they'd press thumbs hard on the world's political scales, and there was a difference between indifference and being the spark that ignited civil war.

He said, "Is Dmitry worth it?"

Jack said, "That's not the question that needs answering."

Holden laced fingers and rested hands on

the table.

Jill crossed her arms again.

Jack said, "From a purely self-preservation perspective, right? We've got the Americans, we've got the Russians, and we've got ourselves caught in the middle. Whether we do or we don't, the Americans consider us a threat and want us dead, so they don't factor. That leaves the Russians. If we don't do this, they're also going to want us dead, and we can pretty much write off ever meeting Dmitry, which means we basically get to repeat Clare's life for the past twentysomething years.

"If we do go through with this, we keep the possibility of meeting Dmitry open, and assuming we survive, we'll have a safe haven in Russia. Problem then becomes the Russians own us, and there will always be one more thing they need us to do. And there's also the inconvenient fact that the whole reason the Americans are trying to kill me in the first place is that the Russians pointed them my way."

Jill said, "Seriously?"

"Gave them my flight details out of Dallas. There's a kill team in Houston now, waiting for me to surface."

She said, "You led them there."

"I did."

"So you're saying what? We do a Clare, twist this to our advantage?"

"No. Clare spent her best years paranoid and on the run. To come out on top, we've got to arrange the board so the powers that be are better served by keeping us alive. It's not Clare we want to pattern after. It's the Broker."

Holden said, "You see a way to do that?"

"Yeah," Jack said. He looked right at him. "Bolivia."

CHAPTER 30

Prospect Hill, San Antonio
Texas, USA

Holden

Three miles west as the crow flew, a ten-minute drive from the downtown River Walk or, if one was inclined to travel on foot, a straight-line one-hour stroll, the city had another face, a poor and tired face that even few denizens ever saw. Here, chain-link-lined houses were old and small and proudly maintained, and the streets were cracked, and windows barred or boarded up, and favors in any flavor were cheap and easily found, and rooms could be had for thirty dollars a night instead of hundreds.

Here was where Jack would trip the radar.

The motel he'd chosen was more of a compound than a building, two old bright blue cinder-block structures set perpendicular to each other on a corner lot surrounded

435

by a weed-strewn privacy fence with just a single entrance. Across the street a convenience-store rooftop offered a direct view into the compound and a clean line of sight on half the doors and windows.

It was a perfect setup for suicide by sniper. The kind of place anyone with a modicum of tactical sense would avoid, even if they didn't have a target on their back. That they'd come here deliberately screamed trap so loudly that about the only thing they could have done to be more blatant was add an Acme arrow and a birdseed sign.

"Mental games upon mental games," Jack had said.

By his reasoning, the kill team expected a trap regardless. Making it obvious would mess with their equilibrium, and the vulnerability worked both ways once the attackers got beyond the fence. So, here they were in the middle of a gallery, waiting for the shooting to start.

Jack had already gone.

Holden was on the bed, killing time by studying watermarks on the ceiling, and Jill sat in the corner chair, working something over on a notepad.

They had arrived together in Jill's Fiesta, the three of them, and had unloaded the trunk onto the bed, adding to what Jack had retrieved from the sizable stash they'd left behind in Houston last month. The X-Caliber was what he'd gone for, a gauged and scoped CO_2 projector used for tranquilizing large animals from a distance.

The rifle was part of the history that had brought them together, and it felt right having it here, more so given that this time it'd be in Holden's own hands.

Jack had dosed the syringes for weight in twenty-pound increments and had labeled each accordingly. Too much and Holden would kill the killer, too low and the killer would feel nice and happy while trying to kill him.

Eyeballing for accuracy was the best he could do.

Jack had run them through a map of nearby buildings and the surrounding streets, diagramming positions and strategies the way he'd mapped out Republic Square in Prague, and they had gone into crawl spaces and had timed distance, and when they'd prepared as much as they could, Jack had tripped the countdown, taken the car, and gone.

The kill team would come, because they had no choice but to come.

When and how many and how hard the fight, were yet to be determined.

Holden had spent the first hour disassembling, cleaning, reassembling, and loading weapons, busy work that didn't substitute for boresighting and zeroing a scope and making a rifle his own, but it had kept him occupied to a point. He was a mechanic relying on another man's tools, and on a high-stakes night like tonight, where an inch could mean the difference between life and death, it left him with a sense of foreboding and dread.

That wasn't helped by whatever was going on with Jill, who hadn't volunteered a word to him since leaving the restaurant and had met each attempt at conversation with deliberate monosyllabic indifference.

If she were anyone else, if there wasn't so much riding on his participation this evening, he'd have already gotten up and left.

Instead he shoved a pillow beneath his head and closed his eyes.

The silence dragged on.

He had no patience for passive aggression, not even on a good day.

Jill left the chair and dug through a bag, carried it to the sink area, dumped the whole thing on the floor in a clattering heap, and repacked it, each movement louder and more extreme than the last.

Holden said, "You wanna talk about it, or

do you prefer throwing things?"

She pulled out whatever she'd just stuffed in the bag, and shoved it back. Voice sweet, mellow, she said, "Talk about what?"

"The jealousy," he said.

"Oh?" she said. "What are you jealous about?"

Holden opened an eye, followed her a bit, and closed it again.

The closer they'd gotten to San Antonio — the closer to Jack — the odder she'd behaved, and he'd seen the way her face darkened when Jack had shaken his hand, and was aware of how she'd grown sullen every time Jack had spoken to him directly, and of the subtle attempts to cut him out of the discussion, as if strategy talk was meant for just her and her brother. For someone who'd spent a lifetime wearing character masks and disguises, she was easy to see through when she thought no one was looking.

He said, "My friendship with your brother takes nothing away from you."

She said, "Whatever that's supposed to mean."

He sat up and swiveled to face her. "What is it you need to be happy? You want me to stop speaking with John? Ignore him, refuse to respect him, not be his friend?"

She looked him dead in the face and, with spite he'd never heard out of her, not even in Prague, when she'd been murderously angry, said, "I want him to not win."

It took a beat to process that.

"Win?" he said. "Is that what I am to you? Some object or trophy you've claimed, and that you're afraid your brother is going to take away?"

She went back to stuffing the bag.

He said, "You're a vortex, Julia, sucking everything into your storm, destroying anything you could possibly have that's good, and it'll never stop until you're willing to face the thing that scares you so bad."

Her lip curled in visible disgust. "I'm not afraid of anything."

"Oh, but you are. Fear drives everything you do."

"All right, smart-ass," she said. "What's it I'm so afraid of?"

"That maybe your mother was right."

She glared, and he hesitated, truly pained, because the things he'd say would hurt, and she'd had enough hurt in her life, and he didn't want to be the one to add to it, but she needed to hear it, and he might be the only one who ever had the chance.

"You spend so much energy taking from your brother, not because you want what he has, but because you don't want him to have what you don't, as if keeping him from having will keep him from being worth more than you. You treat relationships, connections, people, as if they're disposable, because it's safer that way because no one can ever confirm how little you matter if you never let them matter in the first place. And Dmitry, you're terrified John might actually find him, because what would it say about you if after all these years, it turns out even your own father loves him more?"

With each added word, the whole of her had darkened.

Her fists had clenched. Her jaw had clenched.

She'd stood and inched toward him, and he'd kept going, because this would be the one and only time he could say what needed saying, and he had to say it all, but on that last sentence she came at him, swinging.

He dodged the first hit. Dodged the second.

Clipped her hard on the third, and she went out cold.

He shook his hand, irritated at himself, not for hitting her, per se — in a world like this, notions of chivalry were sexist bullshit that'd get a man killed — but because genuine connections in this life were hard to find, and he genuinely liked her, and he'd hoped . . . he'd hoped. But this was too toxic, even for him.

He flexed his fingers.

His knuckles were already bruising. He knew better than to use his hands. A head like hers, he was lucky if he didn't fracture something.

She groaned, rolled to her back, and opened her eyes.

He stood over her, scanned her over to be sure she was okay, and said, "You've forgotten who the fuck you're dealing with."

She pulled herself up and stayed motionless for a woozy minute.

He kept a cautious distance, dug a bandage out of his bag and, wrapping his hand, said, "Just because I like you, just because I *get* you, doesn't mean I'm your doormat. You want to hurt me, you're going to have to find a better way to do it."

She moved to the chair and sat, sizing him up, and he could see her brain plotting, scheming, unable or unwilling to quit, because all she knew was how to brawl dirty and she had no concept of tapping out.

"Don't make me fight you," he said. "The last thing I want is to hurt you — it's the whole fucking opposite of what I want — but I will if I have to, and that's not how you want this to end."

He wrapped a final twist and tucked the bandage tail under.

"You had a shitty childhood," he said. "You were treated horribly, unfairly, abusively, but you know? At least you had a family. Your mother, brother, they might be crap at showing it, but they actually do love you."

"I don't have to listen to this," she said.

"No," he said. "You don't." He reached for his bag, tossed it on the bed, dumped in the shirts he'd left hanging over the floor lamp. "If you're happy with your life the way it is, you don't need me in it."

"You're right," she said. "I don't need you."

He zipped the bag shut. Strode to the bathroom, flipped on the light, checked for anything he might have missed, flipped it off, headed for the door, and stopped there, facing it. He said, "You think I don't know what it's like to fear abandonment? I never knew my father, and the only memory I have of my mother is her bullet-riddled body. I was handed over as a trophy to the guy who ordered her dead, and he left me to wander his villa like a dog. I would have starved if not for the maids who snuck me food, or died from exposure if they hadn't brought the little they could spare from their own homes until I was old enough to learn how to steal for myself.

"Me as a fourteen-year-old? Yeah, I *was* pickpocketing on the streets of Bogotá, and also hiding from the murderous bastards trying to claim the bounty put on my head because I'd gutted the asshole who'd had my mother killed. Do you have any idea what I would have done to have someone — just one person — who saw me as more than trash? Who loved me enough to push me the way Clare pushed you? Your mother can't undo the past. Your brother can't undo the past, but the past is where the best parts of you still live."

He reached for the door handle.

She said, "Stay. Stay a little longer."

Debate tore through him, agonizing debate.

He said, "You're fascinating and brilliant, you're funny, beautiful, and fucking insane, and I love every bit of that. But I respect myself and you enough that I won't be complicit in your self-destruction." He turned the knob. "I'll be up on the roof. I'll stick around long enough to see the night through, and then I'll go."

"Please," she said.

Her voice had a tinge of desperation.

He stood there with the door open a crack. She said, "You're right."

His shoulders sagged. With his back still to her, he said, "See, I want to believe you mean that, but I've already been on the receiving end of your play-pretend, and I can't unknow what that's like. You can say the words, act the act, and to me, it'll still be you trying to keep from losing something just because you don't want your brother to have it."

She said, "I'm fucking hard to deal with, Chris, I know.

"And this thing with me and John, I don't always understand it myself. But I can accept, okay? I accept that what he did in Prague was because he didn't trust that I loved him enough to not sabotage him. And it wasn't true, you know. At the time it wasn't. But he couldn't know, because I never let him. And if I can accept that, and let it go, then it means there's hope I'll eventually accept and let go of the rest."

Holden glanced at her, and that one small movement splintered into several — a double take, a door slam, a roll toward the center of the room, a look.

He'd stay because he didn't exactly have a choice right now.

Jill tossed him the X-Caliber.

He snatched it, looked at it, looked at her.
Heartbeats inflated into minutes.
"Okay," he said. "Okay."

Chapter 31

Jill

She grabbed her kit, ran for the sink counter, and boosted herself through the hole in the ceiling and into the crawl space. She dragged her kit behind her, strap looped around her ankle, elbowing forward over insulation and around wiring in a tight race for the boiler room at the far end. Scratches and shuffling told her Holden had followed her up.

He headed in the opposite direction, to a small access window Jack had created beneath the eaves. He'd already been up here twice, confirming and modifying.

The dude was thorough, she'd give him that.

She caught herself, and cut herself off.

Having him in her head would be like having another Clare.

There'd be time for sorting out emotional baggage later.

She reached the marker, slid the ceiling tile aside, dropped her supplies down, and squeezed between bracing and clambered over pipes in an attempt to avoid getting burned in the fight to get to the floor.

Her toes touched ground.

She cinched her pack, inched the door open, scanned the walkway, and stole out into the dark. Twenty feet separated her from the next building. She scurried across the gap, sidled against the cinder block, and slid along the wall for the corner and a better view of the compound's center. Security lighting cast a glare over the shadows.

She studied them, searching for motion.

Bodies came into focus.

She counted four in tactical gear, with tactical weapons, creeping toward Jack's motel room like a SWAT team about to flash-bang a house on a no-knock warrant, except they were overcautious, deservedly wary, hugging the edges to avoid a direct line of sight on the building. They all knew they were the bait to draw fire, but reluctance on the right flank said at least two of them were here against their will.

She observed body language, watching for hand signals, searching for the team leader, and found her on the right, and paused. *Her.* Team leader was a *her.*

Of all the detail Jack had laid out, much of which didn't matter, he'd somehow failed to mention what actually did. Jill retreated for the de facto alley that ran between the two-story building and the fence, a five-foot strip of storage and clutter, and she snaked through the dark toward the exit. Movement stopped her.

She'd heard it more than seen it.

She froze, crouched in the dark, listening to the night.

The shadows moved again, two bodies at least, gauged and scoped, slipping over the fence with the grace of big cats on the prowl.

She tucked in behind a garbage can, calculating distance against risk.

Footsteps turned her way, and in her mind's eye, she saw the shooter, scope swinging, hunting for anything with heat, anything alive.

She was at the point of weakness, hidden from Holden by a two-story building and invisible to Jack, who, no matter what he'd said about timing and urgency and places to be, was here just as certainly as she was. She could feel him, the way she always did when they worked in tandem, knew he was up on that convenience-store roof, waiting to put holes in any fool stupid enough to try to stake out the high ground.

The footsteps drew nearer.

A hundred times she'd been here, a hundred nights, a hundred strategies, Clare pushing her over and over. *What were you thinking? You weren't thinking. Dead again, Julia. Go. Do it better.* Clare at her day after week after month after year until reaction was instinct and instinct was instant.

The objective had always been survival by any means necessary.

Tonight survival meant getting to that woman team leader, and that wasn't going to happen if a barrage of bullets ripped through the silence before all the pieces were in place. She pulled the infrared torch from her kit and unsheathed the bowie, a full tang, ten-inch blade forged and custom tempered by her own two hands.

The thing weighed nearly a pound.

Swung correctly, it could lop clean through a forearm.

Jack had collected it from Houston with the X-Caliber and had brought it as a peace offering. She cradled the hilt, mentally placing footsteps, feeling time compress.

She saw shadow before body, a shift of shade against the fence, shooter stepping aside to clear the space in which she hid. She was coiled energy, counting seconds, waiting for death, and when death arrived, she flicked the infrared beam up into its face, arm high, light blinding, body low, rolling beneath the muzzle.

She dropped the light. Came up fast on the other side of him. Brought the blade down across his shooting wrist, cut into bone, yanked the rifle free, drove blade point up beneath his chin, and stopped with the tip resting inside his mouth, beneath his tongue. She tugged the earpiece from his ear, pulled the mic free, tossed both on the ground.

"This thing heads straight up," she said. "One shove, one slip, and all the way into your brain it goes. Struggle, you die. Try and fight me, you die. Make any noise, and I have no reason to keep you alive."

She left off the part about how fast he'd bleed out if that wrist wound wasn't stanched. She said, "I'm going to walk backward, and you're going to follow me. You don't keep pace, and this thing will slice into your jaw."

She took a step. He followed. She took another, and so did he.

Foot by foot, they progressed down the alley, blade in his chin hurrying him on as much as he could be hurried, and time raced on without her. She'd kept this guy alive because his body was a heat-signature shield and a bullet blocker, and he was too damn heavy for her to lug as deadweight, but this was too slow.

She needed to get to that woman.

She had to cut him or cut him loose.

He made that decision for her, slamming forearms down onto hers.

The bowie sliced his jaw. The tip slipped free.

He gripped her wrist with his working hand, strong, not afraid of pain.

Clare, cold and ruthless, was in her head. *Empathy and mercy for killers always gets you killed.*

She kicked his stomach. Shoved him off. Lowered the blade point.

He charged her, good hand lunging for her neck. She arced the bowie, twisted her wrist, swung into a backcut. Impossible to see. Impossible to avoid. A skilled bowie fighter could deliver a five-slash sequence in barely half a second.

She wasn't that fast. Didn't need to be.

Velocity. Continuing force. Angle of attack. Ten inches of leverage went clean through the arm closing in on her neck, and the blade arced again, back up under his chin, into a sinus cavity, and she shoved right up into his brain.

She pulled the knife free.

He collapsed. She wiped the blade on his pant leg, shoved it back into the sheath, turned, and ran for the corner. The pop of suppressed semiautomatic fire followed.

Bullets chased her, whining past her ear, kicking up gravel, grazing her thigh. She rounded the corner, made it to the fence, still had to get across the street exit to get behind the woman. The world exploded with the lightning and thunder of compression grenades tossed into the compound.

Inside her head she said, *No, no, no, no, no.*

She'd been so close.

Orderly, quiet movement turned to chaos. The two men on the left flank jerked in quick succession, as if they'd been stung — Holden with the CO_2 projector, shots he'd held off on taking while waiting for the entire team to draw in closer. That wasn't going to happen now.

Stealth had become pointless.

The woman, who'd been halfway to their motel door, tensed.

Her focus shifted. She looked right up to Holden's position. Her mouth moved, and she changed trajectory. And just like that, Jack's plan was fully off the rails.

Jill slowed, skidded, changed direction, and barreled directly for the woman.

Speed was the only advantage she had.

She came up on her fast, boots pounding gravel, and the woman turned and, in that turn, exposed her neck, and Jill brought the blade of her hand down hard over the greater auricular nerve. Brachial stun. Three to seven seconds was how long it took the body's nervous system to recover, longer if she'd hit too hard.

The woman's legs went out, and she dropped hard and fast.

Jill grabbed her collar, dragged her backward into the light.

Five seconds was what it took to get that deadweight into Holden's range.

The night around her turned into a war zone.

A tranquilizer hit the woman's upper thigh.

Jill let go and rushed for the motel-room door.

No time, no time, they had no time.

The noise would have raised the neighborhood. A law-enforcement response wouldn't be far away, and any engagement on their part — deadly or otherwise — was out of the question if the rest of this was going to work.

They needed to get gone.

The ceiling rattled, and Holden dropped

down to the sink counter.

"There are more of them out there, coming over the fence," she said.

"Go," he said. "Go, go, go."

Outside came another burst of gunfire, and then another after that.

She reached for his gear, slung the strap over her shoulder, hefted her own bag, strapped up the CO2 rifle, grabbed hold of the weapons case and supplies, and heaved her way out like a laden donkey, headed for the fence opening to the street.

In the rooms around her, doors remained closed, and curtains motionless.

Guests would have to be insane to do more than roll to the floor and reach for their phones. She lugged her way to the vehicle next door, which Jack, in his many-steps-ahead thinking, had secured for them. It was disposable. One-time use. That meant plates from a clean vehicle had been swapped out for those on this stolen one.

By morning it'd be a death trap.

Silence took her past bodies of the men who'd come over the fence, dead from shots she hadn't taken, that Holden hadn't taken. That'd been Jack on the rooftop, using whatever their compatriots had carried up there, turning their own weapons against them. He'd never been one to let a good setup go to waste.

When the cleaners moved in and pored over the scene, all data would point to a defector in their midst, and the analysts would reject that narrative, but the idea would be planted, and it'd be there, infecting every skirmish that followed.

She reached the beat-up RAV4.

The keys were beneath the passenger seat, same place she stashed those for the Fiesta, because that's how things worked.

She off-loaded the equipment into the rear.

There were already bags in the back, courtesy of Jack, and she stole a few quick seconds to run through the inventory.

Women's clothes were there with the rest.

Brother dearest had most certainly known team leader was a woman.

She ran for the driver's seat, turned the ignition, pulled the vehicle out onto the street, and blocked the motel entrance.

The woman still lay on the ground where Jill had left her. The other sedated bodies were missing, and the motel-room door stood open. Holden stepped out, shut the door behind him, headed for the woman and, with barely a break in stride, hefted her over his shoulder, body armor and all.

Jill shoved the transmission into park,

jumped out to get the rear door.

Holden dumped the woman onto the backseat and slid in behind the wheel.

She didn't have the energy to fight him for it.

She climbed into the passenger seat and locked the seat belt in.

He hit the gas, took the vehicle out in the opposite direction of the sirens. A few blocks down he hung a right into a neighborhood of sleepy houses and quiet streets, following Jack's directions for the fastest camera- and license scanner–free route to the freeway. Distance between them and the motel grew.

Jill's heart rate settled. They both knew they were clear.

Holden glanced at her.

"Your brother's a real piece of work," he said.

In the silence and aftermath and adrenaline dump, those were the last words she'd expected from him, and in the shock of them, she let out a bark of laughter. He laughed, too, and just like that, with the kidnapped woman in the backseat, all of them barreling forward in a race to insanity, they'd made peace.

Chapter 32

Johnson County
Texas, USA

Kara

Her senses surfaced, summoned from oblivion by merciless pounding in her skull. Her eyelids fluttered, catching glimpses of muted color, and a blur slowly took shape and formed into a small table, and across from the table, a sofa chair, and on the sofa chair, her pants, neatly folded, and beside them, her shoes.

Conscious thought was groggy, slow to engage, struggling to reconcile incomplete and scattered memories of the motel — the door, darkness — with *this*.

She was on a mattress, a shaking mattress.

Pillow, blankets, clean sheets. Hands and feet both cuffed.

The click of wheels against tracks reached in from the fog, and the disparate pieces came together. Train. She was on a train, in a private sleeper cabin, sofa pulled out to make a bed. But sleeper cabins were for long-distance routes.

She edged onto an elbow, peered beyond the window shades, and winced against a clear, cold late-morning light. East out of San Antonio would have taken them into the piney woods, and west would have taken them into the desert, but what she saw here was oak and ash, mountain cedar and low, rolling winter grassland, which meant north. But the only thing that really told her was that target had timed the lure and attack to suit a particular travel schedule, and *that* just made her head hurt worse.

She dropped back to the pillow, body aching, memories clashing, holding on to the insane hope that her team was alive, and fighting despondency and despair, because even if this ended well for them, there was no way it ended well for her.

Headquarters would be looking for someone to blame.

It wouldn't mean shit that she'd warned Hayes about the trap. She had been there in Prague and was now unaccounted for at the hit site, which made her the only common denominator, and Liv Wilson was still running the show.

459

Kara rolled toward the wall and shut her eyes.

Behind her, the door slid open, and a soft floral fragrance wafted in.

She'd feign sleep if it would do any good, but anyone smart enough to engage the twists these guys had knew how to time sedatives, and trying to pretend otherwise would just make her look like she was dumb enough to think they were dumb, and she had a hard enough time convincing people she wasn't an idiot without inflicting that label on herself.

The door slid shut.

Kara rolled onto her back.

The blonde stood at her feet, tray in hand, face bare and sun kissed, hair tied back in a messy ponytail bun, wearing jeans, sweatshirt, and Converse shoes, like some peppy freshman straight off the varsity cheer squad, still used to being fawned over and adored, because life hadn't slapped a KICK ME sign on her back yet.

She offered a hint of smile, as if to say hello.

Kara groaned on the inside and fought the urge to roll right back over.

After all she'd done to escape the popular girls, she'd been outwitted and grabbed by one. She'd officially reached the lowest circle of hell.

The blonde placed the tray on the table. "I'm always thirsty after sedation," she said. "Thought you might be, too. Wasn't sure if you'd feel like eating, but brought a few things in case. You have any allergies? Nuts? Dairy? Eggs?"

In her head Kara said, *Highly allergic to bullshit,* but that would earn no favors, so she said nothing and let silence do the speaking.

The blonde picked up a bottle, broke the seal, held it forward.

Kara took the water and glugged it down, and the blonde slid onto the sofa chair and tucked her legs up, like they were gal pals just hanging out, or what the ever-loving heck this was. Kara said, "Where are my men?"

"They're fine. Alive, I mean. They're alive, and they're fine."

"Here on the train?"

"At the motel. There might be a concussion or two, maybe some bad bruises, but other than that, they should all be okay."

Kara capped the bottle, uncapped it, capped it, diverting brain resources, slowing down thought just enough to separate anxiety from relief.

Her guys were alive. That's all that mattered.

But for her personally, this was bad.

Blondie, as if reading her mind, said, "This won't come back on you. We made sure all the evidence pointed to you as hostage, not perpetrator, and left a message for them to stand by, because we'll be in touch for more."

Kara's brain seized up.

Blondie said, "Crap. Look, I'm sorry. I wasn't meaning to make you beg for information. This train is headed for Chicago. We've still got about twenty-five hours left on the trip, and we'll get all your questions answered soon, I promise."

Kara's fingers gripped the cap and worked it right, left, right, left.

Women who looked like Blondie did, and who held the type of power Blondie held, were only ever nice to her when they needed something or were setting her up for something. The word choices and empathetic tone set her on edge.

Blondie said, "It's only fair that you know up front that I'm capable of killing you and getting your body off this train without anyone knowing you were here. I don't want to hurt you, but can, and will if you push me. Please don't."

Kara twisted the cap another hard right and left.

This made no strategic sense, no tactical sense.

Blondie herself made no sense, abductor warning abductee the same way Kara would have begged Nick not to do anything stupid, if these had been their roles, and she'd have had to hurt him. The respect of equals messed with her head.

She had no frame of reference for an appropriate response, so reverted to safe and social and said, "Do you have a name?"

The blonde smiled. "You already know several. Take your pick."

Her warmth was infectious and alluring and made it difficult to see past the words for what she'd really done, letting on that she knew what Kara knew and prompting her for more. Skills like that didn't come without a lot of practice working over strangers and learning how to make them like you.

Kara stopped there, thoughts hovering over *strangers.*

What had made no sense flipped upside down.

Blondie made no sense because paradigms were contextual, and in context, mean girls and their cliques were territorial social hierarchies. Put that same behavior in a lone kid in an unfamiliar place and all you got was an immediate social outcast.

If Steven Hayes was right about Karen McFadden, and if Blondie was really McFadden's kid, she would have spent her entire life on the move.

Friendships, if she'd had them, would have been temporary and fleeting.

No territory. No social hierarchy. No queen bee.

What you got instead was a cultural chameleon adept at reading people, quick to pick up unfamiliar social cues, capable of rapid integration. That's what this was, and with understanding, Kara's insides unclenched and clarity followed.

She said, "If it's on me to pick a name, I'll go with Jen."

"I like that one."

Kara said, "Thank you for letting me know my guys are safe, and for explaining the rules of engagement. What I really need most right now is to use the restroom."

Jen nodded toward the sealed-off space within the cabin.

"Toilet's in there," she said. "Shower, too, if you want to clean up. Just let me know when you're ready, and I'll set your feet loose." She stood. "I'm not going to stay to keep an eye on you, so we can do this one of two ways. You can use the time alone to try to get out of your restraints and make a jump for freedom, which won't work and will force me to hurt you. Or you can accept the situation for what it is and deal with the inconvenience as best as you can."

Kara said, "And what exactly is the situation?"

"Just a long, boring train ride, unless you try to mix it up."

Kara parsed the words for source and context, searching for completeness and meaning, just as she would have if they'd been handed to her as a transcript. Within the many unknowns, this much she knew:

Her captors were capable of inflicting great harm but preferred to avoid it.

They responded to violence with violence but didn't initiate it.

They were rational, methodical killers averse to killing, willing to take prisoners, but not sociopathic, ideological, or even evil — though morality was wholly defined by who did the moralizing — and try as she may, she couldn't get this to fit the narrative headquarters had handed her. Not that she discounted the narrative entirely. Political assassination might very well be the end goal, but that assessment was oversimplistic.

From nearly the beginning she'd known there was more.

More was why she'd been grabbed.

Kara said, "Are you planning to let me go?"

"When this is over, yes."

Kara snorted. "As long as you're wanted, this will never be over, and you'll always be wanted." She laid back and stared at the ceiling. "You don't strike me as someone who'd struggle to understand the long game."

Jen reached the door, waited a beat, and slid it open.

"Have a little faith," she said.

The door rolled closed. The latch was secured. And Kara could have sworn Jen had whispered, "In yourself," and left that addition hanging in the air.

CHAPTER 33

McLean County
Illinois, USA

Jill

She woke in the dark to the ambient glow of the laptop screen, train still rhythmic and rattling, Holden still watching the camera feeds, and no recollection at all of having drifted off. To fall under like that while they'd been talking meant she was still running a serious sleep deficit. She'd done what? Thirty-six, forty hours awake?

She groaned upright, eyes burning, body protesting.

Holden pulled the headphones off. Tone hushed, as if speaking normally might formalize things, he said, "You've still got forty-five minutes. Go back to sleep."

There were too many pending pieces to just let go.

She said, "Has John found her yet?"

"Yeah, looks like it. I'll show you later."

"What about girl next door?"

"Reading. I've got this. Go sleep."

She tipped back over, her eyes closed against her will, and she drifted down again, strategy and conversation, the things she had done and still needed to do, playing and replaying until dreams and reality blended.

Nearly thirty hours they'd been riding the rails.

She'd brought Kara warm meals from the dining car and handed off abandoned books and magazines she'd found, and stopped by just to sit and talk, entering and exiting at will courtesy of a conductor's key, but the key was an illusion. Kara's sleeper cabin, like every sleeper cabin, locked and unlocked from the inside. Shackles alone weren't enough to stop her from trying to walk out on her own. But she hadn't tried, and wouldn't. Not because she was too dumb for it to have crossed her mind, but because she was smart enough for it not to.

Jill knew this, because she knew people.

They'd put the cameras in, anyway, and kept an eye on her in alternating shifts. The miles had dragged on, and Kara still hadn't touched the door, and they were almost to the end, almost, almost, and there was coffee. . . .

Jill's eyes opened again.

A steaming mug sat on the table, not far from her head.

Holden glanced her way and smiled. He was still at the computer, still watching the cameras, but the headphones were off. He said, "Good morning."

She dragged her feet from bed to floor, rested her arms on the table, and dropped her head onto them. Eyes closed, she said, "On which continent?" and then, "How close are we?"

"Couple more hours."

She felt for the mug and dragged it to her face, summoned the energy to get her lips to the rim, and took a sip. Neurons lit up inside her head.

Holden slid a tablet across the table in her direction.

A bottle-enhanced redhead filled the screen, late forties to early fifties, pantsuit, minimal makeup, hair pulled back in a no-nonsense bun, caught mid-stride on her way to a black sedan. She was a picture of power in motion.

Two men in suits walked beside her. Another waited at the rear passenger door. Jill pinched and zoomed and assessed the accoutrements.

Radio earpieces. Service weapons.

By all appearances, John had found what they were after.

The strategy now rested on her getting the confirmation.

For nearly thirty hours she'd been laying that groundwork, every conversation and every visit to the cabin next door, practicing an art that Jack, for all his brilliance, had never fully appreciated.

He thought she manipulated people to get what she wanted.

He was wrong.

People manipulated themselves. If you acknowledged their deepest desires, guarded their secrets, soothed their hidden shame, and reaffirmed their worldview and self-image, they tripped over themselves in a race to their own doom while thanking you for the favor. She'd first internalized that insight as an eight-year-old in Sofia, Bulgaria, after their apartment had been burgled and Clare, being Clare and refusing to accept it as a random act of thievery, had hunted down one of the men who'd cleaned them out and had positioned her kids where they could watch the interrogation.

She'd never threatened, never raised her voice.

Instead, she'd cut the man loose, straddled a chair facing him, handed him a beer, and drunk with him. He'd talked — cautiously, at first — and she'd listened and empathized, and by the time she'd sent him on his way, she'd mapped the entire hierarchy of a local ring of thieves.

Not that he knew that's what he'd done, exactly.

"I could have hurt him," Clare had said. "People will tell you anything they think you want to hear if it will make the pain stop, but they'll tell you what you *need* to hear if they like you and if it's in their own best interest."

That was the difference between her and her brother.

She caught on to self-interest a whole lot faster than he did.

Faster than Holden, too, it seemed, because that first short conversation after Kara had woken had been enough to get her started. Holden, who'd been listening and watching, had still needed an explanation. "Look at it this way," she'd said. "Here's this woman who's been chasing John for over a week. *He's* the one who led her team into the trap in Prague. *He's* the one who led them to the motel. By any measure, *he* should have been the one to walk through that door. But she wasn't surprised to see me. She was irritated, maybe disappointed, but not surprised. What's that tell you?"

"She knew you were part of the trap at the motel."

"Yeah, and I'm betting she knew you were there, too."

Holden had scoffed. "That was the shittiest attack strategy known to man if they thought they were going after more than one person."

"I'm not saying *they* knew. I'm saying *she* knew." Jill paused. "And then there's that bag of stuff John set up for us. Nobody randomly provides women's clothes instead of men's, especially not him. He knew she was running that team and that *she'd* be there looking for him and he just supposedly *accidentally* forgot to mention it?"

She swung her feet off the bed and sat.

"No," she said. "Those two have met. Maybe not, you know, actual conversations or anything, but for the past week it's been his brains against hers, and she's given him a run for his money, so, yeah . . ." Her voice trailed off.

Holden said, "I'm missing whatever your real point is."

She smiled at the floor.

Jack had always been insanely private

when it came to things like *feelings.* He'd had to be, she supposed, to protect himself against a meddling mother and a sabotaging sister, but as a result, it'd been twenty years at least since she'd had an inkling of who he was interested in, or whether he had any interest at all.

That he deliberately let on now was his version of an apology.

Like the photo of the macaques, it was something only she'd understand.

"John likes her," she said. "I think the feeling might be mutual."

"Because of the clothes?"

"Because of the silence."

She didn't want to go into the history, so she went back to what had driven the point in the first place. "A woman in Kara's position doesn't withhold that kind of information without a damn compelling reason," she said. "And it doesn't take Jack's level of genius to figure out what that was." Like Clare had said, people would tell you what you needed to hear if they liked you and if it was in their own best interest.

One quick conversation had given her that.

Jill had slept, just enough to take the edge off, and then returned to Kara with a change of clothes and sat back on the sofa chair, legs tucked up in that same friendly pose, and she rambled like someone who hadn't had a friend to talk to in years, which was true, but like so much else, beside the point.

She talked because Kara was content in silence, and because Kara wasn't a game player, which made straightforward and unpretentious truth far more effective than any lie. She spoke about the places she and Jack had traveled to as kids, and the increasingly strange people Clare had left them with, and the hijinks they'd gotten up to when, as kids with kid brains and adult skills, they got bored.

All of it was a vehicle to talk about Jack, so much about Jack and the training that had made him what he was, and she segued from there to the strategy that had brought them to the motel and from the motel to the attack itself. "You knew it was a trap," she said. "I'm trying to figure out why you kept that information to yourself."

"Everyone knew it was a trap," Kara said.

"Yes, but everyone else believed they were hunting just one person."

Kara was slow to respond. "I don't always catch subtleties," she said. "Are you asking me to tell you how many of you I thought were there?"

"Nope." Jill smiled, and she pushed. "Just trying to avoid feeding you information you might not already have."

The corners of Kara's lips turned up, and with the same confident, almost cocky tone Jack got when he knew beyond all doubt and in the face of contrary evidence that he was right, she said, "There were three of you. Christopher Holden confused me at first. I thought he was competing with us to get to you. But by the time we made it to Cleveland, I understood. Your brother had already pinged in Texas, so the rest was easy to deduce, but by then I was just better off not knowing anything."

Jill said, "Do *they* know?"

Kara shrugged. "Who's to say?"

Fatalism filled her tone, her posture.

She went back to staring out the window, and Jill sighed in commiseration. "You remind me so much of my brother," she said. "You've got that same crazy, wicked smart way about you, but, if your world is anything like mine was, it doesn't really matter how smart you are, it's some idiot guy who's gonna get the praise and promotion."

Kara winced ever so slightly.

Jill, slipping through that opening, asked what being a woman in a bureaucracy was like, and she listened and empathized. Having never had female coworkers other than her mother, she was authentically curious about the drama.

Stories and examples followed, and those produced names, and of those names, *Liv Wilson* kept coming back.

She was the redhead whose face filled the tablet screen right now.

Wilson didn't hold the most senior position in the kill-team hierarchy, but as second in command and the one responsible for so much of Kara's current predicament, she would be the easiest for Kara to give up without violating her conscience, and conscience mattered. Karma could be a bitch like that.

Jill drank down the last of the coffee and carried the tablet next door.

Kara looked up, closed the book she was reading.

Jill said, "We'll be arriving in Chicago in a few hours."

"Is that where you plan to let me go?"

"It'll be another few days before this is over."

Kara shook her head, as if reiterating what she'd said at their first meeting just wasn't worth the effort, and she looked away.

Jill sat, tucked her feet up, placed the

tablet on the table.

Kara, like Jack, valued information more than just about anything, and information was what she'd held back.

Information was where this was headed now.

Jill said, "Explain to me why your people want to kill my brother."

Kara hesitated, as if she wasn't sure if she'd been asked a trick question or if she needed to state the obvious. She said, "He's an assassin they can't control, and they want to eliminate future risk."

"Yes, but in the immediate sense."

"To prevent an immediate assassination."

Jill said, "Do they know who the target is?"

Kara didn't answer.

Jill said, "Yeah, I didn't think so. Makes sense, really, because my brother isn't the assassin they should be worried about. The same guys who, quote-unquote, 'hired' him — and trust me, there's no money involved, only blackmail — they're the ones who pointed you to him in the first place."

Kara's gaze slowly tracked her way.

Jill could see her mind running, reorganizing, and categorizing existing intelligence to accommodate new data, so much like her brother's. She said, "You don't think it's odd that you've known what cities he flies into and where he's meeting but not who he's killing? Moscow has been playing you — your branch, division, whatever it is you guys are — keeping you focused on him so you don't look at me."

She paused for effect, waited until silence became painful, and said, "At some point within the next three days, I will put a bullet between the eyes of a sitting member of Congress, and all your guys out there running themselves ragged trying to find my brother will never see me coming. Even if I turned you loose right now and you went straight back and told your bosses everything, you couldn't stop me. I am *that* good. Not bragging. It's just the way it is. It'll be a public spectacle, something impossible for TV cameras to miss. Those are my orders. I'll give you a minute to connect the dots and figure out why."

Kara said, "I don't need a minute."

"To be clear, we don't want to do this, but your people are making it really hard not to. Whether we do or don't, your guys still want us dead. You've seen my brother work. You know what he's capable of. So you get how big a deal this is when I tell you he has a way to shut this whole thing down. It'll require a channel to where the backroom deals are made. We need you to make that call."

Kara studied the table and then her hands, as if plotting the many directions this could lead. She said, "Even if I manage to get the right person on the phone, there's nothing I can say that will make them take me seriously."

"No," Jill said, "but they'll take *him* seriously."

She opened the tablet, punched in the code, pulled the image up on the screen, and flipped it forward. "Liv Wilson, right?"

Kara didn't speak, but she didn't have to.

"We already know how to find her," Jill said, "but we'd prefer a call. A switchboard number will do. Just a few words . . . proof-of-life type stuff."

Kara said, "Are you planning to grab her, like you did me?"

"Maybe."

"Are you planning to kill her?"

"Would it bother you if we were?"

"I don't like her. You already know that," Kara said. "I probably wouldn't care a whole lot if I didn't know and didn't play a part in it. But I do know. I don't want her blood on my hands."

Jill closed the image.

Conscience mattered to Kara, and that's

why she played to it.

"We don't know what kind of resistance we'll face," she said. "Our goal is to do this with as little violence as possible."

Kara said, "I guess in the end it's all the same. The goal is to stop the chaos. If you want the guy who runs the shop, I have his cell phone, too."

"I'll take whatever you've got."

Kara recited. Jill typed.

She'd needed the numbers, needed them the way they'd needed access to coms in Bolivia, and she'd needed confirmation that Jack had tracked down the correct Liv Wilson, but what she'd really come for was the same thing that had made it crucial that they ensured no blame fell on the wrong shoulders.

Whatever Jack's personal reasons for looking out for the woman, and no matter how much Jill personally liked her, and no matter that she didn't deserve to take the fall for other people's sins, Kara was going back — back to the kill team or to an analyst position or to her old station in the navy. Where didn't matter, because *where* was irrelevant. She was a woman who had access to people who knew things, and having given this to them now, she'd primed herself for giving more.

Not next week or next month or maybe even ever.

But if and when that time came, she was a string to pull.

Clare had taught that lesson well.

Acknowledge a person's deepest desires, guard their secrets, soothe their hidden shame, and reaffirm their worldview and self-image, and you got yourself a back door.

CHAPTER 34

Bethesda
Maryland, USA

Jack

The house was a modern take on a Pennsylvania colonial with a heap of McMansion thrown in, five bedrooms, seven baths, fully finished basement, three-car garage, large backyard, and a secluded pool, set back from the road and surrounded by mature trees on a half-acre lot in a stately, low-traffic neighborhood that made home security systems redundant, because even if random crime did stumble in, it'd get lost trying to find its way back out. Getting in unnoticed meant yet another night on the rough.

He'd laced into the trappings of a fitness junkie, parked a mile away, and headed out for a predawn run that took him to the homes on the rear parallel street. He loped through the shadows between them, working his way from backyard to backyard to reach his target, a far different environment than those Clare had thrown him into, but the basic rules never changed.

Don't be seen. Don't get caught.

He paused at the perimeter, searching for signs of dogs or young children.

No toys, no water bowls, no poop.

Were the weather warmer, more inviting, he'd crawl the exterior, hunting for an open window.

In this damp December cold there was no point.

He headed around the corner for the bay doors that faced a privacy fence.

He needed a silent entry.

That ruled out picking locks.

Even an unarmed security system still chimed when the doors opened.

The garage was the second easiest point of entry.

It took effort, and a fight against the chain lock, but he got the smaller of the two roller doors raised high enough to wedge beneath. With his back to the ground and the full weight of the door resting on his chest, he ran a penlight along the ceiling, walls, floor in a search for cameras and motion sensors and let himself in.

Silver and black, his and hers Range Rovers filled two of the parking spots.

In the third was a workshop with an eighty-inch, double-stacked Snap-on tool chest, a ten-foot workbench, and a Peg-Board, on which high-end power tools were mounted the way he would have mounted weapons, and not a hint that any of it had ever been used. On the back wall a rack held two trail bikes, both of which looked like they'd never made it farther than the box, and in the corner was an array of gardening tools, mostly untouched. The large, empty chest freezer beside the interior door was the closest he'd get to a place to hide. He sat on the cold concrete, looking out over thousands of dollars in wishes and wants, all of which spoke to an idea of life with no time to live it, the type of detail his sister would have used to worm her way into a person's good graces, assuming they had something she wanted.

He'd never had patience for the head games, but he'd never really had to.

It'd always been easier to wind Jill up and set her loose.

They'd wreaked a lot of havoc, the two of them, and in spite of the insanity, they'd had some good times. Those had always been worth holding on to.

Footsteps from inside the house broke the reverie.

The door opened, the alarm chimed, and a man strode into the garage.

He was six feet flat, trim, midfifties, sharply dressed, on the phone, barking at someone about Taiwanese markets. The black Range Rover backed out. The garage door went down. Jack crept toward the door that Mr. Taiwan Markets had been in too much of a hurry to lock. The handle turned for him.

That would save him time gaining entry when seconds mattered most.

Today, the silver Rover would stay in the garage.

Instead, a town car would arrive at the front, and security would arrive with it, and men with guns would escort Liv Wilson from door to backseat. The message Jill had left with the tranquilized foot soldiers in the motel room should have seen to that, and on the chance that hadn't been enough, the phone call from Kara would have pushed things over the edge.

He needed these precautions.

Needed the false sense of safety they provided.

Needed the change in routine.

He sat with his back to the door, waiting,

listening, and in the wait, impatience grew and time became the enemy. He was tired. Tired of not sleeping. Tired of running. Tired of spending nights in chairs and bus seats and on cold garage floors.

Thirty minutes passed, forty. He debated letting himself in and handling the whole thing here and now, but prudence and planning warned him against it.

The security men didn't concern him much.

Ten seconds or less was all it'd take to remove that threat. He could haul Liv Wilson off, use her own car to spirit her away. But as soon as she failed to turn up for work, the whole world would start chasing. They needed more time than that.

Timing was everything. Timing was why he'd routed Jill and Holden by train and why their journey required a ten-hour drive after reaching Chicago.

Traveling by rail had allowed him to erase Kara's trail and gave his sister the time and space for mental games while on the move, but that had been a bonus. What he'd really purchased was the time to get ahead of them, to hunt from a parallel path, and to conjure the bridge beneath their feet.

He was a magician raising bricks before each step touched ground.

Inside the house, a doorbell rang.

The security system chimed, signaling an open door.

Voices carried low and distant, and then the system chimed again, intoning the countdown of a house alarm arming, and the same thirty- to ninety-second grace period that allowed owners to come back in for a forgotten item if needed allowed someone like him to slip in through an unlocked door unannounced.

He let himself into a mudroom that had never seen mud, and scanned the ceiling and floor in a search for motion detectors. In keeping with the neighborhood's sense of quiet safety, the security system seemed limited to door and window sensors.

He stole into the kitchen, checking corners and niches.

The cameras were here, somewhere, wireless devices to capture the goings-on while the homeowners were away. They had to be. Every other home had them these days, and even in a household without kids or pets, they'd exist to keep track of whatever domestic help kept the vast inside dust free and sparkling. He kept his head down, moved quickly up the stairs, found the master bedroom and, from there, the master closet. Unless someone watched in real time, that's all they'd have of him, a record.

He perused clothing and shoes and personal items, and eyeballed distance between furniture, bathroom, and balcony, and closed himself inside and settled into the thick plush carpet. For two days he'd been on the go, pushing pieces into place, and all he had now was time to sleep and time to wait, and he drifted down, down, deep down into the oblivion of timelessness, and woke to the vibration of an alarm going off in one pocket and a minute later a pager going off in the other.

He pried his eyes open, glanced at the pager readout.

The technology, once big in the eighties and early nineties, had mostly vanished as cell phones became smaller and cheaper, but it still had a thriving niche among emergency personnel and was reliable in ways cell phones weren't. Batteries lasted weeks, if not months, and more importantly, the old-school tech couldn't be tracked. He'd collected the devices from their stuff in Houston, along with the X-Caliber and Jill's knife.

His sister carried one.

Holden carried another.

The number on the screen, a prearranged code, told him that Jill had called Liv Wilson to request a meeting, and Liv Wilson had taken the bait.

She'd mobilized a tactical team.

All they'd find was Jill's phone.

It'd ring, and rank would answer, and Jill would tell them they'd been very, very stupid, and Holden, who'd be in position long before the chase started, would put a bullet through the guy's kneecap. And Jill would call Wilson again and say she'd try again tomorrow, and then she'd disappear. Barring some other emergency, there'd be no reason for Wilson to stay late at work.

He dozed and waited.

The pager vibrated again, confirming all moved forward as planned, and he slept again and woke to notification that Liv Wilson was in motion, vehicle last seen headed in the direction of home.

A minute later, the pager buzzed with Holden's response.

Mr. Taiwan Markets was still at the office.

Jack stood and stretched, limbering muscles that had stiffened during sleep, and he upped the tempo to get blood moving through sluggish veins. He sucked on dextrose to compensate for too many hours without food, and right on cue, according to the traffic map in his head, the front door opened and the alarm pad sounded.

A number sequence killed the countdown.

Two voices — male and female — headed up the stairs.

That wasn't right.

Inside Jack's head, the mental maze shifted.

He hadn't planned on Liv Wilson soothing defeat with angry, adulterous sex and had no doubt that's what this was, because Wilson, now in the bedroom, confirmed it, telling Security Dude that her husband wouldn't be home till early morning, because of something-something product launch, something-something time zones.

The bed groaned. Dirty talk turned vicious.

The noise of body slapping against body ramped up speed.

Jack led with the weapon, closet to room, pulling in detail in rapid order.

Security Dude, shirt unbuttoned, pants around his knees.

Wilson, stripped down to bra, ass up, face down on the bed.

Service weapon, holstered, a couple feet to the left of her head.

Security Dude noticed him first.

Shock registered before hips stopped thrusting.

He lunged for the holster.

Jack fired, bullet to the bed, bullet to the guy's shoulder.

Liv Wilson jerked upright in a mad scramble to disentangle.

Jack said, "Freeze."

It was the cliché of every cop show ever, but it had the desired effect.

The room held motionless, suspended in time.

Jack moved in closer, muzzle aimed at Wilson's head, and he snagged the holster strap and tossed the whole thing off the bed. He motioned to Security Dude. "Hands up. Step out of your pants." And then, "Walk backward till you reach the window and turn."

Liv Wilson inched toward the nightstand.

Jack put another round into the bed.

"Last warning," he said. "Next one will hurt."

He could see her face now.

Whatever was on it wasn't fear, and that was stupid.

Security Dude reached the window, turned, as instructed.

Jack motioned Wilson off. Under other circumstances it might've been hard not to look at her, but right now all he cared about was where her hands were and how far he could get her from whatever weapons she

491

had stashed around the room.

He motioned her opposite the window.

"Walk backward," he said. "Turn when you reach the wall."

He retrieved Dude's weapon and, with one muzzle pointed toward the window and the other toward the wall, nudged a foot into the guy's pants and kicked them to the center of the room. He checked pockets, emptied contents into his own.

To Wilson, he said, "Where are your cuffs?"

She said, "I don't . . ."

This would be so much easier if killing wasn't such a last resort.

He put a bullet into the wall, inches from her head.

She said, "Bedside, top drawer."

He inched to the bed, nudged the drawer open. Reached in, felt the underside, found a small revolver and also the cuffs. He pocketed the gun, dropped the restraints at the end of the bed. To Wilson, he said, "Walk backward. Pick up the cuffs, hold your hands out where I can see them, and continue to the window."

This time she did as instructed.

He had her secure one of Dude's wrists, sent her back to the wall, ordered Dude bedside and then to the floor, and secured the other end of the cuff to the bed's metal inner frame. One threat now less of a threat, he snatched a bathrobe from the closet, tossed it at Wilson, told her to put it on, and had her lead the way downstairs. Concerns he'd had about cameras were gone now, at least insofar as the bedroom, stairway, and kitchen were concerned.

Even a woman with balls the size of Wilson's wouldn't be brazen enough to bring a man under this roof while recording the evidence.

Either she'd shut the cameras off or they didn't exist.

He directed her to the kitchen, grabbed her purse from off the island, used her phone to dial Jill's pager, hurried a barefoot Wilson to the mudroom, had her reset the house alarm, and then pushed her onward, into the garage, and onto the backseat of the Range Rover. He kept her there, muzzle directed at her head.

Jaw clenched, nose flaring, she glared.

She'd tried to speak, first in the bedroom, with threats; and then on the stairs, with calculated calls for civility; and then the kitchen, with faux curiosity about what Jack wanted; and finally with pleas for help in the mudroom.

Each time he'd shut her down.

She'd gotten the point.

She was quiet now — murderously angry, but quiet — and he stood beyond arm's reach outside the vehicle door, glaring right back and more angry than she could ever be, considering she was the one who ran the war room trying to hunt him dead.

The pager vibrated.

He used the vehicle remote to open the garage.

Jill strode in wearing a pantsuit, carrying an oversize purse, red hair up in a bun, facial features altered enough that she could easily pass for Wilson.

Like Jack, she wore high-dexterity gloves, and the wig did for her what the beanie did for him. She handed Jack a bundle of industrial zip ties and an earflap beanie. He handed her Wilson's wallet and the vehicle key fob, then used the zip ties to secure Wilson's hands and feet, shoved the hat atop her head, and stuffed loose strands of hair up beneath it. The house had no signs of forced entry. It'd be a cuffed naked man's word against Wilson's prints on the cuffs, and Wilson's face behind the windshield for any cameras that caught the trip out of town. That was about all it took to disappear a person, at least for the short term.

Jill took them north along the interstate,

out of Maryland and into Pennsylvania, then off the highway for the backcountry, and she stopped at the edge of a field.

Jack ordered Wilson out and onto the dirt.

She slid to the ground and righted herself, and stood there in her bathrobe and bare feet, head high and haughty. He said, "You know who I am?"

She nodded.

"No," he said. "Who I *really* am."

"Karen McFadden's kid," she said.

"Good," he said. "That means you know who I was trained by and have an idea of what I'm capable of. So tell me, why are you trying to make me your enemy?"

Wilson didn't answer.

He said, "This. You. Here. Do you have any idea why?"

She blew a frustrated raspberry, as if the possibilities were endless.

He said, "You think killing me will stop the assassination? There's more than one assassin and more than one target. The only person who can stop it is me. I've been try-ing to do that, but you keep giving me reason after reason to move it forward instead." He cut her hands loose. "Clearly, you're an idiot. I want to talk to your boss. Make the call."

Wilson coughed out a laugh. "That's not

going to happen."

Defiance in both laugh and words said she was immune to threat and pain and death, and with that declaration, the past imposed itself on the present, and he was twelve again, living in Athens with Raymond Chance, the closest thing he'd ever had to a father, dropped off on his doorstep for *safe-keeping,* which was the word Clare used when she needed to abandon her kids again so she could jet across the globe.

Ray's past had caught up with him while they'd been there, a past that should have died in Prague at the same time Ray had officially died, and it'd come in the guise of a former Stasi agent who'd never believed the stories and never stopped searching.

Jill had stumbled upon the man first.

She'd knifed him and called for Ray, and Ray had hauled the guy south, to where homes were sparse, and had marched him to the edge of a barren cliff, put a bullet in his head, and shoved the body into the ocean.

Ray had stood there for a solemn moment, and said, "I know your mom ain't one for killing if there's a way killing don't need doing, but there ain't no turning an ideologue, you understand?"

Jack hadn't, but Ray hadn't expected a

reply, either.

"You can't persuade or buy a man driven by the righteous belief of his cause. Show mercy, he'll stab you with it. Threaten and torture, you strengthen his resolve. This here is the only way to keep him from coming back."

In time Jack had learned to see what Ray had seen, and he saw it now.

Liv Wilson was an ideologue.

But he hadn't brought her here to persuade her.

Jack offered Wilson her phone.

"Make the call," he said.

She straightened her shoulders, balled up her fists, said, "No."

He shot her in the foot.

She screamed and crumpled.

Jack grabbed her hair and pulled her up.

Her hands and feet and bathrobe were muddy.

"Make the call," he said.

She gritted her teeth, her nostrils flared, her breathing picked up tempo, and she refused to look at him or the phone, so he shot her other foot, too.

She screamed again, crumpled again.

"We've still got hands, knees, and elbows to go," Jack said. He shoved the phone in her face. "You'll be doing your country a favor by making the call."

She grabbed the phone, scrolled through the contacts, dialed.

Jack tugged the device from her hand, put the call on speaker, gave the phone back. Steven Hayes answered. Wilson told him she'd been kidnapped by the people he'd been trying to find, driven off in her own car, and shot twice, and now they wanted to talk to him. Jack told Hayes what he'd already told Wilson.

He was trying to stop this assassination.

He had information to offer. Hayes was welcome to look at it first, before deciding if he valued it enough to barter for a life. They should meet.

"Where and when?" Hayes said.

Jack hung up, pulled Liv off the ground, and shoved her onto the backseat. "I already had that number," he said. "You could have spared yourself two crippled feet by not being such an asshole."

She spit at him.

He smiled, pulled the SIM from the phone, pocketed it, powered the device back on, and left it lying in the field. He climbed in beside her and slammed the door. "Don't need you anymore," he said, "but gotta keep you until it's over. Let's hope your boss is better at playing this game than you are."

Jill pulled back on the road and hit the gas.

The Range Rover, like most modern vehicles, was hackable and trackable and probably had had a target slapped on it before he'd gotten off the phone. The big guns were coming, and he was going to outrun them with a naked woman who couldn't walk.

CHAPTER 35

Brush Creek Township
Pennsylvania, USA

Kara

The room had one window, high and narrow, and if she angled off as far as the chain would reach and then stretched, she could catch just a glimpse of the porch and the spot where the car had been. The rest was sky and trees. Nearest neighbors, best as she could tell, were a few miles down the road, and she'd been left alone, ankle shackled to a chain that ran through a boarded-up hole in the floor to some kind of concrete anchor beneath the house. Ten hours by car from Chicago for this, an old pier-and-beam on the edge of nowhere Pennsylvania, where she could scream for days and never be heard.

There was a fancy-ass composting toilet in the corner, but no heat.

For that Jen had given her all the coats that were waiting for them with the car in Chicago, and all the blankets that were waiting in the house, and as some token toward warm food, a tiny microwave, and enough water and packaged edibles to make a prepper properly proud. "I don't expect we'll be gone more than a couple days," she'd said, "but I know how fast food runs out when you're sitting out time without much to do, so I brought a lot of extra."

Kara had nodded thanks, hated herself for it, and hated herself for hating it.

This was how Stockholm syndrome set in, thanking kidnappers for basic necessities, but it wasn't that, exactly. What she'd acknowledged was the genuine kindness. And then Jen had left, Jen and Christopher both.

Chris was a whole other side of this.

Kara had suspected since Cleveland that he was involved, but Jen had never mentioned him, and only when he'd rolled that wheelchair into her cabin a few minutes before they reached Chicago Union Station had she finally laid eyes on him. He was taller in person and so god-awful charming that the choice he'd offered between sitting and behaving or taking a long chemical nap hadn't been a choice at all.

It'd been interesting watching him and Jen interact.

A jealousy-making thing, or maybe what she'd felt was envy.

From so young an age, she'd had to fight for every scrap, every skill.

She'd escaped into the navy for the education, and to help her sisters into better situations, but it'd just been a different version of the same nonsense. She'd never had a chance to be a kid, or even a girl, really, and yet here was Jen, glittered and glammed, charming and feminine, younger by a half dozen years at least, treated like a full equal by a man as skilled as she was, a man who also treated *her* with that same respect of equals, minus the handcuffs, of course. And that was the thing, goddammit.

She worked for the good guys, these were the bad guys, and yet they were kinder and treated her better than anyone she'd worked with other than Nick.

That ate at her, made her wonder what it said about who she really was.

She paced the floor, blanket wrapped tight, and for the umpteenth time strained to see out that narrow window. The sun would soon set. She hated the idea of being alone here in the dark. Not because she was afraid of the dark or afraid of being alone, but because this was day two and they were still gone. To be able to release her, they had to survive, and so here she was again, wanting the wrong team to win because her fate intertwined with theirs.

She dragged the chain across the room and stopped mid-step.

She had most certainly heard an engine.

She strained for the window, caught a glimpse of color, recognized the car, and tried counting heads but didn't have the view.

Footsteps tromped up the porch steps.

She crossed the room, leaned into the door to listen, caught movement and Jen's voice in a few scattered words.

A door down the hall opened. The door shut.

Footsteps headed in her direction, and she backed away.

Knuckles rapped against the door — more of that respect thing, Jen treating her as if the space was hers, giving her the illusion that as captor, she couldn't just come and go as she pleased.

Kara said, "Come in."

Jen peeked her head inside.

She said, "You holding up okay?"

Kara shrugged. Just because she was grateful for the little things didn't mean she had to be happy she needed the little things in the first place.

Jen said, "We're going to have to go again soon. I just want to make sure you're as comfortable as can be."

"I'm okay," Kara said.

"Also," Jen said, "I don't know if maybe you want to meet Jack?"

Kara's stomach somersaulted.

Her brain hung up, and her mouth stopped working.

She wanted to meet him, yes. Had wanted to meet him since he'd followed her to her hotel in Prague, and had wanted to meet him every day since, wanted to meet him the way someone might want to meet Alan Turing or Katherine Johnson, but she didn't want to meet him like *this,* hair greasy, two days since her last hot shower, sitting on a mattress on the floor with a goddamn chain around her ankle. But to admit to any of that opened her up to questions even she wasn't ready to answer.

She shrugged again, said, "Sure."

Jen closed the door. A minute later there was another knock, and then a pause, and Jack walked in alone, and seeing him up close, face-to-face, brought on a torrent of inner conflict that sent all the old disfluency rushing through her head.

She thought through the words, said, "I guess you won."

He knelt so he was at eye level.

"This isn't winning," he said.

He glanced at her ankle. "May I?"

She nodded.

He ran a finger between shackle and sock, checking the spacing, looking for chafing, and, apparently satisfied, let her ankle drop. "You don't deserve this," he said. "There aren't many people I'd say that to, but if I could have seen another way, some path to avoid this, I'd have done it."

She said, "I'm worth nothing to them. Someone as smart as you has to know that, so what could you possibly hope to gain from all this?"

"Freedom," he said.

Not the answer she expected.

He said, "Our mother is — was — a paranoid nutcase. Straight up pathological, probably should have been institutionalized, delusional. Until, you know, she wasn't, and it turned out all the crazy was just a difficult version of truth. I don't want to be her," he said. "But it's not easy to walk away from that legacy when everyone either wants you dead or wants to use you to make other people dead."

"They're not going to give you what you

want," she said.

"I think they will."

"Not as some sort of trade for me."

"No, but because of what you symbolize."

She sighed on the inside. She'd seen too much to view him as naive or credulous, and for that reason alone, she refused to write off hope completely, but even still, she found it difficult to see a path forward.

"I wish I could stay longer," he said. "It'd be nice to talk."

She nodded and tried to ignore the Stockholm quality in her agreement.

He said, "We might still get that opportunity."

She gave him a wry dose of side-eye. "As much fun as that might be, it'd mean I'd still be here," she said, "like this. And I'm ready to be done."

"Well," he said, "you never know."

He headed toward the door and stopped.

"I'm sorry about your friends," he said.

She glanced up.

"In Prague," he said. "I'm sorry for your loss."

He stepped out, and she was left staring at the floor, confused and hurt, but a strange kind of confusion and a strange kind of hurt, and she didn't have words and had no way to explain. She swiped angry tears from off her cheek.

Outside, the car doors slammed and the engine rolled over and she was alone again, and then a voice reached out from the silence, high pitched, distant, muted, almost as if it'd come from behind soundproofed walls.

Kara cocked her head to listen.

Pounding came from far away, and a woman's voice screaming for help.

Kara beat fist against wall, spelling out an SOS in Morse, the one pattern that even the densest, most panicked person would recognize. If Liv was smart, she'd catch on that this was a path to communication. The yelling stopped. Kara raised her fist to begin again, but a reply came back. *Name? Who?*

Kara spelled out her name, but beyond that what was there to say?

She'd been offered assurance that freedom was imminent, and she believed the promise would be kept, but she had no idea what fate held for Liv — hadn't even known they'd already taken Liv until she'd heard the yelling — and had nothing to offer the woman other than the knowledge she wasn't alone.

She rested her head against the wall.

Through her bones, questions came. *Where?*

Why?

The first made sense. The second surprised her. Surely any leader running multiple teams of assassin hunters would expect that sooner or later, a killer would take offense at having been targeted and come seeking in murderous, retaliatory rage.

It'd be gratifying to write Liv off as a self-deceiving fool and toy with the reversed power dynamics, but that would make her the bigger idiot.

Her heartbeat spelled out *revenge.*

Her fist answered, *Unknown.*

Chapter 36

Six Flags America
Woodmore, Maryland, USA

Jack

The chain lift ratcheted overhead again, and metal rushed against metal, and empty seats accelerated through a banked turn, and the pattern of preopening safety checks that had been going on for nearly an hour now started anew.

The clock on his wrist said early afternoon.

Five days of hard hours on the rough, grabbing sleep in whatever small increments he could, said it was so-over-it o'clock.

He'd hauled eighty pounds of gear through the night to get here, following the transmission lines that cut a swath through woodland and suburban enclaves and woodland again, ten miles of hugging the easement edge like his own private walking trail, and then off into the untamed forest to cut his own path to the park's outer boundary. He'd waited out the bone-chilling damp in the branches of a white oak not five hundred yards from where he was now, watching the lights, listening to screams of delighted terror, until the holiday hours ended and the employees and food vendors closed out and security staff were the only souls left.

All those bullshit years with Clare had led to this, these hours crawling in and out of restricted areas and building shells and down into overgrowth and bushes, hiding supply stashes. This was Colombia and Greece, Bulgaria and Indonesia and Germany and Belize, it was his entire life compressed into twenty-four hours, and today it all ended, or he did, because one way or the other, he was done.

Recorded announcements and music rose over roller-coaster rhythm.

Another day begun. Another park opening.

Inside the mental maze each beacon moved into place.

Feet tromped up the stairs and sent dust from the platform into his face.

The pager vibrated, alerting him to Holden's arrival.

Jill's alert followed a few minutes later.

They'd come separately, entering through the front gate, carrying what they could safely get past a security team known more for impounding outside food and drink than for anything else. They'd roam, charting paths, scouting positions.

They'd find the drop marks.

He had prepared hard to ensure they all walked out of this alive, and had made contingencies for Kara in case they didn't. Jill had left her with enough food and water to last four or five days — a couple of weeks, if she rationed — and he'd brought her a television and a signal booster so she wouldn't be left in an information void, but mostly because the TV housed a small explosive on a self-powered timer.

If they didn't make it back, the charge would crack the television housing, and she'd find the key, a phone, and a message for the forensics team and bureaucrats.

He didn't care enough about Liv Wilson to do more than provide food and water, and even that felt generous, considering she'd run the mission to kill him and his family and would be first in line to do it again if given a chance. Her fate was in Kara's hands, probably the safest place it could be, because no matter how much Kara detested the woman, she'd still do the right thing, which was more than he could say for himself — or for Holden or Jill.

Kara was where his mind went as he rode out boredom through roller-coaster cycle after cycle, waiting for the crowds to grow and for the winter dusk to arrive. And when the business day neared its end, he shoved the high-tactile gloves back on, retrieved the first burner phone, inserted Liv Wilson's SIM, and dialed Steven Hayes.

Hayes answered with a casual hello, as if he hadn't spent the past twenty-four hours trying to track down yet another team member who'd been snatched and vanished.

Jack, matching turn for turn, skipped the small talk.

"I still have information to offer," he said. "You know where I am. Come find me."

Hayes said, "It's going to take an hour to get there, and I'm in no mood to have my chain yanked the way you yanked Liv's."

"I'll be here," Jack said. "Got no plans to kill or grab you. Just want to talk. I'd tell you to come alone, but we both know you're better at giving instructions than following them, so bring your army if you must, but consider the casualties before you start a war."

Hayes said, "It's a big park. Where will you be?"

Jack hung up.

He shrugged out of the sleeping bag, rolled it tight, and stuffed the bundle into his pack. Then, donning a close approximation to the park uniform, pulled a collared shirt over what he already wore, tucked it into lame-ass khaki pants, slapped a faux name tag over his heart, and clipped a two-way receiver to his belt.

He studied the earpiece that went with it.

Most of the staff wore two-ways, not identical to this, but close enough.

Even still, he'd planned to go without.

He and Jill had worked, lived, fought, and trained as a team for so long, they could predict each other's movements. Instinct took care of the rest. They'd never missed having a two-way, because they'd never had one.

Like so much else, that had been Clare's doing.

They weren't military. They weren't law enforcement. They were fugitives who couldn't predict when trouble would come, or in what form, and unless they planned to wear the tech always, all it'd do was make them lazy.

She'd taught them how to sign instead.

Holden had dropped three units on the kitchen counter.

He didn't have the luxury of being part of their "secret-club handshake" codes, he'd said. At the very least *he* needed a way to know what was going on.

Jack had hesitated all the same.

Earpieces blocked sound, dulled situational awareness, and this was the wrong time to learn to compensate for that.

Holden had unraveled thin wires and shown him a tiny earpiece. "There's no ear fatigue, no sense deprivation," he'd said. "You don't even have to *use* them. Just *wear* them. Let me hear through you. Let me be eyes behind your back."

Jack had been curious enough to nudge the piece into place.

Holden hadn't been wrong.

So here he was now, plugged in, listening to Holden as he narrated progress through the park and found the uniform Jack had left him and the toolbox, and then the maintenance access that led to a towering view.

It felt a lot like listening to the voices in someone else's head.

Jill stayed quiet, but he didn't need words to know she was in costume and headed toward the park's invisible world, the side where delivery trucks and fuel trucks and all the ugly pieces critical to keeping the fantasy alive were shielded from view.

Jack assembled what was left of his gear, placed it in a garbage bag, picked up a stolen broom, and crawled it all out into a night filled with couples and families, bundled-up kids and teenagers in loud, bawdy groups, a crisp cold infused with laughter and color and music, and fragranced by funnel cakes, cotton candy, gun oil, and death.

He left the phone at the head of a snaking line, turned into a staff-only area to gather a cleaning-supply cart, and pulled another burner from the collection.

Hayes answered, less confident than on the first pickup.

"I'm still here," Jack said. "You still coming?"

"Traffic is bad," Hayes said. "Forty minutes."

Holden said, "If the signal's accurate, more like eight minutes."

Jack said, "Were you brave enough to come alone?"

"I brought a few friends," Hayes said. "It has nothing to do with bravery."

Jack hung up and dropped the phone.

Minutes passed.

Holden said, "Vehicle convoy turning east. Three-minute ETA."

515

Jack retrieved the next phone and called again.

Hayes said, "Thirty minutes, Jack. Why don't you give me a number? I'll let you know when I get there."

Jack hung up and continued toward the Grand Theatre.

In thirty minutes, the next show would start.

Holden said, "Convoy bypassing the front for the delivery entrance," and then, "Twenty-eight friends."

Jack sighed on the inside.

Twenty-eight itchy trigger fingers multiplied by however many rounds each man carried in a park filled with families and kids, where the best-lit spaces still cast colorful shadow and a shit ton of glare, was peak stupidity. Even if Hayes planned to shut down the entire park, it'd take a half hour at least to clear it out, and under current circumstances, a half hour was a lifetime.

Jack dialed again. He said, "It's cold, and I'd like to get this over with."

Hayes said, "Fifteen minutes."

Holden said, "They're lit up and headed your way."

No word from Jill, but Holden's confirmation said she'd successfully marked Hayes's men with spy dust.

Not the nitrophenyl pentadien of Clare's Cold War tales, in which the KGB coated doorknobs and floor mats with an invisible substance that, once touched, was nearly impossible to remove. In those stories many a spy had gotten their entire operation rolled and assets killed by unknowingly creating a trail to every place they visited, every hand they shook, and every paper they touched.

Not one of the commercially available antitheft powders, either.

Those all needed UV light to be seen. That made them useless here.

But fine glitter, herpes of the craft world, made a suitable alternative.

Beneath the park's halogen and holiday lights, it could turn a dull head of hair into a telltale chandelier. Every small reflection would help separate security from civilian as Hayes's men attempted to blend.

The men might see it, but like nitrophenyl pentadien, they couldn't get rid of it.

Jill had filled a few dozen bulb syringes with the stuff.

He'd carried them in for her.

According to Holden, Hayes's men were wearing it all now.

Jack kept the phone on, kept it with him

517

as he continued behind a restaurant to the dead end of a staff-only area. He pushed the cart in behind the gate, hopped the fence out the back, cut behind a building whose only purpose was to display animatronics, and popped back into the crowds.

Holden said, "Bait taken."

Jack could see the men in his head, a school of cartoon fish stopping midstream, turning in unison, reconfiguring. And he saw his sister on the edge, predator in the shadows, slinking in unseen to grab those stupid enough to end up on the periphery. She'd always preferred knives over bullets, and preferred hands over knives, and tonight, when winning and walking out of this alive meant more than avoiding a trail of bodies, a lot of Hayes's men would die by those hands. Jack had warned them, just as he'd warned the kill team in Frankfurt and in Berlin.

They never listened.

Jack dropped the phone and circled back for the cart.

In his ear Holden said, "Twenty-three friends."

He retrieved the next phone, dialed again.

"I'm pulling up to the park now," Hayes said.

There was no stress in his voice, nothing

to betray that his team, aided by a war room of experts and analysts listening in real time, observing from the sky, and tapping into park cameras, had already spread out in their hunt for him.

Holden said, "Closing in."

To Hayes, Jack said, "Head for the front gates. I'll find you there."

Jack killed the connection, dropped the phone, slipped onto the main thoroughfare, and broom and dustpan in hand, he swept the street at the edge of the crowd that had gathered outside the theater, waiting for the doors to open.

They'd come this way. The dot-to-dot he'd given had guided them to it.

In his ear Holden kept him apprised of position.

Jack moved slowly, sweeping, dumping, until the man came into view.

Crowd and cameras, location and lighting collided.

The map re-formed inside his head.

He caught sight of his sister, invisible to anyone who didn't know her, walking slowly in his direction. Her hands spoke in quick bursts, telling him from the ground what no amount of distant observation or over-the-wire communication could.

She'd removed nine of the twenty-eight.

There were four following a hundred feet behind him.

There were three a hundred feet behind her.

He told her he needed a distraction.

She passed him by, and he continued sweeping.

To his left, Hayes's men met in the middle.

There were six, instead of the seven Jill had counted.

They turned slow circles, aware that another had gone missing, and they fanned out to search through the crowd.

A commotion started up around the bend.

The spit pop of a suppressed weapon followed, and then a scream.

Hayes and his men hurried toward the noise, passing within feet of Jack's broom, men moving faster than their boss. Jack fell in behind them, weapon in hand, counting down yards, feet, inches until Hayes reached the opening between building and bushes, and Jack shoved him off the path, beyond the glare of ten thousand Christmas lights and into the shadows behind. He shifted the muzzle up under Hayes's chin, yanked the earpiece from his ear, motioned him out of his shoes and jacket, emptied his pockets onto the ground, shoved a hat on his head, and pushed him into the crowd.

He was an easy snatch.

Men who ran the operations were decades removed from activity, assuming they'd ever had an operative skill set to begin with.

Clare 202.

In Jack's ear, Holden said, "Friends in chaos."

Jack prodded Hayes deeper into the mix and up and through the doors of the Grand Theatre, which was a cloyingly hot contrast to the cold outdoors.

Hayes said, "What happened to not having plans to grab or kill me?"

Jack didn't answer.

Someone stupid enough to bring twenty-eight idiots into a park filled with families and children might actually be dumb enough to think he'd have to go to all this effort for a grab or kill, but probably not.

Audience members moved down the aisles toward the stage, removing hats and scarves. Jack reached behind a curtain, retrieved a lightweight, ankle-length, packable down-filled coat, and shoved it at Hayes. "Put this on," he said.

Hayes protested. "It's hot enough in here as it is."

"Put it on."

In Jack's ear, Holden said, "Attention coalescing on the theater."

Jack guided Hayes to the far right aisle, kept him moving until they reached the midpoint, gripped his shoulder, shoved him into a seat, sat beside him, and pulled from beneath his shirt an envelope that held copies of the pages he'd been handed in Toledo.

He thrust the first of them into Hayes's hand.

The theater lighting was dim, made it hard to read.

Hayes angled the page to be able to see, but seeing was hardly his point.

Jack jabbed the muzzle hard into Hayes's side, snatched the page back.

Hayes brushed sweat out of his eyes and fought against a nose run brought on by the extreme temperature shift. Jack handed him a new page, said, "Keep it in your lap," and waited long enough for Hayes, sniffling and sweating, to scan the details, then took it back and handed Hayes the next. He continued that way until the man had handled them all, and he had Hayes return the lot of them to the envelope and shoved the envelope back up under his shirt.

In Jack's ear, Holden said, "Friends at the doorstep."

Jack tapped center chest above the envelope. "I have your target and can confirm a time window of twenty-four hours."

"So you're what?" Hayes said. "Bragging?"

Jack filled his expression with incredulity. "Jesus," he said. "Are you stupid, or do you just think I am? I know I'm not the real assassin, just the decoy. Secretary of state, right? That's who you're really trying to hit. Is that why your killing crew is chasing so hard after me, so no one looks where they should be looking?"

Sweat continued its slow drip, but for the first time, Hayes looked truly uncomfortable. "I don't know what you're talking about."

"Oh, I think you do."

Holden said, "Eight friends inside. Others blocking exits."

Jack could see them in his head, bodies moving forward down the aisles. He said, "Take off the coat. Do not stand. Do not look up. Do not speak."

Hayes tugged out of the coat, bundled it onto his lap.

Jack said, "I'm being forced to do this against my will, so fine, you have my guarantee that absolutely nothing will prevent these killings from taking place. But I'm begging you, Hayes, whatever you decide to do next, at least get ahead of the story. You still have a chance to control the media spin and keep this country from devouring itself in a new civil war. If you don't at least do that much, then maybe the real traitor here isn't me. It's you."

Hayes's focus twitched right.

Jack felt the heat of threat at his back. He said, "If it's your life or mine, there's no question who dies."

Hayes stayed motionless, silent.

A shadow passed through Jack's peripheral vision and continued on. They weren't looking anymore. They knew where to find him.

They were circling, tightening the noose.

In his ear, Holden said, "Get out now."

In his head, the clock counted down to show opening.

Jack said, "I'm also offering you an opportunity. Once this deed is done, you'll have a man Moscow trusts who's willing to keep the information flowing both ways. Ignore me, continue hunting me and my friends, and I guarantee that you and your family will never be able to stop looking over your shoulders."

Hayes said, "Twenty-four hours isn't enough."

"Yeah, well, you ate all the extra time by forcing me to dodge your killers for the past few days."

In Jack's ear, Holden said, "Doors closing. Go. Now."

Jack tossed a burner in Hayes's lap and slid sideways off the seat.

Inside his head, the maze froze, and the clock stopped.

Background music piping in through the sound system went silent.

The theater lights went fully dark.

Jack backed into the aisle, and the sound system came alive.

Strobe lights flashed across the stage, and Jack moved with the bursts.

Holden was in his ear again, an audible voice talking over the inner voice he'd relied on since his earliest memories.

Jack pulled the earpiece loose, let the wire dangle free.

His entire brain relaxed. Music and lights and bodies formed a multidimensional map that rotated and tilted, allowing him to mentally place each itchy finger. He searched for Jill, found her on the outside, keeping a path free. He headed for the door at stage right, owning every bit of the cheesy park uniform, as if it belonged to him, passed one armed man, avoided eye contact with the other, who blocked the door, kept the semiautomatic as low and as inconspicuous as a hunk of metal ever could be.

Clare's training told him to fire now,

eliminate the nearest enemy.

Gunshots would send the theater into a mad scramble for the exits.

The panic would provide him ample cover to get out.

But panic also got people trampled, killed in the crush, and there were an awful lot of little kids in here. If he could settle this quietly, he would.

He pried knife from sheath.

Clare joined the voices in his head.

Are you mad? Only a fool would gift the enemy his own weakness.

He shut her down.

This was his life, and these were his mistakes to make.

The heat of threat burned behind him, rising, closing in fast.

Time slowed, ticking between strobe pulses, hovering between blinks on rapt audience faces, and Jack felt the weight of footsteps and shifted.

A suppressor rose to meet the base of his skull, but he'd moved first.

Fingers scraped air where his collar had been.

His blade swung over and down, connected with forearm, sliced tendons. The shooter's cry rose with the music and died with his own bullet, muzzle twisted back, spitting into his face due to his own uncontrollable finger, and was drowned by pounding drums.

An eight-year-old boy in the nearest seat turned and watched wide-eyed.

Jack pulled the deadweight close, leaned in toward the kid, said, "It's part of the show," and he dragged the body far enough forward that the kid wouldn't be able to see once the theater began to empty.

The music stopped, and the lights shut off.

The dark was made for speed.

He rushed that stage-right door. Two seconds was all he got, but he closed most of the distance, and when the next note rose and softer lighting followed, he was feet from a man in shooting stance, suppressor aimed six inches to Jack's left and moving toward center chest. Every rubber-bullet bruise and hand-to-hand fight, lost and won, said he'd be dead before he could place a fatal round.

Clare shoved him. Jill shoved him.

He dove into the man's feet, knocking him off balance, and they rolled, tumbling, fighting to incapacitate, to kill, to gain control of scattered weapons, while high schoolers crooned the lyrics to "Winter Wonderland" and the nearest audience members no longer watched the stage.

The man was heavy, strong, and nearly as fast as Jill.

His fingers scrabbled along the carpet, found his gun.

Jack thrust his full weight down on that shooting arm, pinning it to the floor, and he hit and hit and hit, punching neck, elbowing head, landing strike after strike on a body that seemed not to feel the blows.

The man's free hand went for Jack's eyes and nose.

His knees went into Jack's side.

Jack drove forehead into face.

Cartilage crunched. Blood sprayed.

The man shoved, punched, forced range of movement on his shooting arm.

Jack struggled to keep the muzzle pointed away and lost by the inch.

He had been beaten by Clare, had rarely won against Jill, but not since he was thirteen had a stranger bested him.

This first time would be the time that killed him.

Acceptance settled.

The song neared its final notes.

Somewhere on the edge of awareness, the stage-right door creaked open.

He was slow to register the muzzle slipping through the crack.

The body beneath him went limp.

Delayed recognition filled in a pattern of suppressed reports arriving with a snare-drum beat, and he rolled free, gasping, shaking.

Jill hissed, "Hurry up, asshole. I've got places to be."

He wanted to hug her until she couldn't breathe. Instead, he crawled after the knife, located his gun, stumbled to his feet, and pushed through the widening crack.

Jill locked the door, shoved a chair up under the handle.

He followed her through the dark, down a corridor, around a corner, into a tunnel that ran beneath the stage, and out a side door into a restricted area.

The cart with his stuff was parked off in a corner.

She tossed him an XXL sweatshirt, over-priced, tags still attached, probably shop-lifted. "Been listening to their coms," she said.

Her fingers worked buttons and zippers.

"They're shutting down the park."

She pulled off the costume.

"We're both burned, but big boy up there can hold until we're out."

Jack pulled his gear from the garbage bag, strapped the pack to his stomach, and pulled the sweatshirt down over the equipment belly.

Returning to the woods and following the transmission lines back was a no-go. They weren't equipped for a protracted run from eyes in the sky, with their heat-seeking sensors. They'd be dead within the hour.

They needed people.

Lots of them.

That was why he'd chosen the park.

They had to get ahead of the crowd.

"We go front," he said.

Jill said, "You got what you came for?"

"Need one last call."

She handed him a Santa hat.

He shoved it on his head, then felt up his side for the tape that had secured Holden's coms to his chest. He snagged the wire that had gone missing during the fight, pulled the earpiece back up through his collar, and tipped it back into his ear.

Jill said, "Boo-boo is back online."

Jack scowled. "Cute."

She smiled and bumped her shoulder into his.

Holden said, "Welcome back, bro. You're clear for about five seconds."

Jack nudged the staff-area gate open and slipped out.

Behind him, Jill went over the fence.

It'd be a slow man's race for the front gate.

He fell in behind a trio of twentysomethings and stuck close, listening in on the conversation to gain a sense of common ground, and was their new best friend by the time they reached the front gate. They were out of Baltimore. He had an aunt there he wanted to visit. It was easy to hitch a ride. They dropped him off in Franklin Square, and he made his own way toward the harbor and sat on a bench outside Light Street Pavilion, adrenaline dumping, brain unspooling, watching the waves dance.

He couldn't stop yet.

This was almost over, but not quite.

He pulled out the last of the burner phones and, like Jill putting the gun to Clare's head in that Belizean hotel, dialed Hayes for the final time.

The voice on the other end had lost its indifferent calm.

There was exhaustion, concern, maybe an edge of anger, but mostly an interesting readiness to listen. Jack said, "Tomorrow the junior senator from Tennessee and the Speaker of the United States House of Representatives will die. Whether or not their actual bodies take the knife is up to you. You've been given an opportunity to control the narrative, and you should use it.

"The intel that makes assassination possible has your fingerprints and DNA all over it, literally and figuratively. The evidence in my possession has been parceled and, together with recordings of our conversation, is ready for delivery to your peers within the intelligence community, the congressional leadership, and the media. The only thing standing between you and going down in history as a traitor is the choices you're about to make."

Hayes said, "I cannot stand down and allow these assassinations to happen, not even with a body switch. You know this."

"I do."

"Then what, specifically, are you asking for?"

"There are names I want taken off your kill list, and I want all the accompanying data completely removed from physical and digital repositories and destroyed. Think long and hard before you agree, because failing to deliver will be worse than no agreement at all."

"I can put a hold on the kill list," Hayes said. "But not today."

"And the rest?"

"Some of that is beyond my paygrade."

Jack stood and strolled toward the water's edge. "Keep me and my friends alive," he said, "and I guarantee your paygrade will rise."

"Twenty-four hours is a long time for circumstances to change."

"Twenty hours," Jack said.

More precisely, twenty hours and eighteen minutes.

Jack flung the phone into the water, watched it sink.

He turned and trudged back toward Mc-Keldin Square.

Hayes would hunt him, the FBI would hunt him, local law enforcement would hunt him, and they'd run him hard, catching glimpses, getting close, discovering he'd slipped away again, and when the assassinations hit, they'd be confused, because that's what happened when you became so focused on finding the man, you forgot about the idea.

Anyone could be taught to vanish or fight or plan an ambush.

Most anyone could even be good at it.

Not everyone could think ahead of the enemy.

Legerdemain. Mental prestidigitation.

That's what Clare had always been after.

The only person within Hayes's headquarters who'd figured out that Holden was working with them was sitting out this fight in front of a television.

And the only person within Hayes's headquarters under whose leadership the war room operated at its most effective, cohesive best was sitting out this fight on the other side of the same house, away from the television.

And though Hayes could tap into unlimited manpower via official agencies, those requests came with paper trails, jurisdictional issues, and cover-your-ass political jockeying. His own outside-the-law shadow force had been nearly decimated tonight due to peak stupidity. What was left of that shadow force would chase him.

And they'd chase Jill passing herself off as him.

But Holden would make the kills.

Legerdemain.

CHAPTER 37

Atoka County
Oklahoma, USA

Kara

She rode with the window down, sun on her skin, wind in her face, parsing memories with prairie and grassland as the miles rolled by. Jack was behind the wheel, just him and her now on the last of the long-ass drive from Pennsylvania.

They were both comfortable with silence. She liked that about him.

It'd been hours since they'd last spoken.

Another few minutes and they'd turn off State Highway 3, and another half hour and she'd be home — not the house of her childhood, the one she'd built for her parents years later. It'd been too long since she'd been back.

The more judicious choice would have been to return to headquarters, but she

535

wasn't ready, not emotionally, and not psychologically. She had contacted Hayes to let him know she'd been set free, had told him she wasn't okay, that she needed time.

She'd expected an argument, perhaps recrimination.

Instead, he'd been conciliatory, told her that her job would be waiting when she got back, whenever that might be.

Clearly, she'd underestimated Jack's promise.

The one he'd made right before he'd reshackled her to that stupid chain.

He had come that morning with a television and had set her free to shower and step out for fresh air while he ran the digital antenna. It'd been kind of endearing, the way he'd spent so much time trying to get her the best reception the remoteness would allow. After, they'd sat on the porch, eating lunch out of cans and boxes, a proper hobo picnic, and he'd told her what he had planned, and she'd told him that letting Hayes control the narrative was like putting a chicken in front of a terrier and expecting the dog not to chase.

Hayes would use the opportunity to grab more extrajudicial power, and for all they knew, he was as much a partisan hack as the next guy, and there was no guarantee that whatever spin he spun would be in the country's best interest.

"No," Jack had said. "But he'll do what's in his *own* best interest."

He hadn't elaborated on how the two aligned.

Power grabs and politicking would go on regardless, he'd said. He wanted to prevent civil war, and wanted his freedom. Attempting to control more would make him yet another person trying to impose their worldview on the masses.

They talked until Jen stepped out to tell him it was time, and he guided Kara back to the shackle.

"I'd prefer to ask you to stay and wait, and to take you at your word," he said. "But there's too much at stake for that. Not just for us but you. Anyone finds you before we get back and you're not locked up, then you're an accomplice."

She shoved her leg at him, hating that she was forced to understand logic that shouldn't exist in the first place, hating that he'd do it whether she agreed or not.

"We'll be gone three days at most," he said.

She hoped to God he was right, because Hayes was about to go all out in an effort to scratch him off the Broker list. He'd have already called up every kill team not on active assignment, he'd have a small army at his back, and if they made it past round one and continued on to targets, there'd be SWAT teams and Capitol Police and FBI and probably multiple Boomerangs — gunfire locators mostly used against snipers.

That was simply the way things worked.

She would say as much to Jack if stating the obvious wouldn't insult them both. She had her own reasons for wanting Hayes to lose.

For the sake of her freedom, she needed Jack to stay alive.

"I've made sure you'll be okay," he said. "No matter what happens to us, you'll be all right. You have my word."

He left her with nothing but television and time.

It was a hell of a wait.

The first episode didn't break until the next day's late-evening news: A bomb threat. An amusement park forced to evacuate. A false alarm.

Helicopter footage showed armored vehicles and multistate law-enforcement personnel, and she saw Hayes in that strategy, but it told her absolutely nothing about who'd lived or died.

Twenty-four hours later the senator pinged

the news cycle: Emergency hospitalization. Critical condition. Previously undiagnosed health issues.

Twelve hours after that, the world erupted and sent Jen's words from the train round and round Kara's head.

All your guys trying to find my brother will never see me coming.

I will put a bullet between the eyes of a sitting member of Congress.

The Russians wanted a spectacle, and that's what they got.

Every channel played variations of the same clip: Speaker of the House outside an immigration detention center. Bullet strike. Body fall. Chaos.

In the background, beyond the noise, she heard the crack-bang.

Kara listened for it each time the clip replayed.

Sound delay told her the hit had come from beyond 450 yards.

Even with multiple Boomerangs, there'd have been enough time for the shooter to bug out, but so much of this was wrong. Jack had given Hayes a head start, an opportunity to prevent an actual killing, and everything about this was *real.*

The spin machine kicked in all the same: a name, a face, a manhunt.

A suspect with a lengthy criminal record and a long unstable history. An armed engagement. Eventually, suspect suicide.

And a collective sigh of relief and space to grieve.

Kara shut off the television, conflicted, confused.

Hayes could have averted this but hadn't, and that troubled her deeply, and she couldn't point to why, exactly.

It wasn't death. The entirety of her adult years had been spent as a cog in death's machine.

And it wasn't the assassination itself. Her job at headquarters had been to support extrajudicial killing.

And it wasn't even that it'd been a US citizen or on US soil. She'd been preparing to do the same thing before she'd been snatched.

Nor was it the taking of presumably innocent life. She'd argued out that issue with Nick after her first six months.

It took a while to shut off her mind, but finally, she slept.

She awoke with Jack's arrival.

He'd returned before the others, a single set of footsteps tromping up the porch, through the front, and to her room. He looked like he'd been awake for days.

He unlocked the shackle, handed her a couple grand in cash, and told her she was free to roam, or to leave entirely if she preferred, but that would mean walking a long way, and if she was willing to wait until Jen and Chris got back, he'd take her wherever she wanted to go. She didn't know exactly why she stayed.

— Because she liked him.

— Because all evidence pointed to him telling the truth.

— Because she wasn't sure where she'd be safe just yet, and as long as she wasn't locked up, another twenty hours here made no difference.

She wandered while he slept, opening cabinets, peering into closets, everything except Liv's room. The odd assortment of shoes and clothing, suitcases, camping supplies, and first aid confused her until she found the gun safe — locked — and the fireproof boxes, also locked — and she understood what this house really was, and was afraid to touch anything after that.

Jen and Chris arrived in the predawn and headed right back out again, with Liv Wilson in tow. They'd taken her to a hospital in Philadelphia according to Jack.

They could have gone round trip to Toronto for as long as they took.

They returned that evening, loaded up on groceries and supplies, and she kept out of sight at first, unsure of her place in the order of things, listening to them knock about in the kitchen, until curiosity and hunger got the best of her.

Jen was first to see her. She lit up with a welcoming smile and motioned her in, and it felt a lot like being a fly on the wall at another family's holiday get-together, all the inside jokes and rapid-fire banter, Jack and Jen bustling around each other while cooking, and Chris trying to be useful but mostly getting underfoot.

They spoke openly about Frankfurt and Berlin and Prague in her presence, as if their secrets weren't actually secrets. Glimpses of those same events as seen through their eyes were like stepping through the looking glass.

The war room's data hadn't been wrong, it'd been incomplete.

Where headquarters saw a legacy killer about to rendezvous with a handler in a lead-up to an assassination, there'd been a son trying to escape his mother's past and hoping to find a father.

Everything had ultimately been about that, about finding Dmitry.

And Dmitry was still unfinished business.

Jen tugged a piece of paper from her

pocket, unfolded it, and spread it flat on the table. Dot-matrix type and peg-holed edges pointed to a flight manifest printed directly off a gate agent's printer. Jack and Chris leaned in for a closer look, and Jen said, "When I lost track of time in Frankfurt, it's because I'd tailed the spotter to his flight and was trying to get this. If you still think he was Dmitry, then this is where we start hunting."

She slapped a set of keys down on top of the paper.

"Took these off a couple Russians holed up in an apartment overlooking the café in Savignyplatz." She nudged them in her brother's direction. "Front door, apartment door," she said. "They were set up long before we got there. What are the odds those *weren't* Dmitry's guys?"

Jack hooked a finger in the ring and dangled the keys above the manifest. He waited a while before speaking. "We went after answers and got them," he said. "There's no question Dmitry's alive or that he's real. There's also no question that finding him will be the lesser challenge. So do we go, or do we let it go?"

Jen sighed, and the guys seemed to understand what the sigh meant, because the mood turned somber. She said, "I'll go for you."

"It can't be like that," Jack said. "We mess this up, and there are real-world consequences on the other end."

"Baby steps, my brother," she said. "This is my way of getting to that."

They stared at each other, some silent contest of wills, which Kara didn't quite understand and which Chris put an end to by pushing back from the table.

"Well," he said. "I guess that's settled. Keeping you buttheads alive seems to be my new job, so I guess that means I'm going, too." He tugged a small plastic case from the inside of his jeans, removed a microSD card, loaded that into a phone, and fiddled with the device until he had what he was looking for. "While we're still doing show-and-tell, here's my contribution from Berlin."

He turned the screen so they could see it.

It showed a short, pudgy, balding man.

To Kara, he said, "You know him?"

She leaned in for a better look.

"He introduced himself as Luka Marinov," Jack said.

She didn't recognize name or face, but if this was the guy who connected Berlin to Prague, that put him in the orbit of global players, and odds were high the war room had something. She shook her head.

Chris extracted the card and offered it to her. "Keep it," he said. "You've got as much vested in figuring out who he is as we do."

She tucked the card into her sock, closest thing she had to a wallet since she hadn't had anything personal on her when they'd grabbed her.

She had the card with her now, padded in tissue, snug between insert and sole, like a pebble near her heel.

They left the next morning, all four of them in one vehicle.

Louisville was where Jack stopped so they could make the calls.

First was her conversation with Hayes, and once that was settled, Jack used Hayes's SIM to call the Russian who'd abducted and blackmailed him.

The man answered as if he recognized the number.

That surprised her more than anything else in this insane week, and that last conversation on the train came roaring back with raging focus.

"Moscow has been playing you," Jen had said. "Your branch, division, whatever it is you guys are. Keeping you focused on my brother so you don't look at me."

That took her back to the intel in Jack's dossier.

Chatter and intercepted diplomatic cables and information from several assets in Moscow that had all pointed in his direction, but the most accurate detail had come as leaks from an ideological defector within the Kremlin.

She understood then what Jack had meant when he'd said Hayes would do what was in his own best interest.

The Speaker of the House had been assassinated.

Hayes, intentionally or not, had let it happen, and his line to the Moscow leaker also connected directly to the guy who'd arranged the hits.

It looked a lot like treason.

Jack knew, and Hayes knew Jack knew.

To the phone, Jack said, "Not Steven Hayes. Jonathan Smith."

And then, "I want Dmitry. That was our arrangement."

And then, "Have it your way. I'll find you in Moscow."

He hit END and tossed the phone to Jen, and she caught it and smiled.

There was a kind of crazy in that smile, like danger had just been let off leash and turned loose. Kara imagined that had something to do with why Jen had been the Russian's primary assassin and not Jack.

Jen and Chris stepped out of the car, hauled two suitcases from the trunk, and headed off. It felt strange seeing them go just like that.

Her job had been to kill them — maybe still was to kill them.

They'd abducted her and held her captive. And yet off they went with a smile and a wave, like old friends parting after a vacation.

Better was watching the miles go by on the long way home, and that's where she was now, home. Jack stopped where the tarmac stopped. From here the roof peeked out between the trees, but the house was still a quarter mile up the dirt road.

He said, "This is as far as I go."

She sat for a beat, unsure if she should thank him for the ride or, now that she was finally free, tell him to go to hell. She opted for silence and stepped out, shut the door, and started walking. But that wasn't right.

Even for people as reticent as they, this required *some* form of exchange.

But there wasn't exactly an etiquette guide on what to say to a target-slash-abductor, no matter how badly you'd failed to kill him, or how well he'd treated you, or how great you got along.

She made it about ten feet and stopped. She looked back.

He was watching her, window rolled down, elbow on the sill.

She said, "You know this isn't over, right? Just because headquarters doesn't want you dead *right now* doesn't mean they'll stop hunting."

The corners of his eyes turned up ever so slightly.

"Good," he said. "It means I'll see you again."

AUTHOR'S NOTE

If you're new to my books, thank you for being willing to take a chance on the unfamiliar. If you're a fan, or a former reader back for another round, thank you for being a part of this ongoing journey. I so hope you've enjoyed it! If you would like more during the long wait for the next book, you can get:

- Semi-regular updates with the latest news, upcoming events, and details on where things are with each writing project, plus bimonthly essays that include an insider's look at publishing, thoughts on overcoming adversity, personal insights, and everything I've learned on this writing journey via email drip from www.taylorstevens books.com/connect.php
- Real-life writing issues solved and in-

depth story and line editing show-and-tell by weekly podcast at www.taylorstevensshow.com where, together with friend and co-host Stephen Campbell, we kick writing in the butt one word at a time

- Special insider updates, video, Q&A, and *Hack the Craft*™ writing tutorials at www.patreon.com/taylorstevens
- Personal interaction in The Taylor Stevens Fan Club Group on Facebook or at facebook.com/taylorstevens
- And occasionally on Twitter @taylor_stevens

ACKNOWLEDGMENTS

This story would never have come to be without so many who've helped carry it through to the end. To my editor, Michaela Hamilton, thank you for your patience. To my agent, Anne Hawkins, thank you for always being in my corner, and also Annie, I'm so glad you are part of the team. To the many unsung heroes within Kensington Publishing, you guys are rock stars.

To the many authors, friends, and fans who've gone out of their way to support both me and my work, you know who you are, and I appreciate you more than you know, and I can't name you here because I will one-hundred-percent forget someone and I'm just not that brave.

To my children, this book *literally* wouldn't have been finished without your willingness to take weight off a load that had gotten too heavy for me to carry alone. To the Muse, thank you for the space to breathe. And thanks also go to childhood friend Lauren Hough, author of the viral piece "I Was a Cable Guy. I Saw the Worst of America," for a description of Berlin that I would have included in its entirety (with permission and attribution, of course) had it not been so much better than anything I've ever written that the only way I could use it was by chopping it up and dumbing it down.

Special thanks to Allison Brennan, *New York Times* bestselling author of the Lucy Kinkaid and Max Revere books, who threw so much time, effort, and energy into promoting Jack and Jill's first outing that it could have been mistaken for one of her own books. There's just no way I can repay that. Allison, thank you.

To fans and readers, thank you for continuing to let me work at a job that doesn't require getting out of pajamas. And to my Patreon supporters, I am continually in awe of you and your generosity, thank you for believing in me *that* much.

ABOUT THE AUTHOR

Taylor Stevens is a critically acclaimed, multiple awards–winning, *New York Times* bestselling author of international thrillers including the first Jack and Jill thriller, *Liars' Paradox.* Stevens is best known for high-octane stories populated with fascinating characters in vivid boots-on-the-ground settings, and she has seen her books optioned for film and published in more than twenty languages. In addition to writing novels, Stevens shares extensively about the mechanics of storytelling, writing, and overcoming adversity and relates the details of her journey into publishing at taylorstevens books.com. She welcomes you to join her.